# PENRIC'S TRAVELS

# BOOKS by LOIS McMASTER BUJOLD

## The Vorkosigan Saga
*Shards of Honor* • *Barrayar*
*The Warrior's Apprentice* • *The Vor Game*
*Cetaganda* • *Borders of Infinity*
*Brothers in Arms* • *Mirror Dance*
*Memory* • *Komarr*
*A Civil Campaign* • *Diplomatic Immunity*
*Captain Vorpatril's Alliance* • *Cryoburn*
*Gentleman Jole and the Red Queen*

*Falling Free* • *Ethan of Athos*

## Omnibus Editions
*Miles, Mystery & Mayhem* • *Miles, Mutants & Microbes*

## World of the Five Gods
*The Curse of Chalion* • *Paladin of Souls*
*The Hallowed Hunt*
*Penric's Progress* • *Penric's Travels*

## The Sharing Knife Tetralogy
*Volume 1: Beguilement* • *Volume 2: Legacy*
*Volume 3: Passage* • *Volume 4: Horizon*

*The Spirit Ring*

## ALSO AVAILABLE FROM BAEN BOOKS
*The Vorkosigan Companion,*
edited by Lillian Stewart Carl and John Helfers

To purchase Baen titles in e-book form, please go to www.baen.com.

# PENRIC'S TRAVELS

by
# LOIS McMASTER BUJOLD

Penric's Travels

This is a work of fiction. All the characters and events portrayed in this book are fictional, and any resemblance to real people or incidents is purely coincidental.

A Baen Books Original

Baen Publishing Enterprises
P.O. Box 1403
Riverdale, NY 10471
www.baen.com

ISBN: 978-1-9821-2457-1

Cover art by Dan dos Santos

First printing, May 2020

Distributed by Simon & Schuster
1230 Avenue of the Americas
New York, NY 10020

Library of Congress Cataloging-in-Publication Data

Names: Bujold, Lois McMaster, author.
Title: Penric's travels / by Lois McMaster Bujold.
Description: Riverdale, NY : Baen Books, [2020] | Series: World of the five gods
Identifiers: LCCN 2019059812 | ISBN 9781982124571 (hardcover)
Subjects: GSAFD: Fantasy fiction.
Classification: LCC PS3552.U397 P48 2020 | DDC 813/.54—dc23
LC record available at https://lccn.loc.gov/2019059812

Printed in the United States of America

10 9 8 7 6 5 4 3 2 1

# CONTENTS

# INTRODUCTION

THE FIRST THING a new reader who has just picked up *Penric's Travels* needs to know is that the stories collected here will give a complete read right now, batteries included, without having to circle back first to the chronologically earlier collection *Penric's Progress*. (Though I hope folks will become curious enough about the younger Penric to do so eventually.) The Penric & Desdemona tales were originally designed to be a series of loosely linked stand-alones, e-published á la carte as the spirit moved me, open-ended. Among other things, I was thinking of the stories of favorite characters that would pop up randomly in the old pulp magazines, such as Poul Anderson's Polesotechnic League or James H. Schmidt's Telzey tales, to the delight of many readers including me. While each short work stood alone, readable in any order, taken together they tended to form larger biographies of the characters of interest. So it's not altogether wrong to think of my e-novellas as magazine stories without the magazine.

While the á la carte scheme holds, the three stories collected here are more tightly linked than usual with each other, forming what I think of as "the Cedonia triptych". I didn't actually write them in that order, having circled back between "Penric's Mission" and "Mira's Last Dance" to write the earlier-set "Penric's Fox". This not only gave me a chance to work on something else while its ideas were hot, but also space for further developments in the later-set stories to brew up. An author looks over characters' lives from a sort of eternal viewpoint, outside their chronological book-timelines. Characters whose stories play well with an episodic structure can take advantage of this fluidity.

For readers who want to know how all my story puzzles fit together, we've included a handy guide in the back of this volume.

Happy reading!

—Lois

# PENRIC'S
# MISSION

# PENRIC'S MISSION

## I

"DESDEMONA!" Penric breathed, awed. "Will you look at that *light*."

He leaned on the railing of the Adriac cargo ship coasting slowly up the narrowing Gulf of Patos, and stared eyes-wide at the rocky shores of Cedonia. The dry clarity of the air made the distant granite mountains seem as sharp-cut as glassmaker's crystal. The angled sun of morning was the color of honey. He tilted back his head to take in the astonishing blue vault above, so deep it was dizzying; he felt he might dive up through it as into the sea, endlessly, and never drown.

It was what he imagined enchantment should be, in some myth or legend of personified elements, *The Man Who Fell in Love with the Sky*. Mortals, he was reminded, did not usually come out well at the ends of those tales.

"Yes, but by noon it will scorch that pale scholar's skin of yours to blisters. Keep yourself covered. We'll have to see about getting you a proper hat," his demon returned, speaking through his mouth as prosaically as the bossy older sister he sometimes imagined her to be. But he thought she was not unmoved by the sight, shared through his eyes, of the light of the land of—could you call it her birth?—that she'd last departed, what, over a hundred years ago?

"Longer than that," she sighed.

He pressed his finger to his lips, warning her not to speak aloud in company, and moved around to the prow, keeping clear of the crewmen shifting ropes and sails. Half-a-dozen other passengers clustered there to catch a first glimpse of the city that lent the gulf its name. The ship came about and tacked toward the farther shore, climbing a slight headwind.

A tumbled slope drew aside like a stage curtain, revealing their goal. Spread across the wide amphitheater of the gulf's head, Patos seemed built of the bones of this land: stone houses with red tile roofs, stone streets, arched and colonnaded; the familiar angled shape, high on one hill, of a stone temple. A broad stone fortress guarded stone quays reaching out into the clear blue waters, where a dozen other cargo ships crowded, offloading.

The grove of cranes and masts made up for what seemed to Penric's eyes a decided lack of trees, which was in part why his ship's heavy lading of cut timber was expected to be welcomed trade. A bit slow, bulky, boring; a ship for ordinary men with ordinary purses to make passage in. Such as a lawyer's young clerk, carrying a sheaf of unsigned merchants' agreements and a hopeful marriage contract. All entirely bogus. He adjusted the strap on his shoulder and touched the leather case that held them, plus the second set of documents that was much less dull sewn covertly inside its lining.

Velka gave a little wave as Pen joined him on the forward deck. The man was a Cedonian mercantile agent with whom Penric had made friends, or at least friendly acquaintance, on what he had been assured was a remarkably smooth three-day sail from the Adriac city of Lodi, and on whom he'd been happy to practice his Cedonian. Smiling slightly, Velka said, "Still excited for your first trip to Cedonia?"

"Yes," Pen admitted, grinning back, still inebriated by the morning light and not even bothering to be sheepish. The young clerk should certainly be allowed such elation.

"I expect you will find it full of surprises."

"I expect so, too."

Des passed no comment, even internally, but Pen felt she watched the harbor scene as keenly as he did.

Two oarsmen in Cedonian Customs' tabards rowed a green-painted boat out from the quay and swung alongside Pen's ship. He picked up his single valise and followed Velka with the first batch of passengers to disembark, making his way over the side and down the rope net without mishap. When it had rid itself of its human freight, the ship would go on to another quay at the Imperial naval shipyard and arsenal to discharge its timber. Penric mused on the rationale, which rather escaped him, of one country selling essentials for shipbuilding to another country when they might, some future year, be at war or at least in chronic naval clashes with each other. Well, the puzzle did not fall within the ambit of this mission.

Imperial Customs consisted of a long wooden shed housing tables, a few agents in official tunics, some bored guards, and a dull air of bureaucracy. The passengers shuffled into line and turned out their goods for inspection. His clerk, when Pen took his turn, examined his fake papers and wrote down his fake name and age and fake business with only mild interest. His valise was dumped out on the table and his possessions pawed through, as the clerk looked for Pen knew-not-what.

His belongings had been carefully selected back in Adria to fit his travel persona, and included nothing of interest; most certainly not his white robes of a divine of the Bastard's Order, or the white, cream, and silver shoulder braids marking him as a Temple sorcerer. Nor even the four-cord green braids of a teaching physician of the Mother's Order, which had been foisted on him back home in Martensbridge even though he had declined to take oath to a second god. The faint ink stains on his long fingers might well have belonged to a lawyer's clerk.

In any case his most secret and dangerous contraband, his chaos demon who gave him his uncanny powers, passed entirely unsuspected.

Velka, lingering to speak with some port official, waved Penric on, and Pen emerged once more into a light grown even sharper. He stepped away briskly, not wanting to be lumbered with a companion at this stage. He wondered if he should first seek out the man he'd come all this way to bargain with, or go find lodgings. Perhaps locate the fellow, then pick lodgings convenient to him. Asking around the harbor marketplace for his quarry's address would leave a trail of witnesses to his interest. There must be something more discreet.

*Good thinking,* observed Desdemona. *Your best bets will be up by the provincial governor's palace, or some tavern near the army barracks where the soldiers gather.*

It felt strange to have a visceral sense of the layout of a city he'd never set foot in before, but one of Desdemona's previous riders had lived here for some years. Over a century ago, Pen reminded himself. Things would have changed, although probably not major buildings or streets, not with all this stone.

The marketplace, a semi-permanent little village of booths and awnings, smelled of fish, ropes, tar, and spices. Offerings included used clothing, domestic tinwork and ceramics, and food, exotic—to Pen—oranges and lemons, dried figs and nuts and strange bright vegetables, olives and their oils. The vendors and patrons showed nearly as much variety, men and women, and children of both sexes running about adding their notes of chaos. Clothing tended to loose linens, tunics and trousers for the men, demure draperies for the women. Skin colors ranged from almost Roknari bronze to olive to a deep brick tan on those who clearly worked outdoors.

Hair was as varied, curly to straight, sun-streaked bronze, dark copper, brown, but mostly black. He was glad he'd taken the advice to dye his own to an unassuming brown for the journey. His blond-white hair stood out even back home; here, where he found his mountain-average height suddenly half a head taller than most men around him, it would have blazed in this sun like a signal beacon. His eyes he could do nothing about, save to squint a trifle. He attempted to shrink in a clerk's stoop.

Completing his fascinated survey of the market, he began a stroll up a street leading toward the hill hosting the governor's palace. The noise of the harbor—seabirds crying, workmen and vendors shouting, the creak of the cranes, clack of hooves and rumbling of carts—at first eclipsed the steady double-time of booted feet coming up behind him. When he turned, the squad of half-a-dozen soldiers was almost in his face.

"Halt, you!" cried their sergeant.

Penric tensed on his toes, but obeyed, blinking and smiling, free hand out empty and unthreatening. "Hello," he tried in a friendly tone. "Can I help you?" Only then did he see Velka running behind them, pointing at him.

"That's the spy! Arrest him!"

His first impulse, to try to talk himself out of this contretemps, died as he reflected that a more thorough search of his leather document case must surely find its hidden compartment, and the duke's secret letters, and then no amount of talking would help. But his well-filled purse was hung hidden on a cord around his neck, his case strap slung over his opposite shoulder, unsnatchable.

As the sergeant pulled his short sword from his sheath and swung it upward, Pen thought, *Des, speed us!*

From his point of view, his would-be assailants slowed. Pen flung his valise at the sergeant, knocking him backward, and ducked another man's leisurely sword thrust. His own movements always felt as though he were fighting through oil when he did this, but he drove force through his legs and turned, taking the first few steps of a sprint away. *Where*, he would have to work out later.

But *now*, he bounded directly into the other half of the squad who'd turned onto the street just above him, bearing down upon him with raised truncheons.

He evaded four languid blows as sinuously as any striking snake. Jerking successfully away from a fifth swing smashed the side of his head into a sixth, with a lot more power than even the man who wielded it had probably intended.

The world turned to stars and snow as he gasped and dropped, cracking his head on the stones *again* as his flailing hands missed catching himself. Nauseating black clouds bloomed in his vision as he did not, quite, pass out.

Passing out would have allowed him to evade the pain and misery that followed. Plenty of strong hands combined to hoist his long body up and hurry him back down the hill and through the gates of the shore fortress. Shadows flickered overhead, then stone. At first he thought he was swooning for certain as the world darkened, despite the continued drumming in his skull, but they were just going underground; an orange blur of torchlight wavered past him. The passage narrowed, widened, narrowed again. Widened again.

He was held down and efficiently stripped of case, boots, purse, belt and belt-knife, and his outer garments. Someone grabbed him by the hair and growled, "What is your real name?" Pen couldn't even groan in reply, though he panted and then, suddenly, vomited on his interrogator. As defenses or even revenges went, it seemed weak, but at least the man leapt back, swearing.

"Bosko, you hit him too cursed hard. He can't talk in *that* state."

"Sorry, Sergeant! But it was his fault—he ducked into me!"

"Never mind," said Velka's voice. "I daresay this will answer all the questions anyone has." Velka, yes, seemed to have taken loving possession of the leather case. A smile of satisfaction curled his lips. Pen grew sorry he hadn't let Des cheat the man at dice after all, shipboard.

"I don't suppose he can climb down the ladder on his own, now," said a soldier.

"We could just drop him in."

"Aye, if you want to break both his legs."

"So is he going to be needed for anything, later? Aside from his execution?" asked the sergeant of, Pen guessed, Velka.

"Too soon to know. Best preserve him for the moment."

A brief, professional debate among the soldiery resulted in Pen, dressed only in his shirt and trousers, being lowered into darkness by a rope wound painfully under his arms, shepherded by a soldier on a twisting rope ladder. His bare feet, then knees, then the rest of him found cold, raw rock as he collapsed. Rope, soldier and ladder all disappeared upward. The scrape of a heavy stone overhead cut off both the voices, and the last faint reflections of the torch. Utter silence. Utter darkness.

Utter aloneness.

Only . . . not for him.

"Des," he groaned. "Are you still with me?"

A shaken pause. "They'd have had to spatter your brains all over the street for me to be anywhere else."

Despite his current throbbing pain, his curiosity prompted him to ask, "Where would you have jumped?"

A sense of surly thought. "Velka."

All else being equal, a demon forced to jump by the death of its rider usually went to the strongest other person in the vicinity. "Really?"

"He would not have lived long." A pause. "And he would have died in all the lingering agony I could arrange."

Pen wondered if that was how a chaos demon said *I love you.*

*More or less,* Des said in their silent speech, as his lips grew harder to move. *Pen, pay attention. You mustn't swoon. Your skull is cracked and you're bleeding inside it. We can burn closed the blood vessel, but we have to open a hole to let out the clot before the pressure kills you.*

*You want me to trepan myself?*

*I'll do it, but you have to stay conscious. I can't work it if you . . . if you . . .*

*Understood.*

Destructive medicine. Sometimes, it saved lives.

Sometimes it didn't . . .

His head was in so much pain already, exploding open a hole the size of his fingertip hardly made a difference. The spurt of blood seemed small, but a little of the numbness left his lips. *Yes, that's right,* and he wasn't sure which of them said it.

*Can I pass out now? Hurts . . .*

*No. Stay awake. We have to finish shifting the clot.*

That, too, was right. Familiar. And a very unpleasant prospect. Was Des in as much pain as he was? Maybe not, but if his mind and body broke down, she would fragment, too. *Can't be fun for you either.*

*No.*

After a little, he asked, *Des, can you still light my eyes?*

*Yes . . .*

In a moment, the blackness pulled back. With no light at all to work with the effect was peculiar, oddly colorless, but his sense of the space and the shapes around him grew secure. They seemed to be in a round chamber quarried out of the bedrock, about fourteen feet high and seven wide, its chiseled walls curving steadily inward to the small port at the top presently blocked by the heavy stone.

Penric studied the cruel angles, and meditated on the mountain-climbing experiences of his youth. *No. I don't think even I could scale this one.* And certainly not in this condition. In his imagination, on the trip over, he'd confidently posited that no locked door could hold them. *Is this place meant to be proof against sorcerers?* Had Velka penetrated *that* secret, as well as his others?

*It's a standard Cedonian bottle dungeon. A place they put prisoners they want to forget, it's said.*

*Ever been in one before?* And, unsaid, *Ever got out of one before?* Except the hard way, he supposed, minus her rider.

*No.*

In a little while, he crawled to the wall and clawed up far enough to turn and brace his shoulders against it. They paused to tease out the last of the clot, and he felt gingerly at the spreading wetness behind his ear, soaking his walnut-dyed queue. It wasn't going to add up to enough blood loss to kill him. At least, not on this side of his skull.

He sat up and concentrated on keeping breathing. As ambitions went, it seemed much reduced from this morning's, but it was challenge enough for now.

An unmeasurable time later he began to wonder how he had betrayed himself to Velka, how he had failed in discretion or simply in acting, not that he'd cast a hard role for himself. Try as he might, he couldn't remember. Velka hadn't been another sorcerer. Nor a shaman. Nor, certainly, a saint. He'd not used any uncanny means to flush out Pen's secrets.

For that matter, who was Velka really? The patriotic Cedonian merchant he seemed? Or an agent of another kind?

*For what it's worth*, said Des, *I can't see our mistake either.*

It was kind of her to try to make him feel less stupid, Pen thought. This, his first confidential diplomatic mission, had been supposed to be a simple one, and, if he brought it off ably, bore the promise from both duke and archdivine of more such opportunities for travels to new places. A bottle dungeon hadn't been on his imagined itinerary.

Some period after that, he began to wonder if he would die; then, as time ground formlessly on, just how he would die. Executed in some frightful manner? Or simply forgotten to death in the dark? Which wasn't the dark for him. Nor would he die alone; Des was a friend he couldn't outlive. He could grow reconciled to that, he guessed.

*I should have liked to see that sky again, though.*

It was a shamefully long time after *that* when he finally thought, *What will happen to the man I was supposed to meet?* The full cost of his failure began to sketch itself to his vivid and well-stocked imagination, and he cursed some dozens of histories he'd read that suggested exactly how, in gruesome detail. *Five gods. What will happen to General Arisaydia?* It wasn't just Pen who might pay for this fiasco with his life.

*But not Des. That, at least.*

And another small blessing: "No sun blisters, anyway!" He giggled. But his mouth was too dry, and then he choked.

*Pen,* said Des uneasily. *You're starting to fray, down here. If you can't hold yourself together, you won't be able to hold me. Hold!*

*How?* He laid his aching head upon his knees, reminded of why people trapped in unbearable pain sought death at their own hands.

Des said reluctantly at last, *Pray to your god. He's the only other one in here besides us.*

Pen considered this. For a long time. Then whispered, "Lord Bastard, Fifth and White," and faltered. He held up his hands in the black, fingers spread wide in supplication. "Master of all disasters out of season." Indeed. "I lay this day as an offering upon your altar. If it please You, take it from me."

That wasn't any of the prayers he'd been taught in seminary, almost a decade ago, but it felt right. And perhaps it was heard, for at length he slept.

A long time, it seemed to Penric, after he had been dropped into this hole, the stone scraped back, orange light flickered, and a covered pail was lowered on a hook. At the guard's shouted instructions, he rolled over and freed the hook, which rose upward as he could not. The cover was a crude round tray holding a small loaf of bread, only a day stale, a sticky block of dried fruit, mostly figs, and a pale square that Des assured him was pressed dried fish. He lifted the tray to reveal not a slops bucket, but a generous couple of gallons of fresh water and a wooden cup.

Pen drank greedily, then slowed, wondered how long it would need to last.

"I'd guess this to be a daily ration," Des opined. "Drink up anyway. You need it to heal."

He managed part of the bread and some shreds of the fruit, but after one bite couldn't face the fish, for all that Des urged it on him with the concern of an anxious mother, insisting it was common food, and strengthening. It smelled. And had bones in it, albeit as fine as stiff hairs. And, and *bits.*

So he was fed, watered, and left alone which, for the first three days, was all he wanted. The cell's diameter gave him room to stretch out fully on the floor, even as it made impossible the old mountaineer's trick for shinnying up a crevice by bracing one's back and feet against opposite sides.

On the fourth day, he sat up and began to tend to his own wounds in more detail. Des could speed the healing of his abused skull and counteract infection, but it was definitely uphill magic, and she needed somewhere to dump the disorder. Normally there were enough minor vermin around to make this a trivial task, but once she'd eliminated the spiders and a few other shadowy things with far too many legs that rippled across the walls, others were slow to arrive. On the fifth day, they enjoyed a boon when a rat came up the central floor drain that doubled as Pen's slops bucket. Des fairly pounced on it. Pen was afraid he would then be trapped in this bottle with rotting rat reek, but Des, compelled to unusual frugality by their circumstances, not only creamed off the death but reduced the corpse to dust within an hour, and he used the dregs of his daily water to rinse it back down the drain.

For lack of other pastimes, he found himself crouching at this sink hoping for more rats like a winter fisherman back home beside his hole sawn in the lake ice. He missed a flask of warming spirits to keep him company, or friends to trade lies with, but at least there was Des. He studied the drain, which was no wider than his palm, drilled down through solid stone. Maybe he was not that desperate yet...

"Not ever," snorted Des. "Even you are not skinny enough to fit down that pipe. And it only goes to a borehole scarcely bigger."

"Empties into the sea, I expect." The smells and occasional drafts that came from it were more estuarial than cloacal. But no, probably not the drain. Widening a passageway through it by chaos magic could be a month's tedious labor, as lengthy and tiring a process as tunneling with the spoon that he did not have. Up was another unfavorable option. He could work apart the arch around the port, at some risk of dropping large stones on his head and making guard-attracting noises, but levitating up there would still be impossible. Waiting to be hauled up out of the dungeon for interrogation by his captors still seemed his best and easiest chance at escape, certainly until his fractures mended. He was perilously hot with their healing, masking the chill of any incipient prison fever.

He shouted questions upward during the daily visit from his keepers to swap out his rations pail, but they were never answered.

Three rats later, his skull, though still tender, had stopped aching in a way that made him want to cut his own head off. He dutifully managed to choke down the disgusting fish and not gag it up after. Des beguiled some time by telling him stories from her many past lives with her former riders, all women, or rather, ten women, a lioness, and a wild mare. The mare had been the point at which the demon first escaped into the world from the Bastard's hell, or repository of chaos, or whatever it was. There had been many theological arguments back at seminary as to the exact nature of the place, which Pen thought Des should be able to settle as she was the only one who'd been there, but she'd claimed to have no memory of it because its very disorder did not allow memory to form. All her personality—personalities—was, or were, something she had acquired afterward, imprinted on her by the endurance of matter.

Her tales were good, but in this lightless, soundless place, began to take on a hallucinatory quality. He'd usually experienced them as words, if inside his own head, and an impression of animated gestures like a storyteller in a marketplace. Now he began to see flickering pictures. It was much like those disturbing nights when he dreamed not his own dreams, but hers.

The more disturbing as it became harder and harder to tell day from night in here, or dreams from waking.

# II

THE SHADOWS in the municipal magistrates' court-and-prison at midnight made Nikys want to crawl inside her own skin. She drew her dark green cloak closer about her and padded as silently as she could after the jailer she'd bribed to let her in to see her brother. This jailer would do more—or rather, see even less—if she could bring her plan about.

He led her up stone stairs and out onto the third-floor gallery overlooking the courtyard. In the night silence the boards creaking under their feet seemed screams, not mouse-squeaks. No dank dungeon cells with iron bars on this level, just a row of small rooms that could as well have been civic offices, apart from their heavy locked doors with narrow, iron-bound slots.

Nikys tried to extract the political meaning from this choice of confinement: more austere than house arrest; not so vile as, say, those oubliettes down at the old harbor fortress. Maybe it was mere prudence. If they'd attempted to arrest and hold the young general out at the army barracks or in the shore fortress, he'd likely have been smuggled aid before this. For all that he'd commanded in Patos for barely half a year, he was already starting to grow popular with his men, if only for his diligence in getting them paid on time.

Although on the lately disputed southwestern borders, men had followed him for much less. *Victory is the best pay an officer can give his men*, Adelis had once remarked. *And vice versa.*

A brilliant campaign of maneuver and strike, it was said, turning back the Rusyllin incursion with half-forces, wits, and spit. (Adelis himself had called it the Bastard's Own Dysentery.) In any just world, in any other *country*, his labors should have resulted in promotion and reward. Not semi-exile to a minor provincial post, and heightened political suspicion. Doubtless exacerbated by his mother's blood ties to the Imperial House, for all that several prior too-successful army generals had ridden on the shoulders of their soldiers to Cedonian imperial power without such bonds. But if Adelis had such ambitions, she'd never seen a hint, and she'd known him from the day of their births.

The jailer peered through the door slot. He did not startle the night by knocking, but just called softly, "General Arisaydia? You have a visitor." Handing Nikys the shaded dark-lantern, he unlocked the door and let her slip within, but stayed nervously on guard outside.

Adelis, dressed only in a loose shirt and string-tied trousers, sat on his cot, blinking in the sudden spear of light. As Nikys set the lantern on a little table and swept back her hood, he swung out bare feet and bolted upright to embrace her, the power of his grip silent witness to his anxiety. She embraced him just as hard, then pushed away to search his face, hands, arms for signs of torture. Bruises, yes . . . but no worse than he might have picked up at sword practice.

As his wits caught up with the rest of him, he shoved her back, though not slackening his drowning-man's clutch on her shoulders. "What are you doing in here at this hour?" he said through his teeth. "Or at all? Five gods, Nikys! I prayed you'd have the sense to stay clear of all this!"

"*All this* came to me. The day you were arrested, the governor sent men to search my house. They took all my letters from you, and my old letters from Kymis, what could they want with *those* I was so furious—"

His jaw tightened. "Did they hurt you?"

She shook her head. "Just shoved me back when I protested."

Despite it all, the corners of his lips twitched. "Did you hurt them?"

"Gods witness I tried," she sighed. "They knocked down my servants, ransacked the house. Tore up floorboards and pried apart paneling and furniture, especially in your chamber. Turned out all the clothes chests and left everything in piles. Although they were clearly after, oh, I don't know what they were after, but they didn't really pillage us, and no one was raped. A lot of small valuables turned up missing after they left, but you'd expect that." She drew breath. "Adelis, where did this all come from? All I could find out is that you are accused of plotting treason with Adria, which is nonsense."

He shook his head. "I swear I don't know. They said they'd seized my correspondence with the Duke of Adria, detained his agent, but I'd never made any contacts with Adria. They didn't let me see the evidence—said it had gone in a courier pouch to Thasalon days before, and this arrest order was the result. Not that they need be authentic letters for this sort of move."

"Forgeries to entrap you, do you think?"

"Maybe."

She flung up a hand. "Later. We can talk later. Dress, gather your things. I have to get you out of here, right now."

"What?" Instead of obeying, he stepped back and stared. "Nikys, is this some sort of hare-brained rescue scheme?"

"Yes," she snapped, declining to waste time arguing about the embedded insult. "Hurry!"

He shook his head. "Bad idea."

"Staying here is a worse one."

"I agree it's not good, but nothing would convict me in my accusers' eyes—in the emperor's eyes—faster than fleeing like a guilty thief."

"Do you imagine they haven't convicted you already?"

"There has been no trial, no hearing."

"When did *you* grow so naive?"

He smiled sadly. "If I didn't run from four thousand screaming Rusyllin tribesmen, I'm not going to run from this."

"They attacked from the front. This is an ambush from behind, in the dark."

"Oh, the Rusylli did that, too."

She grimaced, fierce in her frustration. "What in the world is your plan, then?"

"Stand my ground. Argue my case. Continue to speak the truth."

"And if that ground has already been cut from under you?"

"I did not commit treason, and I will not. I am not without friends, as well as enemies, at court."

"Argue your case from a safer place!"

"There isn't a safer place, not within the bounds of the empire. And to leave it would turn the false charge true."

She leaned her forehead against his shoulder, so frenzied she nearly bit his shirt. "Adelis. It has to be tonight. I can't do this again. I spent all I had on the bribes just to get this far, and the horses. Suborned men don't give *refunds*."

He sank down on his cot and did a good simulation of a boulder, stolid and immobile. Stubborn. It ran in the family. If she'd brought four men, whacked him over the head, and carried him out in a sack, she might have been able to do this. But when that look grew on his face, nothing less would shift him. She'd sometimes admired the trait, but not when it was aimed at her.

"You have to leave," he argued in turn, "and stay well away. You're bound to be watched, but you're not enough threat to anyone in your own right for them to go after you without provocation. For the love of all the gods and goddesses, for the love of *me*, don't give that provocation."

"You're saying I should do nothing, just freeze to the ground like a hare menaced by a hawk?"

"That would be a good start, yes." He swiped his hands through his dark disheveled hair, clenched them on his knees. "*Please* don't try to engage with something so far over your head as this. The last thing I need is for my enemies to realize how effective a lever on me you could be."

Tears were leaking down her cheeks, and she hated their wet helplessness. "Curse all men, and their pride, and their greed, and their envy, and their *idiocy*." *And their fear.*

He grinned at her, his rich brown eyes crinkling. "Ah, that's my Nikys."

She couldn't scream here. She couldn't even *yell*. Another ten minutes of ferocious undervoiced argument moved him no further. He should have been made a siege commander, she thought.

Only the frightened jailer stopped it. He cracked the door and hissed, "That's enough. Madame Khatai, you must come away *now*. I can't stay out here any longer."

Adelis pushed, the jailer pulled, and she found herself once more on the gallery, bewildered in the dark.

He led her back down the stairs. Out the side archway to the entry with the postern door.

Where they found a troop of six guardsmen and a senior captain waiting for them.

The jailer had not revealed her; he whimpered, too, as they were roughly seized. Another lantern was unveiled and raised, pushing back the shadows.

"Where is he?" asked one of the guardsmen, sounding confused.

The captain stepped forward. Cornered, she yanked back her hood and raised her chin. Protests and subterfuge and lies jammed up in her mouth, choked by fear. *Wait. Give nothing away.*

"Madame Khatai." The captain grimaced. "Imagine meeting you here at this hour."

Oddly, his ironic tone steadied her. This was a man who would talk, not strike. Or at least talk before he struck. "If anyone here had possessed the common courtesy or holy mercy to let me see my own brother in the daytime, I would have. I took what I could get."

His glance seared the shrinking jailer. "So it seems."

"You mustn't blame him. I cried at him, you know." Which was true, if incomplete. The captain, she suspected, was not a man whom feminine tears would soften. But let him think this was just an anxious visit from kin, not an escape attempt, and perhaps the poor man would get off more lightly.

"And where is your brother?"

"Right where you people put him. Unjustly." Her lips drew back in something that was hardly a smile. "He claims the Father of Winter will support him in his innocence."

The captain vented a faint snort, but stepped aside to murmur to two of his men, who departed at a run. They returned in a few minutes to report, "The general is still locked in, sir."

The captain stared at her in some frustration. Had he hoped to catch her in the act? He said, conversationally, "We have your horses and your servant, you know. Rather a lot of baggage for an evening jaunt through town, don't you think?"

It wasn't as though she'd left them waiting at the prison's front gate. So, she'd been spied upon—make that, more *effectively* spied upon—than even she had suspected. Not that anyone who'd really known the general and his widowed sister could have been too surprised at this turn of events, but how many people in Patos was that, really? She lived retired by choice, and seldom taxed Adelis at camp; he in turn was respectful of her privacy.

Betrayed from before the beginning, it seemed.

Her dead silence was apparently not the reaction for which the captain had rehearsed, so he gave up trying to draw her out, replacing his heavy irony with sternness.

"Your efforts on your brother's behalf are understandable, Madame, but pointless. If you return here at midday tomorrow, the general will be given back to you freely, without impediment. In fact ... " He narrowed his eyes at her. "In fact, we will escort you home now, and guard your rest. And escort you back tomorrow. Just to make sure of it." He added after a moment, "We will, however, be keeping the horses."

"He is to be released?" The soaring thrill his words engendered died in her chest. That Adelis was innocent—or, be frank, something like innocent—she had no doubt. But he might mean only that her brother was slated to be summarily executed, yet have, as a pious mercy, his body returned to his family, such as she was, for burial instead of being hung on a gibbet outside the city gates as a lesson to other would-be traitors. Whatever the answer, the captain already *knew*. And the pity in his face frightened her far more than the sternness.

He didn't reply, but just surrounded her with his men and marched her out into the winding streets of Patos.

So, they'd both been right, she and Adelis. Her pathetic escape scheme was doomed to failure. And his remaining in his captivity was a horrible, horrible mistake.

At noon the next day the soldiers came once more for her, as threatened, and escorted her in reverse back to the same side entrance of the municipal prison.

The captain swept through, saw them, and grimaced. "You're too early. Keep her here. You three, come with me." And to Nikys, "Wait."

So they waited, shifting from foot to foot. No one spoke to her—nor to each other, no small talk or barracks chaff or crude complaint. They offered her neither insult nor reassurance. The unnatural silence stretched. Her head throbbed, as if it held too much blood, as if she'd been hung upside down.

One of the soldiers returned leading a saddled horse—one of her own hiring that she'd thought lost last night. He joined the wait, as wordless as the horse, which blew through its nostrils and cocked a hip.

The stillness was abruptly shattered by the most inhuman scream Nikys had ever heard. Even muddled by intervening walls, it rose high and piercing, then broke, then rose again. Then cut off sharp, as if the raw throat from which it reverberated had clenched closed, or been sliced through. The horse tossed its head and sidled uneasily.

It couldn't have been Adelis's voice . . . could it? Even at age ten when he'd broken an arm falling off his pony, he'd vented no more than an odd little *Eh!* Perhaps it was only some thief, convicted for a fifth time and paying a hand in penalty? Such punishments were sometimes administered here, she thought. *Please, please, let it be some thief . . .*

The remaining soldiers had stopped looking at her, or around, or at each other. To a man, they stared at the ground. Afraid? Who wouldn't be, after hearing that unholy sound? She was terrified, her body shuddering as if in the winter wind, though sweat dampened her all over.

No. Stranger than that, she realized. *They stand ashamed.*

At length, silhouettes appeared in the bright archway to the inner court, two men supporting a third stumbling between them. *Adelis?* Not a corpse on a litter, to be sure, but relief didn't wash through her. The solid form was familiar, its constricted posture not. His body was hunched, lurching, as though he were overtaken with winesickness.

It was only as they came near that she saw the pale bandage wrapped around his head, and realized why they were now willing to release the genius general to no more stern a warder than his sister.

*Oh gods oh gods oh gods oh gods oh gods . . .*

*They've put out his eyes.*

# III

PENRIC GUESSED it might have been ten days when the stone was dragged back and not replaced, but no hooked rope dropped to collect his empty pail. Instead, a few feet of a leather hose were pushed over the edge of the hole, though not far enough to be anywhere near in reach. The guards were silent shadows in the wavering torchlight, its wan glow grown as brilliant as the sun's in Pen's staring, dark-adapted eyes.

"Now what?" he called up, not expecting a reply.

"Mercy for you, madman," someone growled back down.

"I'm not mad." *Rather angry by now, though.*

"You babble to yourself all the time."

"I'm not talking to *myself." Just to the voices in my head. All ten of them.* Not, he knew from long experience, a useful thing to mention.

A snort, and the—pair?—of sandaled feet shuffled away.

A few minutes later, the hose bulged, coughed, and began to disgorge a steady stream of what Pen hoped was water. He tested it by thrusting a hand in the flow. Yes, seawater, not, say, rainwater or sewage. Odd . . .

"Are they giving our little home a washing and flushing? It certainly needs one."

His throat constricted strangely as Des replied, "No. That's not it."

The water was coming in faster than the drain was leaking it away. Had they blocked the far end of the borehole? Pen splashed his bare feet uncertainly in the growing puddle.

Des continued, "They mean to drown us in our cell. Like a mouse trapped in a bucket. A means of disposing of a prisoner without leaving a mark on his body."

*Why should they care about that? And* ... "Don't they know we can swim?"

"For how long?"

"Hours? Days?"

"They have days."

"If they have days, they could just stop feeding us, and wait." This suggested ... what? *Something has changed, out there.*

After a few minutes, when the water topped his ankles, Pen said in aggravation, "They never even questioned me." That had remained his primary hope of escape—let him only be lifted out of this stone bottle, and whatever bindings or tortures or hulking guards were offered, he'd have been through them and gone from this fortress like an egg through a hen. Although he'd planned to endure through the first few questions, to gain some idea of the shape of his situation. "It's going to take a lot of water to fill this cell."

"They have the whole sea as a reservoir."

The fortress was above sea level, although only just, and so was the cell, or high tide would have come up twice a day to flush his wastepipe. The hose-water flowed steadily, not in spurts like a ship's bilge pump. It was draining from some prefilled tank, perhaps, not being lifted on the spot by men with muscles, or animal power. His mind darted down a tangent, calculating by his hard-won geometry the volume of the cell and the probable rate of flow from above. *Thank you, Learned Lurenz,* and he never thought he'd remember the sharp tap of that rod on his woolgathering young head with gratitude. "Six hours, maybe? Eight?"

"They won't fill it to the top, just to over your head. Pen, attend! Should I burst the hose?"

That would certainly delay things, although one of those things seemed to be 'the inevitable.' About to assent, he paused.

It was only parlor-magic. When he'd first moved over the

mountains a year ago—along with six mule-loads of books and two of clothing—to take up his duties with a new archdivine, he'd found the heat of Adria's humid coastal plains oppressive. Lighting fires with a muted spark was the first destructive magic he'd ever learned, and the easiest. Running the process backward was a much subtler challenge. But with practice, and some thinning out of the vermin in the archdivine's palace in Lodi, he'd devised a trick for pulling water out of the air into a large hailstone, to drop in his tepid drinks. Prudently, he'd not shown off his novel skill, not wanting to be pressed into work as a magical ice machine for the pleasure of his superior's many highborn guests.

It hadn't kept the archdivine's cousin the duke from purloining him anyway, when he'd wanted a secret envoy with a reputation for cleverness and a native's command of the Cedonian language to effect . . . a disaster, it seemed.

*Don't think about that now. You haven't time.*

Had that been Des, or himself? In any case, yes, he did have time. Several hours of it, he guessed.

"How soon do you think they'll be back to check the cell for drowned mice?"

"No idea."

If they expected him to flounder in immediate panic, maybe not that long? No controlling that. He leaned his shoulders against the cell's curving wall and composed himself in patience, forming his plan.

*Your plan is to freeze us to death before we can drown?* Des asked plaintively.

His lips curled up for the first time in days. "Have you never watched the mountain raftmen in the spring, breaking the winter-cut logs loose from the river ice for their journey downstream?" Both Ruchia, his demon's immediate prior rider, and Helvia before her had been cantons-born just like Penric. "It's like a dance."

"A dance with death! . . . Have you ever *done* that?"

"A few springs, in my youth, I helped the local men in the valley of the Greenwell." Pen reflected on the memory. "Didn't tell my mother, though."

*Hah.* She added grimly after a while, as the water lapped his knees, "This is going to be costly."

"Yes. But consider the alternative."

As the seawater reached his thighs, he wondered aloud, "Do you suppose they know I am a sorcerer?"

Des hesitated. "It's not sure proof, but I'd think if they did, there would be a goat or a sheep or some such tethered at the top."

His head cocked back in momentary mystification, but then the answer slotted in. *Oh.* "To contain you safely after you jumped, till they could decide how to dispose of you?"

"It's an old trick when executing a sorcerer, yes."

"You wouldn't like that."

"No. So kindly stay alive, Penric."

When the water reached his shoulders, he commenced, starting a thin sheet of ice in the center of the cell. Hand to the wall and pushing, he walked slowly around the perimeter, to keep the water moving and his tiny ice floe centered. His body grew warm with the working of his magic, welcome this time since the Cedonian seawater, while tolerable by Penric's standards, was still much cooler than a man's blood, and had been leaching his strength away in increments. Hunger and thirst, too, would start to sap him if he let this drag out.

And Desdemona was growing . . . he was never sure what to name it. More excitable, perhaps, in these early stages. They were still a long way from the uncontrollable mania that overtook her when they tried to work too much uphill magic too fast, but it seemed discourteous to stress her beyond need. *Also dangerous.*

Des muttered an obscene agreement, sign of sorts. "But you realize," she said in sudden cheer, as he plowed through water past his chest, "with this skill, you need never die of thirst in a desert."

Pen coughed a seawater-laced laugh. "Not my most pressing concern, here, Des . . . "

His ice disk grew thicker, descending downward in the middle; he tried to keep the top surface relatively flat. He needed to generate rather more than his own body weight, he guessed. As the water reached his chin, he clambered aboard.

And *up* . . .

The hose end was just beyond his reaching fingers. His bare feet on his floe were chilling, and, worse, melting potholes. He attempted a jump, missed, slipped, and ended up splashing into the water, barking his elbow painfully on the wall and being pinched against it by the pitching ice-brick. Brine in his eyes and nose stung, the taste bitter and metallic in his mouth. He came up spitting and heaved himself atop his float once more.

This time, he waited a little, letting the floe and himself settle as much as they could under the ongoing spout of water from above. Tested his balance more carefully. Gauged. Stretched. Coiled. And *UP*...

One hand closed around the slippery leather, then the next. The jet of water in his face cut off as his hanging weight pulled the hose closed over the edge of the port. One hand over the other, *don't let go, don't fall back*... He flopped an arm over the keystone circle. Then he was out altogether, collapsing across the dungeon's paved floor. He lay gasping for a moment.

Rolling over, he peered one last time down into the watery, deadly well. "You realize," he wheezed, "that once that ice melts"—which it was already starting to do, and swiftly—"they're going to have *no idea* what we just did."

Desdemona borrowed his mouth for a black laugh that echoed very demonically indeed. He clapped his hand across it, but grinned back.

He was still sprawled wet, barefoot, brimming with hot unshed chaos on the prison floor of a guarded fortress. Alone, on the edge of an unknown country. No idea if it was day or night outside. *Not the time to plan a triumphal celebration yet, I don't think.*

Three bottle dungeons lay in a row in this close corridor, the other two thankfully unoccupied, so how special a prisoner had he been? A locked door at one end led, probably, to a guard post. The lock would be easy, the guards perhaps not. He followed the leather hose back the other way to where it issued partway up the wall from a small window, its normal barring unbolted and set aside for the occasion.

"Can we get out this?"

"Maybe. Better chance than the drain. Seems to run about two feet through the wall and open into a window well. I can't sense what's beyond that."

Pen leaned backward, reached through, turned his head sideways, and fitted himself in. A great deal of undignified wriggling later, and he was able to sit up in the outer well without actually snapping his spine. His long legs nearly trapped him, but at the cost of some contusions he managed to extract them without having to break bones. He stood up in the well.

He'd reached a sort of porch overlooking the sea. The stone tank rose nearby, a silent bilge pump standing near; unmanned at this hour, which was night *five gods be thanked*. He'd feared the sudden sunlight might have blinded him as effectively as the black below.

Something scuttled along the edge of the porch, and then exploded with a pop.

He'd not seen a rat do *that* before. *Quieter, Des!*

*Hurts,* she complained. *Also, how many times have I sat in the latrine with* you *sick when—*

Even after a decade, she could still make him blush. *Howsoever. How do we get out of this place?*

*Your job now.*

The obvious way out was to slip over the wall, swim quietly around to the harbor in the dark, and creep up over one of the jetties.

They stared down at the black, lapping sea with equal disfavor.

"No help for it," said Des at last, "unless you want to go back to the bottle dungeon. Carry on."

Penric sighed and climbed down into the foam-laced waters.

An hour later, salt-crusted and footsore, Penric sat in a stone laundry trough that drained a modest marble fountain, sited in a square that fronted a middle-sized temple. He'd drunk his fill of blessedly clean water, and now faced the next task. He tried not to think about the several harbor rats and a luckless sleepy seagull they'd sacrificed in their wake down at the shore; Des, calmer, seemed back to visiting chaos only on less theologically questionable insects. One couldn't call it necromancy, exactly . . .

*Lie back,* said Des, in her practical Ruchia-voice, *and I'll get rid of your hair dye.*

"Really?"

*They'll be looking for a brown-haired escapee. Also, your blond roots are growing out. It will be easier to lift the stain altogether than to try to work it around to match.*

He decided to take her word, and besides, the fresh water was something very like a bath. He would have preferred to burn his prison-reeking shirt and trousers, but until he could replace them, this impromptu laundering would have to do.

So it was, after almost falling asleep in the trough, that he sloshed up and squeezed out his hair, letting it fall down his back—the ribbon for his queue was long lost. Not much time left till first light and people about, he gauged. He left a trail of wet footprints to the shadowed temple portico. Opening a simple lock was so routine by now that he didn't even pause in swinging the tall door ajar and slipping within. After that, it was rather like going shopping in the marketplace. In reverse.

The layout within was similar to home, with altar niches spaced around the walls and a central plinth for the holy fire, banked to coals for the night. Timber-built temples in the cantons boasted fine woodcarvings; here, the plastered stone walls were graced with frescos, their subjects ambiguous in the shadows, and mosaic tiles enlivened the floor. This was a neighborhood temple, he judged, serving the folk in the immediate vicinity, not so large or so well-guarded as the main provincial temple atop some higher hill. Nor so wealthy, alas. He found the Bastard's niche, perfunctorily signed himself, and checked the altar table for offerings. Swept bare for the night, unfortunately.

But this was the sort of prudent place that featured locked offering boxes in each niche. He flipped this one open and peered within. If it, too, had been emptied for the night...

A scant scattering of coins and other oddments lay within. His long fingers rapidly picked out the coins and left the less identifiable prayers, such as a coil of hair.

He contemplated his meager take. "The white god must not be much loved here. Or much feared."

"You wouldn't accept any of my suggestions for targets through town."

"Stealing from the poor is inefficient, and stealing from the rich is dangerous. Anyway, this isn't stealing. It's just ... collecting my pay more directly than usual."

Des snickered. "I didn't think the Cedonian and Adriac Temples practiced such reciprocity."

"Same god." He'd known from the beginning that he served his god first, and the Temple second. So far, he'd not found them often in conflict, and prayed it would stay that way.

Slowly, he circled the chamber. His hand hovered over the box at the Mother of Summer's altar, but then passed on. While he'd no doubt She would not begrudge a loan to her second Son's divine, Pen had refused Her his oath back in Martensbridge; it felt, if nothing else, rude to ask for Her aid now. He'd abandoned service to the Son of Autumn years ago, and the Daughter of Spring had never been his goddess. He finally stopped before the Father's altar.

"Pen," said Des uneasily. "*Nobody* steals from the god of justice."

"Borrows," he corrected. "I expect my collateral is good here. Maybe Locator Oswyl would vouch for me." He smiled to remember his friend back in Easthome, the most earnest devotee of the Father of Winter he'd ever encountered. He flipped open the box and raised his brows. "Goodness me."

"Somebody must be anxious for their lawsuit," Des suggested.

"Possibly both sides. Though trying to *bribe* the god of justice seems missing the point." Or he supposed some poor—evidently not-so-poor—call it *distraught* man might be praying for a child, or for ease for a dying father. He signed himself and bowed his head in any case. *I shall try to use it well, Sir.*

He doubled back to collect the cloth from the Bastard's altar to carry it all in, relocked all the boxes, and slid back out to the portico, closing the door quietly. Sky and sea were growing a strange clear gray. He could hear the clop of a donkey and creak of a cart, and, from open windows roseate with lamplight, people stirring and pots rattling.

Find a used-clothing vendor, find a cheap inn, find a breakfast that did not include dried fish; after that...

After that all this was going to grow harder. It wasn't a happy thought.

Penric quartered the streets of Patos near the army barracks and parade ground, trying to puzzle out his approach. Walking up to the front gate and knocking seemed a poor one. In his new retrospect, it struck him how thin his preparation for this emissary's task had been.

He wondered if he'd been missed from the bottle dungeon yet. Fortunately, he'd found a clothing stall and food from a street vendor before being confronted by his cot in his little inn, for he'd fallen like a tree into the linen-covered, wool-stuffed mattress, and slept in profound exhaustion. When he'd woken in the late afternoon, he'd found he'd not lost as much time as he'd imagined. Unlike home, where people seized the afternoon to get as much done as possible before the dark and the cold closed in, here the citizens evaded the bright hours, crawling into the burrows of their houses to escape the heat and emerging just about now.

He wriggled his feet in his odd leather sandals. His workman's garb was unexceptional, a sleeveless tunic and trousers that were expected to ride short in the legs anyway. He'd knotted his hair on his nape, still blond but not hanging out like a signal flag. A countryman's straw hat shaded his eyes. His accent, broadly archaic from the far northern mountains of Cedonia, marked him as not from around here, so legitimately lost, without making him alien.

*Until you start talking at length, and that scholar's vocabulary begins falling out*, commented Des. *In that country accent, it's like a donkey opening its mouth and spouting poetry.*

*I'll try to be more brief*, Pen sighed.

Curse it, he had to start *somewhere*. He spotted a lone soldier, not an officer, leaving the squared-off barracks grounds, and angled over to accost him before he disappeared into the close, winding streets of the civil side.

"Pardon me. Can you tell me where to find General Arisaydia? I was given"—*Bastard's tears, don't say* a letter—"a package of figs to deliver to him."

The soldier stopped and stared. "Hadn't you heard? He was arrested. Four days ago, by the governor's guards. By Imperial order, it's claimed. I don't know where they took him, but he's sure not here." He jerked his thumb over his shoulder at the military quarter now suddenly not Pen's goal.

Pen swallowed in shock. Seven or so days after his own arrest— if the two were connected, why the delay? Gathering other evidence?

"On what charge?" Pen managed.

The soldier shrugged. "Treason, I guess. They can slap that on anything. Sounds like shit to me." He hesitated, as if wanting to call back his unguarded words. "But what do *I* know?" He shouldered away from Penric and strode on, surly. Disturbed.

Seven days. Time for a speedy courier to ride to the Imperial capital, a day or two for debate, persuasion—plotting—a couple of days for an arrest order from high enough up to be returned? Very high up, it sounded like. Officers at Arisaydia's level could be moved around like game pieces only by the most powerful of hands.

However it had come about, it was plain that rumors were running through the army like dye through wool. If Pen wanted answers without bringing attention to himself by asking questions, he needed to find a place where the military talked to each other. Handily, several taverns catering to the soldiers' trade clustered in the nearby streets. He glanced into a few until he found one that was more crowded, and where his countryman's dress would blend in, and slipped inside.

He held a tankard of vilely sour ale and wandered about, listening for key words and especially for the key name. He found it at a table with half-a-dozen low-grade officers, a couple captains-of-hundreds and their lieutenants. He slid onto a stool by the wall and pulled the brim of his hat a little farther down over his eyes, and simulated a workman's tired doze. Well, simulated the doze; the tired was authentic.

"It was never peculation, not him," one scoffed.

"I'd not heard that one," said another. "Plotting betrayal with the Duke of Orbas, I was told. Or the Duke of Adria. Or of Trigonie. Some frigging foreign duke or another, anyway."

Universal scowls greeted this claim.

"Or no duke at all," growled a grizzled captain. "Some trumped-up charge by those eunuchs at court, more likely."

Another made a crude joke at the expense of mutilated men, which his comrades seemed to find more black than funny.

"Yes, but what's Arisaydia *have* that that crowd of mincing bureaucrats would want to steal?"

The grizzled captain shrugged. "The loyalty of the Army of the West, for starters. Enough high-born bureaucrats, whether they still have their balls or not, have military nephews who might like to filch a rank they can't bloody earn."

"Surely the emperor," began another, but his captain held up a stemming hand. He began again more carefully, "Surely those Thasalon *courtiers* are not to be trusted . . . "

Men at this level could hardly know more than Penric did, but their talk was alarming.

*No*, sighed Des. *All standard army-issue bitching about the civil government, so far. It doesn't seem to have changed in a hundred years. Huh.*

The talk had turned to other complaints when a new man joined them, and Pen had to keep himself from sitting bolt upright. He was a younger fellow, broad and brawny, and had the sunburned brick-colored skin of most of the men here, but his face was strained and ghastly, drained to a sallow tinge. Wide-eyed and breathless, he fell into a seat on the bench, where his comrades obligingly shifted to give him room, and said, "Five gods, give me a drink." Not waiting, he seized one from a comrade, who yielded it up with a surprised eyebrow-lift. "I just heard—" He tipped back the tankard, and his mouth worked, but he couldn't seem to swallow. He had to struggle for a moment before he could choke it down.

"Arisaydia," he gasped out. "Yesterday noon in secret at the municipal prison. Imperial order."

"Released?" said a man hopefully, then faltered.

"Executed?" growled the grizzled captain, voice grim as iron.

The new man shook his head. "They blinded him with boiling vinegar."

Shocked silence. Bitten lips.

Pen bent on his stool and swallowed back vomit.

*Don't you dare*, said Des. *Don't give a sign.*

"Princely," observed the gray captain, in a weird sardonic lilt that might be rage, or grief, or swallowed curses. "Thought us army mules usually got hot irons through our eyes."

"Not an honor I'd care for," muttered another.

The other captain leaned back and sighed. "Well, that's done him. What a gods-forsaken waste."

"Is he still in the prison?"

The new man shook his head. "No. They gave him over to his twin sister, what's-her-name, I heard."

*So what is her name . . . ?!*

The men were easing back as they took this in, scowling but not, apparently, moved to leap up and start a military mutiny at the news this afternoon. Someone secured the messenger his own tankard, and he gulped deep. Some moved their food aside, but kept their clutches on their drinks.

"Hope she's a good nurse," said a lieutenant.

"Or will help him to a good knife," said another. "Either one."

Pen panted in horror, so, so grateful for the straw hat, its brim now down to his chin.

"Are they really twins?"

"Who knows? Story I heard was that *he* was the son of old General Arisaydia's highborn wife, and *she* was the daughter of his concubine, whelped on the same day. Unless the midwife swapped them in secret, to give the old man an heir."

"That's an old rumor."

"Funny, you never heard it around till he was promoted so high, so young..."

"Well, he's a poor blind bastard now. Whether his parents were married or not."

The mood of the table blighted, the party broke up, most men finishing their meals and drifting out, a couple settling in for deeper drinking. Penric, as soon as he could stand without shaking, made his way into the street, now half-shaded in the angled, descending sun, and found a wall to prop his shoulders against.

*Gods, Des, now what?*

*Start back to Adria, I suppose. Not through the port of Patos, by preference.*

Acid bile burned Pen's throat at the thought of such an empty-handed retreat. No, far worse than empty-handed.

It made no sense. The Duke of Adria had fancied to hire the demoted and presumably disaffected general as a mercenary captain for his own endemic and inconclusive wars against his neighbor Carpagamo. The private letter he'd received from Arisaydia himself had suggested it, and the duke had taken him up on it...

Taken the bait?

But it wasn't *treason*, no more than Penric exchanging his service across the borders from the new princess-archdivine of Martensbridge to the archdivine of Adria. The duke hadn't planned to use Arisaydia against Cedonia, after all. It was just...a little delicate.

It shouldn't have been much worse than that, unless, unless, what?

There had to be a hidden half to this somewhere that Pen was not seeing. As he'd not seen how that Cedonian, Velka, could have guessed Pen's real mission. Unless, of course, he'd already known...

But, Bastard's tears and Mother's blood, *blinding*. He'd seen burns and bone-deep scalds when drafted into his apprenticing-and-more at the Mother's Hospice in Martensbridge. Up close, in some bad cases. He didn't have to *imagine* anything.

"I have to do something about this."

*Five gods, Pen, what? The damage is done. It's time to cut our losses and fly.*

"I don't know yet." And then, in the next three breaths, he did.

He would need particulars on the sister, her name and domicile, and then a better used-clothing merchant. A better bathhouse, too, that offered services of a barber and a manicurist. An apothecary. A knife-maker's shop serving some very specialized needs. And more. How providential was it that the Father of Winter had filled his purse...?

It was going to be a busy night. He pushed off from the wall. "Let's go find out."

# IV

NIKYS SAT IN THE GARDEN of her rented villa and tried to eat... breakfast, she supposed it must be, this being morning. A morning. Which?

It had been, what, two days?—since she'd brought Adelis back here, clinging to his saddle, his labored breathing as frightening as weeping. Half her servants had fled after the visitation from the governor's men and not returned, so, to her loathing, she'd had to employ the soldiers who'd escorted them to support him stumbling to his upstairs bedchamber and lay him down. She hadn't wanted them *touching* him. She'd ejected them from her domain as swiftly as she could thereafter, without thanks, but a provincial guardsman still lurked outside her front door, and another beyond her back wall.

After that, the nightmare had commenced. She'd sponged her brother's body, dressed him in clean linen, coaxed him to eat, with poor luck, forced him to drink. He'd not cooperated much. She'd seen Adelis in a dozen bad moods in the past, exhausted or frustrated or enraged, though generally with the army or the Imperial court rather than with her. She'd never before seen him *broken*.

It was lovely in the garden in this first light. Water trickled musically through clever stone channels from the tiny spring that had made the villa, though old, such a wonderful find, half a year ago when Adelis had invited her to join him at his new posting. On the pergola that shaded her little table and chairs, grapevines shot forth leaves that seemed to expand by the hour, with green sprigs of new grapes peeping shyly through them. Bees bumbled among the flowers. On the far end, where the kitchen garden grew apace, dew sparkled off a spiderweb like a necklace of jewels carelessly dropped by some passing sprite. The space breathed charm, grace, ease, surcease from troubles.

This morning, its lying beauty *offended* her.

She ate the other half of her boiled egg, with a bite of bread to force it down, and a swallow of cold tea to force down the bread. When she finished, she'd have to return to Adelis's bedchamber and try again with the bandages stuck to his face. He'd screamed when she touched them, and struck out—blindly, of course, and so he'd connected at his full strength in a way he'd not done since they were squabbling children. His full strength had been much less, then. She rubbed at the deep bruise on her cheek, and buried her face in her hands.

She couldn't weep. Or sleep. Or eat. Or breathe . . .

*Control yourself anyway. You have to go back now.*

When she looked up, an apparition sat across from her.

She was so bewildered she didn't even jump, though her jaw fell open as she stared.

Her first thought was not *man*, or *woman*, but *ethereal*. Luminous eyes as blue as the sea in summer. Hair an astonishing electrum color, drawn back in a knot at the nape but with a few strands messily escaping to catch a sunbeam in a wispy halo. And nothing human should have skin so milk-pale.

She dismissed her furious fancies. It was most certainly a man.

Her gaze skipped down the long, folded body. Wiry arms, hands too large and strong for a woman, nails cut blunt and scrupulously clean. Sandaled feet too long to be feminine, chest too flat, hips *much* too narrow. Drawn back to the face, she discovered an inexplicably cheery smile and white, sound teeth.

He wore an undyed sleeveless tunic to his knees, belted at the thin waist, with a sleeveless jacket in dark green over it, suggesting, without quite being, the garment of an acolyte of the Mother's Order.

In a soft, friendly tone, her hallucination spoke: "Madame Khatai, I trust?"

She swallowed and located her voice, sharp-edged with alarm: "How did you get in here? There are guards." Less to keep people from going in and out, she suspected, than to mark and report who did so.

"Perhaps they went off-duty? I didn't see any."

"My servants should have stopped you."

"I'm afraid I didn't see any of them, either," he said as if in apology.

*That* she could believe, she thought grimly.

"Pardon me for startling you," he went on in that same soft voice. *Stunning me.*

"—my name is Master Penric. I am a physician."

She rolled back in her chair. "*Apprentice* Penric, I might believe. You can't be a day over twenty-one. Less."

"I'm thirty, I assure you, lady."

He claimed an age the same as hers, and she was a century old, this morning. "I might grant twenty-five."

He waved an airy hand. "Twenty-five it shall be, then, if you prefer."

"And *Master* . . . ?"

"In all but final oath." His smile grew rueful.

"Hnh."

"My credentials aside, some of your brother's officers took up a collection to hire me to attend upon him. For reasons you may understand better than I, they strongly wished to stay anonymous." He raised his blond brows, and she grimaced, unable to gainsay the likelihood. "But my fee is paid, and here I am."

"For how long?"

He shrugged. "As long as I'm needed." He gestured at the large case by his feet. "I brought supplies, and a change of clothing." After a moment he conceded, "I might not have been anyone's first pick as a physician. But I was the one who would come. ...And I'm fairly good with burns."

That last did not so much decide as dismast her, setting her adrift on dangerous shoals of hope. Her gaze caught on those scrubbed, thin-fingered hands. She might believe those hands, though she was none too sure of his tongue. She had no trust in this sudden stranger, she had no trust in anyone, but she was so benighted *tired*...

Perhaps he read her surrender in her posture, for he continued, "I should examine the general as soon as possible. I'm so sorry I couldn't be here earlier."

"Follow me, then." She pushed herself up, frugally drained the dregs of her tea, and led him into the house. "But he's not a general anymore, you know." She had come to hate the very sound of the betraying— betrayed—military title, which her brother had so cherished.

"What should I call him, then?"

"Arisaydia. I suppose." She did not invite this Penric fellow to *Adelis*.

As he lugged his case up the stairs after her, he asked, "Has he spoken much?"

"A little."

"What has he said?"

She stopped before Adelis's door and scowled up at the physician. "*Please let me die.*"

He hesitated, then said quietly, "I see."

As she opened the door he took a very deep breath and squared his shoulders—she revised his age downward again—and followed her inside.

Adelis lay as she'd left him to go down to breakfast. Nikys glanced at the scullion she'd set to watch him. "Any changes?"

The boy ducked his head. "No, lady."

"You may go back to the kitchen."

The blond physician held up a hand. "When you get there, boil a pot of water and set it to cool. And then another. We're going to need a lot."

"The water left from my tea should be cool by now," Nikys offered tentatively.

"Good. Bring that first." Master Penric nodded, and the boy retreated, staring back curiously over his shoulder.

Nikys went to the bedside and took Adelis's hand. Its tension told her that he did not sleep. "Adelis. I've brought you a physician, Master Penric." The man had brought himself, more like, but she doubted Adelis would respond well to that news, either.

Below the cloth wound around his face, still not unwrapped from that first awful day, his lips moved, and he growled, "Go away. Don't want him."

Nikys perforce ignored this. Her hand hovered over the grubby makeshift bandage. "I'm sure this should come off, but it's glued itself to his skin. My maid said it should be ripped off, but I didn't let her."

Adelis spasmed on his bed, one fist wavering up; Nikys dodged it. "Is that cack-handed hag back? Get rid of her!"

"Shh, shh. She's gone. I won't let her in here again, promise."

"Better not." He subsided.

Penric, coming to the bed's other side, let his hand pass over the cloth and cleared his throat. "In the woman's defense, there is a treatment, debridement, for the reduction of burn scarring that involves... something like that, which she might have seen sometime and misunderstood. Not for this, though." His voice went tart. "If the fool woman had done that here, it would have ripped his eyelids off."

Both Nikys and Penric clapped their hands over their mouths, she to keep her breakfast down, he as if to call back the blunt words. Adelis jerked and groaned. Penric grimaced in weird irritation, and added hurriedly, "Sorry. Sorry!" casting Nikys an apologetic head-duck. "Burns are a gruesome business, I can't deny. I hate them."

A faint snort from the bed.

Penric eyed the heavy supine figure under the sheet. "What have you given him, so far?"

"I obtained some syrup of poppies. I'm almost out, though." Adelis loathed the opiate, but he'd accepted it from her hands this time. She didn't think it had quelled the pain enough for him to sleep, but it had kept him too quiescent to fight them, lying in sodden silence. Too quiescent to rise and seek to do himself harm?

"I brought a good quantity. He can be given some more before I start."

The physician cleared space on the wash table, opened his case, laid out a cloth, and positioned supplies upon it in a precise, organized manner that subtly reassured her. He began by measuring out his syrup into a little vessel with a spout; then he held up Adelis's head and tipped it into his mouth, stroking his throat with a finger as he swallowed it down. His movements were gentle, but firm and sure, practiced-seeming. Mindful, but not in the least hesitant.

The scullion returned with the first of the water, and Penric laid a towel under Adelis's head and commenced dribbling it over the blindfold. "This will take some time to loosen," he remarked, "but it won't be difficult. And I promise all his skin will stay on."

A fainter snort.

It seemed an optimistic prediction, but Nikys longed to believe it, so said nothing. As she sat in her chair, watching the man watching her brother, her head nodded, and she jerked it back up. As much to keep herself awake as for any real curiosity, she asked, "Are you from the northern peninsula? Your speech is a little odd."

He hesitated, then smiled again. "My mother was. My father was a Weald-man, from the country over the *other* mountains, to your far south and east."

"I've seen men like you in the emperor's guard in Thasalon. They were supposed to be from islands in the frozen southern sea. Fierce warriors, I was told, but ill-behaved visitors." Well, not just like him, as he didn't look the least like a warrior. But some of the big brutes had been similar in coloration, if not so, so . . . so much so.

"I'm a well-behaved visitor, I assure you."

"Where did you study medicine?"

" . . . Rosehall. It's in the Weald."

Her brows rose. "I've heard of it! A great university, yes?" Despite her reservations, she grew more hopeful.

He looked at her in surprise. "I didn't think Cedonians knew much about my father's land."

"I've lived in the capital, and seaports. People get around. Like you."

His smile grew a bit strained. "Yes, I suppose so."

At length, done fiddling with water and oils, he took sharp scissors from his case and cut through the cloth on either side of Adelis's face. He undid the wrap from around the back of his patient's head and dropped it out of the way, laying his head back on the towel. Adelis groaned in fear. "You need not watch this," Penric said over his shoulder to Nikys.

"I'll stay."

"Hold his hands, then."

She went to the bed's other side. "To console him?"

A long finger flicked out and tapped her purpled cheek. "So he can't hit me."

She half-smiled and did so; Adelis gripped her spasmodically back.

Penric took a breath, closed his hands on either side of the stiff cloth, and lifted it delicately. The vile mask seemed to puff away from Adelis's face like a dry leaf, pulling... nothing at all.

She swallowed hard at the destruction that was revealed.

Blisters, huge puffs of membrane-thin skin bulging with liquid, ranged over Adelis's upper face and *quivered*. His eyelids were a horror, rising out of his eye sockets like round bladders. What was not white and swollen was violently red and pink. As Nikys recoiled, sickened, Penric leaned forward, staring fiercely into what had been her brother's eyes as if he were trying to see right through his skull. But he said only, "Huh."

He caught Adelis's hands on their way to feel his own face and yanked them down hard, the first ungentle gesture she'd seen him make. "No. No touching. Stay on your back. That skin is barely stronger than a soap bubble, and we want to preserve those blisters intact for as long as possible. They're protecting you, little though it may feel like it."

Adelis panted, but obeyed.

The physician's brilliant blue eyes seemed filled with jostling thoughts, but Nikys couldn't begin to guess what they might be. "I think what I most need now, Madame Khatai, is for you to go get some real rest. I'll stay here and keep watch. Come back and relieve me at nightfall." He beamed sunnily at her.

"I'll bring you both food, later. Or have it brought."

"That would be excellent." He hummed, as if mulling something, then said, "If I'm going to be living in your household for a few days, we'd best give some thought how I am to be explained to your other servants. I'd suggest you tell them you've hired me on to be your brother's male attendant. Which is not actually untrue, among its other benefits."

While she couldn't imagine why anyone, even the politically hostile, could object to Adelis being seen by a physician however oddly he'd been delivered to them, she was reminded that among her erstwhile servants was one certain spy. She nodded slowly. "All right."

She went out to make preparations in the kitchen, and see to the arrangement of the small spare bedchamber. She didn't think she could sleep, but when she reached her own room on the other side of the atrium and sat down on her bed, she felt as if the weight of an oxcart, complete with ox, had been lifted from her shoulders.

She was still crying from the sheer relief of it when she fell asleep.

She returned as instructed at sunset. When she eased open the door, Master Penric leaped up holding a finger to his lips and reeled out of the room. He clutched her hands and shook them up and down like a long-lost relative. His palms were feverish. His wide grin at her was nearly lunatic.

"He's asleep, miraculously. When he wakes up, get more water down him. Don't let him touch his face. I'll be back in a while and measure out the next dose of poppy syrup."

And then she wondered if he'd been drinking, or maybe sampling the poppy juice himself, for he called over his shoulder as he bounded down the stairs, " 'Scuse me, but I havetogokillsomerats now."

"What?"

"Mice? Mice would be all right, but you need more of 'em." His voice faded as he dodged not to the front door, but out the back way. "Has to be something useless lurking around this neighborhood. Stray dog would do a treat right now. Sweet lord god Bastard, deliver us *something*..."

She blinked, closed her mouth, shook her head, and went within. Sitting and watching the slow rise and fall of her brother's chest beneath his sheets as the shadows deepened, she decided she didn't *care* how strange the blond man was, if he could get Adelis to sleep like that.

# V

PENRIC GAUGED HIS DISTANCE in the dark from the neighbor's roof to the garden wall, leapt lightly, and settled himself down atop it for some composing meditation. The sleepy provincial guards, it appeared, had been instructed to attend to the villa's entrance and the postern gate in the rear wall, and that was just what they were doing. The one at the back had curled himself up against his assigned door and was currently napping, combining two tasks.

A bat fluttered by against the stars, but Pen let this one go, since his body had finally cooled. This neighborhood outside the city walls had lacked the swarm of big, aggressive rats like the harbor's, but he wasn't going back down *there* tonight. Des had left a trail of destruction through all the small vermin within her range, but with this much chaos to divest, insects had scarcely repaid even the moment's attention they took. Private middens had yielded more red-blooded prey, including a few slinking suburban rats, and what he thought might have been some kind of hedgehog. Pen regretted the mangy, worm-riddled street cat, but they'd been desperately hot and at least the poor beast no longer suffered.

"Eyes," muttered Pen. "They're so small. Why should this engender so much more chaos than making several times my weight in ice?"

His demon couldn't wheeze, exactly, so maybe it was just him as Des replied, "It may be the most subtle uphill magic you've yet attempted. The ice was big but simple. This mad healing you've thrown us into is *complex*."

Penric's initial plan, more selfish than charitable, had been simply to assure Arisaydia would survive his blinding, to evade the burden of yet another unwanted death in the pack Pen carried. It was only when he'd examined the man with all of Des's perceptions focused to their greatest intensity that he'd realized that the *backs* of his eyes, in all their impossible delicacy, were undamaged. And, suddenly, the hopeless had become merely the very, very tricky.

His first task had been the finicky release of beginning adhesions as Arisaydia's injured eyelids tried to grow themselves onto his steam-lashed eyeballs; then, rapid reduction of the ocular swelling, his skills and refined belladonna tincture working together. Pen had poured all the uphill magic he could into Arisaydia's own body's powers to heal, but that was a narrow channel that could only accept so much help at a time before it burst in a destructive back-blow. It was like trying to relieve a man dying of thirst using a teaspoon, but at least he'd kept the sips coming all the long day.

Arisaydia's survival was no longer in question, perhaps never had been. Pen had discovered the man in the bed to be above middle height, muscular and fit, obviously healthy before this catastrophe had struck him down. His face and arms and legs were that attractive reddish-brick tan common to the men of this region, though the parts of his body routinely covered by clothes more matched his sister's lighter, indoor version. His aquiline features, rough-cut in granite, were in her echoed in fine round marble; both shared the same midnight-black hair, his cut short, hers drawn back from her face and curling over her shoulders. Pen wondered what color his eyes had been. He could ask Madame Khatai, but it might distress her.

Speaking of which... "Do try to be more sensitive around the sister, Des. She's quite upset already."

Des snorted. *You have more than enough sensitivity for us all. To excess, as I have pointed out before.*

*Bloody-minded chaos demon*, Pen thought back.

The impression of an amused purr. *I do sometimes wonder how you ever survived, Pen, before you were us.*

*Whereas I more often wonder how I am to survive after...*

He stared down into the shadows beneath the pergola, where he had first seen and studied Madame Khatai from just about this vantage at dawn. She'd borne something of her brother's air of sturdy health, after a delightfully plump female fashion, but Pen didn't think he'd ever seen a woman's posture so expressive of utter despair. *I imagine she'd be quite pretty if she smiled.*

Des's response was sardonic: *So what is she when she isn't smiling?*

Penric contemplated the conundrum. "Heartbreaking. I think."

Was Des taken aback? *Oh, Pen, no. This isn't the time or place for one of your futile infatuations. This isn't a place we should be in at all. We should be making our way back to Adria.*

"...I know." Pen sighed. He pictured the man in the upstairs bedchamber whose life his fumbled packet of papers had somehow destroyed. No—he eyed the pergola—two lives, it seemed.

*You hardly destroyed Arisaydia all by yourself. You had some expert help.*

*Aye to that.* The increasing suspicion that he'd been *used* was a growing itch in Penric's mind. But by whom, and where, in this tangle of events? "Who around here would know who Arisaydia's enemies are?" He answered his own question before Des, this time: "Arisaydia would. For a start. If I could get him talking instead of just groaning." And, he was now sure, not *if* but *when* he did, who might a man trust more than his physician?

Des's silence would be tight-lipped, if she'd had lips. After a while she remarked, *I know you have no Temple orders for this. And I've felt no god move. You have embarked on this entirely on your own, Pen. How great a step from independent to renegade?*

Or how many little slippery ones, more probably. And Des could not, would not, stop him, though she wasn't beyond making him stop to think. "Shall I pray to my god for guidance, then?"

They both fell silent, considering the fifth god each in their own way.

*What would you do if you got it, and it wasn't what you wanted to hear?*

"...Maybe I'll wait for Him to call on me."

Des shuddered. *I suppose you think that is an* amusing *joke.*

Pen's lips stretched in something almost a real smile as he dropped over the wall.

# VI

OVER THE NEXT FEW DAYS, Nikys's household settled into a strange, limping new routine. Their safety was balanced on the knife's edge, she knew, of the continued inattention of the provincial governor and whatever cabal in the capital—and she could probably guess the most likely men—who had engineered Adelis's downfall. They were doubtless waiting out there for the word of his death, from the shock or infection or despair. She was disinclined to give them the *satisfaction*. Although she supposed a long, silent convalescence followed by a retreat into some hermitage, religious or secular, would serve their purposes just as well. From here forward, Adelis would carry his imprisonment with him, at no further cost to the empire.

She'd made no move to replace the servants who had prudently scattered after the arrest; she wondered how soon the ones who'd lingered would realize how little coin she had left to pay them, and follow. Well, not the maid, the gardener-porter, and the scullion, who'd come with the villa rather like the furnishings, and would stay after the current tenants decamped. Which would be when? Adelis had paid her rent through the half-year, but the end of that term was coming up in a few weeks. Possibly why their landlord had not moved to evict his politically poisonous lodgers already.

Not that any woman could scheme how to hold household when she had *absolutely no idea* what her resources were going to be. Still, Nikys could make some shrewd guesses. Adelis's army pay would be cut off, of course, and all the property he'd inherited from his mother and their father attainted. Would the Thasalon imperial bureaucracy snap up every bit, or leave him some pittance? Would the small remains of her own dower and the military pension from Kymis be seized as well? That would be like a hawk, having taken a fat hare, returning for a mouse.

Their entire lack of visitors told its own tale. Some of his old officer cadre in the Western Army might have had the courage to come, but Adelis had been most cannily separated from them, now, hadn't he? Although given that some of his new men had sent that extraordinary (if extraordinarily odd) physician, she must hoist her opinion of them back up.

She and Master Penric had quickly found their way to a division of labor in the sickroom. The physician had taken a pallet on the floor, attendant-fashion, and guarded Adelis at night. Nikys relieved him twice a day: in the afternoon, when he rested in the garden or went out to discreetly restock his medical supplies, and in the evening after supper, when he departed on errands he never explained, though they seemed urgent to him. She'd almost swear she'd once encountered him coming back in through Adelis's *window*, which made no sense at all, so she'd dismissed the impression from her burdened mind. She wondered what other professional duties the man was leaving undone, to linger so diligently in this stricken villa.

The cook being numbered among the deserters, and the housemaid having proved as clumsy in the kitchen as she was in the sickroom, Nikys took over that task, not least because she trusted no one else with the preparation of invalid fare. Five gods knew she'd had plenty of practice cooking such for Kymis during that last miserable year. She finally managed to draw the physician to a midday meal with her under the pergola, hoping to quiz him frankly on Adelis's progress out of Adelis's earshot.

After they delivered the platters and jugs, she dismissed the scullion and sat herself down with a tired sigh, staring dully at her own plate feeling as if she'd forgotten how to eat. Master Penric poured her wine-and-water, offering the beaker along with a smile fit to compete with the sunlight spangling his hair.

While she was still mustering her first question, he said, "I noticed your green cloak on the wall peg in the atrium, Madame Khatai. Is yours a recent bereavement?" He appeared poised to offer condolences, if so.

Dark green for a widow, yes, though she owed no other allegiance to the Mother of Summer. Sadly. "Not very recent. Kymis died four years ago." As his look of inquiry did not diminish, she went on: "He was a comrade of my brother's—something of an older mentor to him, when he was a young officer. Adelis felt he owed him much."

His blond brows pinched. "Were you payment?"

Her lips quirked. "Perhaps, a little. Our mothers were widowed by then, in reduced circumstances, so helping me to an honorable marriage to a good man whom he trusted seemed the right thing to do. Ten years ago . . . we were all younger, in a terrible hurry to get on with our lives. I wish I could have . . ." She faltered. But talking to this mild, pretty man seemed curiously easy, and he *was* a physician. His claim of *in all but final oath* seemed borne out, so far. "I wish I could have given Kymis children. I still don't know if it was some, some subtle physical impediment, his or mine, or just that he was called too much away to the border incursions. Adelis moved the world to get him back to me when he was wounded and maimed, as if I could somehow repair what the war had destroyed. But all I tried to do to save his life only prolonged his death. He cursed me, toward the end. I thought he had a point, but I didn't know *how* to let go."

It was the most honest thing she'd said about Kymis's dreadful last year to anyone—it was certainly nothing she could ever confess to Adelis—but Penric merely nodded, and said, "Yes."

Just *Yes*. Just that. It was nothing to burst into tears at the table about. She swallowed, hard. And awkwardly returned, "I suppose, as a physician"—in training, anyway—"you've seen the like. How it is to try and fail to keep some valued thing alive."

The flicker in his light eyes might have been from the movement of the dappled shade; he smoothly converted his flinch into a shrug, and she cursed her tongue, or her brain, or the day. Or her life. The smile he reaffixed was so like his usual ones, she began to wonder about their validity as well. But he said, answering her fears and not her words, and how did he *know*, "Adelis will live. I expect to get him up walking later today. He may not thank me at first, mind you."

Nikys gasped. "Truly?"

"Truly. He's a sturdy man; I think he'd have got that far on his own. If not, perhaps, quite so soon."

*That far* as compared to what? But he continued, gesturing with his fork, "So eat, Madame." He followed his own advice, munching with evident relish. For all his spare frame, he had an excellent appetite, of the sort that suggested starving student days were not long behind him. "You have a good cook. Shame to waste her art."

Nikys was about to protest that she was the cook, then realized Almost-Master Penric had certainly observed this. She smiled a little despite everything, and copied his example. After a few bites and a swallow of watered wine, she said, "That was what Adelis brought me to Patos for. To try to help me to a second marriage with another officer, if older and richer this time. I was happy to be here, but I hadn't the heart to tell him his efforts were a waste, that I would never again marry a military man. When we were talking last night, he apologized, the idiot. He seemed to think if he'd wedded me away to the protection of another, I would have been out from under all"—

she waved a hand about—"this. Never mind the feelings of the poor hypothetical husband, to find himself suddenly kin to an accused traitor. Or what if he'd refused to admit Adelis to his household, when I brought him back blinded? I couldn't suggest that to Adelis, but it felt like how he describes ducking a crossbow bolt—you don't even know what you've escaped till it's over."

Penric scratched his head and smiled. "I quite see that. You *do*?"

"What?"

He coughed. "Nothing."

She grew graver. "I hate all this madness. But I can't help thinking about what it might have been like for Adelis if there had been *no* one loyal to him here, in this extremity." Would his tormentors have just cast him blinded into the street? The like had happened to other traitors. "I'm frightened all the time, yet I can't wish myself elsewhere."

"Frightened?" His brows flicked up. "Surely the worst is done, over."

It was her turn to shrug, mute with the weight of her dread. "Dying is easy. Surviving is hard. I learned that with Kymis." And no wonder she'd been thinking about her late husband so much these past few days, like a healed scar broken open again. "What will we do in the *after*?"

"That . . ." Penric sank back, sobered. "That is actually a very good question, Madame Khatai." And, mumbled under his breath: "About time somebody asked that one, Pen." He shook his head as if to clear it, and went on, "I am reminded. If Arisaydia is to be up and moving about, I want to devise some sort of protective mask for his upper face that we can easily take on and off. Line the back with gauze that I can soak with healing ointment, or change out and keep dry and clean, as needed."

"I think I might have something that would do. I'll look for it and bring it to you."

He nodded.

Somehow, while they were talking, she had emptied her plate. She drained the last of her beaker and studied the young physician. Abruptly, she decided he deserved to be warned. "I suspect there is a spy in my household."

He choked on his wine, coughed, mopped his lips. "Oh?" he

squeaked, then finally cleared his throat and dropped his voice to its normal timbre. "What makes you say that?"

"The night before Adelis was blinded, I had devised an escape. I had mounts and a groom secreted near the prison. It was all for nothing, because Adelis refused to come with me. Which was also for nothing, as it proved, but anyway, my horses and servant were taken even before I left Adelis's cell, and soldiers were waiting in ambush for us at the entrance. They didn't even bother to arrest me. But someone had known my arrangements, and passed the news along, and it wasn't the jailer I'd bribed. I've not seen the groom since, so it could have been him, or any of the other servants who fled. Or it could have been one who stayed. I don't know."

"I see. How very uncomfortable for you."

"It's maddening, but it seemed the least of my worries at first." She frowned at him. "I don't know if any of this could follow you home, Master Penric. Perhaps, like me, you are too small a mouse for their appetites. But I should not wish to see you suffer for helping us. So, I don't know . . . be discreet?"

"I did know what I was getting into before I came," he pointed out kindly. "More or less."

"But still."

He waved a conceding hand. "As you say, still. I will undertake to be a very demure mouse."

She stared at him, thinking, *There's a hopeless plan.* But at least she'd tried.

# VII

ARISAYDIA wasn't easy to coax out of bed. Penric fancied the man knew it was the first slippery step in undertaking to stay alive, instead of holding on to his imagined—begged-for—death like a starving child clutching food. But his dizziness, once he was upright, was no worse than anyone abed for a week might experience, and as he inhaled and straightened, it was plain that his body's native strength had been little impaired by his ordeal. He was still in pain, but Pen had found himself able to reduce the opiates more quickly than he'd anticipated, Arisaydia's slurred and muzzy mumbling giving way to crisper speech. Even if it was mostly swearing, so far.

Pen guided him out to the second-floor gallery circling the dual atriums, front and central, that admitted so much light and air into the villa, unlike the tightly boarded houses of the far-off mountain cantons. Did they ever get snow in this country? Arisaydia's hand trailed along the walls; Pen took the balcony side. Pen was almost sure the man wouldn't lunge for the rail and over, trying to finish the job that his enemies had started. Almost. It would make a dreadful mess on the mosaic floor of his sister's nice house, for one thing; for another, so short a drop was uncertain of outcome. So they strolled along arm-in-arm, like two friends out for a postprandial airing.

To distract Arisaydia from his surliness, Penric essayed, "Is it true that you and your sister are twins?"

It worked; Arisaydia's lips puffed in almost-a-laugh. "It was something of a joke among our mothers and us, when we grew old enough to realize we were unusual. If a woman could give birth to children of two different fathers on the same day, no one would hesitate to dub them twins. Why not the same for two mothers and one father?"

They came to a corner where the wall fell away; Arisaydia's free hand hesitated, clenched, then fell firmly controlled to his side. Only his slightly tighter grip on Pen's arm, as quickly reduced, betrayed his refusal to show whatever fear he must feel.

"A wife and a concubine are often bitter rivals in a man's house, but our mothers always seemed more like comrades-in-arms to us. Our father was flanked and outnumbered, but at least he had the wit to surrender. After he died, they continued to share their household—goods and grief and tasks portioned out all the same."

*I wonder if they shared a bed, too?* Des put in brightly. Pen clenched his teeth to be sure *that* didn't slip out, and asked instead, "Were they close in age, or by blood, or some such ties?"

"Not at all. Nikys's mother was twenty years younger than mine. My mother and father had evidently tried for children for years with no luck—it was long after he died that my mother ever mentioned her miscarriages in my hearing. So a child to share was certainly hoped for. And then, by whatever joke of the gods, there were two at

once. We never knew whether to blame the Mother or the Bastard."
Another turn brought a wall back within reach; Arisaydia barely
traced it this time.

Nikys came out into the central atrium, holding something in her
hand. She looked up at the sound of their voices. Her lips parted, a
thrill illuminating her features as she saw them walking. Pen had
guessed right; she was very pretty when she smiled. He felt a queer
flutter in his stomach, to know that his work had put such a look on
her face. And a following clench, to consider what she might look
like to learn the whole story of Pen's involvement with her brother's
woes. He heard the sound of her quick slippers on the stairs as he
guided Arisaydia back into his bedchamber once more.

As he helped his not-very-patient patient sit up in bed, notably
straighter than heretofore, Pen studied his face. The blisters were
much reduced, shrunken and wrinkling; those that had broken were
healing cleanly from the edges inward. The rims of his eyelids were
silvery-damp—tear ducts, gods, how many rats had died for those
tear ducts to open and work once more? Pen was still in grave doubt
about the delicate irises. And nothing was more likely than for the
brutalized lenses to go to cataracts, trading one form of blindness for
another. Pen had heard of a horrifying operation tried in Darthaca,
of cutting out clouded lenses and replacing their function with glass
spectacles, but he hadn't heard that the success rate was high, and
Bastard's tears, how could a person lie down and let someone take a
knife to their eyes? Then he wondered how they'd held Arisaydia
down for the boiling vinegar, and then he tried to stop thinking.

Arisaydia's lids were still too swollen to open, but it wouldn't be
long now. Soon, Penric would find out what he'd done. More to the
point, so would Arisaydia. Penric had not one guess how the man
would respond. Except, probably not mildly.

Nikys entered, holding out her hand. "I wondered if this would
do? It was an old masquerade mask. The beak should come off
readily. Adelis went as a raven. For the battlefield, he said, which I
thought at the time was morbid." She reflected. "Or a sly dig from
the army at the bureaucrats. If so, they missed the point."

"Perhaps fortunately," Arisaydia murmured, turning his head
toward the sound of her voice, the mask visible, apparently, to his
memory. "But I was young and angry."

Penric accepted the object, turning it to check the side he cared about. It was made to cover the upper half of the face, and its dimensions closely matched the ravages of the scalding. No problem to pad it with ointment-saturated gauze, changeable according to each day's needs. And, while feigning to Arisaydia that it would hide his disfigurement from unsympathetic eyes, it would also keep the man from discovering prematurely what Penric had been doing to him, before the work was done.

*What will we do in the after?* Nikys had asked. Pen still had no answer, but the problem would soon be upon them all, and it wasn't going to be the one she was imagining.

Penric turned the mask over. The front side was black leather, cut and stitched in elegant lines, decorated with striking sprays of black feathers a little ragged and brittle from age and a sojourn in some chest. "And what did you go as?" he asked Nikys. "A swan?" White to her brother's dramatic black?

She laughed. "Not I! Even back then I had more sense. I went as an owl. A much rounder bird." She waved a hand down her body, which was indeed more owl- than swan-shaped. Pen thought she looked wonderfully soft, but he didn't suppose he dared say so.

"Wisdom bird," said Arisaydia. The ghost of a smile twitched his lips. "I remember that. Did I tease you?"

"Of course."

"Foolish raven."

Curious, Pen held up the mask before Arisaydia's face. And blinked.

"My word," said Des. Pen quickly closed his mouth before she could add more, and more embarrassing, commentary.

With the eye-diverting damage obscured, the man sprang into focus as not exactly handsome, but arrestingly powerful. Pen had met men and women like that, from time to time; it was nothing a sculptor could ever capture, not residing in the line or the form, but when one saw them, souls ablaze, one could not look away. The raven mask emphasized the effect, unfairly.

*No, keep looking!* Des demanded. *For all the stares you've been sneaking at his sister's ample backside, you can give us this. He's not going to object.*

They'd had this argument in bathhouses where, in general, Pen went because he wanted a bath. Seven-twelfths of Desdemona found the places fascinating for more prurient reasons, although not including, curiously, the imprint of the courtesan Mira, who knew more about what might be done in bathhouses—besides bathing—than Penric had ever imagined, and shared it whether Pen wanted to know or not. Mira was professionally unimpressed with prurience. Some of the rest of the sorority were inclined to goggle—Pen swore Ruchia was the worst—which, since they seized Pen's eyes to do so, had a few times early on got him either punched or propositioned by his fellow bathers. Once, both.

*You'd be propositioned anyway,* Des objected. *That part is not our fault.*

Firmly, Penric set the mask aside. "That will work," he assured Nikys, keeping his eyes lifted. "Thank you." He was rewarded with another faint smile, like glancing moonlight.

A little later, when Nikys had gone off to see to preparations for the next meal, and Pen was working on modifying the mask, he judged Arisaydia sufficiently disarmed by their excursions into his family history to try more troubling questions. He definitely had to ask them before the return of Arisaydia's vision upended any belief that his secrets no longer mattered. *And you accuse me of being ruthless,* Des sniffed. Arisaydia had been apprised of the little fiction about his anonymous military benefactors, whose names Pen had steadfastly refused to divulge because they didn't exist, and he didn't dare make any up. But this had lent Pen a useful air of rectitude. Pen decided to deploy them again.

"Your secret friends who hired me were very upset with the rumors about your arrest," he started. "Outraged by some, worried, I think, by others. Did all this come out of nowhere, from your point of view?" Surely the general had been taken by surprise or he else could have fled, or flung up some other evasion or resistance.

"Not . . . nowhere," said Arisaydia slowly. He held out a hand palm-up, as if measuring some unseen threat. "Accusation and counter-accusation, rumor and slander, are staples of the Thasalon court, as men wrestle for advantage and access to the emperor's favor. I thought I was well out of it, and just as glad to be so, up here in Patos."

"Do you know who your enemies are?"

Arisaydia's laugh held little humor. "I could reel off a list. Although in this case, my friends were likely the greater danger."

"I ... don't understand?" Pen scarcely needed to fake a confused naiveté.

"The Western Army was not well treated by Thasalon in our last campaign. Supplies and reinforcements were almost impossible to extract, pay was in arrears ... In an offensive campaign, an army can pay itself out of the spoils of the enemy country. But we were defending, on our own ground. Pillage was discouraged and, when it occurred, complained of to the government. And punished, which set up its own tensions. In some encounters we were scarcely better organized than the barbarians we fought, and we were well-chewed by them. Our victory was more desperate than triumphal.

"The army always complains they are insufficiently rewarded for the burdens they undertake. It was more true than usual this time around, and the muttering in the tents and barracks fed on itself and turned ugly. There are invariably military men who believe if only they could replace whatever emperor is on the throne with one of their own, their injustices would be remedied."

"That seems to have been tried, judging by the histories I've read." And Pen had read rather more of them than he was going to let on, not that one could trust their writers. "Successfully, sometimes."

Arisaydia grimaced. "Ten years ago, even five years ago, I would have believed that myth wholeheartedly, that we needed only the right man to quell all wrongs. But, as you say, it's been tried, and nothing seems to change in the end. I had to see a lot more of the court to learn what we are up against, and it isn't just the corruption of courtiers, for all that we're well-supplied with that, too. Taxation is a mess, for one thing. The sporadic plagues have chewed holes in the fabric of the realm. At some golden periods the shortfall was made up for by conquest, I suppose, but it seems every generation we lose more territory than we gain. Reform is resisted by everyone who has an interest in it not taking place at *their* expense. Including the army, I'm sorry to say. To set one man, no matter how heroic or well-intentioned, up against the whole vast weight of that ... and then to excoriate him for his inevitable failure ..." He shook his head. "I would say *five gods spare me*, but there was a cadre of my officers who thought otherwise. And started to go beyond muttering.

Evidently, half a year and Patos were not distance enough to save me from their admiration. And the reaction it engendered."

Arisaydia, Pen noticed, was naming no names, and likely not for the same reasons Pen hadn't. In his present state it seemed less calculation than habit, and a curious habit it was for a man to have developed.

"Did you not write to the duke of Adria asking for, um, greater distance? That was one of the rumors." Penric had held the letter in his hand in the duke's cabinet and read it. The chancellery of Adria was expert in forgeries, both detecting and creating them, but it had been in a scribe's handwriting, with only Arisaydia's signature appended. The duke had been frank with Pen about the dubious possibilities, which was why he'd been supposed to sound out the general most discreetly at first. And, should it not prove Arisaydia's idea, implant it anyway.

"Adria! Certainly not. Why would I treat with Adria? Their sea merchants are little better than pirates, sometimes. Rats with boats, nibbling at our coasts." Arisaydia's mouth set. He couldn't glower yet, but his eyelids tensed, and then his lips parted in pain. "Agh." He sighed and huddled down in his sheets, obviously tiring.

Well, that wasn't encouraging for Pen's secondary plan. He had begun to wonder, if he could restore Arisaydia's sight, if he might persuade him to flee east after all. Not that letting the duke aim Arisaydia at Carpagamo, a country that had never done harm to Pen, seemed a very holy mission, but politics were generally unholy, and that had never kept the Temple from dabbling in them. But he could not have stayed in Martensbridge and kept his sanity, and the archdivine of Adria had promised him a place that did not include duties to the Mother's Order.

*Yet here I am, practicing medicine again all unwilled. Is the Bastard laughing?*

This left the question of who in Cedonia had forged the initial letter, as the duke was fully convinced it had originated here. Clear entrapment, it seemed. Vicious both in its intent and its results. Velka might have brought it; he'd certainly escorted the very real reply back into the right wrong Cedonian hands, which had to have been outstretched waiting for it.

Penric was really starting to want some time alone in a quiet room with Velka. He was theologically forbidden to kill with his magic, but there were other possibilities. So very, very many. And oh gods he surely now understood why physician-sorcerers were the most tightly controlled of all the discreet cadre of Temple mages.

Desdemona couldn't lick her lips, but she could lick his. It brought him out of his furious fugue with a start. Her little frisson of anticipatory excitement faded, and she sighed.

*Don't tempt me*, and he had no idea which of them said it.

# VIII

AS SHE AND THE PHYSICIAN walked Adelis around the garden between them, just two days after he'd first been persuaded up, Nikys was pleased to see how much steadier he was on his feet. It was plain that the overwhelming pain of his scalding, so precisely and cruelly placed, that had driven him close to madness was vastly reduced. He was healing with amazing speed.

She did not know what mysterious Wealdean techniques the half-foreign physician was bringing to his task, but her respect for his skills had risen and risen. Even as he went on being rather odd. He talked to himself, for one thing, when he didn't think he was overheard, in what she guessed was his father's tongue, or sometimes in snatches of what she recognized as Darthacan. And then argued back. He always smiled at her, yet his bright eyes were restless and strained, as if masking a brain busy elsewhere.

As they turned and paced along the wall, Adelis unwound his arm from Master Penric's, but not from hers; his hand drifted up to touch his cheek just below the black mask. The sly design made him look strong, and dangerous, and not at all invalidish. It made him look quite like himself, in fact, at least when in one of his more sardonic moods. But his voice was uncharacteristically tentative as he asked, "Does my face look like a goat's bottom?"

Her heart clenched, but she returned lightly, "I always thought your face looked like a goat's bottom, dear brother. It appears no different to *me*."

Penric's brows lifted in concern as he turned to her across Adelis. But Adelis just smirked, looking mordant below the mask, and gave her arm a squeeze, returning in a matching tone, "Dear sister. Always my compass." His voice fell to quiet seriousness. "In the darkest places. It seems."

She swallowed and squeezed back.

Penric offered, "Your blisters looked much better this morning. Almost gone."

"Are you a connoisseur of blisters, Master Penric?" asked Adelis.

"It goes with my trade, I suppose. Yours were superb."

"That's Adelis for you," said Nikys. "Always has to have the best."

A huff of laugh. "Your latest ointment has tamed the itching, thankfully."

"Good. I don't want you scratching."

They turned once more and negotiated the steps up to the pergola, and Nikys said, "Go around again? Or rest?"

"Go around again," said Adelis, definitely. Nikys smiled.

But before they could continue, a brisk knocking at the front door echoed through the atriums, and they all paused, listening intently. The gardener-porter answered and admitted the supplicant. Supplicants; two voices quizzed him. If it was a friendly visit, it was the first since they'd been plunged into this political quarantine. If it was not . . .

A sharp, indrawn breath from Master Penric drew her attention. "I know that voice. One of them. I need—he mustn't see me!" The voices approached, the aged gardener shuffling slowly in escort, the others stepping impatiently short to match. Penric looked around frantically; he was quite cut off from the house by the visitors' entry route. "No time."

To Nikys's astonishment, he scrambled up the corner post of the pergola like a cat climbing a tree to escape a dog. He swung back down to add, "He's no friend to you. Be careful." And then ran lightly along the top, making the grape leaves bounce and quiver. Adelis, lips parted in unvoiced question, turned his head to track the thumps and rustles. Reaching the second-floor balcony overlooking the back garden, Penric vaulted over the railing and melted to the floor. Nikys could spot one blue eye peeking back through the uprights.

Uncertain, Nikys guided Adelis to the outdoor table. He seated himself stiffly. The porter and his charges arrived, a pair of men in civil dress followed by a sharply turned-out provincial guard. If Penric had recognized one voice, Nikys recognized one man: the provincial governor's senior secretary, Master Prygos. Neither friend nor enemy, she would have thought, just a punctilious functionary, his ambitions restricted to his own domain. The gray-haired, dyspeptic bureaucrat half-bowed to each of them, more habitually polite than truly respectful, as Adelis could not see it. Prygos cursorily introduced his trailing clerk as Tepelen. This was a younger man, shrewd-faced, evidently not in his trade long enough for his body to soften and grow pale like his superior's.

"I am charged today to deliver your copy of your bill of attainder," he told Adelis, formally. He nodded to Tepelen, who rummaged in his documents case and withdrew a thick sheaf, evidently a list of all the property Adelis no longer owned. Tepelen handed it to Prygos, who turned to hand it to Adelis, then paused and said, "Er."

Penric, by whatever impulse, had lined the eyeholes of the mask with a double layer of black silk, giving it an unsettling effect of gleaming bird eyes. The light played over the silk as Adelis nodded toward her. "Pray give it to Madame Khatai," he murmured. "She is my scribe these days."

"Ah. Yes."

Nikys took it, glanced through the cramped governmental calligraphy and legal cant, and set it down under her elbows.

Adelis inquired shortly of Prygos, "Do I have anything left to live on, or should I find a begging bowl for the marketplace?"

Prygos cleared his throat. "Madame Khatai's pension was left alone, as was the property of her mother that your mother left to her. Your dependents will not be houseless."

"Small mercies," said Adelis.

"They suffice," murmured Nikys. It would be a constrained little life, the pair of them crammed back into her aging mother's house in its small inland town. Betrayed. Defeated. *But not dead. Therefore, not hopeless.* Call it, in Adelis's lexicon, a retreat to regroup.

Prygos's hand rose, then fell; he looked to his clerk, who cast him a steely frown. He cleared his throat again, and said, "My apologies, but I am also charged to inspect and report on General Arisaydia's injuries and recovery." Adelis's military title was a slip, Nikys thought, unusual for so precise a man. "Uh, Madame Khatai, might I trouble you to help remove his mask?"

Adelis's jaw set; his hands clenched on the tabletop. She let her own hand reach out to cover his fist in silent inquiry. Barely perceptibly, he shook his head. "If humiliation is to be my bread," he murmured to her, "best I grow accustomed to the taste."

She sighed, sickened, and rose to step behind him and unlace the strings holding his mask and dressings in place. She reached around him to lift it as gently as she had seen Master Penric do; she felt a slight tug as the ointment released, but his skin seemed much less fragile today. He didn't even flinch, reverting to that stubborn I-am-a-boulder stolidity.

Then he gasped.

She flitted instantly around to his side. "Oh, gods, did I hurt you?"

A flash of startled red gleamed between his shrunken lids as he turned his head toward her, then his eyes squeezed closed again. His hands tightened on the table's edge, knuckles paling. His teeth set and his body trembled. "Maybe a little," he managed.

She sank back down in her seat, setting the mask on the table. Prygos gulped and looked away. Tepelen, by contrast, sat up with a muffled oath. He leaned forward, eyes narrowing as he stared into the half-wreck of Adelis's face.

"Pray excuse us for just a moment." He rose, and his hand fell to Prygos's shoulder, gripping it, pressing him to rise and follow. Prygos looked up, surprised, but obeyed, and wasn't that odd? Tepelen motioned at the impassive guard, who had propped himself against the pergola post. "Stay. Keep them here." The two men trailed away through the house and out the front. Nikys pricked her ears, but neither spoke till the door closed between, cutting off sound.

"Nikys," said Adelis, his voice taut, "I'm getting a little tired. Perhaps you could escort me back up to my bedchamber."

"Of course."

She started to rise again, but the guard put in sternly, "Please stay seated, General."

Adelis's hands wavered out, found her, patted their way up to her head. He turned her face close to his. His eyes slitted open again. The whites were bloodshot nearly solid red, his irises were a strange garnet color, but the tight black circles of his pupils *looked back at her.* "Dear Nikys," he said. "In that case, perhaps you could fetch refreshments for our guests, and for me. Get my attendant to help you." The lids pinched closed once more, concealing... a terrible wonder. And an exactly equal terrible danger.

Her head felt so bloodless with shock that she feared she might pass out, but she said, "Certainly," and scrambled to her feet. The guard frowned, but evidently decided that her mouse-self, mere nursemaid to the important man, was too frail a threat to concern him.

She walked firmly into the house, not looking back. She did not turn aside toward the kitchen, though she mentally reviewed the residue of wine in the pantry, fit only for servants and therefore too good for these visitors, and her stock of ready poisons, sadly lacking. She walked, did not run, *don't run*, up the stairs to the gallery. Master Penric was no longer lying prone on the back balcony, but she heard faint noises coming from Adelis's chamber.

She entered and closed the door behind her to find him swiftly packing the last of his medical kit. He'd pulled on trousers under his tunic. He looked up and cast her the most contrived smile yet.

Of the dozen alarms jostling her mouth, one escaped first: "He can see!"

"Yes."

"How long?"

"Since yesterday. Or if you mean when did I know I could recover his eyesight, since nearly the beginning, or I'd have been gone long ago."

She gaped at him. "Are you leaving now?"

"No... I don't know. I'm not *finished.*" He grimaced and snapped his case closed. "More to the point, Velka saw. Worst possible time for the man to show up, I swear."

"Who?"

"Tepelen. The clerk who isn't. I don't know which is his real name. Maybe neither. He's a high-level agent from the cabal in the capital who entrapped your brother. I don't know how high, but he isn't stupid, and he doesn't waste time." He looked around. "And neither should we. Is there any money in this room? Anything Adelis or you would want to aid your flight from the city?"

She would cry *What flight?* but his intent, and their need, were too plain to argue. "We haven't enough coin left to pay the *laundress* tomorrow. I was hoping she would take something in trade."

"Can you ride?"

"Yes. But I haven't a horse."

"Hnh." He stood up and tapped his lips with his thumb. "I would so prefer to be discreet about this. May not be possible." They both froze as the sound of the front door slamming, and the tread of too many heavy feet, penetrated faintly from the atrium. "Bastard's hell, no good. Go back and stay by your brother. I won't be far away. Don't panic."

If her glare could have blasted him where he stood, he would be floating ash. She whirled and ran for the stairs.

She made it back to the table barely before the new invasion. Prygos and his not-clerk were followed by four guardsmen, the two who'd been posted at her doors and two more. The one who'd been left pushed off from his pergola support and looked his inquiry not at the senior secretary, but at Tepelen. Or Velka. Or whoever the cursed man was.

Tepelen gestured at Adelis. "Seize and bind him."

Adelis's chair banged over backward as he surged up out of it. No question of tame surrender this time. Nikys realized too late that she should have detoured by the kitchen to grab a carving knife, or two, but she snatched up her own chair and used it to charge at least one of the men. She caught him so by surprise she actually managed to knock him backwards, but he grabbed the legs and yanked and nearly took her down with him. When she tried to stomp him with her feet, he clutched her ankle and toppled her. She landed painfully, the world spinning, and then he seized her hair.

Adelis was more adept, and more professionally vicious, but the four other guardsmen and Tepelen combined against him. And while it was plain he could see *something* now, it was equally plain his sight must still be blurred and indistinct, and when one of the men managed a hard blow against his tender upper face, he gasped and staggered, and then they were all upon him.

She and Adelis both struggled and fought to the last, but the last came swiftly when swords were drawn. They were roped tightly to two opposite pergola posts, panting and bruised, staring at each other in dismay. And where was Master Penric and his promises in all this? Not that the skinny physician could have been much more help in a fight than she had been, but he might have dropped the odds against Adelis from five down to four.

Tepelen, out of breath, huffed upright and straightened his clothes. Prygos, who had stood back from the brawl in understandable terror, came up to his side, and both approached the bound Adelis. Adelis's head jerked back as Prygos lifted his hand to touch his burns.

"As you said," Prygos remarked, apparently to Tepelen. "The man who administered the vinegar must not have had his heart in the task. Someone is going to have to question him, later."

"He seemed diligent to me," Adelis gritted between his teeth. His mouth was bleeding, but then, so was Nikys's. She licked the metallic tang from her swelling lips. "But by all means, feel free to question him. To the last extremity."

"Enough of this," said Tepelen. "Let us amend the lapse and go. No merit in dragging it out. The fine judicial show was all over a week ago." He gestured to a guard. "You—no, you two—hold his head still." Two guardsmen came up to either side of Adelis and grasped his head. The tendons stood out on Adelis's neck as he strained against their hands, and his breath whistled through his teeth. Prygos stepped well back, gesturing assent though looking rather ill. Tepelen grimaced in distaste, drew his belt knife, and raised it toward Adelis's eyes.

Nikys screamed.

"Oh, now," came a soft voice from above. "I really can't allow that."

For no reason that Nikys could see, Tepelen hissed and dropped the knife as though it seared him. Clutching his hand, he whirled and stepped back to look up.

Master Penric stood atop the end of the pergola above Adelis's head, one hand cocked on his hip, looking peeved.

Tepelen's jaw dropped in disbelief. "You! You're supposed to be drowned!"

"Really?" Penric's head tilted as he contemplated this. "Perhaps I was."

Horror flashed in the man's face, to be replaced swiftly with dawning anger. His mouth clopped closed, opening again to shout to the bewildered guardsmen, "Seize him!"

That sounding a more reasonable order, they all started forward. Penric's features set in a look of inward concentration, and one pale hand waved, fingers tapping like a man directing a group of musicians. One after another, the five guardsmen dropped to the floor with cries of pain, their legs sprawling out every which way, helpless to stand as a new foal. Tepelen lurched and followed them down.

Prygos, his eyes bulging, yelped and turned to run.

Penric bent to gaze after him. "Oh. Forgot about you." He waved his hand again, and the secretary tripped and fell, seeming unable to get up again, although he attempted to row himself along the floor with his arms, casting terrified looks over his shoulder.

Penric heaved a sigh and climbed down from the pergola. His face shifted and he vented a weird, silent laugh. "So much for discreet, Penric." He then strode among the guardsmen, now flopping feebly like dying fish, and kicked swords away. As he bent to touch each man's throat, their cries squeezed to squeaks, although his hand drew back from Tepelen's, who was the only man not screaming. "Not you, yet."

All the clamor died away. Nikys's ears rang with the silence. Penric stood up straight. He grimaced and gestured again, and the ropes binding Nikys and Adelis to their respective posts loosened and dropped around their feet.

Nikys thudded to her knees. Adelis staggered forward, grasped Penric by the shirt, and slammed him up against another post. His face was wild, and not just from his squinting, bright red eyes, as he shoved into Penric and cried—wailed, almost—"*What are you?*"

"Now, now." Penric favored him with his sunniest grin. "Mustn't look a gift horse in the mouth."

"That's not an answer!" He shook the physician, who allowed himself to flop bonelessly, unresisting. Nikys suspected him capable of resisting very effectively indeed, if he chose.

Shaking, she used her post to haul herself to her feet, and rubbed at her bleeding mouth, her numb jaw. "Why didn't you let us loose sooner?" *Or do* anything *sooner?*

"I thought about it, but it would have put one random element too many in an already complicated situation. Our attention does have limits. Actually safer to leave you where you were, temporarily."

As Adelis released him with a curse, he brushed down his scarcely rumpled green jacket, and stretched like a cat. His mouth didn't stop smiling, but the smile didn't reach his eyes, which flickered constantly over the scene of not-exactly-slaughter.

Adelis seemed intent on correcting that, as he bent and snatched up a sword.

Penric's hand fell atop his. "No, you can't kill them. They're helpless, you know."

"*So was I.*"

Penric gave him a conceding nod, but said, "You have a more urgent task right now. You have to get your sister to safety."

Nikys, who'd been frantically wondering how she was to get *Adelis* to safely, was offended by this blatant tactic, but it worked; her brother's head cranked around to find her. *Reminded of my existence, are you?* Granted, Penric was a very distracting man. Adelis, still gripping the sword, hurried over to hug her to him.

"Are you all right, Nikys?"

"Just knocked around."

He glared thinly down at the guardsmen, as if reconsidering his prey. But, stepping over the bodies—Adelis kicked a few in passing—Penric hurried them both into the atrium, lowering his voice.

"There are two horses tethered outside. Madame Khatai, if you have riding trousers, go put them on. Grab whatever moneys you have, no more clothes or treasures than will fit in a sack, and be back down here as fast as if the house was burning."

"The house isn't burning." Though it felt as if her life were on fire.

"Yet."

Compelled by his infectious insanity, she ran. A stack of cloth and his medical case were already sitting at the bottom of the stairs, she noticed as she galloped up them.

She returned to find Penric belting one of her longer gowns around a hotly protesting Adelis. He then pulled her widow's green cloak off its peg and settled it around her brother's shoulders, and yanked the hood up over his head. "There. Your magical cape of invisibility. Keep your face down."

Penric peered out the front door, then bundled them into the quiet street, dozing in the bright afternoon. He gave her a leg up onto the larger of the two horses, both marked with provincial government brands and bearing military saddles. A short delay followed while he argued in sharp whispers with Adelis about the widow's clutch on the sword, settled by sliding it semi-discreetly back into its saddle scabbard, but inciting another dispute about getting him up behind her.

"There are two horses," said Adelis. "One for each of us."

"You are not as fit to ride as you think you are, which you are going to find out shortly when the excitement wears off, and there are three of us. I need the other to follow on."

"You're coming with us?" asked Nikys. She could scarcely describe her own reaction. Though not *sorry*, no.

The blond man nodded. "I wasn't done yet, you see. Leave town at a sedate walk, nothing to draw attention to yourselves—not to mention easier on this poor horse—and take the south road. I have a few things to clean up here, and then I'll catch up to you."

"How will you find us?"

"I can find you."

"You and who else?" began Adelis in exasperation.

Further protest was cut short when Penric stepped back and slapped the horse on its haunches, Nikys found her reins, and they . . . fled at an amble.

They were both quiet for a little, as the reverberations of terror running through Nikys's heart slowly died away. She could barely imagine how Adelis felt about it all, twice-betrayed as he was. She could sense it, though, as the fight began to leak out of him and he leaned more heavily against her.

They'd threaded through three streets and found the main road before Nikys said, "I wonder if he really means to burn down the villa?"

After a brief consideration, Adelis offered, "It's rented."

"I should be sorry anyway." And then, "What in the gods' eyes did we see him *do*, back there?"

Adelis's voice went grim. "Something uncanny."

"Hedge sorcerer? Do you think? You saw him more nearly than I."

"It would explain a great deal. In retrospect."

But why had such a man come to them? She considered Penric's airy tale of their military benefactors with a new dubiousness, but she had no better one to put in its place. His brief, bizarre first exchange with Tepelen also hung without explanation. "Do you think he'll really catch up to us?"

"No. He'd be a fool to. Far smarter to take this chance of escape to safety."

She considered what *safety* might mean to a man who could do the things they'd just witnessed, and wondered.

Also, *fool.*

# IX

PENRIC DASHED BACK through the house, trying to track all he must control. *Too much.* In addition to the assailants laid out under the pergola, and the whining senior secretary, the maid and the porter were presently cowering in an upstairs room, and the scullion had vanished. Well, first things first, then whatever else he could do, and then fly.

He passed through and collected all the weapons, not forgetting the secretary's belt knife and also taking a moment to harvest his purse. Then he renewed the pressure on his prisoners' selected nerves to keep them down and quiet. He didn't suppose anyone else would appreciate how *delicate* and *clever* all this was, least of all his victims, but he was rather proud of it himself. *Good work.*

*I could have ripped all those nerves apart* much *more easily,* grumped Des, *and we'd never have to worry about them getting up to come after us again.*

Which was true, but theologically fraught. Penric dumped his heavy armload of edged steel down the privy at the end of the garden and trotted back to the pergola. The soldiers lay in whimpering heaps. One brave man made a feeble snatch for his ankle as Pen skipped around them, but missed. Pen grasped the panting Velka-Tepelen-Whoever—he decided he'd stick with Velka—by the tunic and began dragging him into the house. There were already too many witnesses to his antics. This conversation needed to be private.

A sort of lumber room off the front atrium seemed remote enough to be out of earshot. Penric laid Velka out supine on the floor and perched on his abdomen, knees up, and touched his thumb to his lips in his habitual prayer for luck. His god, he was reminded, was the master of both sorts. He leaned forward between his up-folded legs and smiled.

"Drowned, you say," he began. Des growled aloud in memory.

"The guards reported you drowned in your cell and your body disposed of in the sea," said Velka through his teeth. "Your skull was broken. You *should* be dead. Twice over!"

"And Arisaydia should be blind, aye. So many mysteries."

"No mystery to it. You escaped, and they reported the other to hide their failure and avoid punishment."

"Well, that's one explanation. But wouldn't it be more interesting if they were speaking the truth?"

Velka glared. This was not a man inclined to babble in fear, alas. Or talk much at all.

"There is so much I could do to you," mused Pen. "Take your hearing, as you plunged me into silence in that cell..." He leaned forward and cupped both hands over Velka's ears, then moved them to cover his eyes. "Or your vision, as you plunged me into darkness." He sat up again, palms on his knees. "Who is your master?"

"Who is yours?" Velka shot back. "The duke of Adria?"

"Ultimately, no," said Pen judiciously. "He just borrowed me. And when you borrow a valuable tome from a friend, it doesn't do to carelessly drop it in the privy. But enough of that." It occurred to him that anyone following up from Adria on Pen's disappearance would be most likely to encounter the official tale, at least until he could make his way back to gainsay it, and believe him dead. *Bastard's tears, what will happen to my books?*

*Pen, he's getting more out of this than you are*, complained Des. *Attend!*

"So which shall it be? Ears?" Pen clapped them, but did nothing destructive. He tried to replicate Velka's own look of bored distaste when he'd lifted his knife to Arisaydia's face, while simultaneously mustering the intense concentration needed to compress one of the body's most elegant nerves without permanently damaging it. He suspected he just came out looking constipated. "Or"—he moved one hand over Velka's left eye, made carefully sure of his invisible target, *pinched*—"your remaining eye?"

Velka's scream of anguish was entirely sincere, Pen thought. Despite the pain already placed in his body blocking his range of movement, he tried to thrash under Pen, his head whipping back and forth, and Pen was thrust in his imagination back to the scene of Arisaydia and the boiling vinegar. He hoped Velka was, too.

Pen leaned forward again, and hissed, "*Who is your master?*"

"Minister Methani," gasped Velka.

Methani was prominent in the first circle of men around the emperor, and from a high and wealthy family, Pen recalled from his readings and conversations back in Adria; he didn't know offhand if the man was one of those who had volunteered, or been volunteered, for emasculation so as to rise in imperial trust, or not. Pen's lips pursed in bafflement. "Why would he want to destroy his emperor's most effective general? Seems treasonous in itself to me. Not to mention grossly wasteful."

Velka wheezed, "Arisaydia was a danger to us all. Too independent. Too attractive. Already military conspiracies were starting to swirl about him. We couldn't penetrate the intrigues that had to be reaching him, so we made one to serve in their place."

Which was... pretty much what Arisaydia had said. For all his theatrics, Pen didn't feel he was moving forward, here. Though he wondered if that *too independent* translated to *wouldn't lie down under the thumbs of the right men.*

"Didn't it occur to any of you people that the reason you couldn't find a line was that there wasn't one? That you weren't destroying a disloyal man, but creating one?"

"If he wasn't disloyal yet, he was ripe to fall," Velka snarled back. "And then the cost of stopping him would be much higher."

Well, one couldn't say Velka didn't believe in his mission. Not the wholly cynical tool of some wholly cynical master, quite.

*Cynical enough,* said Des. *Spies have to be.*

*I suppose you would know. Ruchia.*

*A touch.* Des aimed a grimace at him, and subsided.

"Also," Pen added a bit more tartly, "if you didn't treat your armies so badly in the first place, they wouldn't go out looking for some poor sod to stick up on a standard in front of them and fight you for their favor. It doesn't seem to me the root of this is *Arisaydia's* fault. It's, it's, it's... just your own masters' *bad management.* Circling back to bite them. If you'd spend half this effort fixing the real problems, you could stop all the disaffected generals before they started, instead of, of blinding them piecemeal one by one. You're worse than evil. You're *inefficient.*"

Velka stared at him through his one good eye, so taken aback he stopped whimpering. "What are you really sent to Cedonia for?"

"I'm beginning to wonder," Penric admitted ruefully. If he was sent to be *Velka's* spiritual advisor, it seemed a supremely unfunny joke on Someone's part. Which didn't make it unlikely.

He also thought of the unexpected treasury found in the Father of Winter's offering box in the temple. *Maybe the duke of Adria wasn't the only one who has borrowed me?* The suspicion was simultaneously heartening and horrifying.

The Father wasn't Penric's god, but He might be Velka's. "Do you have children?" he asked, then, at Velka's flinch, added hastily, "No, don't tell me. I don't want to know."

Revenge was tempting, but not his mandate.

*I don't know why not,* said Des. *Arisaydia was ready to slay them all, and leave no witnesses.* A sense of reluctant admiration. No . . . not reluctant.

*You know we can't do that.*

I *can't, with our sorcery. You* could, *with your right arm, if you hadn't thrown all the blades down the jakes.*

Penric decided to ignore this. He sat up, considering his congregation of one.

"My time is short," he said at last, "so my sermon will be, too. When a man witnesses a miracle of the gods, the prudent first response should not be to try to *undo* it." A long finger reached out to tap Velka between the eyes; he jerked back. It had actually been a lot of meticulous, tricky, uncomfortable chaos-sluffing uphill sorcery, but Velka didn't need to know that. Though given Desdemona's ultimate source, perhaps it was true after a fashion. "So consider me a messenger from a higher power than a duke, and let me help you to remember this. To use the machineries of justice to commit injustice is the deepest offense to the Father of Winter."

He pressed his thumb to the middle of Velka's forehead. As he knew so well from his mountain childhood, cold could burn as brutally as fire. The work was vastly finer than his ice floe, not nearly as subtle as the labor he'd been doing all week. He lifted his thumb to reveal thin, frozen white lines in the shape of a stylized snowflake, surrounded by a red bloom of hurt. It would heal, ultimately, to a red then a white brand on Velka's skin.

It didn't come close to the amount of scarring Arisaydia would bear. But as a pointed memento, Pen fancied this wintery mark might serve.

He dismounted from Velka, collected the man's purse to keep company with that from the provincial secretary, and pressed himself to his feet, suddenly very tired. Time to go.

*Past time*, Des agreed.

As he made for the door, Velka wrenched himself around on the floor and cried, "Hedge sorcerer! You're *insane!*"

*Your fine sermon doesn't seem to have taken, Learned Penric*, said Des. She was much too amused.

Pen took two steps out, aiming to collect his medical case and his soon-to-be-stolen horse, then whipped around. He stuck his head through the lumber room door and yelled back, "I'm not a *hedge* sorcerer. And your government policies are *stupid!*"

He was still fuming when he rode to the end of the street. From the edge of his eye, he caught a glimpse of the scullion coming back, leading a pelting posse of guardsmen. Which answered the question of who had been the spy among Madame Khatai's servants, he supposed, rather too late to do any practical good. He pressed his horse into a quick trot, rounding the corner safe from their view.

X

"WE NEED TO BE MOVING FASTER," said Adelis. Although the way his chin had sunk to Nikys's shoulder suggested he was growing as fatigued as their doubly burdened horse. They'd come about twelve miles out of Patos, she guessed.

The traffic had thinned from the bustle around the city, where they'd threaded their way past builders' ox-carts, donkeys laden with vegetables for the markets, animals being driven to the butchers, sedan chairs and open chariots, and private coaches whose drivers had shouted them out of the path. They'd passed a road-repair crew whose lewd catcalls at the two unescorted women had made Adelis growl, his hand twitching for his sword, and, once, a troop of soldiers marching the other way, which had made him hunch and lower his face, squinting sidewise from the shadow of the hood trying to make out markers of regiment and rank.

Out here, fellow travelers had dwindled to the occasional farm wain or herdsman with pigs. The sun was slanting across the countryside, spreading buttery light over the small farms and larger villas tracking the watercourses, the grapevines and flickering gray-green olive groves on the slopes, the rocky heights given over to scrub and goats and sheep.

"We're moving faster than your army."

"*Anything* would move faster than an army," he returned. The spurt of remembered aggravation gave him the energy to sit up, at least.

"How are you bearing up back there?" She hesitated. "How much can you see?"

"It's ... blurry. I can see colors. It's too bright. Makes my eyes water. Your cloak is too hot."

"Yes, I know." She felt oddly glad to be out of it. She'd once imagined the widow's green would protect her from unwanted attention, but there'd proved to be a certain cadre of men who imagined it marked her as available to them, instead. She'd quickly learned not to be unduly gentle in repelling their advances, and had held her borders where she wanted them. Of course, she'd always been backed by the tacit garrison of Adelis's rank and reputation— that, too, now attainted. She added, "Faster to where?"

"I'm thinking about that."

She said tentatively, "I was wondering if we should try to make for my mother's." In which case, they needed to find a different road.

"Five gods, no."

She glanced over her shoulder to catch his grimace.

"It's one of the first places they'll think to look, and harboring me would bring disaster down upon her." He paused. "You could probably take refuge there unmolested."

She answered this with the long, unfavorable silence it deserved. He evidently took her point, for his return grunt was muted.

He'd been alternating between keeping his face down and his eyes closed, trying to protect their inflamed sensitivity, and looking around, testing and retesting his returning sight as if fearful it would vanish away again. She interrupted this cycle to ask, "Did you realize Master Penric was uncanny? I mean, before that unholy show in the garden."

"I . . . as physicians went, he seemed more sensible than most. He had a trick of massaging my scalp that he said was for headache, and it certainly seemed to work. I don't know." He seemed to consider. "He could have been lying. About the healing, I mean. Perhaps I was not so badly injured as it felt like."

"No. I saw your face when he first lifted off the prison wrap. You were that badly injured." *And then some.*

He added somewhat inconsequently, "He didn't look like what I'd imagined. From his speech, I never guessed he'd be barely out of his youth." He peered around again, and stiffened.

"Pursuit?" asked Nikys. Could they get off the road and hide?

"In a manner of speaking."

She stood in her stirrups to look, but then eased back when she recognized the single horseman, puffs of pale dust kicking up in his wake on the dirt track that ran alongside the paved military road. In a few minutes, Master Penric trotted up beside them, both he and his horse sweating and winded. His face was flushed pink under a countryman's straw hat.

"Ah, good! I caught up with you."

"If it was that easy for you," said Adelis, "it will be that easy for them."

"Ah, probably not right away. They'll be quite a while sorting themselves out back there. And I had the advantage of knowing which road to try." He smiled cheerily, but it won him only dual glowers of suspicion. "But they know what they're dealing with in me now, which is, mm, unfortunate. Doubt they'll come so unprepared again."

"You didn't kill them while you could," said Adelis. It wasn't a question. "You left witnesses."

"Well, really, that would have been a problem. Would you have had me slay the maid and the porter, too? The scullion? The laundress? The butcher's lad? How about the apothecary . . . ?"

Adelis scowled and looked away, discomfited.

"Take heart," Penric advised. "The next best thing to no witnesses is many, who will all contradict each other. Or else arrive at a consensus that has more to do with their needs than with what they've seen."

"Did you burn down the villa?" Nikys asked, thinking morbidly of her good floor loom, left behind along with so many of the tools of her life.

"What? Oh. No."

"So was his name Velka or Tepelen?"

"You know, I forgot to ask. He was the same man as—" Penric broke off, smiled, waved a hand as if to drive off a fly.

"Same man as who?" asked Adelis.

"Doesn't matter. He did say his master was a Minister Methani. Does that name mean something to you?"

Adelis shrugged. "Methani? Yes, that's very likely."

Penric looked disappointed at this tepid response. "Not a surprise, I take it."

"Not especially. We've been clashing at court for a couple of years, now."

"Had you ever done anything to anger him personally? Traduce his mother, steal his slippers, ravish his goat?"

Adelis cleared his throat. "I may have said a few intemperate things. From time to time."

Nikys snorted. She looked again sidelong at the strange blond man. "So you're really a sorcerer?" Was he really a physician, for that matter? "Why did you follow after us?"

He lifted a hand from his reins and tilted it back and forth. "A number of reasons. Mostly because I hadn't finished treating your brother's eyes. It was upsetting to be so close to bringing off . . . what I mean to bring off, and be so rudely interrupted."

Adelis blew out a non-laugh, short and sardonic.

Penric turned in his saddle and added to him, "Also, I promised Des I would try to restore your eyebrows. She was rather set on it."

"Des?" said Adelis, beating Nikys to the question.

"Ah, ha, Desdemona, my demon. I suppose it's about time you were all introduced, given she's been living with you right along, within me, for the past week." He looked at them both, hopefully. "You do know that it's the acquisition, the possession, of a chaos demon that turns a person into a sorcerer, yes?"

Nikys didn't think she'd reacted visibly, but their horse yawed farther from Penric's.

Adelis said warily, "Is it ... ascendant? That's a great danger for hedge sorcerers, I've heard."

"No, certainly not. I mean, yes, it's a significant hazard, but it's not the case here."

"How can you tell?" said Adelis. "That is ... how can we tell?"

"A sorcerer or sorceress whose demon has become ascendant will exhibit far more chaotic—erratic—behavior."

A long silence. Twin, level stares.

Penric seemed stung. "No, really, not! Though Des does leak out from time to time. You've both heard her speak. With my voice, of course. It would be quite unkind to keep her wholly prisoned."

Adelis said slowly, "You ... share your body ... with this unnatural being?"

"Share and share alike, yes. It's an intimate relationship."

Adelis looked revolted; Penric was beginning to look offended by his reaction.

Nikys put in hastily, "It seems natural to me. Every mother does it, and every unborn child. Even Adelis and I once had to share another's body and blood."

"Unmanly, then," Adelis muttered.

Penric touched his thumb to his lips and gave a little bow in his saddle. "There are compensations. As you ... can see." His thin smile put the point to the wordplay.

Nikys tried again to divert the tension: "Did Adelis's officers know you were a sorcerer when they hired you for him?"

"Ah, not exactly. By the way, do you know how far we are from the nearest largish town? Because we would be more remarked in a small village. And I'd prefer to find some inn that's quiet and clean to continue the eye treatments tonight."

"Doara is about eight miles off," said Nikys. "We should be there by sunset."

"Perfect. That will be a good time to get rid of these incriminating horses, too."

"You have a plan for that?" said Adelis, sounding distrustful.

"Oh, yes."

❖ ❖ ❖

They were in sight of Doara, and dusk was closing in, when Master Penric pulled them off the road into the cover of some scrubby trees and had them dismount.

"I believe the best, and most confusing, thing will be to send these beasts back to their own stable. Better than just turning them loose to be found along our route."

As Adelis detached the saddle scabbard, Penric unbridled his mount, scratched its ears, and began rubbing its forehead, crooning under his breath in a strange tongue. Turning away to secure the bridle to the saddle, he remarked, "I once spent a year in Easthome, the capital of the Weald, studying their style of magic with the Royal Fellowship of Shamans. A geas of persuasion doesn't come at all naturally to a chaos demon, but we learned to simulate it. A real shaman can lay a geas lasting weeks or months. The best I can do is hours. Well, it's only a horse, and the compulsion lies in line with its own inclinations. I expect this will do."

He repeated the mystifying performance with the other animal, then turned them both loose with friendly slaps to their haunches. "Off you go, now." They snuffled and trotted away down the road together. "Ah." He bent over, looking distracted. A patter of wet red fell from his sunburned nose into the dry dirt.

"You're bleeding," said Nikys uneasily, wondering if she should fetch him a cloth out of her sack. She would have to sacrifice one of her few garments.

"Yes," he said, muffled. "Don't be alarmed. It will stop in a moment. A sorcerer pays for magic, uphill magic, in some greater amount of disorder. A shaman pays in blood. The shedding of which, I argue, is also a form of disorder. Shaman Inglis and I tried to work out the implications of that . . . " He glanced up to check their reactions. Nikys leaned forward, a hand tentatively raised but with no idea what she could do. Adelis had retreated a pace, the tree guarding his back, fists clenched. "Ah, I might as well be talking in Wealdean to you, I suppose. Never mind."

The gush tailing away, Penric rubbed his upper lip with the back of his hand, straightened, and smiled rather flatly. "Let's go find that inn. I'm tired, aren't you?"

At a lodging place on a side street in Doara, Master Penric

negotiated for two adjoining rooms, while Adelis kept his head down in surly silence and pretended to be a stout, standoffish widow. The awkwardness of concealing the sword under the cloak lent him a convincing aged hunch. The moment their chamber door shut behind them he shucked out of the cloak and Nikys's dress, tossing them aside with a muffled oath. Nikys rescued her abused clothing and nobly refrained from comment. Feigning that his female employer's widowed mother was ill, Penric had arranged for their dinner to be brought up, which happened thankfully soon. It was eaten mostly in tense silence.

After the meal was cleared away from the small table, Penric, growing serious, laid out his medical kit and turned at last to Adelis. He first carefully cleaned away the day's grime from his patient's face, a sticky mess from the ointment, sweat, and road dust, and from around his eyes, but Nikys didn't think it was just from the firm touch that Adelis flinched away.

Penric evidently didn't think so either, for he said lightly, "Oh, come now. I've been helping you to your chamber pot for a week. If you trusted me in the darkness, you can trust me in the light."

Adelis grunted and, rigidly, endured the ministrations. After a while, he said, "You're a hedge sorcerer."

"Something like that."

"With a talent for healing."

Penric's voice went drier. "Something like that."

"Not a physician at all."

"I said I'd taken no oath. It's ... complicated. And not relevant here."

Nikys, seated closely and watching it all, said, "I would like to understand."

Penric hesitated, then shrugged. "Two of my demon's prior riders—possessors—were Temple-trained physicians. Their knowledge came to me as part of the same gift as their languages. Plus what I've added myself since acquiring Desdemona. Which she will carry on in turn someday to a new rider, after my death, which is a strange thought. Rather more useful than being a ghost, sundered souls not being good for much. They mostly won't even talk to you."

Nikys blinked at this last offhand observation; Adelis shifted his swollen red eyes.

"Have you tried to talk to ghosts?" she couldn't help asking.

"A few times. One feels they could answer so many questions, starting with *Who killed you?* but they almost never do." Standing behind the seated Adelis, Penric spread his fingers over his patient's scalp and paused in his chatting, though he sent her a faint smile evidently meant to be reassuring.

Nikys thought about all she'd seen. "Why do you call this... creature of chaos *her*?"

"Desdemona's prior ten human riders all chanced to be women. Plus the lioness and the mare, however you count them, but that goes back to her very beginnings. Right here in Cedonia, as it happens. This resulted over time—two hundred years of time—in a sort of composite personality that I named Desdemona, when she came down to me." His gaze grew pensive. "Your first gift to me, Penric. Though not your last."

Nikys, listening to the subtle shifts in his tone, was torn between fear and fascination. Had he always been doing this, disregarded? "Could—could I talk to her? Directly?"

Penric stared in surprise over Adelis's head. "I don't think anyone has ever asked us that before." His lips twitched. "Well, why not?"

Nikys swallowed, looked him in the eyes, and tried, "Hello... Desdemona."

Penric's smile transmuted to something more bemused. "Hello, Nikys."

"So... so you really live inside Master Penric? Like another person?"

"Or another dozen persons. It is our nature."

"How long, um, have you been... in there?" It felt absurdly like asking a new neighbor, *So, how long have you lived in Patos?*

"Since he was nineteen, and stopped to help my former mistress, Learned Ruchia, when she fell mortally ill upon a roadside in the cantons. Ruchia called him the Bastard's last blessing. We... thought we needed to learn what better to do about bad hearts."

"How long have you been together, then?" As if the neighbors were a married couple.

"Eleven, twelve years?" Master Penric—or was it the demon?—waved a dismissive hand.

To be certain the man wasn't just having an arcane jape at her expense, Nikys supposed she should think of some question to which the demon would know the answer and Penric would not, but none at once occurred to her. *Do you like being a demon? Is Penric a good master? What is it like to live for centuries?* Not to mention, *What was it like to be a woman, and then a man?* Did demons even think that way? She tried for something that seemed more answerable. "Why is Master Penric—Penric—not a proper physician?"

His expression seemed to conduct a brief war with itself, but he—or she?—replied, "A good question, child, but not mine to answer. Though if he ever does explain, you'll know he's come to trust you." His voice went sharper. "I think that's enough, Des."

Adelis, still sitting stiffly, rolled his eyes as best he could, as though he considered this offering dubious coin, and his sister a gull for accepting it. Nikys, watching those long fingers barely move through her brother's hair, wondered if she was witnessing some delicate sorcery being done right now. By Penric's abstraction, maybe so?

But Adelis, after a while, had a question of his own. "Can you kill with your demon magic?"

Penric grimaced—yes, this was Penric again now, and was this going to be like learning to tell two identical twins apart? "No."

"Fight?"

"Within limits. Did you think all those soldiers trying to arrest you earlier today tripped over their own boots?"

"What if your attackers were more than you could overcome?"

"Running away is always my first choice. After that, disable and run away. As you saw."

"What if you were truly cornered? A you-or-him contest?"

Penric's eyebrows pinched. "You've killed in warfare, presumably."

Adelis nodded shortly.

"Have you ever murdered? Slain one helpless before you?"

Adelis shrugged. "There were cleanups on the battlefield. More speeding a death already underway than a killing. Not a pretty business, nor heroic, but needful sometimes."

Penric, after a thoughtful moment, gave a conceding nod, and said, "I suppose. But every death, howsoever accomplished, opens a doorway to the gods. If I die, my soul goes to my god, if He'll have me. But should my demon murder, whether under my command or ascendant and rogue, she would be stripped from me through the victim's soul-door by her holy Master, her two hundred years of life and knowledge boiled back down to formless chaos in an instant. Worse than burning down a great library. So my mortal calculation is never just me or him. It's me or him or *her*. Do you see the conundrum?"

"...No."

"Imagine...I don't know, imagine Nikys was your demon. And, in slaying, would be not just slain but sundered. Could you see it then?"

Reluctantly, Adelis said, "Maybe. I see that you would lose your powers."

"And thus, I run away."

Adelis, his head drooping, vented a little unconceding huff, but did not pursue the matter further.

He did revive to protest when Penric made to place his mask—and when had he retrieved it?—relined with clean gauze and ointment, upon him for the night. "If you want to end up with working eyelids, you'll cooperate," said Penric sternly, and overbore him. Nikys didn't think he'd succeed in doing that for much longer.

When he'd finished cleaning up and restoring his supplies in their case, Penric told her, "I'm going out for a little."

"Why? You did that every night back at the villa, and I wondered."

"Ah." He paused at the door. "It's not a great mystery, if you recall what I told you of the price of uphill magic. Creating order, such as in healing, generates a greater burden of chaos, which I must promptly find a place to shed. The more efficiently I work out ways to do this, the more uphill magic I can safely accomplish."

"Wait. Does working this, these healings put you at some risk?"

"Not necessarily," he said cheerfully, and whisked out the door, shutting it firmly behind him.

"Not *necessarily*," she echoed aloud, hovering somewhere between baffled and peeved. "That's no answer!"

"If you haven't yet noticed that the man is as slippery as a fish," Adelis remarked dryly from his bed, "it's time you did. Also mad as a boot."

"Fish," Nikys returned with what dignity she could muster, "don't wear boots." It wasn't much of a rejoinder, nor much of a rebuttal, but it served to see her off to her own room.

# XI

ARISAYDIA'S EYES LOOKED BETTER the next morning, and saw better, too, Penric judged. Also more shrewdly, although that wasn't the eyes, exactly. For the first time, he refused even the reduced dose of the syrup of poppies, and insisted that his sister, not Penric, shave him. Which suggested he hadn't quite wrapped his military mind around how little a medically trained sorcerer needed a weapon, but it was perhaps not prudent to point this out.

Working the lather and razor carefully around the nearly healed burns, Nikys asked, "Will the brown come back?" Arisaydia's irises were still that peculiar deep garnet color, although the whites were clearing to merely a wine-sick sort of bloodshot.

"I'm not sure. I've never done a healing this delicate before." Pen didn't know if anyone had.

This triggered Arisaydia's demand for a mirror, which Nikys had to go fetch from the innkeeper's wife downstairs. It was good silvered glass, though, and its small circle reflected back a clear image of half of Arisaydia's face at a time. "Huh," he said, frowning and tilting it this way and that, but he seemed much less appalled than Penric had feared. Pen supposed the man had witnessed injuries more devastating than this in the course of his career. "I can work with this."

Without Pen's labors, the upper half of his face would have become a knotted mass of yellow, ropy scar tissue, but, of course, without Pen's labors Arisaydia would never have been troubled by the sight of it. These scars would eventually work out as flatter, paler, with redder skin between, in a sort of spray pattern not unlike an owl's feathers. Strange, but nothing to make children scream, and any woman who would recoil likely wasn't tough enough for Arisaydia anyway. Nikys managed to seem completely unruffled, a mirror Arisaydia had to find more reassuring than the glass one.

He emphatically refused to redon the blinding mask, so Penric made do with gauze wrappings above and below his eyes, which gleamed out like coals. By tomorrow, even those light dressings might be dispensed with. Pen's efforts last night had been intense, but the results were at last making themselves visible to less subtle senses than his own.

The other advantage to stopping at a larger town was that it could support a public livery, which Pen had located when he'd been out shedding chaos. Arisaydia made no objection to Pen's proposal to hire a private coach to carry them all farther south, which doubtless meant that he harbored his own ideas about their route in that direction that he wasn't sharing. The vehicle would restrict them to the road, dangerously, but also be swift.

Pen disemboweled Prygos's purse to make sure the coach was the smallest and lightest available, the horses a team of four to be managed by a postilion riding one of the front pair, out of earshot. He feigned it would allow him to continue his healing en route, but its overwhelming advantage was the privacy it would give him to open the next stage of his negotiations. Which were going to go somewhere past delicate and through awkward to, possibly, incendiary.

Because by the time they reached Skirose, some one-hundred-eighty miles farther on, he must somehow persuade Arisaydia and Nikys to turn east with him to the coast. There to find some fishing vessel to deliver them to the island of Corfara, and from there, passage to Lodi in Adria. And if he couldn't . . .

*Then we still need to turn east*, said Des.

Arisaydia refused to be dressed again in his sister's clothes, but did, grudgingly, consent to be muffled in the green cloak and hurried through the inn to the waiting coach. Once inside and started on their rattling way, he instantly divested it, bundled it up, and thrust it back at Nikys, seated next to him. "You are never to speak of this."

She returned a musical sort of "Mmm!" that promised nothing, and Penric discovered how enchanting her round face grew when she smiled deeply enough to dimple. Thwarted, Arisaydia switched his glower to Pen, more convincingly.

Penric had taken the rear-facing seat across from them, along with their meager baggage. Making sure his feet were firmly planted on the sword scabbard laid on the floor, he tried to evolve a plausible way to open his negotiation. Which must also entail his confession. Arisaydia took the problem out of his hands.

"What did Prygos's clerk—Tepelen, Velka, whoever he was— mean when he said you were supposed to be drowned? He knew you. And you knew him."

Penric cleared his throat. "Ah. Yes. That's something we need to discuss. I'd been putting it off till after I was sure I could restore your sight. That time has come."

Arisaydia made an impatient *so get on with it* gesture.

Penric signed himself, tapped his lips twice with his thumb, and gave a short, seated bow. "Permit me to introduce myself more fully. I am Learned Penric of Martensbridge, formerly court sorcerer to the late princess-archdivine of that canton. For the last year, I've been in service to the archdivine of Adria. Who, for my command of the Cedonian language and certain other skills, loaned me to his cousin the duke, to dispatch as his envoy in response to your letter begging honorable military employment in his realm."

Nikys's eyes widened.

Arisaydia barked, "I wrote no such letter!"

"Forged, yes. Velka confirmed that. It was a plot from the start. Velka, who had been following me in the ship from Lodi, seized the duke's quite authentic reply as soon as I set foot ashore in Patos. Velka knew I was the envoy but didn't know my real name nor, I suspect, my real calling. Although I'm not sure they would have treated me any differently if they had. They cracked my skull and tossed me down a bottle dungeon in the shore fortress. The night after you were blinded, they tried to drown me in my cell. Tying up a loose end, I expect."

Nikys gasped. "How did you escape?"

Penric, who had worked out in his head a scholarly letter on his novel method during his nights in the sickroom, almost opened his mouth to start spouting the preamble, then realized that wasn't really the question being asked. "Magic."

Arisaydia sat back, glaring fiercely. "More likely he was let go. Agent or unwitting cat's-paw, could be either."

Penric, affronted, snapped, "If you must know, when the water was halfway up the cell I turned some of it to ice and stood on it to reach the opening."

"I don't believe that," scoffed Arisaydia. Nikys looked more doubtful.

Penric sighed and sat back. "Just a minute..." He held up his pinched fingers and concentrated. Des had been right in her theory about water in the desert, or at least in Cedonia, he was pleased to see, as the tiny, intense spot of cold grew to a hailstone half an inch across. He leaned forward, pulled out Arisaydia's palm, and dropped the chip into it. Arisaydia, looking vaguely horrified, shook it hastily out of his hand. For good measure, Pen made a bigger one for Nikys; she, at least, rewarded him with a more appropriate look of awe. And, after a moment, bent forward to taste it.

"Don't—!" her brother began, but she crunched it between her teeth and smiled.

"It really is ice! They had ice sometimes at court in Thasalon," she told Penric, "but they brought it down out of the mountains in winter and stored it underground." She narrowed her eyes. "If you are a Temple sorcerer, you must owe final allegiance to the Bastard's Order, yes?"

"He is my chosen god, yes." Or choosing one—Pen had never been quite sure. "I did really attend the white god's seminary at Rosehall, which is associated with the university corporate body there."

"But not its medical faculty?" *You lied?* her eyes asked.

Penric waved this away. "I had enough on my plate then just with the theology, since I was doing everything backward, and in a hurry. A Temple sorcerer is supposed to train as a divine first, and only then be invested with a demon. Everything caught up with itself eventually."

She tilted her head, lips firmed with a different flavor of doubt than her brother's. "You are neither quack nor charlatan. Your skills, even if uncanny, couldn't have come out of the air."

And *there* was a place he didn't wish to dwell. "They were hard-earned, just not all by me. But this is beside the point. I was sent here as a go-between, not as a physician. The duke of Adria was quite sincere in desiring to take you into his train, General Arisaydia, and would be pleased if I were to return with you. And your sister. At present you are running away, but that's not enough; you need to be running toward. If we turn for the coast at Skirose, I think I can get us all aboard a ship for Adria."

"Ship captains don't like to take sorcerers aboard," Arisaydia observed, in a temporizing tone. "They say it's bad luck."

Not nearly as bad of luck as being caught helping an Imperial fugitive, Pen suspected. "Eh, hedge sorcerers, certainly. The Temple-trained know enough not to shed chaos in the rigging, and, further, know how not to."

"Can mariners tell the difference?"

"Generally not, which is another reason why I travel incognito."

Nikys was staring back and forth between them, clearly taken aback by this new proposal to dispose of her life unconsulted. "I don't speak Adriac. I speak a little Darthacan."

Pen smiled hopefully at her. "I could help. I could translate. I could teach you."

By their dual frowns, Pen didn't think he was making much headway. He tried again to bring things back to the issue: "The duke really does want you. He thinks with your skills and experience you'd slice through the forces of Carpagamo like a knife through butter, and I concur. Although even you might break a tooth on their canton mountain mercenaries. Unless the duke hired you some canton troops of your own, I suppose, although that could get very awkward and messy and probably is not a good idea. Certainly not for my poor cantons." He added after a moment, "Adria and Carpagamo do no end of horrible things to one another, as opportunity presents, but at least I can promise you blinding is not public policy there."

It was Nikys who pulled the unravelling thread from this. "You aren't really half Cedonian, are you? That was another lie."

"Ah, no. I'm from the valley of the Greenwell, in the mountains about a hundred miles east of Martensbridge. I don't think you would find it on a Cedonian-made map." Or most other maps, truth to tell.

"Are the cantons even a country?" said Arisaydia in unflattering doubt.

"Mm, more a patchwork of . . . *city-states* is too grand—call us town-states. Conquerors from the Old Cedonian Empire to Great Audar of Darthaca to Saone and the Weald have all tried to hold various of the cantons, but none have succeeded for long. We have no tolerance for foreign misrule. We prefer our *own* misrule." A little homesick grin twitched Pen's mouth. "Not that there's much profit in conquest. Our mountains have few productive mines, and our fields are worse. Unless you like goats and cows. Our main exports are cheese and mercenaries. Both quite good," he added in a faint spasm of patriotism. "It snows a lot," he ran down. "When it isn't raining. Perhaps that's why I'm good with ice." Gods, he was tired.

"Mad as three boots," muttered Arisaydia, cryptically.

"Adria," said Pen, "would pay you well."

Arisaydia's mouth twisted in disgust. "No doubt." He raised his chin, his garnet eyes glinting. "I was never in correspondence with the duke of Adria. I was in correspondence with the duke of *Orbas*."

Pen's eyes widened; Des murmured, *Aha!* Now, *there* was a missing piece fallen into place...

"I'd not got so far as telling him to go jump in the sea, although that was next. A happy interruption, in retrospect. When we arrive at Skirose, you are welcome to go home to Adria, with my best curses. Nikys and I will strike south for Orbas."

He sat back and folded his arms, stony. Nikys's lips parted, and a hand lifted, but fell back, whatever she thought given no voice.

Arisaydia added, "And if you try to lay a geas on me like those bloody horses, I'll run you through."

Surreptitiously, Pen put a little more weight on the scabbard under his foot. "That would be harder for me than it looks. And harder for you than you think."

Arisaydia snorted and closed his eyes, shutting out... everything. Pen could see his point.

# XII

A STRAINED, exhausted silence filled the coach, broken by the bustle of changing the horses at the first fifteen miles. A servant sold them cups of thin ale, which Nikys drank for lack of any better beverage, and they took turns at the livery's privy. She seized a moment when the physician... sorcerer... *Learned* Penric, an oath-sworn Temple divine *ye gods*, was out of earshot to draw Adelis aside beneath a tree overhanging the coach yard.

"It's all very well to spurn the duke of Adria, but have you noticed that Penric is the only one among us with any money?"

"I thought you had some." Adelis, certainly, had been hurried out of the villa with little more than her clothes on his back.

"Enough for a night at an inn and a few meals, maybe. Not enough to get us to Orbas. If that's our destination, the man emptying out his purse to buy us passage all the way to Skirose was a boon." And the continuous travel through the coming night, purchased at a premium, would give them a significant edge on any pursuit.

"I believe that was Secretary Prygos's purse, but yes. Getting it away from the sorcerer could be tricky."

"I wasn't actually suggesting we repay his bounty by robbing the man," Nikys said a little tartly. "He could be an extraordinary resource." The fact that he'd served princesses, archdivines and dukes hinted at a high level of standing that the man himself concealed. "You don't wish to be conscripted by Adria..."

His laugh was short and humorless. "My Adriac is poor, I get sick on ships, and I have no desire to let those sea rats use me against Cedonia, which I don't doubt they'd try to do sooner or later, Carpagamo be hanged. No." He added in a lower tone, as if embarrassed by the hope, "From Orbas, I might have some chance of eventually reinstating myself with Thasalon. From Adria I'd have none."

Nikys considered this. "Something dire would have to happen to Minister Methani and his hangers-on, to allow you that."

Adelis's teeth glinted, feral below the wreck of his face. "Probably."

She took a steadying breath. "So what do you say we turn it around and try to conscript Penric to Orbas?" *Or to ourselves?*

"I'm still trying to figure out how to safely shed him. As I've refused to make myself his duke's man, he has no reason not to betray us."

"I think that's about as likely as an artist setting fire to his master-painting. For all that he mumbles around it, he seems wildly proud of what he's done for your eyes." *As well he should be,* she suspected. If she hadn't known it was magic, she'd have dubbed it miracle.

"Nikys, he's an Adriac agent. Self-confessed!"

"He's a lot more than that."

Adelis snorted. "Are you sure it's Orbas you desire him for?"

Her lips twitched up; she hoped she wasn't flushing. "It's true I've come to like him. He's just . . . different. Strange, but not unkind."

"That was a *jest*." Adelis's eyes narrowed in new suspicion. "Has he offered you any offense? He's not been . . . trying to seduce you in some sorcerous way, has he?"

She had to laugh at this. "I don't think he'd need sorcery for that, but no." *Alas* was probably not the best thing to add.

Adelis being Adelis, he heard it anyway. "Of all the—! I introduced you to any number of honest officers, yet you want to make cow's eyes at some foreign little, little . . ."

"He's taller than you," Nikys pointed out, as he groped for a word to sum Penric. She thought he'd need an oration at the least.

"Skinny then, twitchy, lying . . . he has a chaos demon inside him! If he were doing something to you, could you tell? I can't!"

"Then maybe he's not. Wasn't. Whichever." Was that alarm the root of his antipathy? Or was the antipathy his alarm's disguise? She took a breath to tame her temper. "We can certainly both see what he has done *for* you. That ought to give you a comparison." She could grant that the very invisibility of Penric's magic was disturbing—how could a man defend against an attack he could not see? But she didn't usually need to squeeze fair judgment out of Adelis like oil from an olive press. "I'd think Thasalon just gave you a sharp lesson in the hazards of imagining threats where there are none."

He did flinch at that one, and backed down a tiny Adelis-inch, worth a yard from any other man. "I just believe he could be dangerous. To you."

She folded her arms, her head tilting at this blatant hypocrisy. "Then you shouldn't have taught me not to be afraid of dangerous men, hm?"

He knew enough not to step into this quagmire, but he soon found another, saying grumpily, "I'd think you'd be jealous of a fellow who's prettier than you."

"Why, are you? Really, Adelis!" She spotted the man in question emerging around the side of the stable, and had to admit that last fraternal jape was part-right. Not about the jealousy, though, which would be as futile as envying the sunlight. "Hush, here he comes back."

They climbed once more into the close confines of the coach and were off, rumbling and bumping along at a smart, steady trot.

A few miles farther on, they were passed by a galloping provincial courier. Penric glanced out the window and frowned. Minutes later, the horse came cantering back down the track, bucking and kicking at its saddle turned under its belly, followed at length by the panting, swearing courier. Adelis craned his neck to look after them as they fell behind.

"Did you do that?" he asked Penric.

"Yes," he sighed. "I'm not sure it will actually help anything."

Adelis drummed his fingers on the window rim. "I don't like being trapped on this road."

Penric shrugged. "We can count on a one-day start at least. I guarantee Velka won't be recovered enough to ride yet. And then, if he means to pursue me, he'll be put to requisitioning a sorcerer from the Patos Temple, or wherever one might be obtained. If the Temple in Cedonia is anything like the ones I know, the delays will be maddening. Although if they think I'm a hedge sorcerer, they'll take the request seriously. Controlling hedge sorcery is in their mandate regardless of the politics."

"If we could find a coach, so could Velka," said Adelis. "With or without his own pet sorcerer."

"Hm."

"You didn't cripple him permanently." The least Penric might have done, Adelis seemed to imply, even if his status as a learned Temple divine finally explained why he would not kill.

"No."

"Why not?"

"I suppose the simplest answer is... to avoid accumulating theological damage to ourselves?" Penric frowned. "I understand the drift of your questions, Arisaydia. Every realm's army tries to tap the Temple for destructive sorcerers, even as rare as we are. I won't say my superiors never give in, but someone is always sorry later. Generally the sorcerer. It's a known hazard."

Adelis accepted this with a provisional "Hm," of his own. Nikys was increasingly sensible that there was disciplined thought behind what the sorcerer would or would not do, even if the hidden rules of it escaped her. To the point where she was starting to wonder if his claimed age of thirty might be a lie in the *other* direction. Though there was Desdemona, at two-hundred-and-something.

It was deceptively easy, but wrong, to overlook Penric's permanent passenger. And then Nikys wondered what all this looked like from the demon's point of view.

At the third change they downed a hot meal at the tavern associated with the livery, then fitted themselves into the coach for the next stage. It really wasn't possible to keep up the morning's tension when Nikys wanted no part of it and Penric folded himself in a boneless slouch, vaguely amiable once more. When he offered to fill the time with another healing session, Adelis wavered.

"What if I pledge to stick to restoring your eyebrows?" Penric said.

"How can I tell what in the Bastard's hell you're doing anyway?" asked Adelis, though his aversion was plainly flagging.

"What does it feel like?" asked Nikys, curious.

Adelis shrugged and admitted, "Strangely soothing, usually."

"This is going to be a long ride," Nikys pointed out, and Adelis allowed himself to be persuaded. They switched seats, and the two men worked themselves awkwardly around to give Penric's hands access to Adelis's head. This left rather a lot of sorcerous leg to be disposed of somehow; his feet ended up nearly on Nikys's lap.

At length, Adelis's eyelids drifted closed.

"Is he asleep?" Nikys whispered.

"No," growled Adelis, and the corner of Penric's mouth tweaked up. So, his guard was not so far down as that. But the bonelessness seemed to drain out of Penric and into his patient. Penric, by contrast, seemed to grow tenser and more jittery, his brow sheened with sweat.

At their next change, Penric gave them both a tight smile. "I need to take a turn around the stable. Back in a bit. Don't leave without me, heh."

Nikys, inquisitive, got down and followed after him. The stable was cool and dim, pleasant with the bulks of the horses resting in their stalls, munching rhythmically at their fodder. She saw his lean silhouette pass out the far doors.

She emerged at the manure pile, its acrid aroma saturating the air, where the buzz of flies was dying down. Along with the flies. Penric leaned against the stable wall with his arms folded, watching their devastation somewhat glumly.

"What *are* you doing?"

"The disorder harvested from the healing has to go somewhere, and death makes the most efficient sink of chaos. Killing flies, or fleas, or any other vermin assigned to the Bastard, is theologically allowable sacrifice. Most red-blooded animals are the province of the Son of Autumn, but there are a few exceptions. Rats, mice, other creatures making pests of themselves where they shouldn't be. My god's elder Brother may owe me a favor or two, but I shouldn't like to presume. Thus, flies. Which are tedious but always abundant."

It was possibly the most bizarre conversation she'd had in her life but, oddly, not frightening. She leaned against the wall beside him and folded her arms too, a silent offer of company. He cast her a quick, grateful smile.

"But never people." It was comforting to reflect on that.

His smiled faded. "Well . . . "

She glanced up, letting her eyes speak her doubt.

"Not quite never. For the Bastard is the god of exceptions, after all, and the son of His Mother. In the highest levels of medical sorcery, there are a few exemptions. Not at all the sort of *him versus me* contests your brother pictures, so don't tell him. He'd get excited and try to make something of it that it isn't. When the choices are one life or another, or one life or none . . . " He trailed off.

She let her silence stand open, waiting to be filled with whatever he chose. Or didn't. Not for all the world would she press him. It might be like pressing too hard on glass.

"After which the physician gets to spend his nights face down on the temple floor, praying for a sign and receiving silence. Not devotions I'd wish on . . . anyone."

"I . . . " Could she honestly say *I see*? She changed it to, "I'm sorry."

The yard before them had fallen deathly still.

He drew breath. "Aye, me too." He shoved off from the wall, his smile carefully reaffixed, and they turned back through the stable.

And what, exactly, did this erratic-seeming, young-seeming man know about *the highest levels of medical sorcery*?

She was beginning to suspect that the answer might be *Everything*.

Which trailed the question, like a net behind a boat, *How?*

❖ ❖ ❖

In the late afternoon the Patos plains gave way to climbing hill country, and their progress slowed. Nikys's only consolation was the reflection that the rugged slopes would delay pursuers equally. A third pair of horses was hitched to their little coach, at a price, to haul them over the highest pass.

The sorcerer alternated between more healing sessions, growing intense now that his patient seemed soon to be parted from him, and staggering out to shed his chaos however he could at every stop. With her packed so close, and the labors so relentless, Nikys began to see the effects not only on Adelis but on Penric. *He's draining himself.*

Freed at last to talk about his craft, Penric did. He didn't sound much like a spy, but he did sound quite like a frustrated scholar with a favorite subject and a captive audience. She wondered if he was one of those inexplicable people who talked more, not less, as they grew tireder. Adelis was bestirred to open curiosity at last, despite his reservations, although his probing questions tended to revolve around military applications.

No, no one could muster a troop of sorcerers. Demons did not well tolerate each other, which was also why one only heard of a single court sorcerer at a time. No, one sorcerer did not differ greatly from another in raw power; all were limited by the amount of chaos a human body could safely hold and shed at a time. The differences in skill were mainly due to cleverness and efficiency, which age and experience enhanced. The inefficient working of magic generated, among other things, heat; a clumsy sorcerer might pass out from the heat or (a vile grin) perhaps burst like a grilled sausage, who knew? Nikys wasn't sure she believed that one, nor, from the look on his face, did Adelis. If the latter were true, Penric temporized, no one had lived to report on it, so proof was hard to come by.

No (a wistful sigh), no sorcerer could shoot fireballs from his or her fingertips. The two men looked equally disappointed at this. "Although I'm a pretty fair hand at shooting flaming arrows," Penric added. "But that's archery, not sorcery."

*No, no, no,* and through repeated discouragement Penric gently led Adelis away from hypothetical military schemes involving sorcery, or at least this sorcerer.

Nikys wondered how all this negative certainty sat with the god of exceptions and exemptions. Slippery as a fish, indeed.

Her own questions seemed to fall on more fertile ground. Yes, physician-sorcerers were rare. Only the tamest and most domesticated of Temple demons, cultivated over several demon-lives, or rather, the lives of their learned riders, were considered suitable and safe to be paired with an already-trained and skilled physician. Yes, two hundred years was unusually old for any demon. Most new elementals did not last so long in the world, being hurried out of it by a saint of the Bastard's Order dedicated to the task, or some other accident. The longer a demon survived, the more likely it was to seize ascendance in its rider's body, and without its rider's disciplines its fundamental chaos would come to the fore, to disaster all around. Yes, demons took the imprints of their personalities from their human partners, for good or ill. Given some humans, this could turn out very ill indeed, making it quite unfair that it was the *demon* who suffered instantaneous sundering and utter destruction when its god caught up with it at last.

Nikys wasn't sure if this last gloss came from Penric or Desdemona, though it was delivered quite fiercely.

As night fell in the rocking coach even the chatty Penric ran down to miserable endurance. Adelis put on his campaign face and went stolid. Nikys drooped.

She and Adelis took turns leaning on each other, napping badly. Penric folded himself this way and that in his seat, each position looking more uncomfortable than the last, finally lifting his legs to prop near the roof, more-or-less bracing himself in place.

She might have brought more comforts if this flight had been planned, conducted in suitable secrecy, instead of forced pell-mell, with pursuit pelting hot. *If wishes were horses, we all would ride,* the old nursery saw went, and remounts were another thing she was going to be wishing hard for when they reached Skirose.

Where they would be running out of time, money, stamina... everything.

They came to Skirose at the next day's dusk. Stumbling out of the coach at last, Nikys wondered if Penric had felt anything like this escaping the bottle dungeon. At a cheaper, grubbier inn they found only one room to share, but it offered water to wash with and a flat, unmoving bed to fall into. The innkeeper dragged in a thin, wool-stuffed pallet to lay on the floor. Penric grimaced and casually rid it of crawling, biting wildlife, for good measure passing his hand over the bed. She and Adelis took the bed and Penric took the pallet. Her head was swimming, Penric's blue eyes were clouded with fatigue, and Adelis's stolidity was ossifying. Danger or no, a few hours of sleep could no longer be put off.

Deep in the night she awoke to see Penric, who like all of them had lain down half dressed, pull on his jacket and slip out through the shadows. Adelis was snoring. Was the sorcerer making his escape to Adria? Planning some final, belated betrayal? Alarmed, she slid into her shoes, whipped her cloak around her, and followed him on tiptoe.

He exited silently through the inn's front door; she waited a moment and did the same, flattening to the wall and looking around for that narrow form, without torch or lantern, flickering in and out of the moonlight. She pulled up her hood and tracked him down the street and around a corner. He crossed a paved square and disappeared under a temple portico. She waited for the second creak of a heavy door, then dared to run to catch up. What did he want inside?

He'd left the door ajar; she eased it open with no betraying sound, and found a deeper shadow to stand in. The moon, just past full, shone directly down into the sacred atrium, pulling short the blue shadow of the fire plinth. A few red coals gleamed in the ashes. As her eyes adjusted, she spotted Penric making his slow way around the perimeter from altar to altar, signing himself, then cursorily opening what she'd thought were supposed to be locked offering boxes and helping himself to the contents, tipping the coins into his purse. Which did explain how he'd been finding funds since his escape from the bottle dungeon, apart from pickpocketing provincial officials. He skipped the Mother's offering box, although he signed himself and bowed his head before Her place all the same.

At the Bastard's offering box, he murmured, "Hm. They must love You better in these hills." He topped off his purse, but, instead of merely bowing, went down on his knees before the altar with its white cloth. He raised his hands palms-out in an attitude of supplication; after a minute, he instead lay prone on the tiles, arms out in the attitude of deepest supplication. Or possibly exhaustion.

Quiet fell. Yet not, she thought, quietude, for in a minute he mumbled, "Who am I fooling, kindest-and-cruelest Sir? You never answer me anyway."

His voice went acerbic. "Fool indeed, to invite His attention. This is not something we want. Really."

Nikys had no wish to interrupt a prayer, but this seemed more like an argument. She walked over and sat herself down cross-legged beside the... physician, sorcerer, divine? Which of his bewildering multiplicity of selves had laid itself down in such hope-starved humility?

He rolled over on his back and smiled at her, seeming unsurprised. "Hullo, Nikys. Come to pray?"

"Maybe."

He bent his head back toward the white-topped altar. "Is this your god too? I think you said so, once back in Patos."

"For lack of answers to my prayers from any others, yes."

"My condolences."

She wasn't sure how to take that. "I've been wanting to tell you. I had another idea, back in the coach."

"Oh?"

"Instead of Adelis going to Adria with you, which he will not, why don't you come to Orbas with us?"

The little noise he made was altogether uninformative, although it sounded vaguely like a man being hit. Then he paused, doubtful. "Does Arisaydia endorse this?"

"I'm sure I could talk him around," said Nikys, a little airily. "Once we are established there, Adelis could help you to some honorable appointment. Maybe even court sorcerer."

"Likely the duke already has one. That's how I lost my last position, you know. When Princess-Archdivine Llewen died so suddenly, the replacement archdivine brought her own trusted sorceress from Easthome. I offered to stay quietly apart among my books and papers—I wasn't even done with my latest translation— but no one seemed to think there was room in the palace for two chaos demons. Not even the chaos demons."

Wait, was that last delivered in his other voice? But he was going on, speaking his reminiscence to the night sky framed by the inner architrave.

"They all tried their hardest to shift me into the Martensbridge Mother's Order, which wanted me as much as the Palace suddenly did not. Very tidy. Everyone happy but me. No man should have to bury two mothers in one year."

Her neck felt wrenched with this last turn. "What?"

He waved a hand, dismissing she-knew-not-what. "Princess Llewen had been like a second mother to me. My own mother's death happened not long after, back at Jurald Court. I wasn't there for either one. Not sure if that was a blessing or a curse."

"I'm sorry." Surely more inadequate words were never spoken, but his hand waved again, this time in understanding acceptance. She tried to find her way back to her proposal. "If not court sorcerer, Orbas must surely be willing to make you court physician." Eager, once they learned what he'd done for Adelis.

Without heat, and with some precision, Penric said, "I would rather die." His smile grew small and strange.

Nikys sat up, gathering her determination. "I've been trying to work out why a man of your obvious—extraordinary—skills would not take up the healing trade. I think I know."

"Do you? Tell me." His tone was ironic, but not malicious. There didn't seem to be a malicious bone in his body.

"You lost a patient. Maybe someone important to you"—could it have been his princess? his mother?—"maybe just someone you tried too hard for, and it broke your heart, and your will to go on." She tried to gauge his reaction out of the corner of her eye. Was she too bold, too offensive? Would he be angry at her probing?

She hadn't expected to evoke a crack of laughter, cut off sharp, and she flinched. *Mad as a boot*, Adelis had said. Was the observation shrewder than she'd guessed?

"If only that." Penric stretched back on the temple floor, folded his hands behind his head, and squinted up at the moon, which bathed his pale face in pale light until he looked carved of snow. "Try three a week. More, some weeks."

"What?"

"This is a place for confessions, why not? After tomorrow we are unlikely to see each other again, even better. Like lancing an infection, and as ugly yet fascinating as what drains from one, aye. Might be good for me."

*Three boots?* She bit her lip.

"Everything started well. I was happy in my scholar's work for the princess-archdivine. But due to my transcription and translations of Learned Ruchia's germinal volumes on sorcery and medicine, the Mother's Order at Martensbridge found out that two of Desdemona's former riders had been physicians. The princess was eager to add another string to my bow, and so was I, when she sent me over to their hospice to learn. Apprentice, we all thought, until all of Learned Amberein's and Learned Helvia's knowledge began to awaken in me, and suddenly I was doing as much teaching as learning. Not that every new patient isn't a lesson for every physician, lifelong. I did enjoy instructing the apprentices in anatomy.

"I brought off some difficult cures. It all depends, you know, on underlying conditions. If they'd taken your brother's eyes with hot irons, it would have left me too little to work with. But from the outside, no one could tell why I sometimes succeeded and sometimes failed.

"The hospice began to ask more and more of me because, after all, it *sometimes* worked. Worth trying, you know? I was stretched, but still holding my own, when the princess passed away and I lost a defender I didn't realize I'd had.

"You see, the Order's idea of conserving me was to save me for only the worst cases. I never got to treat, I don't know, a hangnail, or even worms anymore, I never was allowed any *easy* victories. Always and only the direst injuries and illnesses, over and over. Far more died than not. When I found myself walking to the hospice each day devising . . . well, it doesn't matter now."

"It matters to me," Nikys dared.

His moon-silvered brows flicked up. "Whyever? Whatever. I did promise a full confession, didn't I. As I sit—lie down—speak before my god. Not that He doesn't already know." A snow-smile, barely bending. "So, when I spent my walk to work each day thinking up methods for a sorcerer to kill himself—which is not an easy thing to do, it turns out, when his demon opposes the idea—I realized perhaps it might be time to stop. I made application to the archdivine of Adria for work in translation, and other Temple scholarship, and ended my career as sorcerer-physician in Martensbridge. It was good, traveling north over the mountains. It felt like a narrow escape."

Nikys tried for a friendly silence. Because the alternative was to cry out in horror and protest, and that would certainly not be helpful. Just how far had that *devising* gone? *I'd bet Desdemona could tell me.*

Penric continued, "And thus I learned the difference between a skill and a calling. To have a calling with no skill is a tragedy anyone can understand. The other way around . . . less so."

"Oh. I . . . see." She took a breath and cast her own challenge. "You know, I should really like to hear Desdemona's version of this."

She'd startled him; his eyes went wide. In an uncertain voice he said, "I suppose . . . we could do that."

She could catch, now, when that inner twin shifted the tensions in his face. The demon spoke: "Hah. *We* blame his superiors entirely. Amberein and Helvia both trained up in the greatest centers of the medical arts in Saone and Darthaca, in their days, where their skills and limits were properly understood, together with the reticence needed to sustain them. Backwards Martensbridge saw only that a magical boon had fallen to them, and wanted to milk it for all it could give. Like a greedy trainer putting a high-blooded colt to race too soon, to its ruin. And Penric, the fool, wouldn't say no and wouldn't quit, till we both ended up on a hillside at dawn seeing if I could heal his arms faster than he could slice them open, which was *not* my idea of how we should part ways."

"It wasn't *serious.*" His voice shifted to a tone of dissent. "There was a precipice near enough if I'd been serious. As you have several times pointed out, you can't make us fly."

"Fortunately, he passed out before he could win the contest. A small landslide and an unlucky elk paid for the rest, and when he woke up, we had a *talk.*"

Penric may have been confessing; this sounded more like ranting.

"And he *still* won't say no and he won't quit, which is how we ended up in a bottle dungeon in Patos instead of a nice, comfortable study in Lodi overlooking the canal. What he *needs* is a superior with the backbone to say *no* for him." His voice went sly, and his eyes shifted toward her. "A woman with experience keeping fool men alive might do the trick."

"Des!" He convulsed to a sitting position.

"What, you're the one who's been mooning after her hips for the past fortnight. So do something about it."

His jaw snapped shut. In this light, it was impossible to tell if he blushed, but his cheeks darkened a little.

Nikys gulped, not doubting she'd caught the demon's drift. Though not the first, it certainly ranked as the strangest proposition she'd ever received. Also, curiously, the least insulting. "Experience I have," she said quietly. "Success, very little."

"Worth asking," came the mutter, and she wasn't sure which of the people in his head said it.

His spine straightened. "It *is* worth asking." Now his voice was his own. He turned his head toward her, eyes silver in the shadows, and unreadable. "I have a counter-proposal for you. What if you came to Adria with me? Let Adelis make his own way to Orbas, which I think he now might do."

She rocked back. "I couldn't do that, I couldn't leave . . . "

"He left you, to go off to his wars how many times? He might even travel more safely alone, and certainly faster."

"Your duke doesn't want *me*." Her heart was thumping, uselessly.

"I didn't say it was for the duke." He'd gone a little breathless.

"It would make me a hostage against Adelis."

His lips parted, closed. His voice went small. "Wasn't what I had in mind."

"But it would follow. Inevitably. Things being as they are."

"Oh." He slumped back supine on the floor again, staring up at the advancing moon. "I might protect . . . "

"When one's own liege-lords turn on one, we have all lately seen how hard *protection* is to come by."

"I suppose that's so."

His was the cruelest kind offer she'd ever received, hopelessly misaimed, like pressing gloves on a handless thief, or flowers on a starving woman. She returned the favor. "There's still Orbas."

His face jerked away, as if dodging a dart. "All my books are back in Adria. I hope."

"Beloved hostages?"

"After a fashion. Which says something sad about me, I'm sure."

She considered this oblique evasion. "There are books in Orbas. The duke has a fine library, I've heard. Books you haven't read. Maybe some you've never heard of." He had not, she recollected, said

*No* to Orbas, not in the unyielding way Adelis had refused Adria. Even slippery fish jumped into nets sometimes...

His mouth curled up. "Wisdom bird. Madame Owl. Your brother dubbed you aright."

Yes, and what if Adelis woke up and found them both gone? "We should get back. If you are done here."

He looked pensively around. "No one talking here but us, so I would seem to be." He clambered colt-like to his feet, and offered her a hand to heave herself up.

# XIII

PENRIC TOOK NIKYS'S... Madame Khatai's arm in escort as they walked back through the shadows to the inn. He suppressed a wince at the thought of her having trailed him to the temple alone this late at night, in a strange town.

*It was no great distance,* observed Des.

*Des, just don't... embarrass me with this woman.*

*Rather do it yourself, would you?* An impression of a huff. *If I have to listen to you pine after her, so can she. And rather more usefully.*

It was bad enough that he'd made Nikys listen to his fractured confession. *There are impediments. Starting with my Temple oath to the archdivine of Adria.*

*Your god is the same everywhere, Adria, Cedonia... or Orbas.*

*My god was just now silent on the subject of my direction, you will note. As ever. And everywhere. A sameness of sorts, I suppose.*

*What, you prayed for guidance and in the very next moment that nice child came and sat down beside you. I thought she was going to pat you on the head. I could have told her a board would work better. What do you expect from Him, a letter signed and sealed and hand-delivered? A parade with trumpets?*

Penric said hesitantly, *You like her? You don't always like the women I, er, meet.*

*They don't always like me. But she seems willing to learn. Not so sure about the brother.*

*I thought you all found him quite scenic to look upon.*

*Yes, till he opened his mouth and was so rude to us.*

*We've met worse. I thought him teachable. Give him time.*

*The time you aren't planning to allow? Contradictory, Pen.*

He smiled tightly. *If consistency is what you want, I've taken oath to the wrong god.*

They made their way as quietly as possible through the inn's front door, Penric turning the key again behind them. The place afforded no night-porter, fortunately. They creaked up the dark stairs and made their way to their chamber, marked by a faint orange glow under the door. He was therefore not too surprised to enter after Nikys and find Arisaydia sitting up in the room's one chair, glaring at them by the light of a tallow candle, his eyes red sparks. His unsheathed sword lay across his lap.

He kept his voice low, but fierce. "Where have you been?"

It must have been alarming for him to wake up to the empty room. Or at least to the absence of his sister; Pen hadn't planned on that. Good that he hadn't gone charging out into the town in some wrong direction and repaid them the jolt. "The temple," he answered, equally quietly.

"At this time of night?"

"The gods will hear prayers any time."

"Actually," said Nikys, doffing her cloak and hanging it on a peg, "I found him robbing the offering boxes."

At Arisaydia's stare, Penric said, "You want to hire horses tomorrow, don't you?"

"I was afraid we would be pressed to forage for mounts like an army in enemy territory," he admitted reluctantly. "But buying would be better still, to leave no witnesses to our direction."

"You were thinking of stealing them?" said Nikys, her brows rising. She glanced sidelong at Pen. "It's hard to imagine Cedonia as an enemy country."

Arisaydia's hand touched his temple, as if to say, *Not so hard for me now.* But he clearly still mourned this hostile transformation, even as he set his face to the wind. "No horses for sale in this crossroads village at this time of night anyway." He sighed out his tension and rose. "Try to sleep."

At least he sheathed his sword before he lay down again, but he did pass Penric a special brotherly glower as he blew out the candle.

Pen lay on his pallet and sorted out his options.

There weren't that many. From Skirose, a lesser military road ran east to the sea, and west over the spine of Cedonia to link up with the net of roads around Thasalon. A minor local road ran south into the hills, branching into tracks unfit for wheeled vehicles over the stony passes to the neighboring province. It was another hundred or so miles across that province to the next range of mountains. Beyond them lay the lands of Orbas, Cedonia's sometimes-client-state, sometimes-ally, sometimes-enemy, presently attempting a neutral independence. Thasalon would be happy to forcibly reconvert it to a tax-paying province, if the emperor didn't have a compass-turn of other pressures to attend to: Adria to the east, the Roknari to the north coast and islands, the Rusylli to the southwest.

Penric's most direct route home was east to the sea and across it to Adria. Overland, it would be a longer journey, south around the arc of the coast through Orbas and Trigonie, before he came to Adriac lands once more. Although once to Orbas, he would no longer be running as an outlaw of sorts, and could presumably report to the Temple and seek aid from a local chapter of the Bastard's Order. So heading south with Arisaydia and his sister—all right, with Nikys and her brother— wouldn't be *deciding* anything, necessarily. An alternate course would be to find a coastal ship to take them to one of the few ports of Orbas, although Pen doubted his ability to persuade Arisaydia aboard a form of transport he could neither control nor abandon at will.

Nikys would, of course, follow her twin. Not some possibly-lunatic stranger she'd just met a fortnight ago. Arisaydia was correct, if not right, to take that for granted. Did he realize how much he assumed of her?

Not that oh-so-Learned Penric was in a position to offer her anything better than a different dangerous flight and uncertain welcome, now was he?

*Pen*, said Des, exasperated, *what you are in a position to do is to stop fretting and go to sleep, so we aren't all worthless for any action in the morning.*

She wasn't wrong. He grumbled and rolled over.

❖ ❖ ❖

They ate breakfast soon after dawn in the inn's common room, as apart from its other patrons as they could arrange, and silently. Fare included porridge, unexceptional, dried figs and apricots, decent, a small ration of white cheese, horrifyingly familiar squares of dried fish which Nikys and Arisaydia consumed without comment, and an excessively generous bowl of tough half-dried black olives, which Penric sampled suspiciously and passed along to his companions. After, they returned to their room to count out Pen's coins on the washstand, and plan.

"If we make for the coast," Pen reasoned, "and then pick up passage on some local vessel, we could as soon reach the ports of Orbas as the island of Corfara. Which must surely be easier on Madame Khatai than an overland flight through these hills." And it would give Penric several more days to argue for Adria, if he could evolve some better lever to shift this human boulder. A frown from Nikys indicated that this slight on her endurance was not entirely appreciated, but an appeal to Arisaydia's own convalescent state would have been worse received.

Arisaydia appeared not totally unmoved by the argument, or at least his scowl grew more thoughtful. He glanced at Nikys and seemed to consider. "Our funds might purchase one maybe-sound horse. Not three," he said at last. "Give the purse to Nikys, and we'll go dicker for hired horses. You go and buy us food to last for a two-day ride. We'll meet back here and decide on our direction then."

It wasn't a *yes*, but it wasn't as firm a *no* as usual. Penric elected not to push, or push his luck, just yet, and went off to find whatever passed for a day-market in this town. And marshal his next set of points. Debate had never been his best skill, back in seminary.

He returned with a sack of variously preserved foods, including more leathery olives, and settled on a bench in the inn's entry atrium, tilting his straw hat down over his face, to await the siblings' return with horses.

And waited.

Growing restless, he went up to check their chamber. No notes. Arisaydia and Nikys had taken their scant belongings with them to pack in the hoped-for saddlebags, and Pen's case stood ready to go. Arisaydia was not a man to waste time.

*Indeed, not.*

A weight settled in Pen's stomach that had nothing to do with porridge and olives, and he hastened downstairs and around to the main street that hosted the livery and coaching inn serving the military road. A quick survey of the ostlers came up only with no, no sir, a man and a woman had not tried to hire three riding horses in the last couple of hours, nor even two horses. Was there any other livery in town? Oh, aye, sir, there was a little place just off the west road, but it only offered local hires, not good coach teams like ours, twelve miles an hour on the flats! Reflecting that this country was not oversupplied with flats, Penric lengthened his stride as he found his way to the west road.

The stable on the west road was small but tidy, featuring a dozen stalls, mostly empty. Oh, aye, sir; a man and his wife had hired two horses, together with the requisite groom-guide, and left upwards of two hours gone. Which way? The south road. Something about visiting relatives in a village up the far head of the valleys.

*Arisaydia, you son of a bitch*, Penric swore, internally. For the stable owner he managed a thin smile. What was left in Pen's pockets wouldn't hire a pony for a ride up and down the street.

He waited till he was out of earshot, stamping back up the road, to curse aloud. It didn't relieve his feelings much. The blasted man hadn't won wars, Pen supposed, by sitting around waiting for the battle to be brought to him. He should have remembered that.

*He was smooth*, agreed Des, unhelpfully. *If he'd demanded that purse for his own hands, you wouldn't have been near so quick to hand it across.*

Pen growled.

And had Nikys agreed, or argued and been overridden? Gone along eagerly, or regretfully? Pen supposed the clench to his heart made no practical difference either way.

Returning to the inn, Pen cleared his case and sack from a room he could no longer afford, and tried to come up with his next scheme. Walking after his quarry in an attempt to overtake them would be futile. More futile, he suspected, would be catching them. Horse theft, even if a temporary borrowing, would be tricky. *Not impossible, though.* But if that was his plan, he needed to carry it out quickly.

He'd have to wait for nightfall to revisit the moneylenders of the gods in the temple, although raiding the same place twice in a row seemed imprudent. If anyone had noticed the sudden shortfall, they might set a watch tonight. Alternatively, he could give up and start walking to the coast. His worn Cedonian sandals were not his idea of marching gear, but he could replace them at the next town. Where there would be another temple, likely, although perhaps more impoverished. He gnawed a piece of dried fruit from his sack, and fumed.

Mulling feasibility, he hoisted his case and sack and returned to the first livery. It harbored more horses to choose from, but also more people about. Sneaking an animal out in broad daylight would certainly pose a challenge, even for a sorcerer. Waiting for the cover of darkness would be pointless, if the entire purpose was to catch Arisaydia and Nikys. If he were going east afoot, better to start now.

He stood concealed across the street in a niche between two whitewashed houses and, slowly, tore his own hopes in half. He'd done all he could. East it was.

A pair of coaches rolled up, noisy and dusty, each pulled by a lathered team of six. Someone had been paying for speed, to be sure. The ostlers and servants, interpreting the signs of impending largess, swarmed out to take charge. About to step forward Pen instead jerked back, as the vehicles disgorged a troop of ten soldiers and a sergeant, a man in the loose white robes of the Bastard's Order in Cedonia, and the all-too-familiar figure of Velka.

Heart hammering, Pen scrambled up the side of the house, fingers and toes scraping raw on stonework and sills, to take a concealed vantage on the flat roof, peering down into the street and a bit of the inn yard. Of *course* coaches. If Velka had tried to march a troop after Arisaydia, they wouldn't be more than forty miles from Patos by now.

After some milling about and a rush on the livery's privy, and the successful sale of some tankards of ale swiftly quaffed, the sergeant rounded up his men, counted them off, and sent them spreading out in pairs through the town. "You know what questions to ask by now," he shouted after them. Penric bet he knew, too. *Bastard's teeth.*

Velka, who bore a thin white bandage around his brow, was stiff and limping. It might be the lingering effects of Pen's rough treatment of him three days ago at the villa, but the gray-bearded man in the rumpled whites moved almost as stiffly, so maybe it was just the coach. The glint of silver from the man's shoulder braid would have told Pen what he needed to know even without Desdemona's tight, *Well, Pen. We have a colleague.*

*Can you tell anything more without revealing yourself?*

*Not yet.*

Velka began interrogating the ostlers and servants, who answered readily, pointing in various directions. A handing-out of coins reduced the directions by maybe half. Penric wanted to thump his own head—their memory of his recent queries must send Velka on to the other livery much sooner than he would have found it otherwise. Although he would certainly have arrived there in due course. Arisaydia and Nikys couldn't be more than ten miles up the track by now. Maybe there were a lot of possible side trails? Penric hoped for dozens.

It would take Velka some time to collect intelligence, decide on a course, hire or conscript thirteen riding horses. Though the sergeant was already bargaining with the inn servants to get his men a hasty meal, which might well be accomplished while horses were found and saddled. Their demands would strip this stable of mounts, apart from the dozen spent coach horses, useless to Pen. The Temple sorcerer passed within, perhaps looking to his own sustenance.

Velka would shortly know that Pen had been seen separately from Nikys and Arisaydia, and more recently. Pen wondered briefly if he should show himself to get them to chase after him instead? They could well catch him, he recognized ruefully, although they would soon regret doing so. But Velka had enough soldiers to split his forces if he were forced to. He only needed the sorcerer and a couple of men to go after Pen. The rest could ride south, unsparing of their mounts.

Arisaydia would fight to the death before allowing himself to be captured again, Pen suspected, and where would that leave Nikys? Fallen into the hands of some remnant of enraged men, out for revenge for their dead and wounded? Unless the twins should decide to travel together one last time. It seemed a horribly plausible nightmare either way.

Pen swallowed, swung back down the side of the building, collected his case and sack, and slipped through to the next street, not that Skirose had many streets to choose from. He loped west, parallel to but out of sight from the military road. Sneaking up opposite the small livery through someone's scanty grove of olive trees, he spotted two of Velka's men coming back already, marching double-time with their news.

He swore under his breath, waited until they'd angled out of sight, and darted across the road to the stable.

The stable boy rose in far too much alarm to be greeting a potential customer. Pen made one futile attempt to motion him to hush, then, as he turned, yelling and starting to run, tweaked the nerves in his legs and, as soon as possible, his throat. The lad recoiled in terror as Pen rolled him to the side of the aisle, whispering, "Sorry—sorry! It will wear off in a bit." He hoped. He hadn't as much time to prepare his strike as with the soldiers in the villa.

Only one horse was left, a rangy bay gelding turning restlessly in a box stall. *Looks good*, said Des. *Its legs are even longer than yours.*

It also had a spine like a sawblade; ten minutes of bareback trotting would slice a rider up the fork. Pen searched feverishly for a saddle and bridle, and saddlebags, into which he stuffed his case and sack. Back in the stall, he discovered the reason for the beast's lonely state was that it was a biter. And a kicker. And generally uncooperative. At its second yellow-teethed snap, Des gave it a good sting on the nose, mysterious to it since the human it was trying to savage hadn't touched it, and again at the third. It stopped trying after that.

Fitting the bit into its mouth involved ear-wrestling and a near-loss of valuable sorcerous fingers. Pen rechecked the girth—aye, it was a blower, too—and prudently mounted while still in the stall. He let Des undo the latch and swing open the door, and concentrated on keeping the animal's head up on a short rein, and his head down instead of smacked into the door lintel, as it pronked out into the light of the afternoon.

He fought it out onto the road, where it was at least pleased to convert vertical into horizontal motion. Only a sketchy illusion of wolves, a fragment of geas learned from his shaman friend, allowed Pen to force the turn—more of a shy—onto the south road. At that point, he could crouch in his stirrups and let the blighted beast run itself out of piss and vinegar.

It took five miles. Pen, gasping for breath, was impressed. *Bastard's blessing, are you?*

The gallop fell to a bounding trot almost as hard to sit, then a blowing walk. The road followed the winding valley as it rose toward the hill passes. Between patches of tangled woodland, little farmsteads clung to the creek. At one, a woman was out working in a vegetable garden, and Pen dared to stop and beg a drink of water and word of any prior passers-by. She scowled at him in alarm but then, at her second glance, smiled unwilled. The water was forthcoming, but no news; she'd been working inside earlier. Pen cast her a blessing, which made her blink, but then wave back.

He watered the horse when the creek crossed the road, after an argument about whether it was going to try to flop down and roll him off among the rocks. He was only sorry he couldn't give it to Arisaydia. The two deserved each other.

# XIV

ADELIS, NIKYS THOUGHT, was champing at the bit far more than their sluggish horses. Pressing their guide for more speed had only won them grudging brisk trots. He was excessively tender toward his employer's beasts, she thought, till they arrived well-timed to stop at what proved a cousin's farmhouse, and an offer of a purchased meal. Adelis whispered, in a furious undervoice more than half serious, that it would be faster to run the man through and steal his horses after all, but yielded to a chance for food that they *only did not have* thanks to leaving Master—Learned—whatever-he-was Penric behind.

The broad, smiling cousin set them out a lunch at a shady table by the stream, in what would have been an idyllic setting and interlude under any other circumstances. As it was, it gave Nikys her first private chance to pick up their argument from back at the livery.

"I still think we were wrong to leave Learned Penric behind. If not tactically, although that too, morally. What if something happens to him?"

Adelis made an exasperated noise through his chewing. "He's a sorcerer. And a spy. He'll land on his feet. Like a cat."

"That's not actually true of cats." Or sorcerers? "And last time, he landed in a bottle dungeon."

"If it's true he was tossed into one, it's also true he escaped. Which is ... let's just say unprecedented. He can make his way back to Adria faster and safer without us. That he's an Adriac agent is the one part of his jumble of tales that I certainly believe to be real."

Nikys swallowed watered wine and drummed her fingers on the boards. "I watched him, and talked to him a little, during those first days when you were too lost in pain and syrup of poppies to track much. Whatever else was going through his mind, he cared passionately about what he was trying to do for your eyes."

"Which says only that the man had a conscience, which I will not argue about, and that it was guilty. Whether because what he told us was true, or for some other secret up his sleeve, I can't guess. That he was still trying to the last to persuade me to Adria, after all our disasters, that he expended such heroic effort on healing me, suggests that his duke must want me far more than seems reasonable, and I have to wonder why. Nikys, we had only his word for his whole fantastical story. He only claimed to be a Temple sorcerer, and all the rest. We don't know."

"All his actions so far were not proof enough for you?"

Adelis shook his head. "I swear, you swallowed down everything the man said without choking because, what, you liked his blue eyes?"

"You don't deny he's a sorcerer, you can't deny he's an extraordinary physician—what he told me in the temple last night—"

"*He* told," Adelis put in. "Again."

She waved this off. "Well, that was in confidence anyway. As for the other ... he thinks better of people than he should. Better than is safe for him. That says more learned divine than spy to me. He thinks differently."

"He and his invisible twelve-headed demon, yes, very differently." A wry grimace as he leaned back.

She still boggled trying to imagine what must be going on inside Learned Penric's overcrowded head. All the time. Whatever else was happening, his mind had to be very, very full. The wonder was not that he was mad but that he wasn't.

"Anyway, we can move faster now," said Adelis.

"Not at present," Nikys noted.

"Aye." He shoved the rest of his bread in his mouth and rose, still chewing. "I'll go prod that groom. And see if I can secure a water bottle. And some food. We'll want them, going over these hills." He went off into the old stone farmhouse.

Nikys thought her greatest want was going to be human, and demonic. Would she ever see the strange sorcerer again? Would he really be all right, as Adelis insisted? His last time—first time, she also gathered—wandering about Cedonia on his own had included some horrifying turns. She hadn't felt this sick with helpless worry since, well, Kymis. And then Adelis, until Penric had appeared. And now Penric. Her chain of alarming men was getting longer, but no better.

Would there ever be any way to find out if he'd made it home safely? She didn't know a soul in Lodi, had barely met a few Adriac merchants. She supposed one such might carry a letter, but to whom?

But wait, Learned Penric was a Temple-man. If he truly was all he'd said, an inquiry sent in care of the archdivine of Adria might well find him. The ill-fates of recent letters to and from Adria were daunting, but should she and Adelis arrive safely at last in Orbas, she abruptly determined to dare.

There, a plan. Better than crying limply under a persimmon tree any day. As Adelis emerged from the farmhouse, more-or-less strong-arming the groom, she rubbed her eyes and hurried to the horses.

# XV

AS THE LIGHT leveled toward evening, the woods dwindled to scrub, the farmsteads gave way to shepherd's huts, and the road narrowed to a winding, stony track. At a bend, Pen encountered a rider leading two saddled horses back the other way.

The rider stopped to stare in surprise. "Five gods, man, someone rented you Pighead? And you're still atop?"

That alone was enough to identify the man as the small livery's groom-and-guide. "Is that its name? Very fitting. We've had some debates along the way, but I've won so far. Tell me, were you escorting a man and his wife, traveling? Where did they go?"

"Oh, aye. I told them they'd never get over the pass before nightfall, better to find shelter and continue in the morning, but they were having none of my advice, so I suppose they deserve what they find. I took them as far up as the horses could get, where they insisted I leave them off."

Pen was still on the right track, five gods be praised. "How much farther? I need to catch up to them."

"Maybe a mile?"

Pen nodded relieved thanks. "Oh, I should warn you—there's a troop of soldiers behind me that are conscripting horses for the army. If you don't want to end up walking home, you'd probably best get your beasts off the road and find a place to hide them till they pass on."

"Oh!" The man looked startled, but he swallowed down the lie. "Thanks!"

"Ah . . . " Pen's conscience prodded him. If he could only ride a little farther anyway . . . "Do you want this one, to take back as well?"

The groom grinned. "Naw. Let the army enjoy him."

They each hastened on, in opposite directions.

Indeed, after about a mile of scrambling over slippery scree, footing more suitable to a donkey than to a tired, nervy horse, the trail gave way to outright climbs over stair-like stones, narrowing to a scrubby defile. To Pen's relief, he saw a flash of movement above: a pair of figures, one in a green cloak.

To his dismay, as he turned to look back down the valley before dismounting, he could just make out a troop of mounted soldiers, trotting relentlessly single file. He counted—yes, the whole thirteen. A flicker of white confirmed that Velka had brought his sorcerer. Pen sucked breath through his teeth. The horse, its head hanging in weariness, made one last halfhearted attempt to bite him as he dragged out his belongings from the saddlebags, unbridled it, and turned it loose.

He hoisted his burdens and began clambering up the slope. In a few minutes, Nikys glanced back, spotted him, and touched her brother's sleeve. After a brief debate, they sat on boulders to await his arrival. They both looked nearly spent, but equally determined. Arisaydia still had the sword, naturally.

Penric heaved his way up to them, brandishing the sack. "You forgot your food," he wheezed. "Among other things."

Arisaydia glowered, but Nikys looked tentatively delighted, saying, "After Adelis—after we left you in Skirose, we thought you would certainly go back to Adria. You decided to join with us after all?"

Her smile at him, Pen decided, made up for that vile horse, if not quite for her brother. Not much question whose idea Pen's abandonment had been. "Not exactly. But Velka and a troop arrived in town barely an hour after you'd left. By coach, just as you predicted." He allowed Arisaydia a conceding nod, not received with any discernable gratitude. "They're only a few miles behind us right now."

Nikys's breath drew in. Arisaydia's expression turned a much cooler shade of grim.

By silent, mutual consent, they shelved their differences for later in the face of this news. Arisaydia surveyed the landscape, ending by looking up toward the narrowing defile. "Then we keep climbing. There might be a cave."

"To hide in? He brought his own sorcerer. So maybe not," Pen cautioned.

"Huh." At least Arisaydia took in the warning without argument. "I admit, I don't like putting myself in a bottle."

"Neither do I," Pen agreed, heartfelt.

"Climb, then."

They did so. It took nearly all their breath, but Arisaydia spared what he could to ask after the numbers and condition of their pursuers, seeming peeved that Pen had no more detailed inventory of their arms.

"You took down, what, seven at the villa? That would leave six for me. It may be better to turn and face them here than letting them catch us later, at a worse vantage, even tireder, in the darkness."

Pen didn't care for Arisaydia's arithmetic. Alone, he thought he might be able to bolt up the hill, turn and dodge, climb, vanish. Run away. *But not the three of us. And so the tactician prevails. In a sense.* He observed, voice flat in his concession, "Velka's Temple-man is going to tie up a lot of my attention, once we get within range of each other. This isn't going to be the kind of fight you think."

Arisaydia's red eyes narrowed. "Can you take him?"

"I... won't know till I see what he brings to the table. We won't exactly be trying to kill each other. Jumping demon problem, there." Among other theological concerns. *Bastard's teeth, what a mess.*

At last Arisaydia stopped, glanced around, and said, "Here. We won't do better."

Pen copied his inspection. The steepest part of the trail zig-zagged down behind them, giving them a height advantage not unlike being atop a rampart. The scrubby slopes to either side allowed no cover for a man to advance and circle them in secret. The defile ahead might not be a good place to be pressed into if anyone did manage to get above them, but it wasn't entirely out of the range of some rabbit-sprint retreat.

Reminding Pen a bit of the prudent sergeant, Arisaydia had them all sit down and share out bites of food from Pen's sack, and mouthfuls of water from the leather bottle he carried, and when had he acquired it? He glanced at Pen's case. "You dragged that all this way?"

"Its contents were expensive, and would be hard to replace. Good steel needles and scissors and scalpels. Clean gauze, the remains of my ointments... had some trouble getting them compounded correctly, you know."

Nikys eyed it, and him. "I'd have thought you'd be glad to leave it behind."

*Yes, no, I don't know, maybe sorry later...* "Frugality is a hard habit to break."

Looking thoughtful, Nikys bestirred herself and began gathering up a pile of throwing rocks. Adelis blinked, then went to assist her. Penric wished wanly for his good hunting bow, back in Adria, but joined the foragers.

He stopped when the first of Velka's party, their horses slipping and snorting, cleared the last ridable turn below, looked up, and saw them. Shouts, excitement, bustling back and forth as the ten men and the sergeant dismounted, secured the horses, arrayed themselves and waited. Four of them were archers, Pen saw, even now stringing their short bows and looking up warily, awaiting orders. All their quivers bristled with arrows.

"That's going to be a problem," sighed Arisaydia, watching them.

"Not really," murmured Pen. Nikys glanced at him sidelong and picked up a rock, turning it in her hands. She, too, seemed to be waiting for orders.

"Now I'm sorry you were drawn into our disaster," she said quietly to Pen.

"Wasn't you who did it. And I mean to share that regret around, if I can."

Her little smile reminded him of that scary smirk of her brother's. "Good."

They were just out of bowshot, at least for men shooting uphill. The archers were also out of range for Pen's sorcery, certainly of the finely tuned variety he hoped to use. Landslides remained an option, although there wasn't a great deal of scree poised in just the right places.

More debate below among Velka, the sergeant, and the sorcerer. Then the man in the white robes turned, seemed to steel himself, and began climbing the jagged trail with the aid of a stout staff.

He looked everything a Temple sorcerer and learned divine should be. Tall, grave, mature, powerful, his beard trimmed neatly around his face, though he could have stood to take the scissors to his eyebrows as well; black eyes glared up from their bristling shadows. Both Arisaydia and Nikys stared down in muted alarm.

"This one's my part, I guess," sighed Pen, without enthusiasm. *Des, are we ready?*

*Ooh,* she cooed, *what a cute little baby demon!*

*What?*

*The lad with the beard as well, but his demon is just a youth. Only two animals before him, and this is its first human incarnation. All it will know is what* he *knows.*

"Bastard be praised," breathed Pen, and tapped his lips twice with his thumb. Then twice again, because everyone here was going to need His luck to get through the next minutes alive. He stepped out a few paces from where his companions crouched, letting the approaching man get puffed closing their mutual range. He wondered what he looked like in turn. A tired, skinny, sunburned young man with hair escaping its knot—he blew a strand out of his mouth—wearing an odd assortment of castoffs, sweaty tunic, green jacket, mismatched riding trousers all over horse. Long feet unhappy from his hike in these falling-apart sandals, and he had to get some good boots soon.

"Hedge sorcerer!" the man stopped and shouted up. "I am Learned Kyrato of the Bastard's Order in Patos, and in the god's name I order you to surrender to me. Come peacefully, and no harm will come to you!"

"Demonstrably not the case," Pen shouted back. "Ask Velka what he did to me in the bottle dungeon!"

The man's head went back in perplexity, quickly mastered. "For the second time, I demand your surrender! Or your life will be cast from the Temple's shelter!"

Penric glossed to those at his back, "It's a ritual he's obliged to try. No point in interrupting him before he gets through it."

Kyrato repeated his warning three more times, each more strongly worded. Arisaydia drew his sword and looked even more untrusting. Nikys's dark brows bent in dismayed curiosity.

"I am sorry," said Kyrato solemnly, signed himself, and opened his hand as he attempted to set Pen's clothes and hair on fire.

Pen snapped up the arriving impulse with his cold skill. Kyrato's body jerked slightly, then he tried again, to the same end. And a third time.

*It only took that horse two bites to learn better*, Des observed, amused.

The sorcerer stared nonplussed at his own hand, then made to ignite Nikys and Arisaydia. Pen whipped those efforts aside even faster, and flipped out the chaos to land where it would; a few rocks worked loose around them and began to tumble downhill. Kyrato dodged, startled. Des was humming like a bowstring released, *Let me, let me, let me...*

"What are you?" Kyrato cried, his eyes widening in real fear at last.

"I *told* Velka I wasn't a hedge sorcerer," Pen returned impatiently. "Didn't he pass you the word? That was really unfair. I swear the man doesn't listen to a thing one says to him."

Pen wondered how inexplicable this intense contest looked to outsiders. Two eccentric men standing on a slope making faces and gesturing at each other...

Velka bellowed up the hill, "Arisaydia! Surrender or be slain!"

Arisaydia muttered, "He meant 'and', there." He gripped his sword in an impatience to match Des's.

The Patos sorcerer put in loudly, "Surrender and your sister will be spared, and be made safe under my authority." Which he probably imagined to be true.

"*Sod* you," snarled Nikys, and heaved her first rock. It was well-aimed, but burst into fragments before it stuck its target. Another followed, to tumble aside in its arc.

"Why don't they hit him?"

Pen wasn't sure if that was plea or complaint. *Both, really.*

Arisaydia dropped a hand on her arm to hold her next launch, muttering, "Useless..."

"No, keep them coming. They're a good distraction." Pen cast her a sunlight smile over his shoulder. "Make him work. Heat him up."

Her eyes flared with understanding. Ha, at least *someone* had listened to him, and remembered. The next rock whistled through the air. Arisaydia woke up and joined her effort, his rocks hissing more viciously.

The sergeant hadn't been an idle spectator. The archers, in two pairs, had edged their way up each side of the slope into tolerable range, and loosed their arrows at last.

*Have fun, Des.*

The arrows, variously, burst into blue flame as they arced, to arrive on target as harmless puffs of ash, or tumbled end-over-end to clatter on the stones. A second flight met the same fate.

*Why doesn't he move faster? Doesn't he have the trick of it?* asked Pen, his senses racing along with Des's.

*He's controlling his demon tightly. They can only do one thing at a time. It's almost sad, really.*

*Remember, he's a fellow divine, not your plaything.*

*Then he shouldn't have threatened you.*

The archers had almost worked close enough for Pen to reach, but as long as they were content to waste arrows, Pen was content to let them. A little closer, and he could clip their bowstrings at will, and their hamstrings nearly as easily. Pen trusted Kyrato had more defenses than thus seen, but since Pen hadn't really attacked him yet, he'd had nothing to demonstrate them upon. Pen was growing adroit with that brutal tweak to the sciatic nerves, if he wanted to render this enemy unable to run away, not really his preference here. But the axilla offered equally distracting possibilities...

The sorcerer shifted the dusty pebbles under Pen's feet, trying to dump him on his backside presumably; Pen danced aside to solider stone. A formless flurry of hallucinations whirled before Pen's eyes; an interesting natural talent, suggesting the man could create extraordinary visions someday, with practice. Though not today, alas. Even without Des's aid, Pen had no trouble ignoring them. The sorcerer was momentarily distracted averting one of Arisaydia's sizzling projectiles—during which Nikys's latest lob came down square on his head with a satisfying *thunk*. That had been a heavy rock she'd heaved, two-handed. He fell half-stunned, sliding down the path and grabbing at his staff to stop himself. With a distraught cry, he flung out his hands.

Pain boomed in Pen's chest as his heart tried to tear itself apart. He went over backwards as if hit by a ram. Des was abruptly nowhere else but inside him, wrapping herself around the organ, holding it back together. The next flight of arrows fell unimpeded all around them, missing by inches.

Yells from below as the soldiers, taking his fall as their signal, started forward.

Pen climbed to his knees, chest bucking for air, mouth gaping in astonishment. That had been a *killing blow*.

Kyrato was also on his knees, mouth open in dismay and horrified triumph. He hadn't quite, Pen thought, intended to do that forbidden thing, but he didn't look as though he wanted to call it back. His gaze jerked all around, as he struggled to guess where Penric's demon would jump as Pen drew his last breath.

Chaos *spewed* from Desdemona.

Half the hillside shook itself apart and thundered downward.

Kyrato slithered several yards with it, ending half-buried in scree. Sweating and scarlet, he heaved, twisted, drained suddenly pale, and then... passed out.

*Heat stroke*, Pen diagnosed, from some strange detached plane of continued consciousness, as uncomfortable and unwelcome as his trip to the bottle dungeon. His chest *ached*. The rest of him wasn't doing terribly well, either, although there was a nice moment when frantic hands gathered him into a soft, soft lap.

Arisaydia's boots passed him by; a sudden scrape and clang of steel rang descant over the throbbing echo of the slide.

"Don't kill the sorcerer!" Pen cried in warning.

A grunt, a scuffle. "I remember," Arisaydia's voice floated back, sounding irritated. "Didn't he?"

"Oh Mother's blood, Pen, are you all right?" Nikys choked above him. Wet drops splashed his face, although the early evening sky was an impossible deep blue, cloudless. Could tears be also a blessing? But gods, he loved the sky in this country.

"Will be." *I hope.* "Don't you need to keep throwing rocks right now?"

"You just threw all of them. I think Adelis has it under control... the rest are running away. I mean, the ones who can. The sergeant is yelling for them to come back, but he's running just as hard."

"Huh. Good." *Des...?*

*...Des...?*

*Hsh. B'sy.* But then, after a moment, in muzzy indignation: *Kyrato was going to* sacrifice *his demon, in killing you. Let the god take it with your soul. He would have lived.*

*Aye. War-rules magic. S'why I want nothing to do with war.*

*...Good.*

# XVI

NIKYS CLUTCHED PENRIC, whose mumbling had drifted into well-enunciated but not particularly sensible rambling, and watched Adelis's figure move methodically around the slope below. The sun had retreated behind the hills, leaving the sky still luminous, only a few stars pricking through, and the dry ground drenched in shadowless blue. Adelis had chased off the only two swordsmen still willing to stand up and try to fight after the landslide. Both of them cut and bleeding, their considerable courage had broken, and they'd turned to run down the trail after their fleeing comrades while they still could. Nikys was relieved.

Adelis paused at an indistinct shape at the bottom of the slide.

Muffled voices, a cry of protest, a meaty *thunk*. Silence. Nikys shuddered, inhaled, looked away.

Penric convulsed up in her lap. "What was that? He's not dispatching all the wounded, is he? I have to stop him—"

"No. Or only one, I think. Lie still. How badly are you hurt?"

He sank back. "Not too badly, I think." His inner twin's voice overrode this, puffing, oddly, more: "Nearly killed just now. Would have been, except for me."

"Des!" objected Pen, and shut his jaw on this.

What did it say that Nikys had better luck getting a straight answer from a chaos demon than a man? *Nothing new, more's the pity.* "Desdemona, what's really going on? Tell me!"

Penric clenched his teeth, but then gave up, or gave way. "That accursed Bastard's divine tried to rip apart his heart, by forbidden magic. I have it under control for now, but Penric should stay flat in bed for the next week."

Nikys stared around the dusky hills at the marked absence of beds, and sighed. "Was that . . . normal magic?"

"No," said Desdemona, and Penric, one hand wavering up to touch her face, added, "No one should be allowed to break my heart but you, Madame Owl."

Her breath caught, but before they could continue this promising exchange, Adelis came clumping back. He paused below to study the unconscious sorcerer half-buried in the scree, then bent to wipe his sword clean on the loose sleeve of the man's white robe, and sheathed it. Mounting the hill to Nikys's side, he let down a pair of bows and a quiver of arrows. With a tired grunt, he dropped next to them and gazed out over the unexpected battlefield.

Penric levered up on his elbow. "What all has happened? Is happening . . . ?"

"The sergeant, two archers, and two men ran off, for now. And the two wounded, after. The rest are half-buried in the rubble. A few may get out without help, and help the others. I expect their comrades will come creeping back to their aid by-and-by. The horses tore loose and ran off during what I take to be your landslide. At least one fell. Broken neck, fortunately. Broken legs would have made for a messier cleanup. For somebody, not for us. We need to move along."

Penric's brows pinched. "What about Velka?"

Adelis shrugged. "He'd tried for me twice. Three times, if what you say is true. I decided not to give him a fourth chance."

"Oh." Penric sank back, signing himself. "I regret . . . not doing better with him."

"Well, he's his god's problem now. Don't promote your troubles beyond your rank."

"That is actually theologically sound advice."

"Works in the army, too."

"Ah." Penric hesitated. "Did you ever find out his real name?"

"Didn't ask. Didn't care, by then."

"It seems strange to kill a man without even knowing his name."

"Seems usual to me." Adelis rolled his shoulders. "Though in his case, we may find out later. Anyway, with the head cut off, the body will thrash. Best guess it will take this lot some days to dig themselves out and limp back for help. More confusion after that. Unless that one"—he nodded downhill to the pale lump that was the Patos sorcerer—"recovers faster than I think. Which, given his demon, your god only knows."

Penric, who had slumped into Nikys's willing lap, struggled up again. "I should try to treat the wounded—"

"No, you shouldn't," said Nikys, pushing him back.

"No, and I won't help," Desdemona put in. "I have other priorities right now. They'll all live if their friends return."

"I agree with the demon," said Adelis, unexpectedly both for the agreement, and for spotting just who had spoken the words coming out of Penric's mouth. "I swear the thing has more sense than you do, Learned Fool."

Which was, all right, a small step toward acknowledging the truth of Penric's account of himself. An Adelis-inch. Nikys bent her face and smiled.

"Any being learns a lot in two hundred years," Penric conceded shakily.

Adelis picked up one bow and tested it. "You said you could shoot flaming arrows, sorcerer. How about regular ones?"

"Usually. Maybe not right now."

He handed the bow to Nikys. "Check the draw for you."

Seated on the ground, she took it a little awkwardly, twisted and pulled, and grimaced. "It's fairly hard for me, but I could do it in a pinch." She leaned over and set it with the other.

"We'll keep both, then." Adelis turned and shifted his gaze upward. "I'm not sure how much steep we have left, but if we can get through that narrow place before full dark, we should be able to stop safely till moonrise."

Nikys bit her lip, wondering how this squared with Desdemona's recommendation of rest for Penric's safe recovery. It did not sound good.

The pile of pale cloth below them shifted, then moaned.

This time, Penric rose in greater determination. "Help me. I have to get some water down that one, or he won't last till morning. It matters, trust me."

"Jumping demon problem?" inquired Adelis, in a kind of wearied concession.

"At the very least. Not that he deserves to keep his."

Nikys hoisted the leather bottle, and Penric. They slid down the few yards and settled by the half-buried sorcerer.

Penric took the bottle and dribbled water over the man's head, rubbing it into his hair. "I need to cool him down the hard way, if he's still too stunned to shed chaos," Penric told her. "Here, Learned Kyrato." He patted the man's bearded cheek. "Wake up, now. You have to drink this." He tilted the spout to the man's lips.

Kyrato swallowed, choked, spilled, and seemed to come back to full consciousness. He heaved his trapped body, without effect.

"Stop struggling," Penric told him, a stern hand to his shoulder. "You'll just make yourself hotter. I haven't much time—"

Kyrato's voice went sharp in terror. "I won't tell you anything!"

"Good, because I only want you to listen," said Penric.

"Is this safe?" asked Nikys in worry. "If he just tried to kill you?"

"Now that I'm on my guard, yes. . . . Maybe. You'd best sit back a way." Penric gestured.

Nikys retreated perhaps two feet, and felt around for a good big piece of scree, ready to knock Kyrato in the head with it again if he made some sudden move. Although it wasn't the moves she could see but the ones she couldn't that were the real danger, she supposed. She'd have to trust in Penric and Desdemona for those. This was . . . curiously not-hard.

Kyrato's eyes flickered from her back to Penric.

"The fight's over," Penric informed him. "Your side lost. You have surrendered."

Groggily, Kyrato said, "No, I haven't." He mustered resolve. "You may get away this time, but the Bastard's Order will track you down."

"Which will be ridiculously easy, as I work for the Bastard's Order. And the white god."

Kyrato managed a shaky sneer. "Who are you to speak for the white god? Have you met Him?"

"Once, about eleven years ago. Not an experience a man forgets." He shrugged. "Nor does a demon. You can call me Learned... Anonymous for now, although if we ever meet again in less troubled circumstances I promise I'll introduce myself properly."

Kyrato looked as though he didn't believe a word of this. No—as though not-believing was less *frightening* than believing. Most curious. Nikys watched in increasing fascination.

"I have not much time," Penric went on, "but I need to speak to you about the way you are treating your demon. Because it's both theologically incorrect—and rude and cruel," someone added aside, "and very poor management, frankly.

"Your demon is a gift of the god and the Temple, you know, an elegant opportunity for mutual growth, not a beast to be dominated, imprisoned, and enslaved. To it, you are model, mentor, and the only parent such an elemental being can have. As the holder of a Temple demon, you have an obligation to pass it on at the end of your life improved, not ruined by your selfishness, inattention, or, as in this case, fear, bad judgment, and panic." Penric waved a hand. "Although I grant you were led astray."

Learned Kyrato's stare of terror was slowly transmuting to a stare of utter disbelief. *Oh good*, thought Nikys, *it's not just me*. Even the Temple-trained found Penric confusing.

"I don't know if or how you will be able to make things right with your demon," Penric went on, "although I would certainly suggest repentance, prayer, and meditation for a start. Forgiveness will likely be beyond it until it is not beyond you, and as for absolution, you'll need to petition a higher authority. But I would suggest, by way of a first apology, and also a good idea for your future association, that you start by gifting it with a nice name." Penric sat up and smiled cheerfully at the trapped divine. Kyrato responded by heaving again against his stony prison, to no effect. No—heaving away from Penric.

"You are mad," choked Kyrato.

"My brother says he's as mad as three boots," Nikys put in from the side, agreeably, starting to get into the spirit of this. "But he's also a very learned divine, with a very wise demon. You should attend."

In a hoarse voice, Kyrato said, "It is ascendant!" Then a rather cross-eyed look. "No . . . but it is monstrous dense. I thought it must be ascendant." His voice rose sharp again. "*Why isn't it ascendant?*"

"That's just what I'm trying to explain," said Penric patiently. "Now, names. Can you think of one you'd like?" He looked hopefully at Kyrato, who was starting to wheeze. Penric frowned and forced him to swallow another drink of water.

Abandoning the divine, Penric turned his expression inward. "Des, do you have any ideas for naming a young fellow demon?" A pause. "That's absurd." Another pause. "And that's obscene." And another, "No, we're not naming it after me, either." He sighed and turned to Nikys. "Madame Khatai? What's a Cedonian name that you like?"

*Nikys, in your mouth,* she thought, but offered aloud, "Reseen? Kuna? Sarande?"

"Des," said Penric, "does Learned Kyrato's demon have a preference? No?" He frowned again at Kyrato. "Really, how long have you possessed the poor thing that it doesn't understand the simplest of nomenclatures?"

He appeared to think, although not very long, then sat up. "All right." Penric signed himself and placed his hand on Kyrato's brow, following to do so again as the man recoiled. "In the white god's name I bless you and name you Kuna. A somewhat catch-as-catch-can name-giving ceremony," he added aside to Nikys, "but you and Des are two adults and can bear witness, so it's sufficiently sanctified."

As Kyrato was no longer struggling to escape, or much of anything apart from lying there limply in a state of receding heat stroke and advancing Penric, Nikys retreated uphill while Penric continued sermonizing. Adelis had finished organizing their belongings.

"Does he ever shut up?" Adelis inquired in mild gloom.

"I think he talks more when he's tired. Makes less sense then, though." She collected the few undamaged arrows that had fallen in their vicinity, adding them to the quiver.

Penric finished his lecture at last, signed the distraught man, tapped his own lips twice with his thumb, and climbed—well, crawled—back up to them, where he lay on his back and tried to catch his breath. Adelis studied the too-rapid rise and fall of his chest, and shook his head ruefully. "Aye. I see the problem."

"Shall we each take an arm?" asked Nikys.

"Better, I think, if you take the food, water, bows, and . . . yes, my sword."

"And his case?"

"If you choose. I'll lug the blond fool for you. Consider it your belated Bastard's Day present, sister."

"Ah, yes, you missed the last one, didn't you?"

"Busy with a war at the time, which I'm sure your god would understand. I almost dedicated it to Him."

Penric argued, but he was outvoted three to one, and at last he was coaxed up onto Adelis's back. Adelis's legs bent a little, then straightened. "Heavier than he looks," he grunted.

"I'm sure I could make it on my own—" Penric began, to which Nikys and Adelis replied in unison, "Shut up, Penric." Nikys thought Desdemona would have chimed in to the chorus if she could.

In the defile, the shadows were growing purple. This stretch, rough underfoot, was a hard slog by any standard. Nikys and Adelis saved their breaths, although Penric was still talking, going on about something in Wealdean until Adelis threatened to drop him back down the hill. His head drooped to Adelis's shoulder, and then there were only the deepening twilight sounds of the hills: small insects, a nightingale calling, the crunch of the dirt and gravel below their feet, and then the faintest flutter of a bat. As they came up out of the winding rift, an owl swooped by not ten feet overhead, wings spread in vast silence, and Nikys could see the white glint of Penric's teeth as he looked up and smiled.

A question occurred to her. Happily, she had just the person to answer it right here. "Desdemona," she said, "if Penric had been killed"—horrid thought—"and you had been forced to jump, where would you have gone? If the demon always chooses the strongest person in the vicinity, it would have had to be Adelis, right?"

Adelis jerked, then paused to heave his slipping passenger back up and labor on. It was too dark to see his expression, but Nikys imagined it a study in dismay.

"No, child," said Desdemona. "It would have been you."

At this, Adelis stopped short. Nikys stopped with him. "Me! Why me?"

"We have been with Penric for eleven years, and are now well imprinted with him. We could have made no other choice."

Penric breathed out, and Nikys could see the faint sapphire gleam of his widening eyes, but for once he was struck silent. After a moment, they hiked on.

No sounds of pursuit arose behind them.

A prayer of supplication to the Bastard was begging for trouble, in many people's views, but Nikys thought a prayer of gratitude for His better gifts was not likely to go wrong. She hummed the old hymn of praise under her breath as they reached a flatter trail. "Sing it aloud," entreated Penric from his perch. "I've never heard it in Cedonian."

She looked up to find no up left; before them, now, the land fell away in velvety darkness. A hundred miles distant it rose again, like a black blanket rucked up upon the horizon, the promise of Orbas.

"Far enough," huffed Adelis, and let down his burden. They all found seats upon the stony ground, under the sweep of the stars. She shared the water pouch around.

Then Nikys straightened and took up the old words, as Penric had requested. Adelis came in on the chorus in a bass harmony, as he had not done since they'd sung in the temple as youths, before . . . everything. Penric murmured in a pleased way, and then, at Nikys's demand, offered up a hymn of his own in his native Wealdean, in a breathy but surprisingly true baritone.

His words fell strange and sweet upon her ears, and so, trading mysteries, they sang up the moonrise.

# MIRA'S LAST DANCE

# MIRA'S LAST DANCE

# I

NIKYS WAS WORRIED about their sorcerer.

They'd fetched up at this little hill-country farmhouse two days ago, passing off their disheveled party of three as a man and his wife, plus their friend who'd sprained his ankle when they'd lost their way on the rocky trails in the dark. Their coin spoke more convincingly than they did, she'd suspected. What seemed to her a small sum had bought them shelter, displacing the farmer couple from their whitewashed bedroom to the loft and their half-grown children in turn to the stable. Such rural hospitality would cost their hosts a great deal more trouble than that if Imperial pursuers arrived here, Nikys reflected uneasily. She rocked her hips to bump open the bedroom door, and carried her tray within.

Learned Penric was dutifully lying flat in the bed, as ordered, but not asleep. He hitched himself up on one elbow, blinking glazed blue eyes at her, and favored her with one of his strange sweet smiles. Quite as if he hadn't *almost died* three nights ago, defending her and her brother Adelis.

"Ah. Another meal, already?"

"I'm sure you need it. Or Desdemona does." Penric might just be one of those maddening long, lean people who could eat like a horse and never gain a bit of pudge, but she guessed his chaos demon, riding inside him like a second personality—a very complicated second personality—drew on his body for nourishment as well. "Do you have to eat for two?"

"Mm, maybe a little. Here, I can get up—"

"Lie back!" Nikys and Desdemona commanded together. Since Des spoke through Penric's mouth, the effect was quite peculiar, but Nikys fancied she was getting used to it. "Listen to your demonic physician," Nikys said, to which Des added, "Yes, and listen to your lovely nurse. She knows what she's about in the sickroom."

"When did you two combine forces?" Penric muttered, as Nikys set down the tray on the washstand and drew it to the bedside, plumped his pillows, and permitted him to sit up. "Here, you don't need to spoon-feed me."

"It's not soup, so I can't." Nikys plopped down beside him, spread goat cheese onto circles of coarse country flatbread, added sliced onion, and rolled them up, alternating handing them across with holding the beaker of watered wine. Penric tried to take the vessel one-handed, but ended up having to use two, as his hand shook. He cast her an evasive look through those unreasonably long blond eyelashes.

Not for the first time, Nikys wondered exactly what it *meant* that the rival sorcerer, whom Pen had defeated in that bizarre twilight fight, had tried to rip his heart apart inside his body, and how much magical work Desdemona had been doing every moment since to keep it beating. Her own and Adelis's father, old General Arisaydia, had survived half-a-dozen bloody military campaigns in his life, only to die of a sudden seizure of the heart. That final, fatal blow had made no mark upon him. Bad hearts frightened her.

Nikys finished coaxing the whole of her culinary offering down the not-unwilling man. The fact that Penric was out of breath from eating lunch was more telling than his panting protestations of recovery. She checked the artistic bandage around his right ankle, mainly placed there to help him remember which one was supposed to be sprained, and tightened it up again.

The discreet blond knot at his nape had unraveled into a tangled mess. "I have a comb," Nikys went on, drawing it from the pocket of her borrowed apron. "I can straighten out those snarls of yours." She'd wanted an excuse to touch that amazing electrum hair for weeks, ever since he'd appeared like an improbable guardian spirit in her villa garden, offering healing for her unjustly blinded brother.

He started to indignantly refuse, and then either his wits or his demon caught up with him. He swallowed his manly declaration of self-sufficiency, converting it into a hopeful smile. "That would be very nice."

She had him sit up on the edge of the bed and knelt behind him. The rope net strung on the bedframe, topped by the wool-stuffed mattress, was not the firmest of seating, and his narrow hips rather sank between her knees. She began at the bottom of the tail of hair that reached to his mid-back, working out the knots as though carding fine flax. He'd kept himself as clean as a cat back in the villa in Patos, as became a physician, but they were all the worse for wear after a week's flight. She wondered if she could persuade him to let her wash it for him. She just might, judging by the way he was making low humming noises, as close to a purr as a human could come, as the tortoiseshell tines reached his neck and scalp and began slow, repeated strokes.

Alternating the comb and her gratified fingers, she began to separate the soft length into three strands for braiding, only to discover that somehow there was no room left for the task between his bony back and her... un-bony front. She cleared her throat and inched back, and he seemed to come awake and lurched forward, bowed spine straightening, once again the tidy Temple divine. Albeit a divine sworn to the Bastard, the fifth god, whose emblematic color was a white in real life usually ambiguously stained. She'd sometimes wondered if that was the white god's idea of theological humor. Laundresses should be in His flock, really; they probably served Him on their knees more often than did divines. Learned Penric cleared his throat, too, and she caught a glimpse past his ear of milk-pale cheekbone faintly flushed.

She set to finishing the queue and tying it off—she'd snipped the bit of white ribbon from one of her few garments that she'd managed to grab when they'd escaped the soldiers in Patos. An undefeated enemy, still out there on the hunt. The memory was enough to chill her brief warm comfort. Just as well; she had barely time to slide off the bed and tuck Penric back into it as the distinctive clunk of her brother's boots sounded across the farmhouse floorboards and through the door.

"There you are."

Adelis looked, really, almost his old self, at least from the mouth down. Standing straight again, sturdy, muscular; his thirty years sat lightly upon young General Arisaydia. Young former-general Arisaydia. Only when he took off his countryman's broad-brimmed hat did the horror of the burn-scarring on his upper face spring out. A barely healed spray of red and raised pink welts bloomed like malign flower petals around his eyes, though Penric claimed they would someday fade pale. His formerly dark brown irises had been resurrected a garnet red from their acid destruction. But thanks to Penric's sorcerous healing he could see again, and well, apparently, which in Nikys's view went somewhere beyond magic to miracle.

Adelis ran a hand through his black hair, growing unmilitarily untrimmed, and addressed a point in the air between his sister and the man in the bed. "How is he doing?"

"All right," answered Penric.

"Not as well as he claims," Nikys corrected this. "Desdemona says he shouldn't do any lifting or sudden exertion, so as not to strain his healing heart."

"Hnh," said Adelis. He focused on Penric. "Do you think you could ride tomorrow? Led at a walk?"

"Not on that poor donkey in the yard. My feet would drag the ground," said Penric.

Adelis's shrug acknowledged the truth of this. "I've found a neighbor lad with a mule. He can't take us all the way to the Duchy of Orbas, but he can take us down to a cousin's farm in the valley. Which would at least put us farther from the pass that they know we hiked over. We're not safe here for long."

Penric nodded; Nikys frowned. Penric put in, "A change of scene wouldn't hurt. Des has pretty much eradicated all the small pests within range, shedding chaos. We could do with a new supply."

His demon traded out the disorder harvested from his sorcerous healings, as Nikys understood it, venting it into the world as safely as they could manage. Killing theologically allowed vermin, the divine claimed, was the most efficient such sink available. Other sinks were less efficient. Or less allowed. She contemplated the dangerous gap between *not allowed* and *not possible*. Did Penric know where the real boundaries lay? She hoped so.

"We'll go at dawn, then," said Adelis.

❖ ❖ ❖

In the event, it was full light when they finally loaded Penric, still short-winded, and their few possessions aboard the tall and placid mule. Adelis's stolen sword and bow and arrows traveled wrapped in cloth, a discretion that didn't content him much. Nikys was just as glad. She didn't doubt her brother would fight to the death before allowing himself to be captured again, but it seemed pointless to send stranger-souls unripe to their gods if it made no difference to the outcome. Penric's glib tongue might be a better defense than Adelis's sword arm. Or indeed, Penric's magic, though his demon was very quiet this morning. Busy within him still healing his hidden damage, she guessed from the occasional flies, buzzing up from animal droppings on the farm track, that fell dead in their wake. She trusted the mule-boy didn't notice.

The presence of this youth leading the mule inhibited conversation on the long trudge, thankfully more downhill than not. The farm track, which eventually grew to a farm road, followed a winding creek with the hills rising on either side. Nikys was hot, sweaty, and footsore by the noon halt, where the boy led them out onto a local promontory shaded by old oaks, evidently a favorite stop. She could see why. It offered a last high view out over the miles-wide valley that made this province such a valuable, and defended, granary for the Cedonian empire.

The mule-boy led his charge off to a distant patch of grass for its own lunch. Adelis strolled to the rim above the drop-off, pushed back his hat, and stared with eyes narrowed. Nikys and Penric joined him.

"This is as good as a map," Penric remarked, following his gaze. "What are we looking at?"

Adelis dipped his chin. "The walled town on that bit of height above the river is Sosie. Not the capital of the province, that's down by the mouth with the port. But it's home to the garrison that guards the top end of this valley." His hand sketched out the squared-off patch, vague in the distance, that suggested barracks. "Imperial troops, not provincial. Part of the Fourteenth Infantry."

"That sounds like something we might need to avoid," said Penric. "Would any of them recognize you?"

Adelis's hand touched his still-tender face. "I wonder."

"The three of us are distinctive, if any description has been circulated yet," Nikys observed unhappily. Even if not together, Adelis's disfigurement and Penric's height and foreign coloration would make them stand out. Only Nikys might pass unremarked.

"Still, Sosie has a large temple," said Adelis. Its stone shape was just visible, rising on a hill within the city walls. "Might you, ah, refresh your purse there?" He cast Penric a sidewise look.

Penric's expression was more grimace than smile. "I should not like to make a settled habit of robbing offering boxes. Although it's still better than robbing people directly. It's money they've already given up, and so presumably will not miss." He mused on, whether talking himself into or out of the suggestion Nikys could not tell, "Hard on the local Temple, though. You would not believe Temple expenses."

"But we could hire horses again, or even some sort of carriage," Nikys couldn't help noting. Her tired feet talking, to be sure, but a carriage might be better for the convalescent sorcerer as well.

"By what route?" asked Penric.

"Only two choices," said Adelis. "Well, three. We could make our way down the valley to the coast road, or even to a port for some local ship to take us south."

"That was my suggestion in the last valley," Penric noted a bit dryly. "We could have saved steps."

Adelis stiffly ignored this, and continued, "Either will be well guarded. And I guarantee any description of us will be sent to the border posts and ports first. The other way would be to find a path up through the mountains to Orbas."

The rocky walls lining the other side of the valley were considerably more daunting than the hills they had just come over. Which was a good part of why the current duke of Orbas was able to maintain his precarious independence from a neighbor who would be very pleased to turn his lands back into an imperial province. Nikys had always felt that Cedonia had the right of that old dispute, before.

Penric stared at the distant precipices, too, and finally said, "Unless we could pass in disguise."

"I am not putting on Nikys's clothes again," said Adelis, scowling.

Penric grinned, provokingly. "True, you did not make a very convincing widow."

"I'm an officer. Not an actor." A brief clench of his jaw suggested to Nikys that he was remembering he was neither, now.

"In any case," said Nikys, placating, "our roads lie together till we reach Vilnoc in Orbas. Penric can as well sail home to Adria from there." *Or not . . .*

"Or we all could," Penric suggested. Yet again.

"Nikys and I are going to Orbas," said Adelis. "You may go where you please."

Penric studied his set face, and sighed.

And if neither man—one as stubborn as a stone, the other too supple to be pinned down—would, or even could, change his mind, where would that leave Nikys? *No place happy.*

After eating, they resumed the downward trek. Penric, watching Nikys stump along, apparently forgot his sprained ankle and offered to trade her his place on the mule. For the mule-boy's benefit, Nikys asked after his fictional crippling, keeping his real one to herself, and he subsided, gallantry thwarted. But the mule-boy allowed as how they might ride double. Nikys was duly boosted onto the beast behind Penric, wriggling her way to comfort atop the blanket strapped to its barrel. Neither the mule nor Adelis seemed best pleased with this cozy new arrangement, but they didn't kick. Nikys slipped her arms around Penric's waist, for security, and he sat back a little, for what reason she did not speculate. Weary in the warm afternoon, she leaned her head against his shoulder and half dozed, the thousand worries coursing through her mind easing their torrent for a time.

Arriving at the next farmstead in the early evening, they negotiated shelter with nearly the last of their coin. The combination of their thin purse and a house full of farm family left the stable loft the sole choice for their new bedroom. Adelis and Penric were both apologetic about it. Nikys was too tired to complain even if she had been a fussy fool, which she was not. This more fertile stretch of country also assured a good supply of stored grain, hence an abundance of the mice and rats that infested such. Desdemona was pleased. Penric, swinging a stick that he occasionally remembered to lean on, puffed off in the dark to hunt them for all the world like a cat.

Adelis hooked the lantern on a nail safely away from the straw, and rather pointedly arranged their blankets with himself in the middle as a bolster. Nikys snickered.

"I haven't been a girl laying flowers on the altar of the Daughter of Spring"—goddess of, among other things, virginity—"for over a decade," she pointed out.

"One wouldn't know it, from the infatuated way you were hanging on that sorcerer's shoulder all afternoon."

"You don't, actually, have a right to tell your thirty-year-old widowed sister who and who not to cuddle." Should it please her to cuddle anyone, which it hadn't for a very long, gray time.

Adelis lowered himself to their straw pile with a grunt, looking unhappy. On the whole, Nikys thought she'd rather deal with grouchy, where she could give as good, or as bad, as she got. "Think it through. I know what wonders the man has done for us, and I'm not ungrateful, but he's an Adriac agent, for the five gods' sake. Sent here to suborn me, till *that* plan went wrong in so many ways. He hasn't stopped being one, for all that I've chosen to go supplicant to Duke Jurgo of Orbas instead. Suppose, in the best case, we all win through to Vilnoc alive. The man will have no choice then but to go on home, empty-handed. Don't get . . . don't get taken in, is all I ask. You don't want to end up with nothing but a blue-eyed infant to remember him by."

Nikys was not altogether sure she'd object to such a souvenir, but she snorted. "I had six years of marriage with Kymis, which left me with less than that. And it wasn't for lack of trying, I assure you. I don't think it's a pressing danger." Although her late husband's frequent and prolonged absences on military duties hadn't helped. "Anyway, I doubt Learned Penric's up to seducing anyone, in his current condition."

Adelis was drawn into a sly smirk. "Quite. We wouldn't want the poor man dropping of an apoplexy between your thighs."

"Adelis!" Deterring image indeed.

"Truth, it's happened! I've heard. Although generally with older men."

She threw straw at him. He threw it back. Before they could revert further to their five-year-old selves, she heard the squeak of the stable door, the object of their argument returning. She bit back retaliating rudeness. But she did think to add, "You should want to keep him with you anyway, at least until you gain a position from Duke Jurgo. It will give you a much stronger position to negotiate from if Jurgo knows, or at least believes, that you have another offer waiting. Not supplicant, but, but..."

"Merchant?" he said dryly. "With myself as both seller and horse?"

"Think it through," she shot his own words back at him, and he raised a hand in concession.

They laid up at the valley farm for two days. Adelis kept out of sight in the loft, growing bored and restless. Penric only descended to vent chaos when the farm folk were abed, though he evidently was able to vent quite a lot. On the bright side, he seemed to be recovering his strength and wind, but Desdemona's labors were creating a growing reek of dead rodent about the place.

Sitting up cross-legged on his blanket in the warmth of the afternoon, Penric sniffed apprehensively at a particularly pungent waft. "Huh. I don't normally leave such an obvious swath in one place. People are going to notice, I'm afraid."

"I should think they'd be grateful," said Nikys. Although it would be better if people didn't learn he was a sorcerer, since their pursuers must by now be looking for one.

"You'd be surprised. Once, when I was a young student, I freed a man of his body lice without asking. He nearly had a fit. I hadn't realized he'd thought of them as pets. He was certain it indicated some terrible loss of health, like rats deserting a sinking ship. I wasn't in a place where I could explain my calling, so I ended up tiptoeing away."

"Why couldn't you explain what you'd done?" asked Nikys.

"We were in a gambling hall. I wasn't cheating, but proving it would have been a challenge."

Adelis snorted. "You'd have been beaten up, more likely."

Nikys tilted her head, trying to picture a young Penric so cornered. "Would you have let yourself be?"

He shrugged. "There was nothing at stake but an evening's entertainment. Heroic measures were not called for. Hence the tiptoeing. We should do likewise, soon."

It was left this time for Nikys to arrange it. Asking among the farm women turned up word of a neighbor taking a wain load of grain to Sosie, which they caught in the gray of the next dawn in exchange for their last coins and the promise of Adelis's shoulder should the wheels bog. It was a long day's ride at the oxen's steady pace, but they entered the city gates before dark. Passing their bedraggled selves off to the gate guards as rustic laborers was no trouble at all. They dropped down from the wagon near the temple and waved farewell to the grain man.

Penric had promised them a night of secret shelter in the temple atrium, once he'd slipped them all inside and relocked the doors. Nikys looked forward to the safety, if not to the discomfort. It seemed to her their bedding as well as their endurance was steadily deteriorating as this flight staggered on. And the refuge of Orbas, so close, still hovered maddeningly out of reach.

# II

IN THE DWINDLING DAYLIGHT, Penric threaded the narrow streets of Sosie to the temple square. Leading his flock of two, though Arisaydia and his sister were anything but lamb-like. The space boasted a small fountain, and some stone benches scattered about, gifts of some pious rich benefactor according to the inscriptions chiseled upon them in the elegant lettering of Old Cedonian. Penric selected the most shadowed bench and settled them all down to wait for the square to clear as full night fell.

Nikys brought out the last of their bread from the farm and shared it among them. Adelis eased up his lowered hat brim, squinting around in a tactical survey as he chewed.

"I doubt the city watch will let us linger here much after curfew," he observed. "If Sosie is like other garrison towns, they'll be in perpetual feud with young soldiers from the barracks, and so be more active than the usual sleepy companies."

"Then perhaps they'll be too busy elsewhere to bother us," Nikys suggested in a tone of bracing hope.

Penric considered the picture they presented, huddled here like skulking vagrants. Just the sort of vagabonds to be suspected of potential thievery in the night. Perfectly correctly, in their case. While being arrested would give them a free place to stay, its other costs were likely to be much too high.

A small throng of townsfolk was assembling under the portico sheltering the temple entry. They spilled down the steps as a pair of acolytes came out and swung the doors wide, hooking them open and lighting cressets high on the stone walls to either side. Soon after, what was obviously a funeral procession emerged from one of the side streets: a pair of liveried servants bearing lanterns up on poles, six grim-faced men carrying a bier with a shrouded figure, kin dressed in hasty mourning following in a gaggle. Instead of entering the temple atrium, they paused. A faint golden glow of a sacred fire not banked for the night, but fed to flames, wavered through to the square. In a few more minutes, another procession emerged from another street. Its shrouded bier was piled about with flower garlands. The two processions came together in a sort of wary truce, then, carefully, both biers were lined up and carried within exactly side-by-side.

A squad of city watchmen followed. Half of them went inside, and the other half took up posts around the portico as the doors were swung shut. From the sacred atrium, the music of a threnody sung in five voices sounded, echoing eerily from the stones. Song, Penric was reminded, was considered an especially acceptable offering to the gods, being a gift of pure spirit. The people in the portico did not disperse, but rather, settled as if preparing for a long wait. Penric couldn't guess if this was good, giving a crowd to blend into, or bad, the extra watchmen having leisure to survey the scene and decide the strangers on the far bench didn't belong here.

After a long, frustrating silence, Nikys finally said, "I'm going to find out what's going on." She unfolded and donned her respectable dark green widow's cloak, and made for the portico. Adelis and Penric both twitched, but really, the gathering remained tame enough, and Nikys was the least memorable intelligencer among them. She spent what seemed to Penric quite a long time chatting with other women on the periphery of the spectators. Finally, she trod back, a dark discreet shape in the fire-limned shadows. At her gesture, the two men slid apart, and she sat down between them with a sigh.

"They're going to be at this all night," she reported. "It's a double funeral for a double suicide. Rather a tragedy. Two young people from a pair of feuding families fell in love and, not allowed to be together in life, decided to be together in death."

"Seems idiotic," said Adelis. Penric, tactfully, did not bring up how recently Adelis had been considering such an exit from his own dark woes.

Nikys shrugged, not disagreeing. "It appears they were very young. Anyway, the magistrates and the Sosie divines ordered both families to pray all night for their souls, and for atonement for their strife. By morning, people expect there to be either a reconciliation, or blood on the temple floor and no survivors, and it didn't sound as if the magistrates much cared which by this time."

"Well." Adelis rubbed his neck. "We can't sleep in there, then." He frowned. "And I won't have Nikys sleep on the street."

Penric agreed with that. His own preference was to scout out a high place to hole up. Desdemona lent him the ability to see in the dark, so that wasn't going to be much worse for him than such a search by daylight, but getting the other two up after him, and in stealthy silence, was going to be tricky. The night was moonless, making the narrow lanes pitch black in most places. All the good citizens would be indoors by this time, leaving mainly the other sort abroad. Granted, any villain unwittingly tackling a Temple-trained sorcerer could be in for a horrible surprise, and he doubted Adelis would make easy prey, either. But it would be far better to slip in and out of Sosie without any incident at all.

*Thank you*, murmured Desdemona, within him.

*Aye.* Cedonia was a beautiful country, Pen thought, but it kept trying to kill him. At some point, his demon might not be able to keep up, and then they... no, *she* would be in real trouble. His troubles would be over, presumably.

But they weren't over yet. He hoisted himself up and led his charges into the dark and winding passages, the paving stones usually dry underfoot but sometimes unpleasantly not. He held Nikys's hand, and she held Adelis's, so he was able to guide them safely around the worst of the hazards. The houses here were in the

Cedonian style of high blank walls around inner courtyards, the few street-facing windows or balconies confined to upper stories. No handy stairs, or ladders, or even climbing vines rewarded his investigations.

*You shouldn't be trying to climb yet anyway,* Des muttered in disapproval. *You might get dizzy again. No sprinting, either.*

*I'm feeling stronger now. Chest's stopped hurting. You do excellent work.*

*Flattery will not avail you,* she responded not entirely truthfully, part placated, part still stern.

Orange light flickered at the next corner. Penric poked his head cautiously around. The light had two sources: a simple candle lantern hanging on a bracket above a doorway, and a brighter oil lantern held by one of a pair of soldiers. Young officers, Penric guessed by their dress and demeanor, captains or lieutenants of hundreds; Adelis would be able to tell at a glance. The other soldier pounded impatiently on the stout wooden door.

"Hoy! Open up, Zihre! Don't leave your best customers standing in the street!"

More pounding. At last the door creaked, and a woman thrust her head out. "We're not open, gentlemen. Come back another night."

"Oh, you can let us in, surely," wheedled the officer. A bit drunk, Pen guessed.

"We're closed for washing. Unless you want to scrub laundry, be off with you."

"All that hot steam could be exciting," the drunken officer allowed, attempting to grab and kiss her. She evaded him without effort or apparent offense.

"Yes, we could hold your head under the suds till you grow smarter," she returned. "Or cleaner. Whichever happens first." His companion guffawed. "If you're not the laundresses"—she leaned out and looked up and down the street—"I can't accommodate you tonight."

A bit more whining left the woman unmoved, and the pair gave up and left. Their voices sounded again at the next corner, a lewd joke and a sharp rejoinder. An older woman, trailed by two others carrying sacks, rejected their inebriated attentions and made for the light, under which the lady of the house, seeing them approach, had paused.

"Ah, good." The woman in the entryway waved and beckoned. "At last."

The presumed-laundress held out her hand to halt her companions. "Yes, we're here, at this unholy hour. But I'm telling you straight out, Zihre, it's double pay tonight or we're not coming in. And your girls can boil their own crawly sheets." She mimed an exaggerated shudder.

Zihre sighed. "Yes, yes, whatever it takes. We can't do business at all till this Bastard-sent plague is eradicated." She tapped her lips with her thumb in a quick averting half-prayer, as if the god himself might be listening, offended at this scorning of His ambiguous gifts.

Penric, rapidly figuring out the situation, grinned to himself. *Bastard be praised indeed.* He whispered to Adelis and Nikys, "Wait here. I may be able to win us shelter for the night." He raised his chin and strode forward, ignoring Nikys's *What?* and Adelis's *We can't take Nikys in there!*

"Madame Zihre?" he called in his most dulcet tones, as she made to pull the door closed again behind the party of stumping, grumping laundresses.

"I'm sorry, sir, we're closed tonight," she began perfunctorily as Penric stepped forward into the light of her door lantern. She looked up into his face, and her eyes widened. "So very, very sorry!"

He smiled back with all his heart. Prostitutes, after all, were numbered among the Bastard's own flock. Along with pirates, Pen supposed, but he didn't think he'd deal well with the latter, oath-sworn divine or not. "Ah. I didn't come to employ, but to seek employment. May I come in and speak further?"

She blinked. "We've not kept lads for the loves of the Bastard before, but that's not to say we might not start. Are you experienced? Not that you'd need to be, necessarily. I could train you." The corners of her mouth crept up.

Penric cleared his throat, to block Desdemona's knowing snicker. "Ah, ha, not that sort of employment. I am given to understand you are troubled with an unfortunate outbreak of personal parasites. I've had experience eradicating such pests before, at houses such as this. I am a Temple sorcerer, Learned... Jurald." He signed himself, forehead-lips-navel-groin-heart for the tally of the five gods, and tapped his lips again for the Bastard's special blessing.

Her dark eyes grew shrewd. She was a decidedly handsome older woman, Pen saw at this closer range. Her dress was more dignified than provocative, aside from a wide green belt at her waist, glimmering with sewn pearls, that supported her bodice in an attractive manner. "You are too pretty to be Learned Anybody," she protested.

"I could make you a scholarly argument, but really, I think it would be faster for me to simply demonstrate my skills. And you can judge for yourself." He kept up the blinding smile. "If I cannot perform to your satisfaction, you will owe me nothing."

"And what would I owe you if you did?"

"No great price, merely shelter for myself and my two"—he made a rapid recalculation—"servants for the night. We've found ourselves unexpectedly benighted in Sosie without the, er, resources we expected to receive here, and must make do."

Her eyes narrowed back down. "Why not go to the Temple, then, oh learned divine?" Unkempt on her doorstep, dressed and probably also smelling like a farm laborer, there was certainly nothing of the divine about him.

"It's a long story." Which he had better make up as soon as possible. "There was a shipwreck involved," he essayed, and then realized he had a better one. "The Sosie Temple, as you may know, is much occupied tonight with settling a tragic feud between two local families."

"Oh," she said. "Yes. That. Young fools. Although the old fools were the worse." She snorted. "I won't say they got what they deserved, because no one deserves to lose their child, but it's to be hoped they've learned a lesson from the gods that they refused from anyone else. Everyone in town was tired of their riot and rumpus." She gave way and opened her door.

Penric thanked her, and hurried back to collect Nikys and Adelis.

"I'm a traveling sorcerer-divine, you two are my servants, and we were recently shipwrecked . . . somewhere," he whispered in rapid tutorial. "Which is why we have no baggage or money. I've just undertaken to rid the house of an infestation of, er, insect pests, in exchange for a night's lodging."

"What kind of pests?" asked Nikys.

Adelis said, repressively, "Bedbugs."

"Oh? From the way she was talking with the laundress, I'd have guessed crab lice."

Penric choked down Desdemona's laugh as Nikys sailed past him. "Could be both, but I can be the bane of either. Remember, you are servants. Tired, quiet servants. A guard and a maid. Who keep to themselves."

"You have the first part right," Adelis growled, following her. "Shipwreck? You do know we're eighty miles inland, yes?"

"We had a long walk," Pen returned, swallowing aggravation. Adelis might resent being cast again as an actor, but a guardsman should be less of a stretch for him than a widow. If he deigned to cooperate.

Crossing the threshold, Penric signed himself again, and murmured, "Five gods bless and keep this house safe from all harm." *And us as well.* Their hostess's fine plucked eyebrows twitched up at the gesture, a tiny concession to belief in his self-proclaimed calling.

She turned, took up a pole with a hook from its wall bracket, and used it to retrieve the lantern over the door before closing it again with a firm thud, setting the bar across. "That's served its purpose," she murmured. "Our porter's job, but he's busy hauling water just now." She motioned her new guests after her.

The house may well have belonged to a rich family before falling to its present purpose. Spacious, but short of palatial. The arrangement, Penric saw as they followed Zihre inside, was typical of this country: stone-built, an entry atrium with a mosaic floor, then a larger atrium also with a second floor of rooms built around it on a gallery. A small walled garden beyond held a separate outbuilding for the kitchen, laundry, and bathhouse. The garden boasted its own well, and a stream of activity as people carried water and wood for the boiling vats, under the stern direction of the laundresses. The general air was cranky and harried. And itchy. Not the sort of evening party that usually graced this garden, Penric imagined.

Hopelessly the diagnostician, Penric asked, "When did your current troubles commence, do you know?"

Zihre shrugged. "Perhaps a month ago. It was either a party of merchants, or some new soldiers from the barracks. Which means the boys will doubtless be gifting them back to us."

Adelis winced, no doubt able to picture the military side of the scene. Penric wondered if he should pass on some tips for diplomatically delousing her customers that he'd picked up back in Martensbridge, when he had been asked out as a physician-sorcerer to take care of a similar plague in certain establishments there. That had started an extraordinary education for him, to be sure, the like of which he could never have imagined back in his canton mountain boyhood. He'd made many new and interesting friends. And come to better know the courtesan Mira of Adria, the image of his demon's long-dead fifth rider who lived, in a sense, along with the rest of her strange sisterhood inside his head. He suspected he'd be asking her for advice again soon.

External parasites did not require nearly the delicacy to dispose of as internal ones. He and Des were so practiced by now he could likely do it with a simple stroll around the premises, but he supposed he'd better make enough of a show that their hostess would realize he'd done anything at all, and credit him for it. Rather the reverse of his usual preference for discretion. They were going to need the credit. Really, when he had time someday he needed to work out a way to make his magics visible at need to ungifted observers, some sort of sham light show perhaps. Maybe the marketplace jongleurs would have some tricks he could adapt.

*Penric*, Des murmured. *Take a look at this.*

His outer vision was abruptly flooded with his inner one, and he glanced around, wondering if she had spotted a sundered ghost. The lingering smudges of those lost souls were common enough that he usually had Des spare him the distraction, lest he alarm companions by constantly dodging around things they could not see. But at his sight's fullest intensity he also saw the souls of those still alive, congruent with their bodies in an eerie swirling nimbus of life and light. It seemed to him such intimate god-sight ought not to be gifted to a mere man, but he'd learned to use it back when he'd been a practicing physician. Far too much practice, but it hadn't made perfect. Right now, Adelis was mostly dark red, stress and anger well-contained, no contradictions there. Annoying as it sometimes was, Pen appreciated the man's straightforwardness. Nikys—he sneaked a peek—was blue with weariness, a snarled thread of thick green worry running through that he quite wanted to wind out of her, if only he had a way, which he didn't.

*No*, said Des. *Look at Madame Zihre. Left breast.*

She was a normal mix of colors, more to the blue and green, but he saw at once the black blot of chaos riding in her breast. That familiar, lethal egg ... *Oh.* He gulped. *Oh, Des, I wish you hadn't shown me that.* Which was the *other* reason he avoided using his inner sight. All that overwhelming pain, pouring in from the people around him—how did gods and saints endure such knowledge?

*The tumor's still encapsulated. There's a chance.* Des let the disrupting visions fade, to Pen's relief. *Or I should not have troubled you. Attend to her later, perhaps.*

*Perhaps.* Pen drew breath and forced his attention back to his external surroundings. Madame Zihre frowned doubtfully at Pen's companions, following in behind them—Nikys with their sack of meager belongings and Penric's medical case, Adelis, his hat pulled down again, clutching a roll that looked exactly like a bundle of weapons.

"Could we take my servants to our chamber, first?" Penric suggested. "They're very tired."

"Mm, yes," said Zihre thoughtfully. She plucked a candlestick from a table by the stairs, lit it from another, and led them up to the small gallery over the entry atrium. Entering a bedchamber there, she shared the flame with a brace of candles on a shelf, and a couple in fine mirrored wall sconces, and gave Penric a sidelong glance. "How about this?"

The place had a rumpled air; after a quick survey, Des reported, *Lively in here. She's testing you.*

"Is it ... clean?" asked Nikys, pausing on the threshold in doubt.

Penric waved a hand, and enjoyed the familiar little flush of warmth through his body as Des divested chaos. "It is now."

"Ah. Thank you, Learned Jurald." Getting into her assigned role at once, hah. She smiled and entered confidently, Adelis trailing.

By the bemused purse of her lips, Zihre was more persuaded by Nikys's belief than by Penric's patter.

Nikys set down the case and hefted the sack stuffed with their clothing, mostly filthy by now. "May I join your laundresses, Madame? What little we saved from the wreck is overdue a washing in something other than seawater."

"Certainly. Come down when you're ready."

A female voice shrilly calling Zihre's name echoed from the atrium, and she grimaced.

"We'll follow you shortly," Penric told her, and she nodded and hurried off to address her next household crisis.

Penric shut the door behind her. A basin and ewer sat on the chamber's washstand; he seized the moment to splash his face and hands, saying to Nikys and Adelis, "Adelis should stay out of sight in this room. We'd best get our story straight. Where did our ship wreck?"

"Cape Crow would make the most sense," allowed Adelis.

"Right, so I coasted down from, say, Trigonie. Trying to get around to"—Penric mentally reviewed the map—"Thasalon. After the wreck, I wouldn't get on a ship again, nor would any captain have me, because of those nautical superstitions about sorcerers aboard being bad luck."

"Apparently confirmed," Adelis murmured.

Penric ignored this. "So we struck west overland. You two have not been with me for long. Which should allow you to say *I don't know* to most questions about me."

"You hired us in Trigonie," offered Nikys, entering into the spirit of this. "We worked cheaply, because we were trying to get home to Cedonia. Should we still be a man and his wife?"

"You've been that for the last while. Better change it around. Go back to brother and sister?"

Nikys, kneeling to sort dirty clothing, nodded.

Adelis folded his arms and looked skeptical. "Why are you traveling?"

"Temple business," Penric returned at once. "Which, of course, I have not discussed with you. You think I'm a ... "

"Spy?" said Nikys brightly.

"Lunatic?" suggested Adelis.

"Called as a physician," Penric suppressed this flight of fancy, or commentary. "To treat someone important. Or moderately important, I suppose. But, really, if you just say *Temple business* and look down your nose at your interrogator, it usually suffices."

Adelis's lips twitched. "Confirming something I've long suspected about Temple functionaries."

Penric waved this off, and bent to help Nikys with her now-sorted bundles.

"No." She tapped his hands away. "No lifting for you till Des says."

"I'm doing much better," Penric protested, but rose empty-handed. "Though I'd as soon get this night's work over with as swiftly as possible. I'm about dead on my feet. Not literally," he added hastily, as Nikys looked up in alarm.

Adelis hoisted her up, and the bundles into her arms, and opened the door for them.

"I'll try to bring us back some food," she told him.

"Don't trip on the stairs," Adelis called after them in an under-voice. "Or Penric's tongue."

Penric caught up with Madame Zihre downstairs, and had her guide him around her house from room to room. The place was surprisingly free of bedbugs, but while he was at it he had Des strip out in passing endemic fleas, flies, wool moths, and all their eggs, from every cranny, cupboard, chest, and fold of fabric, as well as his primary target of lice. Nearly the entire household was collected in the garden and laundry, aiding the washing, which allowed him to stand in the shadows and divest them all more-or-less at once. *Heartwarming*, Des quipped happily, growing replete with balance. Pen dissuaded Madame Zihre from introducing him, or even letting him be seen by his beneficiaries, as he was beginning to evolve a new idea.

Leaning against an atrium pillar in the shadows with his arms folded, he remarked to her, "You, happily, are not infested."

"You can tell this?" Her expression had not shifted much from its initial dubiousness. Like any merchant, she'd likely had plenty of experience with cheaters and charlatans, and was plainly waiting for him to slip up in some revealing way.

He nodded. "Is there someplace we can go to talk quietly?"

Her lips drew back in a half-smile, dryly satisfied, as she braced for whatever sly pitch she now expected from him. "Come this way."

She led him upstairs into a bedroom, richly appointed and obviously her own, and unlocked a door to a small private cabinet. A writing table, quills and inkpots, shelves with ledgers for accounts and tax records, a strongbox—this was her real personal space. She lit the generous candles and settled him on a stool crowded by the wall, turning around the straight chair at the table for herself.

Penric clasped his hands between his knees, smiling to conceal his own unhappiness. He had *so* not wanted to be drawn into this calling again... "Madame Zihre. Do you know what rides in your left breast?"

She gasped, her hand flying to the spot. *Aye, she knows,* murmured Des.

She swallowed and raised her chin, and said in a voice gone grim, "My death. In due course. Such a curse killed my older sister... eventually."

Penric could picture it all too well. He nodded. "I made acquaintance with such things when I was training as a sorcerer-physician in, ah, my home country. I had no luck destroying any tumors that had spread like tree roots, but if they were still encapsulated like an egg, sometimes... I did." But less luck persuading his fellow physicians in Martensbridge, or the patients they brought too late before him, of the critical differences, visible only to him.

"How, destroy?"

"Small, repeated applications of heat, of burning, inside the affected flesh. Although lately I have bethought that burning with cold would be a gentler method."

"Burn with cold?" She stared at him. "That sounds mad."

"Ah, Cedonia is a warm country. I keep forgetting. Yes, it is possible to burn with cold." He sat back, held up his fingers, and concentrated. A tiny hailstone grew from the air between them. He let it enlarge for several breaths, till it was the size of a pullet egg, and held it out to Madame Zihre.

She took the ice lump, her lips parting in surprise. It was the first visible, uphill magic he had worked in front of her. When she looked up at him again, her expression was frighteningly intense, shock and fear and hope intermingled, and a whole new kind of doubt. "Oh," she breathed. "You really *are*. You seem so young."

He nodded, not bothering to feign an offense he did not feel. "I'm thirty, but never mind. Do you wish me to try to treat you?"

Her eyes narrowed and her lips thinned again, as she thought she spotted the hook. "What is your price?"

"For this, nothing," said Penric. "Not least because—and you have to understand this—I cannot guarantee you will be healed, or that the tumor will not return. They did, sometimes." And often worse than before, destroying false hopes as devastatingly as a fire. "My offer stands regardless. Nevertheless, I do have a need. I want to travel on from Sosie as someone else, unrecognizable. My servants also."

She took this in, blinking thoughtfully. "Why such secrecy?"

"Temple business." Not wholly a lie. The archdivine of Adria had assigned him to his duke, who had assigned him to fetch General Arisaydia, and things had spun out—of control, among other things—from there. Bringing him, all unplanned, here. Unplanned by any human schemer, anyway, he conceded uneasily.

*You know, for a divine of the god of lies, you cleave to the truth rather closely*, Des commented.

*It's the scholar in me. Hush.*

But Madame Zihre, for all her wariness, accepted this without demur, awarding him a slightly more respectful nod. "So... what is it that you do for such things?" She motioned to her breast once more.

"As you have observed, the deepest magics never show above the surface. It would be helpful for my precision if I may touch you."

"Right now?" She seemed to expect more preparation. More ceremony, something.

He was too tired to invent any. "Soonest begun." *Soonest done.* He opened his hand toward her. "I should warn you, you will feel some pain."

"Well, that's some proof, isn't it?" She shrugged out of half her bodice with an almost medical unselfconsciousness, a curious parallel between their respective crafts, and leaned toward him.

*Des, sight, please.* The inner vision came up at once. He placed his fingers on her fine soft skin, found the dark blot, and called up the spot of sucking cold in its center as he had just done for the hailstone. Her breath caught as she felt it, but she held still as the chill increased, though her hands gripped her skirts on her knees. She was not the first woman he'd met who endured dire pain in disturbing silence, and he wondered if Nikys would be another such. When the ice reached the edge of the blot, he stopped and sat back.

She inhaled, and allowed herself to pant. "That's all?"

"First treatment. I should repeat it tomorrow, to be sure. As sure as I can be. Then later I'll need to open it and drain the killed matter, to prevent necrosis and infection." And cram the area with as much uphill magic as he could make it accept, but that part would be invisible to her.

She nodded and reordered her clothing. Her breathing was slowing, to his relief. "I can feel it. Maybe it's doing me good."

"It will likely swell and hurt worse through the night. Tell me everything you feel. It will help me..." *To guess what I've done* was perhaps not the most reassuring thing to say. He left the sentence hanging.

"So... how do you plan to make yourself unrecognizable, and how do you imagine I can help? Can't you do it by magic?"

"Sorcery only works that way in tales, to my regret. I would love to be able to turn myself into a bird and fly, wouldn't you? I cannot even manage a cloak of invisibility, but I've found it's possible to manage a cloak of misdirection." He took a breath. "I think it will be best to start from the skin out. Have you, anywhere about your premises, a woman's undergarment that used to be called a *bum roll*?"

"Oh!" She looked him up and down, and her face lit with true delight for the first time since he'd met her. "Oh, yes. I see what you have in mind. ... Oh, I *do* adore a masquerade."

# III

WHEN THE UPROAR of the nighttime laundering and bathing crisis had died away, and nearly all the linens and garments of the household were strung on lines across the garden to await the morning sun, Nikys sneaked a bath for herself before returning to their room. She found Penric leaning on the balcony railing outside their door, looking pensive, though he straightened and smiled when he saw her. "Adelis fell asleep," he told her. "He's really not as recovered yet as he thinks he is."

Nikys wondered if that went for Penric as well; he looked exhausted. She entered the chamber quietly, calculating how they were to divide the bed this time. But she found Madame Zihre had sent up two pallets for the traveling divine's retainers. Adelis already occupied one of them.

"You should take the bed," Penric whispered.

"No, you should," she whispered back. "What if someone comes in? It would look strange to have given it up to your maidservant."

He opened his mouth, but she held her finger to his lips and shook her head. He glanced at Adelis and forbore to continue the argument, to her relief. Her pallet was still an improvement over a pile of straw. They had surely not reached safety yet. But with Adelis snoring on one side, and the gentle creaks of Penric nesting himself into the bed on the other, it seemed a sufficient substitute that all her anxieties failed to keep her awake long.

This was not a household that rose with the dawn the way her well-ordered and much-missed villa in Patos had. But it was not long after first light that a quiet tap announced a servant with wash water and a bit of breakfast for the odd guests. Nikys intercepted it at the door, and swapped out the chamber pot. They gratefully devoured the hot tea, bread, and fruit. Nikys was surprised when the next knock was not the returning servant, but the lady of the house herself.

"Learned Jurald. My bathhouse is temporarily deserted. This is a good moment to begin that task we discussed last night."

"I should be pleased, Madame," Penric replied smoothly.

"Bring your maidservant. I don't want to get my hands all over henna."

They all shuffled after her, through the forest of laundry already half-dry in the day's promise of heat, to the little bathhouse, where Adelis was induced to haul water on the promise that he could be next. He frowned over his shoulder as he was sent off to stay out of sight till then.

Penric shucked off the shirt he'd slept in and started to untie his trousers, then stopped. "Oh. I did not mean to offend your modesty, Madame Khatai. After four years of teaching anatomy to the apprentices, I'm afraid anyone with their skin still on looks dressed to me."

Even Zihre raised her eyebrows at this rueful comment.

Nikys took this in. *Urk.* He wasn't worrying about the other madame's modesty, she noted. "Learned," she sighed, "just get in the bath."

"Ah. Right."

He was sluiced—Nikys stood on the bench to lift the bucket high enough—soaped himself up, sluiced again, and then nipped delicately into the wooden tub. Thin he was, but strappy, not scrawny, she was pleased to note. And that milk skin went all over.

And then she was allowed to fulfill the fantasy that she would not have confessed aloud under threat of thumbscrews, and wash that amazing hair. This was followed with a light henna rinse, which almost broke her heart to apply. But the silver-blond transmuted to an almost equally entrancing copper-blond, not raw red the way the color sometimes came out. Zihre handed him a thin robe after he'd dried himself, and Nikys made him squeeze his brilliant eyes shut and very carefully colored his eyebrows as well. Her hands emerged a somewhat less-attractive orange.

Zihre smiled in satisfaction. "Ah, yes. Very natural. I thought that might do."

"It's better than the walnut dye I started this trip with. I believe it will be best not to overexaggerate anything."

"It's a start. That beard stubble must go, next. Did you bring your own razor, or shall we use one of ours?"

It occurred to Nikys then that for all she'd seen Penric shave Adelis, during his blindness, she'd never seen him shave himself, even in the constant close quarters they'd shared on their flight.

"I actually have a trick for that. A bit of oil and a cloth will suffice."

He rubbed oil over his jaw, then scrubbed it thoroughly with the cloth. The stubble—miraculously—seemed to have transferred to the cloth. Was that uphill magic, or down? Nikys tensed as Zihre ran her hand over the smoothed skin so revealed.

"My word. *That's* effective." She gestured down his chest, faintly dusted with fine gold hairs. "And now the rest of it."

"Er. I had actually planned to keep my clothes on." He waved a wiry arm. "Long sleeves. High neck. And so on. A look of expensive reserve."

"We'll have to experiment with the clothes. I don't have much of that style. The upper half of your chest, then."

He grimaced, but complied. And it began to dawn on Nikys that it wasn't just his hair color he was planning to change for a new disguise. "Are you proposing to set my brother an example in acting, Learned?"

"Something like that. We'll see if it works."

His back being turned just then, she tapped her upcurving lips in a prayer of heartfelt gratitude to the Bastard. And when Zihre said, "We can continue this privately in my chamber," picked up after them like a proper maidservant and followed with zeal.

She collected Penric's smallclothes off the line in passing, threadbare linen drawers almost dry, and, when the door of Zihre's chamber closed behind them, handed them silently across. Penric gave her a smile of thanks and slipped them on at once.

Zihre's . . . workshop, Nikys decided to think of it, was nicely appointed; part, no doubt, of keeping her prices up. Nikys had a shrewd guess of just how much coin it cost to run a household with a dozen employees and a dozen more servants, with nightly hospitality added atop. The cleanliness, recently restored, and the pleasant effects of the decorations no doubt helped as well to keep the house's customers from growing too rowdy, striking a fine balance between inviting and daunting. The furnishings were for the most part simple, storage chests and a wider-than-usual bed. The one personal grace-note was a large collection of masquerade masks arrayed on one wall, inventively decorated.

The bed was stacked with women's dresses and undergarments. Zihre had Penric stand while she held up one and then another against his long body, murmuring, *No, no . . . yes, no*, and tossing them onto alternate piles. She shook out two extended tubes of stuffed cloth; Penric pointed without hesitation at the thinner. "Hm, yes. I thought those snake-hips would need more, but you're right." She fitted its strings around his waist, so that the tube fell to and circled his hips. Another wrap went around his upper torso, and they debated how much stuffing to stick in it; again, choosing less not more.

"Your hands and feet need work. It's the details that do the job, you know."

"Indeed, Madame." Cheerfully obedient to her pointing, he sat himself on the bench in front of a small table with drawers and a mirror.

She dove into the drawers and unearthed several lacquered boxes, full of more grooming tools and makeup than Nikys had ever seen collected together. Zihre set Nikys to work on Penric's feet, and herself tackled his hands. Such a pedicure was not a task Nikys had undertaken for another person since before she'd married, trading services with like-minded girlfriends, giggling together as they clumsily copied the skills of mothers and older sisters. Well, and the care she had tried to give Kymis, in his later illness, but that had entailed no giggling. By the little smile playing about Zihre's lips, Nikys wondered if she, too, had fond memories of such youthful hen parties.

Penric's feet were hard-used. But the routines of files and scrubs and oils came back to her soon enough, aided by a few workwomanlike tips from Zihre. The bright copper nail lacquer that Zihre handed off to her finished the job, and she sat back, pleased, to find Penric looking down at her with a crooked half-smile. She had not the least clue what he—he and Desdemona, never forget—were thinking of all this.

"Hair's dry now," said Zihre, fluffing it; the henna had caused it to curl more than its usual soft waves. "What do you think? Back? Up?" She rolled the mass of ruddy silk in her hands and twisted it this way and that.

"Down, surely," put in Penric, rolling his eyes up in a vain attempt to see what she was about. "To screen my neck as much as possible."

"Mm, but one wants to make the most of those cheekbones." Combs and clips in her clever hands split the difference, resulting in a handful of wisps falling across Penric's forehead, hair from the sides drawn up to a knot at the crown, and a copper cascade falling free down his nape.

"Now let's see . . . " Zihre's hands dove into her makeup box. She inked his lashes brown, was dissuaded from applying more than a hint of kohl to his lids, and finished with a mere brush of rouge to his cheeks and lips. For the first time, Penric twisted around to check the results in the little mirror, his henna'd eyebrows quirking.

"Stand." Zihre gestured and Penric complied. She shook out a loose length of blue-green dyed linen and dropped it over his head, careful not to muss the hair. After guiding his copper-tipped hands through the sleeves, she smoothed the soft folds down. The sleeves were pieced and pierced along the top edges, allowing pale skin to peek through, holding the sea-colored cloth demurely draped across his collarbones; it dipped lower in the back, veiled by his hair.

The hem, unfortunately, only fell to his calves. Nikys pointed mutely.

"Yes, I thought that might be the case. Here, girl, help me." They collaborated on pinning a second skirt, a darker blue with a ruffled hem, around the roll at his hips and under the dress, which made up, or down, the requisite length to his ankles. A belt of copper links cinching the waist finished the job. Zihre stood back to study her handiwork, lips pursed. Penric blinked back, amiably.

"Five gods," murmured Nikys. "That's really unfair."

"Amen," agreed Zihre, with a vast sigh.

"What?" said Penric, as the contemplative silence lingered.

"Never mind, Learned." Zihre turned and rummaged in another chest, retrieving a pair of clogs raised more in the heel than the ball of the foot. "Try these on."

Doubtfully, he sat. "Wouldn't flat sandals be better? Surely I am already too tall."

"Goddesses are permitted to tower." She tapped his pink cheek. "More to the point, it will change your walk. No use in adorning you like this if the body inside still lurches about like a lad."

After a moment, he nodded agreement, and Nikys knelt to adjust the leather straps, careful not to smudge her lacquer-work. He rose again to teeter cautiously around the room. He muttered something in Adriac.

"What was that, Learned?" said Nikys.

"Mira says she used to risk her neck in shoes three times this high, on cobbled streets with the canals waiting for a misstep, and that I shouldn't be such a weakling." On the second pass around the room he was steadier; on the third, natural, and she wondered what swift tutorials his multi-minded demon was offering him.

"And what is this tall and elegant red-haired lady's name and history, Learned?" Nikys asked. "Not to mention that of her servants?" There had been such a rapid succession of tales to account for themselves, she was losing track.

"Ah. Good question."

He headed for the bench; Zihre put in, "Don't *plunk*. Dispose of your skirts gracefully."

He hesitated, then did so quite credibly. "I suppose I had better be Mira. That will be easiest to remember. History... hm. I don't know how long this masquerade must last."

To the border of Orbas, quite possibly, Nikys imagined. How many days? And they still had no money.

After a moment's thought, Penric offered, "I am Mira of Adria, a... retiring courtesan of that realm. Traveling to private service. In our youth, Zihre and I were friends—no, better, we had a mutual friend. We have not met before. In her name, I imposed upon your hospitality when my party was unexpectedly benighted in Sosie. Because, hm, why did we lose our baggage this time...?"

"You sent it by carter," Zihre suggested, "and it has not arrived. In fact, it may never arrive."

"Oh, very good."

"It happens," she sighed. "Lost in a river crossing, they claimed, but *I* think it was stolen." Nikys wasn't sure if this was an addition to their fiction, or a personal anecdote. It certainly sounded more plausible than shipwreck, and much less interesting, thus needing far fewer supporting details.

"And your servants?" Nikys prodded Penric.

"Have not been with me long, but share my destination."

"And my brother's...?" She touched the upper half of her face. Penric gave her a fractional shrug, acknowledging the problem. Any halfway-accurate description of the fugitives circulating by now must mention Adelis's burn scars, unique and condemning. The old masquerade mask that they had modified for him back in Patos to hold his dressings in place was no solution; too obvious a disguise, it would draw the attention of observers just as dangerously as the disfigurement itself. Her eye fell on the collection of fine masks decorating Zihre's wall, and an idea began to niggle at her. *Later.*

Penric—Mira—tapped his, or her, lips with a thumb. He glanced up through his lashes at Madame Zihre. "I should like to repeat my treatment of last night, now. How did you fare by this morning?"

"Sore and swollen, as you said." She shrugged. "Not... unbearable. Is it time again?"

He gave a tiny nod. "There is a balance to be struck between destruction and healing. I provide the destruction, but your own body must provide the healing. Mostly." The rather merry mood between them had suddenly turned sober, and Nikys's brows drew down.

To Nikys's brief bewilderment, though she had the wits not to betray it, Zihre knelt before him and composedly undid her bodice. Penric frowned and laid two fingers upon her left breast at a patch indeed swollen and reddish, and his face fell into that look of inward concentration that Nikys had learned to mark when he'd been healing Adelis's eyes. She bit her lip. Wasn't he supposed to be saving Desdemona's strained powers for his own bruised heart, right now? She must tax him later on that.

Zihre's breath caught as she went rigidly still for a minute, until Penric's hand fell away.

"Still bearable?" he asked gently.

She nodded and rose, looking down at him with that worried mystification he so often engendered in people.

"I'll fetch in my medical case to you later and attend to the draining, and then we'll see," he said.

Another chin-dip.

"I should prefer not to impose upon you any longer than we must," Penric went on.

She waved a hand. "This morning's amusement repays me for a few baths and meals, Learned Jurald. Or—Lady Mira? Madame Mira?"

"Sora Mira, if we are to go by the Adriac style." He pondered. "I must work on my accent. Her accent. Mira spoke little Cedonian. Excellent Darthacan, though. How is my voice, by the way?" He repeated in a higher register, "How is this voice?"

"Don't overdo," advised Zihre. "Tall Mira can be throaty. Or breathy. Just don't go deep, or loud."

"Understood." He started to stand up, paused, and rose with more conscious grace. "Well. Let us make a test." He smiled at Nikys. "Shall we go introduce Sora Mira to your brother?"

Nikys barely controlled her grin, struggling for servility. "Oh, yes *please*, Learned."

Madame Zihre waved them out, turning to restore the tools of her trade to their boxes, and Nikys and Penric exited to the atrium balcony.

"Let's go around a time or two," Penric muttered. "I need to practice this walk."

Nikys nodded, and he laced his arm through hers to stroll along. After a moment, she asked, "What were you doing for Madame Zihre, just then? When you laid on your hand?"

He grimaced. "Just a little healing. I hope."

"What sort? Uphill or down?"

"Some of both. She suffers from a tumor there. Not a tame sort, I'm afraid."

"Oh." She hesitated. "You can do this?"

"Sometimes. Sometimes not." He sighed. "I suppose we will be long gone before it has time to prove not."

"Is it costly to you? Magically?"

He waved away the question, a non-answer that made her suspicious. He lowered his voice. "Not as costly as the risk to Zihre of harboring fugitives, even if unknowingly. If things go ill."

"Well." She drew breath. "We should not let them go ill, then."

"Aye." His voice fell softer still. "I should have been able to understand such things better, back in Martensbridge. Tumors and their ilk. There is an element of chaos involved, that I can sense direct, but no prayer addressed to my god ever returned any useful insight. Despite the fact that several of my demon's first human riders eventually died of related disorders. Including Mira, come to think."

"We are sorry," said Desdemona, even more quietly. "We did not realize, then."

He gave a curiously compassionate nod. "Not your fault, exactly. It couldn't have been until Umelan—Des's sixth rider," he added aside to Nikys, "fell into the hands of the Bastard's Order in Brajar that you even could learn to balance your chaos, and not to shed it internally unawares." He ducked his head to Nikys again. "Which is yet another cause for the Temple to pursue hedge sorcerers and secure them to its disciplines, I suppose. Or else divest them of their demons. Not a reason that is widely known or understood."

Desdemona vented a tiny growl at the mention of the Temple's demonic destructions, but did not press the argument. Nikys gave the arm wrapped in hers a little squeeze, and she was not sure which of the occupants of that complicated head she was attempting to console. Was Penric at any such inner risk now? It didn't sound as if he thought so.

They fetched up at their chamber door. "Why is it, I wonder,"

Penric mused, "that men dressed as women seem more risible than women dressed as men?"

Nikys shook her head. "I don't really know. It doesn't seem fair, does it?" She poked glumly at her well-filled bodice. "I don't suppose it's an experiment worth my time to try. Not since I was twelve. Not even with tight wraps."

"No. Definitely not worth your time. Or your worry. You're perfect as you are." A faint smile curved his rose-tinted lips. "At least Des likes the gown. I don't know how an incorporeal demon should have developed a taste for fine clothing, but she has. At home I try to do my best by her, within the limits of my calling and purse, but evidently she's missed the styles of her own sex." Penric took a moment to compose himself, in both senses, as Mira, then gestured Nikys ahead of him.

Adelis had used the bathhouse while she and Penric had been so long occupied in Zihre's chamber, and was dressed again in his least-smelly shirt and trousers, barefoot. Nikys reminded herself to go collect the rest of their laundered clothes off the line soon. As Penric wafted in behind her, the startled Adelis grabbed his hat, tipped it low over his forehead, and stood up. He shot Nikys a glare of dismay.

"I'm sorry, is this your room?" he managed. "Madame Zihre assigned it to—to my master."

"More or less, but that's fine." Mira cast him a dazzling smile. "I don't mind sharing."

"I met a new friend," said Nikys brightly. "Her name is Mira."

Adelis scowled. "You shouldn't be chattering with people out there. Learned . . . Jurald told us to be discreet."

"Please, sit," Mira said throatily, waving a kind, pale hand. "I didn't mean to interrupt your work."

Adelis, who hadn't been doing any, looked around as if for some task to feign, found none, and sank back into his chair. Mira sashayed to the bed and sat with a cheery seductive bounce, arms back to support herself, chest thrust out. She tilted her head, somehow making her blue eyes seem to glint like sun on the sea. "I met your sister in the laundry. I do love travelers' tales." She kicked a rather long copper-tipped foot against her ruffled skirt hem.

"What tales have you been telling?" Adelis asked Nikys. His

attempted-casual tone did not quite mask alarm. Really, with his hat pulled down like that this might not be wholly a fair test.

"You are indeed a very strong-looking guardsman," Mira purred. "So your sister said. I was sure she must be exaggerating, but it seems she understated. Well, sisters. I suppose she is accustomed to the fine view. What's your name?"

"A—Ado," Adelis improvised. His eyes, in the shade of his brim, had grown quite wide, and his scored cheeks flushed.

Mira clapped her hands. "An Adriac name! Have you ever been there? It's a very fair, rich country, if one doesn't mind that touch of tertiary fever now and then." She favored him with a limpid moue. "You should pay it a visit."

Adelis gave Mira a third look, and a fourth. Nikys could see exactly when the coin dropped, because he yanked off his hat and threw it to the floor. "That," he said, in an entirely different voice, "is horrifying."

"How rude!" Mira sat up, fluttering her hand before her pouting lips. Penric turned his head to Nikys and added in his normal voice, "You know, I think we could really use a fan. Mira knows an entire sign language with them, very nuanced, although it may be out of date. Or Adriac in dialect. There's a translation project for me. I wonder if Zihre has one she would lend, somewhere in those miracle boxes of hers?"

"I imagine she would, and I'll bet you could make her laugh with it," said Nikys. She sat down on the bed beside him. Her. Them, howsoever. She turned to Adelis. "He fooled you for five minutes. Do you think he could fool a troop of border guards for a quarter-hour?"

"Unless they've taken to stripping travelers to the skin, yes." He added after a moment, "And maybe even then. If all he needs is to be not-Learned-Penric, Temple sorcerer." And after another, "I never had any doubt that *he* could escape the country, one way or another. Maybe even he and you together. That... is not the core of the problem." His hand crept to his lurid scars.

Nikys leaned forward, intent. "I had an idea about that." She glanced aside at Penric. "Is Mira the sort of woman who would have the whimsy to dress her servants in matching liveries?"

"Oh, yes."

"Perhaps with matching masks?"

"...Huh."

"One masked servant draws attention to himself. *Two* such servants draw attention to, I don't know, Mira?"

"Mira lived for attention," Penric conceded. "Well, in her public life, at least. Privately too, really."

Not scholar Penric's style at all, Nikys suspected, but he had certainly proved he could rise to any challenge.

Adelis's gaze kept flicking back and forth between Nikys and Penric. Or perhaps Nikys and Mira. Penric caught his eye and flipped at the curling copper hair, smirking. Adelis's lips flattened, and he turned his face away. He was still a little flushed.

"Then I," said Nikys determinedly, "shall do some sewing, if I can get the materials."

"I can help," offered Penric. "Cloth or skin, I make very tidy stitches."

She smiled up at him. *I'll bet you do.*

The part about *You are perfect as you are* she tucked away for later examination, like a child hoarding a sweet that she was afraid would be stolen by some stern grownup. *I have had to be my own grownup for a very long time now, haven't I?*

# IV

PENRIC was impressed with Nikys's foraging abilities, as she gathered supplies for their next project of disguise. They all retreated to their room for the rest of the afternoon to carry it out. Zihre had donated a pair of identical black half-masks, broad across the upper face, modestly ornamented with sequins. Nikys turned and cut up a voluminous old black skirt for two tabards, which, when she draped them over a black shirt and trousers for Adelis and a dark dress for herself, blended well and gave them both a unified air. Done with being fitted, and having run out of sandals to clean and swords to sharpen, Adelis sat and watched.

"These should have matching embroidery and more decoration,"

Nikys murmured, her borrowed needle flashing in and out, "but there isn't time. This bit of braid around the edges must do."

"Everyday garb, perhaps," Penric offered, his fingers trying to equal her pace on the other piece. "I'm sure Mira provided her servants something showier for those exotic evenings, sadly delayed with the rest of her things by the accursed carters."

Nikys smiled into her work. Penric watched her covertly. Bent over in her concentration, she seemed utterly unaware of how enchanting she looked. Surely she was built to be the serene, solid center of... something. *My life*, he tried not to think. Because she would be stopping in Orbas with her brother, and he would be sailing back to Adria, right? He kept his needle moving.

But he couldn't stop picking at the impasse. *Like a scab?* "I know what Adelis plans when we get to Vilnoc," Penric said. "What of you?"

Nikys glanced up in surprise. "What?"

"Have you taken no thought for yourself?"

"While I have," Adelis put in, "Nikys will not lack."

Penric reflected, but refrained from observing aloud, that what Adelis had right now were the possessions they carried and a murderous pursuit. Both of which he was sharing equally with his sister, to be sure.

"Well, then," Pen tried again, "what would you desire? I mean, if you had a choice."

It was a little painful watching Nikys trying to wrap her imagination around the idea of having a *choice*. Or failing to. "What's the point of such speculation?" she asked in turn. "I'll deal with what chance drops in my way when it arrives there." The gesture she made put Pen uncomfortably in mind of a mourner throwing the first handful of dirt into a grave. Three times, he supposed, she had suffered her life to be upended by disaster overtaking those she'd depended upon: her father's sudden death, her husband's lingering one, and now Adelis's flight for his life. She glanced at her half-twin and away, but her needle didn't falter. "I did love the villa in Patos. I used to pretend it was mine. Just as well it wasn't, now."

*She wants her own house?* Pen tried to interpret this.

*Most women do*, Des returned, *at some point in their lives. Getting one without going through some man is made nearly impossible on purpose, I suspect.*

So would two small rooms in someone else's mansion overlooking a canal qualify? Sufficient for himself, they suddenly seemed a scanty offering.

"We won't be this poor for long," Adelis vowed. Less optimism, Pen suspected, than an effort to keep up his sister's morale. Adelis, too, had lost hugely in the late—ongoing—calamity, almost including his eyesight. Did that last recovery put the rest into an altered perspective?

Nikys shrugged. "Safety has nothing to do with being rich or poor. Or good or bad. A person could be as pious as you please, and own a palace, and still lose it all in a moment when the earth shakes its shoulders, or fire erupts." She frowned at her stitches. "Maybe true safety lies not in roots, but in feet. Or wings." She glanced, strangely, at Penric.

*Bower birds*, Pen thought. Didn't that breed try to attract females by producing elaborate, decorated nests?

*Or there's that bird that hangs upside down from a branch by its toes, shakes its wings wildly, and screams for hours*, Des put in with a spurious air of helpfulness. *You could try that.*

*I'm not that desperate. Yet.* Though even a rented villa seemed beyond his purse as a Temple divine.

*Not beyond your ingenuity as a sorcerer, if you didn't continually* underprice *our services.*

*Our powers are a gift from the god. It seems wrong to hoard their benefits.*

*So put up your sign as a physician.*

Penric's amusement congealed. *No.*

After a daunted pause, Des muttered, *Sorry. Not a good jest?*

*No.* Pen drew a steadying breath. *Never mind.*

He came to the end of his length of braid and tied off his thread, automatically using the one-handed technique a surgeon had taught him. Brows rising, Nikys paused to stare, then shook her head and kept sewing.

*So what would* I *desire, if I had a choice?* Pen thought to ask himself. One answer was obvious, and sat in front of him. But was the choice his to make?

*You have many choices*, Desdemona opined. *The real question is, what would you trade for them?*

❖ ❖ ❖

Consulting with Madame Zihre during her drainage treatment, Penric struck a bargain to earn another night's lodging and meals, not to mention their clothing and masks, by taking a seat that evening above the entry atrium and discreetly delousing any incoming clients in need of it. This proved to be a good third of them. In the persona of Sora Mira's own servant, neat in her black tabard and mask, Nikys attended upon him as they sheltered in a spot normally occupied by the upstairs maid. Penric wasn't sure which of them was guarding the other from any untoward notice, but in the event Zihre's customers seemed reasonably inhibited. If excessively inhabited.

It was all downhill magic, and so not costly, but really, such small prey made barely a nibble for Desdemona, given the demands of his own self-healing, still proceeding, and his work on Madame Zihre's tumor. He wondered if he might change clothes later and take to the rooftops in search of some better chaos sinks; and then there was the temple still to mulct. Zihre's house was proving a seductively comfortable respite, but they dared not linger long.

Toward midevening the influx of customers slacked off, and Penric decided he could leave his post and visit the garden, where Zihre provided food and drinks for her clients, as well as music and conversation. It simulated an impromptu, cresset-lit salon under the stars, although Penric expected the personalities and politics of this provincial town were nothing so rarified as in the aristocratic soirées of Lodi that Mira had once dominated.

*They weren't half as rarified as they liked to pretend*, Mira told him, amused.

In any case, it seemed a safe place to practice Mira a bit, before having to flaunt her at the potentially lethal audience of a border guard-post. Plus, he was getting peckish.

Trailed by Nikys, he shortened his stride to something more dainty as he navigated the stairs, managing not to wobble atop the clogs. *Do you have any idea*, sighed Mira, *what I could have done back then given your splendid inches?* Some dozen men and half-a-dozen women occupied the garden; he was a little startled when *all* their heads turned upon his entry. Not a few jaws hung open for a long moment, before their owners recovered them. He smiled benignly and selected a seat, a padded bench beneath a lantern hung on a post. *Good choice,* murmured Mira. *The light will really bring out our hair.*

Self-consciously, he leaned back and fluffed it a trifle, winding a curl around his fingers. Nikys, bless her, guided a servant with a tray to him, and he selected a couple of snacks, aromatic meat wrapped in cooked grape leaves, and some bites of white cheese.

"Aren't you hungry?" he murmured to her.

"Servant, remember?" she whispered back. "I'd be dismissed for helping myself in front of guests."

"Mira, happily, is eccentric." He tapped her chin sternly and popped a grape-leaf-wrap into her mouth with his own slim fingers, and she smiled back unwilled. Possibly not such a wise move; abruptly, not all the men who were staring were staring only at him.

Three fellows circled in upon him, one abandoning his own partner to do so, to her dismay. The two younger ones were glowered off by the older, a broad, stocky man sporting a military haircut tipped with gray. The man had a face to launch a powerful glower, a trebuchet of a visage. Big, hooked nose, big chin, big ears; dark skin peppered with old smallpox scars; it reminded Pen of nothing so much as a well-worn boot, probably with hobnails. Yet it was redeemed from its remarkable ugliness by a pair of shrewd brown eyes, and more so by his slightly grim smile as he slid in beside Penric on the bench. Interestingly, he was not one of the visitors Penric had needed to secretly delouse, earlier. Nikys took up a maidservantly guard position behind them.

He captured Mira's hand. "Hello, there. You're new, are you?"

Penric allowed him to touch his lips to Mira's knuckles, and decided not to attempt a simper. "And you, I gather, are not?"

He chuckled. "Nothing new about me by now, no. Name's Chadro. And yours, lady?"

"You may call me Mira. Alas, I am not new either. I'm merely a guest of Madame Zihre's, breaking my journey here."

His heavy eyebrows went up in disappointment. "Not an employee of the house, then, Mira?"

Pen shook his head.

"Ah. Pity." He set Pen's hand down upon his skirted thigh, and patted it. "How do you know Zihre?"

"We'd not met before yesterday, but we share a mutual friend, in whose name I was able to presume upon her gracious hospitality."

"Do you . . ." He hesitated. "Might this friend, and you, by chance also share Zihre's trade?"

"I used to, but I am retiring to, shall we call it, private service. Hence the journey."

"Really." His smile crept back. So did his hand. "But not retired yet?"

"You tempt me, sir, but I have these pending obligations."

"You lie very nicely. Kind Mira. I can't imagine this face tempts you much."

"One part is not the whole of a man, nor the whole measure of a man's worth."

"Hah." His amusement grew. "You make a prettier philosopher than most I've met."

Mira smiled. "Not a high bar to leap over, I daresay."

"Indeed, not. If you—" But his next foray into this faintly ponderous banter was interrupted by an altercation from the atrium, which spilled violently into the garden.

Two red-faced young men, both with poniards drawn, circled each other, seeking space. The other occupants of the garden gave it to them, scattering back to the walls with alarmed cries. The young men were both well-dressed in the local style, with elaborated hair that suggested neither were of the military persuasion that so many of the clients here shared. A couple of servants dropped their trays and raced out, calling for help from the porter and Zihre.

"Berat scum!" one cried. "A pox upon your house, and you!"

"Parga dog! I'll cut out your lying tongue!"

They barged forward, meeting in a shrill scrape of steel.

"Oh, gods," groaned Chadro. "Who let those idiots in here both at the same time?" Unlike every other more prudent witness, when he rose he stepped not back but forward.

Penric matched him. The last thing his party needed was for a brawl to turn bloody, bringing in the local authorities to question and closely examine everyone present, including the passing travelers. As strangers, they'd draw attention, and with enough attention someone might well put together the manservant with the burn scars on his face, and whatever circular from the capital for

Adelis's arrest that had arrived by now. This had to be stopped, and Penric had the means. To manage it discreetly, not revealing his powers, was going to be trickier...

*Des, speed me.* As slippery as a snake, Penric weaved between the two opponents, managing to grab one knife-clutching hand by the wrist. He dodged a flash from behind, though it clipped a curl from his hair. A quick twist to the nerve beneath the skin, and the hand flew open, dropping the poniard. He swung his leg around behind his victim's knees, disguising a jab to his nerves there and dropping the fellow neatly to the ground. Chadro meanwhile had stepped behind the other man and slid his muscular arms through his armpits, lifting him off his feet with a jerk and trapping him close. One strong shake, like a dog dispatching a rat, and the second poniard followed the first to the paving stones, clattering.

"That's enough!" barked Chadro, his voice deep and loud; parade-ground pitched, charged with authority. "I'll cool both your hot heads upside down in the well if you don't settle!" Penric didn't doubt Chadro could and would do it, too, and apparently no one else doubted it either.

Penric bent and quickly collected both poniards, and another knife concealed beneath his man's jacket at the small of his back, and yet another hidden in the other's boot. Clutching the cutlery, he danced back out of range of it all, smiling and catching his breath. A couple of the young men with military haircuts belatedly stepped forward to aid Chadro, taking his prisoner off his hands, and the big porter arrived at last, looking both alarmed and irate. Penric's man wasn't exactly standing up yet, crouched over clutching his paralyzed right hand with his left, though he would recover the use of his no-doubt-tingling limbs in a few minutes. Probably.

Chadro bent and scooped up something off the pavement, and lumbered to Pen's side. "Lady," he said earnestly, "you should not have run between those two wild men. They nearly knifed you." He held out his hand, in which lay the shining copper scrap of Pen's hair.

About to protest *I was perfectly safe*, Pen was interrupted by the portion of Desdemona that was Mira. *Leave this to me, oh-so-Learned, or you will botch it.* Bemused, he let Mira take over. "Oh, my!" she gasped, as Chadro captured her hand and tipped the curl into her palm. "I never saw. So good that you stopped him."

"Whatever possessed you, to attempt that?"

A true explanation of what possessed Penric would take all night, he thought wryly. "I was thinking only that Madame Zihre did not deserve the disruption to her household."

"Very true." He frowned up at her. "What did you do to the one that you put down? You were very quick."

"Oh"—Mira flipped at her hair—"I was taught a few tricks, early in my trade, for discouraging obstreperous clients." She took Chadro's thick paw and pressed the curl into it. "You may as well keep it. I can't put it back."

His hand closed around it, and he smiled. "I suppose not."

Penric looked around for Nikys, who had sensibly, thank their mutual god, hung back behind the bench. Her dark eyes wide with fear, she hurried forward to his side, gripping his arm tight. He could feel her hand shake. "Sora Mira! Are you all right?" She did not add, *You cursed fool!* but he thought he detected it in the set of her jaw.

"Perfectly all right, thanks to this gentleman here," Mira purred, and Nikys shot her—him—them—an even more scorching look, quickly concealed as she bent her face. She swallowed and regained control of her features, or at least, her distressed gaze was sufficiently in-character for a lady's loyal maidservant.

Madame Zihre appeared, looking rather rumpled, to sort out the contretemps, and Pen faded back a little more. The clash had started when the two young men had both attempted to choose the same lady for the evening, apparently for no better reason than to thwart the other. With the air of a mother sending unruly children to bed without their suppers, Zihre decreed that neither should have the girl, instead assigning them two others, or they could take themselves back out to the street with no refunds.

"My knives!" protested one, unwisely. Indeed, giving them back their weapons even upon their departure invited them to take up their brawl again as soon as they got outside.

"Madame Zihre," said Penric, "might I suggest a servant be dispatched to deliver their weapons to their respective parents, together with an explanation as to why. They can each beg their property back from their fathers in the morning."

Both paled, the one standing shooting Pen a look of extreme dislike, the one still seated a look of dislike mixed with dread. Chadro grinned. Zihre nodded dry agreement, and consigned the blades to a manservant to so dispose of. The angry, but cowed, rivals were drawn up opposite stairs by their girls, whom Penric suspected Zihre had selected more for reliable sense than looks.

"I trust those two will be delivered out the front door, later, at different times," he murmured to her.

"Oh, yes," she agreed distractedly. "Thank you for your aid, Ler—Sora Mira." She turned and added, "And you, General Chadro. Without your quick wits and work, that could have been the most dreadful mess."

Penric blinked. *Well, that explains some things...* At that rank, and clearly active duty, Chadro could only be the commander of the whatever-number-it-was Imperial infantry that Adelis had identified as the local garrison. Fourteenth, that was it. Ye gods, did he and Adelis know each other?

She continued to Chadro, "Consider your entertainment on the house tonight, sir."

"Hm," he said, "about that..." He sent Mira a faint smile and drew Zihre into the atrium. Penric pricked his ears, but could not quite make out their low-voiced consultation, except that they took turns glancing back into the garden. Zihre made some rather helpless palms-out gestures, and shrugged. Chadro grimaced unhappily. After another minute of even lower-voiced exchange, they returned, Zihre looking apologetic, Chadro frustrated.

Chadro seated himself again beside Mira, converting his frown to a wry smile. "Zihre tells me you are your own woman, and if I wish to seduce you, I will have to do so without her aid."

"Well, that's true. Mine was a hard-won autonomy, and I do not hold it lightly."

"Rather cruel, from my point of view. Throwing me back on my meager resources. If I had any kind of skill with women, Zihre would not find me near so profitable a client."

"Take heart, sir. I doubt there is any man in Sosie who could afford me."

Chadro cast Mira an oddly shy sidewise glance. "I could try."

She smiled back, and stroked him kindly on the cheek. Interrupting this exchange, Penric leaned down to Chadro's ear and whispered conspiratorially behind his hand, "It's no use in any case.

It's that time of month when I am compelled to take a few days off."
There, that should settle things without hard feelings. He was just
sitting back, satisfied, when Mira added, "Although I have a number
of pleasant ways around such issues. A man would have to be willing
to place himself entirely in my hands, however."

*Mira . . . !*

"I can think of no fate more delightful," murmured Chadro, "than
to place myself entirely in your hands, Sora Mira." He followed this
up with another brush of his lips upon Mira's knuckles, and Penric
began to think Chadro's humble self-presentation was as sham as his
own. Granted, a man with his looks had strong motivation to perfect
charm.

"If you truly mean that," said Mira, "you might provide me with
as much amusement as I provide you. Making up any shortfall in our
arrangement."

"Oh," breathed Chadro, "I truly do."

"Then negotiate with Madame Zihre for the use of her room, and
I will show you secrets of Lodi that have made slaves of dukes."

Chadro rose with alacrity and made his way over to Zihre, who
was quietly dealing with a servant by the kitchen door.

*Mira, what are you about?* asked Penric in panic. *Are you out of my
mind?*

*Come, come, Penric,* and now she sounded rather like Ruchia,
brisk and practical while proposing lunacy. *We have sat through any
number of your bedroom ventures over the years. Turnabout is fair
play.* She added after a moment, *Also, you will learn some new things.
That should appeal to the scholar in you.*

*We can't let ourselves be trapped in a room with him!*

*On the contrary, I plan to trap him in a room with me. I had his
measure in the first five minutes, Penric. Trust me. You will never take
your clothes off, he will be very happy, and that little problem of
financing the next leg of our journey will be solved.*

Pointing out that he planned to rob the temple felt like a weak
counter-argument, given that there was no certainty the Sosie temple
would yield anything. Also, it did not quite seem the moral high
ground.

Nikys leaned over his shoulder to whisper in alarm, "Penric, what
are you *doing*?"

"Mira has some idea," he whispered back. Mira, in Pen's prior experience, had many ideas, some of them scandalous. "She *is* the expert here..."

Briefly, he considered trying for some consensus, or veto, from all ten of the personalities that made up his chaos demon, but in bedroom matters that tended to be more of a cacophony. Learned Ruchia would vote with Mira, and so would Vasia of Patos. The two physicians, Amberein and Helvia, would just laugh at him. Learned Aulia of Brajar would sit it out, feigning dignity, although he gathered she was entertained by the results regardless. Umelan the Roknari hated men generally, not without cause. Rogaska had no use for anyone. The Cedonians Litikone and Sugane, Desdemona's first human riders, tended to blur together after two hundred years, although he suspected Sugane had liked women. *So do I, blast it.* The lioness and the mare, thankfully, never offered comment; Pen supposed, as creatures subject to heats, they'd never had to deal with such human complications. He was beginning to envy them.

Chadro returned with Zihre, gone wide-eyed, in tow. "Sora Mira," she said hesitantly, "are you certain? I assure you, my hospitality does not depend on you doing anything you... you do not care to do."

Mira favored her with Penric's sunniest grin. She stepped back, her hand going to her throat, and Chadro, watching anxiously, vented a faint *Oh* like a man hit in the stomach. "I promise you," said Mira, and Penric imagined that *you* was inclusive, "everything will be all right."

Zihre raised her hands in a feeble gesture of *upon your head be it*, and led them upstairs. Nikys crowded close behind. As Zihre opened the door to her bedroom, Mira inquired lightly, "Zihre, do you chance to have a supply of silk scarves or the like? Preferably the like; silk *knots* so."

"No chance to it. Top layer of that green chest, together with, ah, some other things. Which may be better to the purpose."

"Excellent." Mira swept inside with the air of a queen reclaiming her country. Chadro followed in hopeful curiosity, like the queen's loyal general sworn to her service.

*Mira, this is madness*, Pen complained, by now half-terrified. Most of the other half of him appeared to be gathering to watch events unfold like spectators to an archery match.

*Not at all*, said Mira serenely. *Back in the later days of my career in Lodi, I made something of a specialty of elderly gentlemen. They dubbed me the Resurrection Woman. I had expected my income to fall with age, but in fact it rose. Very satisfying.*

*Chadro isn't elderly!*

*So much the better.* Mira smirked.

*He could probably break me in half with his bare hands. If he figures out who I really am, he'll kill me!*

*If he figures out what any of us really are, he'll likely kill us all. Compelled to by his orders, if nothing else. This adds nothing to our risk.*

Gods, that reeked of a Ruchia-argument, twisty as a braid and as fitted to hang him. He'd often wondered if that was an effect of her scholarly Temple training, but really, it was probably just Ruchia. Was this a foretaste of his demon ascending?

*You could take back control at any time*, and that was clearly Des altogether, *but I advise against it. After all, you wouldn't jog the elbow of an expert acrobat juggling fire.*

"Sora Mira," the dismayed Nikys choked, "I will remain right outside your door. Call me if you need *anything at all.*" Rescue being strongly implied.

*Bad plan*, opined Mira. *I don't know yet how noisy a man Chadro is. Too much room for mistakes. And I know you like her, but do you really think she could interrupt subtly enough?*

Pen had no idea, besides wanting to keep Nikys as far apart from this misadventure as possible. Like, in another country. Which, in fact, was the end goal. He must not lose sight of that. If events turned to disaster in Mira's hands, he could probably rescue himself despite Chadro's unnerving burliness, although betraying the secret of his sorcerer's status, but . . . "No," Pen said, "go join your brother in our room. Stay there." He wasn't sure how to convey *Get ready to run*, but Chadro was already closing the door upon their two wildly anxious escorts.

Chadro twisted the key in the lock and turned to Mira, smiling wryly. "Sora Mira, I do believe your maidservant is in love with you. I cannot fault her for it."

Penric coughed. "Surely not." Or at any rate, not for much longer.

"She was certainly looking daggers at me. Ready to bite. Clearly, I had better return you without a hair out of place."

Desdemona inquired, half-sweet, half-serious, *If Nikys were not watching, dear Pen, would you even care? Or would you find this just one more odd adventure with us?*

Pen could only manage a sort of mental mumble.

*Because if Nikys is going to take up with you, she is perforce going to take up with all of us. Or do you somehow imagine you can, across years, hide from your most intimate companion everything you really are?*

Are, had become, was still becoming...

*Because that never ends well.*

Two hundred years of experience speaking, across ten very different lives? Twelve, counting the lioness and the mare. Penric went silent in temporary surrender, letting Mira go hunt up her supplies.

# V

NIKYS RETURNED RELUCTANTLY to their room. Adelis, last left dozing on his pallet, was up and pacing from wall to wall. He'd had the least to do, hiding all day in here, and the forced delay in their flight was making him tenser and tenser.

"Finally!" he said to her. "What's happening out there? Where's Penric? Is he still flouncing around in that bloody dress?"

"I have no idea what he thinks he's doing. Adelis, did you ever know a General Chadro?"

Adelis halted. "Egin Chadro?"

"I didn't catch his given name. He apparently commands the Fourteenth, here in Sosie."

"He's out there? In this house?"

"Yes. Is he someone who would recognize you?"

"Yes, very likely."

"How well do you know him?"

"We served together a few years ago. Very level-headed officer, but lacking a rich or well-connected family to foster his career. If he's been promoted to the Fourteenth, someone is finally doing something right."

"Does he have a short temper?'

"He doesn't suffer fools gladly. Or at all. Why do you ask?"

"He was very taken with Mira."

Adelis grumbled something unintelligible. And grudgingly granted, "Penric was very convincing."

"And I think Mira was very taken with him. She's taken him off to Zihre's bedchamber, anyway. I can't imagine what she's up to in there with him." Rather, Nikys could *imagine* quite a lot, but most of it ended in bloodshed.

"Is he *insane*?" Adelis sputtered, and Nikys had no doubt which *he* was meant.

She contemplated the question. By the standards of anyone not a Temple sorcerer, was Penric mad? Or should she only be asking if he was mad *by* the standards of sorcerers? She was beginning to wonder about sorcerers in ways that had never crossed her mind when they were just a distant rumor or a rare glimpse of white robes.

"I don't suppose General Chadro likes lads?" she tried, in a weak sort of hopefulness. "Do you know?"

"Not that I'd ever heard. I can guarantee he wouldn't like being made a game of."

"Oh."

Adelis eyed her. "I think we had better pack up. We may have to run."

She nodded shortly, feeling sick. "How long should we give it?"

"No idea. Although Chadro does not suffer fools quietly, either. If there's an uproar, we'll hear it."

"All the way across the house?" Zihre's bedchamber was in the far corner of the inner atrium.

"Maybe. Bastard's teeth grind us all." And never had the oath seemed more apt. "If Penric's unmasked and arrested, we'll have to leave him to get himself out."

*He's never abandoned us. Not once.* The cry teetered on a see-saw with *What does that long lunatic expect to happen?* trapping Nikys voiceless between her offense and her dread.

They fell into a quick collaboration, bundling their possessions into two parcels. Nikys stacked Penric's scant clothing ready on the bed. Penric's medical case she set apart, though she made sure it was all neatly packed. Adelis kept his sword out. It didn't take long, and

then they had little to do but sit side-by-side on the bed and listen to
the occasional voices or footsteps crossing the gallery, more muted
and infrequent as the night grew old. Nikys rose and pushed the door
ajar, tilting her head intently, but heard nothing more than a
household settling down. Adelis finally stretched himself on his
pallet, fully dressed with his sword by his hand, and dozed, so Nikys
forbore pacing. She jittered in place, instead, flexing her feet and
knees.

It must have been two hours before she heard footfalls
approaching on the gallery—barefoot padding, not the clunk of
clogs. And since when could she recognize those steps unseen? She
jumped up. The door swung open, and Penric appeared, still entirely
Mira from copper-gilt top to lacquered toe, although he held the
clogs in one hand. His dress did not seem disarrayed. No blood. He
shut the door and leaned against it with a tired whoosh of breath.
His eyes were dark and a bit wild, reminding her for some reason of
a clumsy cat they had once fished out of a cistern.

"Well," he said, his voice dropping from Mira's through its normal
register to something that also could have come out of the cistern.
"That was an experience."

Adelis was on his feet. "Where's Chadro?"

"I left him sleeping like the dead. I'm not sure if Zihre will let him
occupy her bed till morning, or wake him up and toss him out."

"What did you *do* to him?" asked Nikys. "Something magic?"
Magic, illusion . . . surely Penric if anyone could manage something
like that. Maybe he hadn't had to do anything . . . real. She glanced at
Adelis's half-healed scars, and his wholly-healed eyes. *But sorcery is
real.*

Penric was silent for a long moment. He finally said, "Mira does
not gossip about her clients. Very rigid rule, I gather. The highest
rank of Lodi courtesans don't; that's part of how they become the
highest rank."

Adelis was giving him a very sideways look, his lips flat, but he did
not choose to press for details. At least not in front of Nikys. It was
maddening.

She said urgently, "You weren't hurt? You took no . . . no insult?"

"Not at all." Penric grimaced and spread his fingers. "It's all right,
Nikys. I kept my clothes on, and I didn't have my hands anywhere

they'd not been as a physician. Better, actually, since this body was still alive. There were good reasons we taught anatomy in the winter. And I washed them before and after, all the same."

Since, as an anatomist, he'd taken bodies *entirely apart*, Nikys did not find this in the least reassuring. And how well was she growing to know him, that she could spot his misdirections so readily?

"More importantly," Adelis cut in, "do you think Chadro saw through your disguise?"

Penric seemed to consider this question seriously, then replied, quite simply, "No." He thumped his head back against the door, stretching his neck and rolling his shoulders. "Ah, gods, I'm tired. Well, no help for it. Nikys, aid me getting out of Mira and back into my own clothes. Carefully; we're still going to need her in the morning."

He took two steps forward, stopped, and slapped his hands against his torso in dismay. "Oh, *shit!*"

Since Penric had to be the least foul-mouthed man she'd ever met, Nikys found this oath quite startling. She gasped, "What's the matter?"

"I forgot to ask for money. *Mira* forgot, if you can believe it. I thought she seemed overexcited. All that for . . . shit, *shit.*" He took a deep, recovering breath. "Well. It may be possible to get into the Sosie temple now. And oh my dear bleached god, I need to dump some disorder on the way. It's been building up in me all day. Like water behind a dam. Tiny insects are useless for this much chaos, and besides, there aren't any left around here."

If he noticed their possessions packed for flight, he made no remark on it. Perforce, she helped him out of his Mira-togs, laying them aside. Nikys had never believed that clothes made the man, but the lack of them certainly did; it was weirdly heartening to see the familiar Penric emerge again from the disguise . . . and, perhaps, from the domination of his demon? Because she was increasingly convinced that Mira had been something more than skin-deep. More than an act.

So . . . so Penric had evidently done some things tonight that would horrify her to have to do. Men did. Shoved swords into people, for example, or sacked towns. But she found herself drawing away from him despite the arguments of common sense. Would she be happier with him if he'd seemed more distraught? That at least would be a reaction she could understand.

Instead, she asked, "How will you get out of the house unseen?"

"There's a tradesman's door in the back wall by the laundry. I don't need a lantern, so slipping out in the dark should be easy."

*And if it's locked?* she started to ask, then realized it was a foolish remark. She'd seen what he could do to locks. There were barriers that could thwart sorcerers, evidently, but ordinary locks weren't one of them.

And then he was gone, flitting out as silently as a cat. But this time, she thought of those big wildcats in the northern mountains, the ones that took lambs and kids in the night. She'd long been aware that Penric was a strange man, but she'd somehow thought him *safe*.

What, as Adelis, or Kymis, or Chadro were safe? For all of Penric's soft-voiced self-effacement, the ignore-me-I'm-harmless smiles, she was beginning to realize he might be the least safe man she'd ever met. Or, certainly, the least predictable... perhaps that was the root of it. Most men kept to their assigned parts in life. If you knew the part, you could reliably guess how they would behave. She had no script for *demon-ridden sorcerer*.

And nor did Adelis, she supposed. Penric had powers Adelis could neither see nor counter by any military skill. She wondered if Pen realized her brother's stiffness toward him had its roots in well-stifled fear. Or if Adelis did, for that matter.

The next hour of fretting was a reprise of the first two, although her exhaustion was such that she lay down in her pallet beside Adelis's. He slept; she couldn't. At last, Penric ghosted back in, not heralded by any night-candle. The one on the washstand that barely kept the room from total darkness was guttering.

Adelis sat up with Nikys. "Any trouble?" he asked.

Penric waved a hand in the dimness. "Yes and no. I wasn't seen. But the Sosie temple evidently clears its offering boxes when they lock up at night. Not a single coin to be found."

Adelis frowned. "There might have been objects of value. Good candlesticks, plate..."

"Yes, and all of it too recognizable to try to pawn in this town." Penric's voice took an unaccustomed edge. "Since the whole point of the exercise is to get out of this town, not a useful thought. Which I already had, believe me." He paused only to strip himself of his jacket and trousers, and flop into the bed in his shirt and drawers. "Ah, gods." He added after a moment, "I did manage to divest all today's chaos. There was a sick street dog. Poor beast."

Taking this in, Nikys discovered a new curiosity. "How did you rid yourself of all that chaos back when you were working for the Mother's Order in Martensbridge?"

A faint snort from the bed. "I struck a bargain with a Martensbridge butcher. I'd once treated his daughter. He let me do his slaughtering. It bore a double benefit; I was able to unload an enormous amount of disorder on a regular schedule, and the animals died painlessly, without fear or distress. It seemed to be theologically allowable, or at least no god chided me. Thankfully. My superiors were delighted with the scheme. It allowed them to use me to my uttermost limits."

And beyond, until he'd broken, as Nikys understood another night-confession, back in the temple in Skirose. Which Adelis had not witnessed, and she had not relayed, she was reminded. She was not moved to explain it to him now.

"It worked well," Penric's reminiscence went on. "Although I stopped eating meat for a while. Odd. I never had that trouble with animals we hunted, or butchered on the farm." His head fell back on his pillow, and he signed himself. His voice seemed to come more from underneath the bed than atop it. "Tomorrow, we need a new plan. This one is growing overcomplicated."

"You think so?" growled Adelis, sardonic.

Penric did not attempt a reply.

The next morning, when they were all still sodden with sleep after the late night, they were awakened by a knock at their door. Nikys dragged herself from her pallet and went to answer it, drawing her role as maidservant around her like a rumpled robe. But it was Madame Zihre, alone. Nikys let her in and closed the door firmly in her wake, as Penric, sitting up blearily in the bed, was still very much Penric, flat-chested and stubble-chinned.

Zihre strode to the bedside and planted her fists on her hips, staring at him. "*What* did you do to poor General Chadro last night, *Learned*?"

Penric rubbed his face, visibly choking back a first defensive protest of *Nothing!* as plainly untrue. "Why do you ask? Did he have a complaint?" He went still, swallowing. "Did he realize what I really was?"

"I have no idea what you really are," said Zihre, sounding exasperated. "But no, he had no complaints. He did send this, by special messenger just now." She thrust out a small coin-bag.

"Oh!" said Penric, surprised. "An honest man, five gods pour blessings upon his boot-faced head!" He took it, fingers jingling the contents through the cloth. "If this is silver, and not copper, which would be a bit of an insult, we may be able to hire a coach to continue our journey after all." He straightened the counterpane across his lap for a tray and upended the bag upon it. Zihre, Nikys, and Adelis with his hat pulled down again, though it was futile for disguise at this range, all crowded around the bed to see.

A chiming stream of metal the real color of Penric's hair poured out into a little pile.

*Everyone* fell silent for a long moment, staring at the glowing gold.

"That," said Nikys, shaken, "could *buy* us a coach."

"And a team," added Adelis. "Matched."

"Well," Penric took a breath, "that was certainly the style in which Mira always traveled."

Nikys gulped for her scattering wits. "Except that would be wasteful."

Penric's lips twitched back in a swift, short grin, though she wasn't sure how she'd amused him.

Learned Penric pointedly declined to entrust the new purse to Adelis, or to Nikys who might yield it to Adelis—Adelis's cheeks darkened slightly at the reminder of his duplicity against Penric back at Skirose, before they'd fled over the hills. So by the time they had broken their fast, and done Penric up again as Mira, and he and Nikys, prudently escorted by a manservant borrowed from Zihre, made their way to a livery to arrange matters, it was nearly noon before they left the gates of Sosie in the hired coach. The postilion swung his team east down the river road at a smart trot.

Penric had delayed their departure yet more by going aside with Zihre for a change of her compress and one last treatment of her tumor. Trying not to admit anything, he'd talked all around cautioning her to say nothing of what she'd really learned of her guests. But Nikys thought the woman received the warning well enough. Her good-byes were ambiguous, though polite. Although she did remark that if Learned Jurald ever found himself interdicted by the Temple, she might find work for him in her house. At least she didn't ask for restoration of her loaned garments.

As the road curved, Nikys looked back at the town on its height. "Do you think you will ever return there in the future, Penric? To see if what you tried to do for Madame Zihre succeeded?"

Penric leaned his head against the worn leather squabs of the seatback, and closed his eyes. "No," he said.

Despite the dress, the hair, the makeup, he did not look very Mira in this moment, and Nikys wondered at the difference, and then at herself for finding it so readily discernible. She hesitated. "Why not?"

"If it worked, I don't need to know, and if it didn't, I don't want to know." He turned aside, pretending to doze. The pose was not persuasive.

Adelis, fingers drumming on his knees, stared out at the river. Sosie guarded the dwindling head of navigation for the stream, the craft that could reach it more skiffs than barges. "We should have caught or stolen one of those boats, day before yesterday," he mused. "Or offered to work our passage like the grain wagon. We'd be nearly to the coast by now."

With none of the appalling risks their recent sojourn had occasioned, it went unsaid. Eyes still closed, Penric grimaced. It might be true. It also, Nikys thought, neatly undercut all that Penric had done for them in the past two days, pushing himself to his peculiar limits.

*Five gods, I cannot wait for this journey to be over.*

# VI

THEIR COACH was three-fourths of the way to the border when darkness overtook them. After some debate, Penric ruled that they should stop at the next coaching inn to eat and sleep, rather than paying extra for night service. Mira would be rumpled and unattractive at the border post if they rode all night, such travel was rare and thus more likely to draw suspicion, and Adelis would do better to present his petition for refuge at the court of Orbas in daylight. Adelis was on edge at the delay. Penric couldn't blame him.

The inn proved modest and clean, but Mira was sulking, and left Pen to play her part by himself. Fortunately, it was brief, the traveling courtesan's gold coins speaking for her, speeding the negotiation for a private chamber and dinner to be brought up. Desdemona as a whole was still talking to him, though she didn't seem to have much to say.

Nikys was scarcely talking to him either, plainly repelled by his last night's—surprisingly successful—ploy. Really Mira's ploy, but what was the point of him protesting? It would just make it sound as if his demon was in imminent danger of ascending, hardly an improvement. It must be enough just to get Nikys and her brother over the frontier safely, which, after all, was the task he'd started out to complete. Anything else, including gratitude, would be a boon that he couldn't do anything about anyway, right? It was better that she was peeved with him. It would make parting less painful. Right?

The reflection that their whole detour to Sosie might well have been the Bastard's answer to prayers none of their own was too disturbing to dwell upon. As they blew out the candles and settled into their beds, Penric turned his mind to more practical matters.

Vilnoc would be his first chance to report in at his own Order since news of his execution-or-escape from the bottle dungeon in Patos. There had been time by now for first words of the fate of their envoy to get back to Lodi, to the duke and to Pen's archdivine, but Pen had no guess what stories they'd received, let alone believed. They might think him dead. Pen wondered morbidly if the archdivine would have claimed all his books, or yielded them to the duke, or broken them up for sale.

And if his treasured volumes were gone beyond recall, what did he have to go back for, really? He toyed with the notion of staying dead. It would be a very clever, tidy escape from all his oaths and disciplines, to be sure. Except that he didn't really want to. He'd no heart to abandon the reputation for learning that he'd spent the last ten years building, and a scholar needed a rich patron. It was not the sort of work ordinary men would understand or pay for, not seeing immediate benefit to themselves.

*Keep it in mind for your future self, then*, murmured Des slyly, enduring his fretting. As if she had a choice to do otherwise than endure him, any more than he did her.

*Des!*

But his outrage was weak.

They made a reasonably early start the next morning, despite delays for making up Mira to her most polished perfection that had Adelis's hand clenching on his sword hilt with impatience. But at last, escorted by her matched pair of masked and tabarded servants, Mira swept aboard, and they were off again. Only twenty-five miles more. One more relay of horses would do it, although they would be compelled to exchange both horses and coach again at the border village, leaving their Cedonian transport behind and picking up men and beasts of Orbas. No doubt at a premium price, but at least that assured such services would be waiting. Skinning foreign travelers trapped by border laws was a happy tradition for such countrymen, in both directions.

They had made their first change, with but ten miles left to go, when Adelis, painfully tense, turned his head. "Hoofbeats. Horses. Galloping behind us."

"Put your mask back on before you stick your head out, sunder it," Pen demanded. Adelis glared but complied. Nikys gave him a glance for this rare black profanity, and took to the other window.

"Cavalrymen. Half a dozen of them," she reported.

Adelis swore. "Bastard's teeth and Mother's blood. It's Egin Chadro. Come for his revenge on you, Penric?"

"Can the coach outrun them to the border? If you offer the postilion gold?" asked Nikys.

"Not a chance," said Adelis. "Still too far. They're bound to overtake us in another mile. We'll have to fight." He readied his knife in his belt sheath and set the sword beside him. Extracted the bow from the wrapped bundle, strung it, and retrieved their scant handful of arrows. Frowned at Penric. "We've taken down that many men before, between us. Can you do your magic tricks again, Penric? Pull the bow, or should I give it to Nikys? Or will you be afraid to muss your dress?"

Penric ignored the trailing insult. He wanted to think fast, but he mostly thought of his quiet study above the canal, suddenly missed. "It would only take one survivor to warn the border against us, and bring back a swarm of reinforcements. He wouldn't have far to ride."

Adelis's teeth set. "Then we had better make sure none get away, eh?"

Penric contemplated the potential chaos. Was this a gift of his god? *If so, I don't want it, Sir.* "It's a busy road. A single passing witness could get away and do the same. Or a coach-load. I don't think we can count on privacy for such a bloody brawl." He slid over beside Nikys and risked a glance himself. The horsemen were close enough now for a deep bellow to be faintly heard over their own team's hoofbeats and harness-jingle and the creaking of the coach. "Wait."

"What?" said Adelis, outraged. "Have you lost your wits?" His mouth thinned. "Or are you betraying us at the last? What were you really talking about with Chadro all those hours night before last?"

"Not that," said Penric, fervently. "Listen."

The bellow became words: "Sora Mira! Stop! Please!"

"Don't you think," said Penric slowly, "that if he'd learned of my disguise, he would be yelling something more like *Stop so I can kill you, Jurald, you lying son-of-a-bitch*?"

Nikys's eyebrows climbed. "Would he?"

" . . . Unless he's being clever. Is he that clever, Adelis?"

"Maybe." Adelis's hand worked on his hilt. "Maybe."

"Because if he still believes I'm Mira, I think I could talk our way out of this." Whatever this was. "Give him his remaining gold back, something." *Right, Mira? Right?*

The return silence was palpable, and pointed.

Pen scrambled to persuade her. *Lovely Mira, if I was insufficiently admiring of all your hard work, I apologize, and I promise to make it up later—but only if there is a later. Besides, if we get slaughtered here on this road, where would you all jump? I mean, I know you liked Chadro, but surely not in that way?*

Desdemona-as-a-whole snorted. *An admirable man, but he does not have a swift and malleable mind. Not like you, young Penric.*

"We can still fight after we talk," Nikys gulped, "but we can't still talk after we fight. I think we'd better let Penric try first."

Adelis set his jaw on fulmination, but choked out, "Perhaps so."

Pen managed a short nod. "Stay in the coach, out of sight, Adelis. Those masks are enough to mislead anyone who hasn't met you, but not someone who has. If things go badly, I'll try to send a couple of horses your way. Or cut loose the leaders, or anything I can. Ride and don't look back."

"Don't try to explain my trade to me," growled Adelis, "and I'll not try to explain yours to you."

The grinning cavalrymen were riding up around them, one of them grabbing for the surprised postilion, another for the coach horses' checkreins. Their hoots for a halt sounded more cheery than murderous. The coach rumbled to a stop over the protests, but not the resistance, of the postilion. Chadro cantered up and swung his lathered horse to the door, blocking it. The animal's nostrils were round and red and blowing. Chadro was in scarcely better shape, though as exultant as a successful runner at the end of a god's-day race. His boot-face was damp with sweat as his chest rose and fell.

Pen signed himself, tapped his thumb five times against his lips, took a deep breath, fixed a smile in place, and leaned out the window.

"Dear Egin!" he cried, endeavoring to sound surprised. "What are you doing here?"

"I thought you'd still be resting at Zihre's place. I didn't expect you to leave so soon. I came last night to speak to you, but you were already gone."

"I do have, as I mentioned, an obligation, and we were already much delayed."

Chadro dismounted, handed off his reins to an attentive soldier, and looked up at her. "Mira, would you walk a little apart with me? What I have to say is for no one's ears but yours."

Pen's lips parted in doubt, but Mira spoke up at last: *Oh, for pity's sake. It's not like I haven't acted in this playlet before, too many times to remember. Stand aside, Learned Fool. I couldn't bear to watch you flounder.*

Relieved, Pen yielded the lead to her, though on guard to take it all back in an instant. She dismounted from the coach into Chadro's helping arms rather more gracefully than Pen could have managed.

Her smile was grateful and soft. Chadro's grip was understandably hot, and Pen quickly captured his hands to keep them from straying anywhere near his underpadding. No convenient bedposts and bindings here, and his costume was only meant to fool the eye.

Mira hooked her elbow through Chadro's as they sauntered up the verge away from the straining ears and avidly curious eyes of both their escorts. An old plane tree stood near the road, and Chadro led her into its speckled shade, a few papery fallen leaves crackling underfoot, then turned to take both her hands in his. Pen looked down into his earnest, ugly features; he was a good half a head taller than the general even without the clogs. Chadro looked up like a man kneeling before an altar.

"What would it take to make you stay with me, Mira?"

"I cannot stay. I told you I was journeying, and why."

"Yes, you've been wholly honest with me . . . "

*Ouch, ouch, ouch.*

"Yet you plan to tarry for one man. Why not another?"

"My course has already been laid."

He ducked his chin. "I expect the lucky fellow only thinks to give you some private portion." He took a breath. "How if I outbid him? Marry me, and all I have will be yours."

"Oh, Egin," Mira sighed. "Do you think I haven't received such proposals before, from other great men?"

*That's laying it on with a trowel, isn't it?* thought Pen.

*No, it's quite true.* Mira tapped Chadro on his big hooked nose, in a friendly but distancing fashion. She continued to him, "When I get to Orbas, I must make a final choice of service between two dukes."

That, Pen realized, was also perfectly true. Although the duke of Adria had never shown any sign of wanting to bed him. Thankfully.

Chadro swallowed, taken aback. But not for long, because he was, clearly, not a man who surrendered readily, or he would not have achieved his present rank. "But I daresay neither offers you marriage."

"No. That is their attraction."

"You don't have to sail so isolate. I could be your harbor. Your rock."

"You're a soldier, Egin. You must serve at your emperor's pleasure, not mine. One unlucky moment in battle, and my rock turns to sand. Or grave dirt."

"A Cedonian general's widow is not without resources."

"Exchanging my wedding garlands for bier wreaths? I like you well, but I am not drawn to such a ceremony."

*You know, this man really is terrible at courting women,* Pen observed in bemusement.

*Hush,* chided Mira. *I think he's very sweet.*

Pen stared at that ugly boot-face, and tried to see what she was seeing. The horrible thing was, he could.

"What do you want, in your heart of hearts, Mira? Anything I can command, I will lay at your feet."

Sadly, fondly, Mira smiled. "My freedom."

Chadro was silent for a good long time, taking this in. At length, he gave an infinitesimal nod. "I'm a man of my word. Shall I escort you to the border, then?"

"That would be very welcome."

Chadro offered his arm again, and they strolled slowly back toward the coach. "If your duke proves sand, would you know how to find me?"

"I would."

"You are young yet—what, twenty, twenty-three? You might change your mind in the future. The future is a long time."

*You have no idea how long,* thought Mira. *I had no idea.* She had reigned in Lodi over a century ago, after all. "Would you still want me at thirty? Forty?" She smiled dryly. "Two hundred?"

"Yes," said Chadro simply.

"Cruel to give you false hopes."

"Crueler to give me none."

"Not really."

*This is excruciating,* said Pen.

*Aye. The darling men used to imagine they'd fallen in love with me all the time. Most of them were actually in love with their own cocks.*

*But not all?*

She sighed, silently. *No, not all. I might have surrendered myself to one of them, but the tumor in my womb overtook me first. I wasn't half past forty when I died.* She brightened. *It's lovely to know I can still hook them in.*

*Yes, Mira. Now please throw him back.*

*I am trying,* she pouted. *He's charmingly persistent.*

"Two dukes, eh?" Chadro vented a reluctantly defeated huff.

"One must seize great opportunities when they come."

"It seems some opportunities come too late. Or too early." He stopped and turned her toward him. "For all we did night before last, I never got a kiss."

Pen barely managed to get an arm up between them, fingers spread on Chadro's chest, as Chadro encircled Mira and drew her to him, leaned up, and pressed his lips to hers. Pen did not interfere as Mira returned it with grace, but chastely, as far from the wickedly inventive Mira of the bedchamber as he could imagine. No wonder she'd made men's heads spin. He was just glad he'd chosen a minimal sort of padding, hard to discern in the folds of the blue-green dress. The watching soldiers whooped and whistled. Pen sensed wide eyes behind the masks in the coach window.

"Freedom can turn to ash as well," murmured Chadro.

"I know," said Mira.

"You are too young to be so wise."

"You are too old to be so foolish. But you are kind, which is a rarer treasure than gold. May the woman you finally bestow it upon be worthy of it." She slipped out of his hold, and Pen skipped toward the coach, terrified lest some incriminating underpadding come loose in the heat. With a strained smile, Chadro followed and handed Mira up the steps once more, giving her copper-tipped fingers a last squeeze of sincere farewell. He clicked the coach door closed.

Pen fell into the seat across from Nikys and Adelis, wheezing. Some low-voiced commands from outside, and the coach started up once more, this time with six armed outriders.

Adelis looked ready to surge across the gap and throttle him. "*What just happened?*"

"General Chadro has charitably undertaken to escort Sora Mira to the border, and see her safely across."

"What?" gasped Nikys. "How did you bring that off?" Adelis jerked around to look out the window, as if making sure they were still headed in the right direction.

"All Mira's work, I assure you."

Nikys stared at him, wary-eyed even through her sequined trim.

"So where does Mira leave off and Penric begin, behind that pretty face of yours?"

Pen thought of how Sugane and Litikone had blended together, after all their years, and Vasia nearly as much, and shook his head. "Should I live long enough, who knows?" Still reeling, he flung his head back against the seat and waited for his heart to slow. That had been *worse* than sprinting. "If my demon doesn't slay me by sheer terror first. Although then she will be someone else's problem. Consoling thought."

Nikys tensed as if she wanted to recoil, but in the close confines of the coach, there was nowhere to retreat.

Penric closed his eyes, and thought, *I swear to my god, Desdemona, if I ever again have to disguise myself as a woman, I'm calling in Learned Aulia.*

*Ungrateful, Penric!* But he could sense Mira's amusement. At him, of course.

A murmur from Aulia: *I'm not sure it's such a compliment to me, either. Are you saying I'm dull?*

Penric imagined a mental figure of himself flailing his hands in apology and backing away, which made Des snicker.

Des went on, *If you wanted a dull life, Penric, you picked up the wrong demon from that roadside out of Greenwell.*

*Ha. Which of us picked up which?* And what were wrong or right demons, anyway? All demons started identically, as unformed blobs of chaos escaped into the world from the Bastard's hell, or repository of disorder, or whatever it was. Each grew more different from all the others with every rider it came to; the differences redoubled as its riders accumulated over time. Des's theological argument that the Temple should not blame the demons for the imprints their riders left upon them was ongoing, and . . . not to be solved on a coach road.

The vehicle rumbled onward. After a few minutes, Pen opened his eyes and gathered his wits enough to caution, "No word of this episode must ever pass anyone's lips."

Adelis snorted. "Embarrassed, Learned? It seems late to find your pride."

"*Not one word*," said Penric, irritated. "If it ever gets out to your enemies at the Imperial court how Chadro let you slip through his hands like this, they'll hang him in your place, Adelis. And he doesn't deserve it." He added, more cruelly, "Or maybe they'll put out his eyes with boiling vinegar."

That won a real flinch, and Adelis dropped his gaze, if not ashamed, at least deterred. Although after a while he muttered, "If we ever end up facing each other across a field of arms, I may well *wish* I'd let him hang."

The last five miles to the border passed in brooding silence.

Chadro's high-ranking oversight saw them past the guards on the Cedonian side with utmost courtesy, and no questions asked. The hired coach ferried them the few hundred yards down and across the stream marking the boundary of the two polities, and up the next slope to the post of the Orbas guards. There the postilion let them off, was duly rewarded with a suitable coin, and turned his horses around to go back.

The men of Orbas, having watched their impressive arrival at the opposite guard-post, gave them a closer inspection. No one broke character yet. The two masked servants trailed dutifully, overshadowed by their dazzling mistress, who gave the guards to understand, without naming names, that she was traveling under the protection of a very high lord of Orbas indeed, who was looking forward anxiously to her safe and untrammeled arrival.

The closest thing to an attack was after they cleared the soldiers, as they suffered the importunities of three rival coach owners competing for their business. Adelis, in the role of Mira's manservant, shouted and cuffed them to silence and chose the one who seemed to boast the healthiest and fastest team. It wasn't till they clambered into the new conveyance that Chadro, watching from the far side of the ravine, gave Mira one last wave. Charitably, she waved back and blew him a broad kiss before he turned his horse and rode away, spine disconsolately bowed.

They were a mile up the road from the border village, with no sign or sound of pursuit, when Adelis at last threw his countryman's hat and the carnival mask to the rocking floor of the coach and bent over with his scarred face buried in his hands. His shoulders shook, and Penric wasn't sure if he was weeping or getting ready to vomit. Or both. Of the three who had shared this journey, Adelis had borne the most frightening burden, and Penric fancied the mask staring up blindly by their feet was not the only one he'd been wearing.

Nikys laid a consoling hand on her brother's arm and squeezed, perhaps knowing better than to speak. Prudently, Penric copied her muteness.

# VII

AFTER THE FIRST CHANGE of horses on the coast road, Learned Penric skinned out of Mira's togs and back into his own, an awkward process in the close confines of the coach. No ... not really his own, Nikys supposed, just whatever plausible garb he'd obtained from some used-clothing merchant in Patos after escaping the bottle dungeon, and before presenting himself to Nikys in her villa's garden. That bright morning seemed a hundred years ago, from this vantage. Undyed tunic, trousers, a sleeveless green coat that had once fooled her eye, or at least her tired mind, into accepting him as a physician of the Mother's Order (unsworn); the clothes, the man, the deceits, and all of their little company seemed worse for wear after their long flight.

"When you get to the ducal palace, Adelis," Penric said, beginning to take down Mira's elegant hairstyle, "there are bound to be a lot of questions about your blinding. I would ask you ... beg you ... " He paused to remuster his words. "It will likely make it much simpler for you if your tale is that the man who administered the boiling vinegar did a poor job of it, and your eyesight recovered largely on its own. Your sister's good nursing did the rest."

Adelis studied him. "You don't desire the credit? The reputation?"

"Not for that, no."

"So what is your role in this play? This time." That Adelis had grown mortally tired of playacting was plain in his wearied tone.

"I don't suppose I need a speaking part at all. When we reach Vilnoc I plan to find the main temple, and report in at whatever house of the Bastard's Order they have there. Once I establish my identity I can find my own way back to Adria." He cast a guarded glance over at Nikys, thinking of who-knew-what. Combing out his hair with his hands, he began braiding it in a single short rope down his back. "Although it might be well for you to come in with me, and use the Order's house as a staging area for your foray upon the palace. Get a wash, a meal, maybe a loan of clothing. Send a messenger ahead announcing your arrival who will not be ignored or shuffled aside. Rather than taking your host by surprise. This not being an attack."

"I suppose," said Adelis slowly, "it would be better not to appear wholly as beggars at Duke Jurgo's gates."

Even though they were? But no. Adelis was a man with a treasure of military skill and experience to offer, as desirable as gold to any leader as beleaguered as Duke Jurgo of Orbas. Penric was right; her brother should do nothing to devalue himself, here at the start. And since she was his whole train, neither should she. Pensively, Nikys lifted the servant's tabard over her head, folding it aside. Adelis had already shed his.

Penric sacrificed the last contents of their leather water bottle to wet a dirty shirt and try to scrub off his rouge and kohl. The effort left him resembling a man who had lost a tavern brawl and then not slept for three days; impatiently, Nikys grabbed the shirt from him and cleaned his face herself. He merely murmured, "Thank you." She merely handed the shirt back rather than throwing it.

The port town of Vilnoc came into sight around the next bend and rise of the road, and Nikys peered out the left window, eager for any orientation in her upended world. She'd caught only brief flashes of the sea in the past few miles, but here the shoreline opened out before her. Vilnoc sat athwart the constantly silting mouth of the Oare river, navigable to larger boats for only a few miles inland before rising turbulently into this hillier country. The town had tracked the river downstream over the centuries, stretching itself to the present waterfront with its fortifications, one of Orbas's few good harbors along this difficult coastline. Which was part of why the duke made the town his summer capital, but really, to Nikys's Cedonian eye the place seemed hardly larger than Patos.

The livery lay outside the city walls, where they dismounted from the coach and paid off the postilion. An ostler gave directions to the local chapter of the Bastard's Order, sited hard by the main temple, which was visible from the inn yard as a looming shape on a height. For once, when they entered the city gates, they gave up their real names to the gate guards, though not their titles; Penric kin Jurald,

Adelis Arisaydia, Nikys Arisaydia Khatai. Penric, Nikys reflected, had not been very careful picking an alias back in Sosie, if that was his real surname.

The local chapterhouse of the white god was readily found, a place for Temple administration rather than worship, occupying an old merchant's mansion on a side street just off the temple square. Penric parleyed them past the porter by sheer assertion, then left them uneasy in the vestibule as he talked his way up the resident hierarchy. He came back just before Adelis was about to bolt. He was accompanied by a gray-haired woman in the white robes of a full-braid divine, with a pendant around her neck that signified some authority, or at any rate the porter and the dedicat set to watch them stood up and braced at her entry in a respectful manner that Nikys did not associate with devotees of the Bastard. She addressed Adelis as *General*, Nikys as *Madame Khatai*, and Penric as *Learned Sir*. The latter made her minions blink, and the copper-haired vagabond grin at them.

Nikys was then taken up to the women's dormitory by a smiling young acolyte, very interested in her tale. Nikys kept her answers brief. But it was such a relief to be in the company of women once more, even if only for an hour or two. The hen party that promptly assembled to get her washed and dressed reminded her of the fuss Zihre had made for Mira, although the results were less spectacular and more respectable. Nikys thought she resembled a plump gray partridge, and wondered if she might have looked less dull had she been able to borrow Mira's dress. Minus the extension below the hem.

As she was being fed and fitted, she thought back over all that Penric had done for them, for no benefit to himself if Adelis did not choose Adria. Or unless Duke Jurgo did not choose Adelis? Was that the chance Penric was waiting for, why he continued to aid them? Their reception here was by no means assured.

She did not want to move to Adria. She hadn't wanted to abandon Cedonia, for that matter, though she could not regret a moment of her support for her brother. *Beggars can't be choosers* the old saw went. So if you wanted choice, you must not beg? There was something wrong with that notion, when Adelis himself would shortly be begging a place from the duke.

What she wanted—well, she couldn't have what she wanted, now could she? Which left her not with choices, but with second-choices.

Or maybe mixed choices, things she desperately wanted inextricably mixed with things she wanted no parts of.

*I want my life to not be one continuous emergency for a while.* Gods. She was so tired her *eyes* were throbbing. But she could not relax yet. This palace presentation still loomed. She must get through it without stumbling, for Adelis's sake.

And if, contrary to all this pointless fretting, the duke granted Adelis his whole desire? Adelis would be off at once to look after his new army, leaving his sister to fend for herself in a strange country. Installed in some safe-appearing box first, no doubt, but still, alone among strangers. She'd returned to her widowed mother's house after she herself had been widowed, four years ago, but that wasn't an option this time, with her mother still in Cedonia. *Safe in Cedonia,* Nikys prayed. That his father's concubine had been as much a mother to Adelis as his own noble dam was not likely to occur to his enemies; only his closest friends were aware of it.

*Safe in Cedonia* was not so comfortable a thought as it had used to be, Nikys couldn't help reflecting, as a breathless dedicat popped into the dormitory and told her it was time to go down to the entry again, the duke's page had arrived, and Madame's brother the general was already waiting.

In the vestibule, she found Adelis dressed in clean, well-fitting tunic and trousers, dark and neat. Without ornament, more soldierly than aristocratic, but that seemed exactly what was wanted; Duke Jurgo must prefer to multiply subordinates, not rivals. Someone had trimmed his hair back to military standards. The owl-feather red scars framing the glaring garnet eyes might be a bit unnerving, she granted, to a gaze not grown used to them. In another lifetime, she might have dubbed the effect *demonic*, except she now had much more informed ideas of what a demon really was.

He gave her an approving nod. "We look as well as we can, I suppose."

She calibrated for Adelis-speech and smiled at the effusive praise, standing taller.

He stepped closer and lowered his voice. Watching her. "Your infatuation with the sorcerer is over now, I trust. After all his antics in Sosie."

Her smile faded, as she contemplated the tangled complexity of all she'd witnessed. The lunatic absurdities of pubic lice and amorous generals aside... *I saw him pull death from a woman's breast as if drawing down wool from a distaff. And then spin it out into the world, following him like a billowing shadow. He sees in the dark.* She shook her head. "I have no idea what to think of him by now."

He gave a little chin-duck, as if reassured. She had no such reassurance for herself.

*Speak of the demon.* A quick, scuffing step on the stair heralded Penric's arrival. Nikys found herself gaping, as taken aback as her first sight of him in the garden of the Patos villa.

He had somehow obtained Bastard's whites in the style of Adria; a close-fitting, long-sleeved linen tunic buttoned high to the neck, with an upstanding round collar, open from the waist down with panels that kicked around his knees. Slim linen trousers. Pale polished shoes. Most riveting, on his left shoulder, the triple loop with silver-tipped ends of a full-braid Temple divine, the usual white and cream colors twisted with a silver cord signifying a sorcerer. Or warning of one...

Unfairly, the official garb made him look even taller.

The copper lacquer was gone from his clean fingers. His hair was still henna'd, if a lighter shade, and drawn back in a tight knot at his nape. His blue eyes were alight, and Nikys realized that she was seeing him for the first time in his real persona, free of dissembling.

A movement drew Nikys's eye to another figure waiting in the vestibule, a nervous youth of perhaps twelve in the tabard and livery of Orbas. The duke's page, presumably. He stepped forward and touched a hand to his forehead in greeting and salute. "If you are all here, Learned Sir, General, Madame, I am charged to take you to Duke Jurgo's secretary, Master Stobrek, who will take you to the duke."

They followed the boy out to the streets of Vilnoc, where the sea-softened light was slanting toward evening. Adelis dropped back beside Penric to murmur, "I thought you were done here?"

"So did I, but I was told I was invited. Which, from a ruling duke, means commanded. I have some small reputation as a Temple scholar, and it seems the duke collects such men. Scholars, writers, theologians, artists, musicians. A cheaper way to ornament his court than masons, I suppose."

Nikys had seen the famous buildings and fabulous temples of Thasalon, some of which had come close to bankrupting an empire; Penric was right about that.

"For display like a menagerie?" Adelis said dryly.

Penric's lips twitched. "As the duke neither rides them nor eats them nor puts them to the plow, very like, I expect."

They walked some four or five blocks following the page, turning twice, before they came to a broader avenue that ran from the top of the town nearly to the harbor. The ducal seat here was neither castle nor palace, but a row of three older mansions run together. Echoes wafted from one scaffolded end: hammering and sawing, the clink of chisels, and men's cries. The page led them through the middle door, unimpeded by a flanking pair of guardsmen who granted him familiar nods. They did stare openly at Adelis's face—and covertly at Penric's shoulder.

Nikys had barely taken her bearings in the marble-lined vestibule when a delighted voice cried out: "Oh, it *is* him! Most excellent chance!"

"Master Stobrek, the duke's secretary," murmured the page helpfully, as the man strode towards them, his arms out in greeting. His sweeping garments were a cut above those of the usual palace functionary, and he wore a badge of office on a gold chain around his neck.

Adelis took a breath and stood straighter, but the man walked right past him and seized on Penric. "Learned Penric of Martensbridge! It is such an honor to have you in Vilnoc!"

Penric smiled in a slightly panicked fashion, but allowed the fellow to capture and shake both his hands. "Learned Penric of Adria, for the past year," he put in. "I exchanged archdivineships. We have met, ah . . . ?"

"At that extraordinary Temple conclave in Carpagamo. Five years ago, now, so I don't wonder you don't remember me—I was just a clerk in the Archdivine of Orbas's train at the time, and your talents were only beginning to be recognized. But I certainly remember you! I am instructed to tell you, on Duke Jurgo's behalf and my own, you are most warmly welcomed at the duke's table tonight."

Stobrek turned around and added, as a palpable afterthought, "And you too, General Arisaydia."

Adelis's return smile was rather fixed. Stuffed, in fact. "Thank you,

Master Stobrek." He rolled his eye at Penric in new question; Penric just opened his hands and shrugged.

Nikys bit her lip. Really hard. Even though she was probably the only person present who could get away with laughing at Adelis. And even though her doubts about Penric still ran as deep as a well. She supposed she could now be sure Penric was Penric. *Among other beings. But I knew that already, didn't I?*

As an afterthought to the afterthought, Stobrek continued, "And you too, Madame Khatai."

She offered up her sweetest smile in return, and murmured, "Thank the duke for me-too, then, Master Stobrek." She was fairly sure only Pen caught the acid edge; in any case, his lids lowered in what might have been acknowledgement.

A woman arrived—no, a lady, Nikys placed her by the fine details of her dress and discreet jewelry. Dark hair bound up, no gray but not young. Stobrek looked up and said, "Ah," in a gratified manner. "May I present Madame Dassia. First lady-in-waiting to Her Grace the duchess."

She nodded graciously to him, acknowledged the two men with only the barest gasp at Adelis's disfigurement, instantly stifled, and turned to Nikys. "The Duchess of Orbas invites you to make her acquaintance, Madame Khatai. Please, come this way."

The woman led Nikys toward the marble staircase, heading up to whatever maze of courts and galleries this improvised palace had acquired.

Master Stobrek added, "And the duke awaits you, General, Learned Penric. By your leave, follow me." They trailed him through a ground-floor archway and out of her sight.

It was becoming apparent already that she and Adelis had reached a safe harbor. So, she no longer had to be afraid every hour, terrified in anticipation of whatever new threat it might bring. Wasn't that enough?

# VIII

DUKE JURGO'S TABLE rivaled that of the duke of Adria's, though Penric had put his feet under the latter enough times to not be intimidated by ducal splendor. But it meant the meal was prolonged, and there were obligatory musicians, after, and so it was not until late that he finally had a chance to catch Nikys alone. He had to intercept her coming back from the ladies' retiring room—not going to, no, and he hadn't *needed* Des to tell him that, thank you. He gestured, well, herded her out onto a gallery overlooking a small courtyard opposite the one where the duke dined. It featured mainly builder's scaffolding, shadows, and, he hoped, a scrap of privacy.

They leaned on the gallery railing side-by-side, frowning into the gloom.

"So, Adelis has his post," Penric began. That, at least, had gone quickly. Jurgo's eldest daughter had lately married the head of the polity to Orbas's west, a man with the peculiar title of the High Oban; his far border was presently suffering Rusylli incursions. Jurgo had been anxious to obtain General Arisaydia's experience with that foe. An expedition in support of the new son-in-law was being readied to march.

"Yes, Adelis seems very... I suppose pleased is not quite the word, since he's not so war-mad as to be delighted by an invasion. Engaged, perhaps. Already. He's not a man built for idleness." Nikys turned and rested her elbow on the balustrade, watching Pen in the half-light leaking from the rooms behind them. "What about you? Has the duke offered you a stall in his menagerie yet?"

"Mm, there were hints. He can't conscript me, nor could I accept on my own word. He would have to get the archdivine of Orbas to extract me from the archdivine of Adria. Who, since he only just extracted me from the princess-archdivine of Martensbridge last year, at some expense, might not think he's yet had his money's worth of me." Penric rubbed his forehead. "I certainly did him no good on my first mission to Cedonia." He looked up. "I asked you this once before. Have you taken any thought for yourself? Because I trust Adelis has better sense than to drag you after him to a war camp."

"Happily, yes. Madame Dassia hints that a place might be found for me as a lady-in-waiting in the duke's household. Not to the duchess herself, but to one of her daughters."

"Oh." Penric was taken aback. "That sounds... quite honorable. Safe enough."

"Yes, Adelis was very gratified by the notion, too. Although since the daughter in question is seven, what it actually translates to is the work of a nursemaid or governess, except with a better grade of cast-offs. The servitor's tabard is invisible"—she sketched a rectangle over her torso—"but one wears it nonetheless. Still, it gives me a breathing space. It's a relief not to have to make any more hasty decisions."

A more alarming thought occurred to Penric then. "Don't ladies-in-waiting rather risk being preyed upon by lords-in-ambush?"

"If they're twenty, maybe. I'm thirty. I've been defending my virtue by myself perfectly well since I was widowed." She made a hard-to-interpret grimace. "It wasn't as challenging as I'd thought it would be."

"Oh." He gathered his courage, and his breath, and turned to take Nikys's hand. "Nikys, is there hope for me here, with you?"

Dishearteningly, she took it back. "You will have to be more clear, if you expect me to understand you. Hope for what?"

"I'm told it's bad strategy to open with one's high bid, but I'm going to. Marriage?"

A long, unwelcome silence greeted this declaration. Nervously, he called up his dark-sight to try to read her expression. Every familiar line and curve and dip of that face remained lovely, but it didn't bear a look of love. Nor was it a look of loathing, which would at least be some strong emotion. It was more the look of a woman confronted with a monstrous pile of chores that she didn't have the endurance to face right now.

*Well, of course,* Des put in, uninvited. In fact, he'd specifically dis-invited her to this dialogue.

*Dialogue: two sides. Not three. Nor fourteen, Des.*

*Penric, the poor woman is exhausted. I swear, your timing is as bad as Chadro's.*

*There is* no *alternate timing that would have worked for Chadro,* Pen objected.

*He was only out by a century,* murmured Mira. Pen chose to ignore that.

"Is it the demon?" Pen asked Nikys, bluntly. It had been so before. More than one woman, attracted at first by his looks and whatever glamour she imagined hung about a sorcerer, had decided upon closer acquaintance that he was a walking quagmire, and wallowed away like a panicked pony escaping a bog.

After a little silence, Nikys said, "Not . . . exactly." It sounded as if her own answer puzzled her. "I suppose I had begun to think of

Desdemona as like what my father's first wife was to my mother. Arrived first, can't be dislodged, supposed to be a bitter rival, in truth her best ally. That may be wrong, here."

"No, it's not!" said Pen. Des purred in amusement, unhelpfully.

"But it's not just Desdemona inside your head, is it? There's Mira, whom I did not expect." By her expression, she might still be getting over Mira. Or not. "And then I realized... that's not all. Well, I suppose I've had glimpses of the two physicians. And Ruchia—you've implied more than once that she was a clever spy. How much of our twisting escape do we owe to her? That's just what I've seen. What haven't I seen yet? Is there not one first wife, but ten? And I can't even imagine what the lioness and the mare might be doing to you."

"Not that much," Pen protested. "They're very old and muted."

She declared, "It is plain madness to fall in love with a man who has more personalities than I have fingers." She wriggled hers, as if in demonstration.

*Is. She said is. Not would be.* Dared he hope Nikys was as much of a grammarian as he was?

*Unlikely,* murmured Des.

"Also, I don't want to go to Adria," added Nikys.

Pen, wrenched by this sideways jink, tried for a neutral-encouraging sort of noise. It was all very confusing, but if he could keep her talking...

She straightened up, tilting her head back against a supporting post, and sighed. "It's not that I have a special aversion to Adria, although I would dread not being able to speak the language. You have to understand. I spent half my life trailing after my father or my husband or my brother to assorted military camps or postings. There are *reasons* some military wives cling like limpets to their homes when they are finally allowed to stop. I feel like a plant that's constantly been uprooted and transplanted, and never allowed to grow, never allowed time to recover enough to flower or fruit. Ready to wilt in despair, denied its nature."

"Some people relish the road," Pen offered, feeling his way forward. "Youthful adventure and all that."

"I'm thirty," said Nikys, flatly. "The desire to escape a home where one will never be more than the child is not the same thing as volunteering to be dragged through every ditch in Cedonia. I'm too old for *either* of those to be attractive." Her eyes narrowed thoughtfully at him. "You, I suspect, are a bird. Even roads won't hold you."

"Only because of the way we first met. You've never seen me at home, with my books," Pen protested. "I'm really quite sessile by nature. The only bird-like thing about me is my quill, flapping away. There are weeks at a time when my greatest danger is a paper cut."

"And the other weeks?"

*You just saw some* was maybe not the best answer. "It varies, depending on what problems land in my superiors' laps, that they think they can tip into mine."

"Something I did not know at twenty," said Nikys slowly, "that I do know at thirty, is that when a woman marries a man, she marries his life. And it had better be the life she wants to lead. Your life seems very... unsettled, to me. Very... " She seemed at a loss for the next word. "Anyway, it's plain I'm safe for now. No longer in need of your escort, or protection. You have finished your task, Penric. Perhaps you can find another woman to rescue."

"You could be in need of my... something else," Pen suggested desperately. "My merry wit. My vermin-extermination skills. My kisses?" Hesitantly, he raised a finger to touch the side of her mouth; she dodged it. "A person can have many different kinds of needs, all as real as rescue."

She shook her head and backed a step. "I wish you fair flight. But I want to put roots in the ground."

"You are not a plant. And I am not a bird. We are both human beings."

Her lips quirked, helplessly. "Well... one of us is."

A pleasant voice from behind them said, "Ah, there you are, Madame Khatai. Your brother is looking for you."

Madame Dassia strolled forward, giving Penric the polite, repelling smile of good duennas everywhere. "We should say our farewells downstairs, and then it will be time for me to show you to your new room. The household is a little disordered at present because of the repairs, but this is actually one of the more spacious of the duke's residences for us." She laced Nikys's arm through hers and drew her away.

"You see," said Nikys over her shoulder, "I shall be well looked-after here, Learned."

"So nice to see you again, Learned Penric." Madame Dassia's nod was a clear dismissal.

Penric gave them both a weak wave, and allowed himself to be dismissed. He made his correct and civil goodbyes downstairs, exited the palace-in-progress, and threaded the streets back toward the chapterhouse.

*She didn't say no, Pen*, Des observed into his despondent silence.

*It felt like no to me. She certainly didn't say yes!*

*Two blighted proposals of marriage in one day for you, then. Poor Penric!*

Pen definitely ignored that one.

The stars overhead were a bright wash in a vault still holding a faint sense of color, some purple or blue too deep to name. Orbas, it seemed, shared the beauty of its sky with Cedonia, even if reluctant to share anything else. Penric still loved this boundless exotic sky, in all its moods. Even though he could never, ever touch it. Grasp it. Bring it down into a bag and carry it home. There were so many splendid things here, it seemed, that he could not carry home.

He'd not taken time earlier to write the letter to Adria reporting himself alive. He'd wanted to include the final report of Adelis's meeting with the duke, he'd told himself. Or had he been hoping, even then, that some last talk with Nikys would show him what he wanted to do?

He had to scribble something yet tonight, so it could go out with the earliest Temple courier tomorrow. Or, he supposed, he could just leave in the morning, and speed back to deliver his bad news in person. Writing home asking for instructions when he could already guess them was really nothing but a time-delaying ploy. A piece of diplomatic subterfuge. Or, to put it plainly, wretched foot-dragging.

In the small but private chamber that had been allotted to him in the chapterhouse, he carefully removed his borrowed whites, lit a brace of candles at the little writing table, lined up paper and inkpot and quills, and sat. The room was hot and close. The quill felt almost unfamiliar in his hand, after so many weeks without it.

He sat for a long time. Scribble or sail? For once, Des offered no opinion.

At length, Pen offered up a curse in the Bastard's name upon the heads of all hapless men who made fools of themselves for women, bent forward, dipped his quill, and began to write.

# THE PRISONER
# OF LIMNOS

# THE PRISONER OF LIMNOS

# I

THE BOOKROOM in the duke of Orbas's palace at Vilnoc was a lovely chamber. The spacious octagon, lined with shelves for scrolls and codices, was capped by a glassed roof. A well of good light for reading fell upon the central table where Penric sat. The quietude smelled of ink and paper, time and thought. It was his own failing that he couldn't concentrate upon a single word of the rare scroll rolled open in front of him.

He sighed and pulled the letter from the inner pocket of his white tunic, unfolded and read it once more. It had been handed to him this morning by the superior of the Bastard's Order here in Vilnoc. So, did he hope its contents might have changed since then? The lines penned by his own master the Archdivine of Adria, across the sea in Lodi, were quite short. And tart. And ordered him, for the third time—given that his mission to secure General Arisaydia for Adria had plainly failed—to stop loitering in Orbas and remove himself forthwith back to Lodi and his Temple duties waiting there.

Penric had written three temporizing missives to this high prelate, suggesting variously plausible reasons why he might linger in Vilnoc or even be assigned some ongoing diplomatic duty in the court of Orbas. All had fallen flat. At no point had he let slip his real reason for delaying, as that, he was sure, would have been even less well-received.

*Nikys.*

Or, more formally, the widowed Madame Khatai, sister to the young general and presently taking up new duties as lady-in-waiting to the duke of Orbas's daughter. Duties, she had repeatedly made clear to Penric, that left her no time for dallying. Nor dalliance. Or at least none with him.

Who knew what other courtiers about the palace might catch her eye? Or vice versa, definitely that. The widow had only her plump beauty for dowry right now, making her more a target for idle flirtation than courtship, though either vision was equally maddening. Even the dubious protection of poverty wouldn't last. The refugee siblings had arrived at the duke's court with no more than the clothes they stood in, but the general, already dispatched in the duke's service, would not long remain penniless.

*Oh, she's still interested in you,* Desdemona countered these glum musings.

*So you claim,* he thought back. *But I can't see it.*

The two-hundred-year-old Temple demon who lived inside of Penric and gave him the powers of a sorcerer was deeply imprinted by the lives of the ten women who had held her before him. He usually imagined this gave him a hidden advantage when dealing with females, but it seemed to be failing in this case.

*You're too impatient,* Des chided him.

*You're too old,* he thought back, grumpily. And not very prudently, but there was no concealing his thoughts from Des. *You don't remember what it's like.*

*I promise I remember far more than you do,* she shot back. It was all too likely. *Grant you, we've not seen this dance from inside the fellow's angle of view before. Though it appears to be equally absurd.*

Patient, impatient, hopeful or hopeless, certainly absurd, his pining scarcely mattered if he was going to have to bundle it all up and throw it overboard from some departing ship tomorrow. He might as well throw himself into the sea as well, and be done with it.

*Now you're just being melodramatic.*

*Bah, leave me to brood in peace.* He tried once more to bring his mind to bear upon the antique Cedonian prose laid out before him.

He should probably be packing. Not that the task would take long, since he, too, had arrived in Orbas with little more than what he wore—apart from his medical case and the folded-up costume of an auburn-tressed courtesan named Mira. Sora Mira, whose cleverness and professional skills had slid them all through the final set of dangers before they'd reached the safety of the border. Mira had been his demon's fifth possessor, a century past. He touched his hair. The last of the henna was almost out of his pale blond queue by now, but Nikys was not yet over Mira.

Not yet? Or not ever?

Desdemona, in all her complexity, was going to be a part of him until the day he died. As a Temple divine, he had a duty to care for his chaos demon; it had been made very clear in his seminary training that all their actions had to be ultimately his responsibility. But he was now beneficiary of two centuries of experience accumulated from ten wildly varied lives. (Twelve, counting the lioness and the mare.) To deny it all was beginning to feel like denying himself.

Which was not the same thing as keeping the direst bits private, true. Any man did that.

*Agh*. He gritted his teeth and reset the weights that held the scroll open.

At the scuff of sandals and a soft knock at the doorjamb, Penric looked up from his manuscript. As if summoned from his own thoughts like an apparition, although magic only worked that way in tales, Nikys stood in the entry to the bookroom. Penric kept his breathing level with an effort.

She was dressed for her day's duties in the Cedonian version of a sober summer gown, a loose linen dress belted at the waist, sleeves gathered in folds. It was dyed a widow's dark green that had lost its saturation to wear and washings and faded to an ambiguous sea-color. All hasty hand-me-downs from other ladies of the court, just as Penric's own white tunic and trousers were borrowings from the chapterhouse of the Bastard's Order, where he was also lent a room.

Her black curls were collected by embroidered bands, holding them off her neck. Her dark eyes were as sober as her garb. She clutched a paper in her hand.

"Learned Penric."

His formal title that she'd used since their arrival in Orbas had replaced the *Pen!* she'd come to call him in their flight across half of Cedonia, and it felt like a slap. Rising politely to his feet, he retaliated in kind: "Madame Khatai. How may I help you?"

She cast him a distraught look, as if his question were not a rhetorical pleasantry, but some toweringly difficult puzzle. His heart perked up in curiosity.

"I just received this letter." She waved the paper and hurried across the bookroom to his side. "Really it was addressed to Adelis, but before he left he made me his executor for all his interests in his absence."

Those were duties she'd held before for her military brother. Given the hazards of his trade, it could all too easily turn into an executorship in fact, and it was a sign of his trust in his twin.

"It concerns me as much or more," she went on, "even though it's plain he's the real target." She bit her lip and thrust the single page at him, obviously meaning him to read it, too. By its cleanliness, it must have arrived wrapped in some outer protecting envelope.

He took it, readily suppressing any faint qualm that perhaps he should not be reading General Adelis Arisaydia's personal correspondence. Or his official correspondence, either.

It was in a spidery but clear handwriting, unsigned and unaddressed unless that salutation, *To the one of the yellow roses* meant more to Nikys than to Pen. It went on: *You need to know that on the second night of the full moon*—a scant week ago—*the dam of your cradle-mate was brought to the spring on Limnos by the order of the one who served you pickles. She is guarded there by his servants. The purpose being plain enough, it is hoped this may reach you in advance of any surprise, if the rumors of your destination prove true.*

*We will try to find out more. Yours in haste and hope.*

"All right," said Pen. "I may read six languages, but I need you to interpret this."

She ducked her chin. "I recognize the handwriting. It's Lady Tanar's eunuch secretary, Master Bosha."

"And if I knew who either of these people were...?"

She waved an urgent hand. "Adelis was trying to court Lady Tanar two years ago, when we were both in Thasalon, before he was dispatched to thwart the Rusylli incursion. After which he was reassigned to the garrison in Patos, and after that, well, you saw all the disasters that overtook us there. In aid of his suit Adelis set me on to make friends with her, and we exchanged visits, oh, several times."

"So the yellow roses were, what, some courting gift from him?"

She nodded vigorously, making her bound-up curls bounce.

"I suppose it's a good sign that she remembered them two years later, but what about the rest of this?"

"*The one who served you pickles* has to refer to Minister Methani, who ordered Adelis be blinded with the boiling vinegar. Limnos is an island just off the coast near Thasalon—the Daughter's Order maintains a retreat there for high-born devotees who wish to withdraw from the world and dedicate their virginity to her. It also serves as a place for those who have grown old in her service to retire."

"Also the high-born ones, I would guess?"

"Not always, but certainly those who have risen high in Her Order. And also"—she took a deep breath—"as a delicate prison for noblewomen whom the emperor has taken hostage against their rebellious relatives. This says they've taken *my mother*."

Pen swallowed. "Oh."

"Oh, gods, I thought she would be safer than this. She's not Adelis's mother, after all, nor high-born. Most people don't know how close they are. Someone must have said too much to the wrong ears, at the imperial court."

"Unless this Methani fellow is clutching straws."

"Possible, but it hardly matters now."

Nikys and Adelis insisted they were twins, being born on the same day to two different mothers and the same father, on the grounds that had it been two fathers and the same mother, none would hesitate to dub them so. Old General Arisaydia's first marriage to a noblewoman with imperial connections had sadly been without issue for years, until he took a second wife, or concubine—Pen was a little unclear on Cedonian domestic legalities—and by whatever joke of the Mother and the Bastard, found himself with two offspring at once. Typically such women were expected to be rivals, but those two seemed to have united, instead, taking house together after the death of their husband in Nikys's late teens. According to Nikys, her mother had mourned the loss of the senior wife, a few years ago, even more than she'd mourned their husband.

It had all left Adelis's enemies at the imperial court with a dearth of potential hostages to hold against him, certainly.

"And what have the duchess or the duke to say to this?"

"I don't know yet. I came to you first."

Pen felt more alarmed than flattered. "Er, why?"

Her gaze upon him intensified. "You're a sorcerer. You smuggled Adelis and me out of Cedonia to Orbas. You escaped a *bottle dungeon*, and no one does that. I believe you could save my mother."

Penric gulped down his first impulse, which was to protest that those all had been flukes, unrepeatable. "We must take this to Duke Jurgo, to start. A threat against the loyalty of his new general concerns him closely, after all."

"Yes." Her hands clenched. "We have next to no resources, even between us, but he could help us if he chose."

Just exactly what she might have in mind, Pen shuddered to imagine. Perhaps Jurgo would be a voice of reason? Leaving the scroll open on the table, Pen folded and repocketed his own letter of the morning.

"What's that?" Nikys asked, seeing this.

"Oh"—Pen exhaled—"nothing of importance now. Let's go find Duke Jurgo."

They exited the bookroom together, Nikys's shorter steps for once outpacing Penric's leggy stride.

# II

THEY TRACKED THE DUKE, eventually, not to his cabinet but to the east end of the palace, where he was examining some renovations in progress. The work-crew foreman sent Nikys an unsolicited look of gratitude when she drew Jurgo off to a quieter courtyard.

Jurgo was a pleasantly ugly, mostly-affable man in his early forties, duke for some fifteen years and as solid in his position as possible for lord of such a beleaguered realm. Shrewd, or he wouldn't be so solid. If Nikys could present her needs as lying in line with his, she thought she might have a chance of gaining his support. At cross-purposes, she'd be weak indeed.

Jurgo settled on a shaded bench under the colonnade, Nikys standing stiff before him as he read her note. She strove to organize her thoughts through a head throbbing with more tension than since Adelis had been arrested back in Patos. And to shove aside, for the moment, a thousand thronging visions of what dire things might be happening to her mother *right now*. Women prisoners were almost never blinded, for example. Castration did not apply. The cutting-off of breasts, promising not only agony to the woman but starvation to her infant, was not usually threatened to women past childbearing. Retreats of the Daughter's Order did not feature dungeons.

*Is she very frightened? Has she been cruelly treated?* Nikys swallowed hard to keep control of her voice.

Penric leaned against a post and listened soberly as she again explained the strange message's import.

Jurgo tapped the paper in his hand, and asked, "Do you trust this? How certain are you of its senders?"

"Master Bosha's handwriting I know well, from other correspondence with Lady Tanar. Along with the roses, it's full of private things that Adelis would be expected to understand at once, just as I do."

"Not very full. It's quite short."

"The shorter, the better, for this sort of thing," Penric put in from the side. "Every unneeded sentence is another chance for betrayal, should it fall into the wrong hands on its journey."

Jurgo gave a conceding nod. "Could its writing have been bribed, or suborned?" His hand circled. "Compelled?"

"Lady Tanar Xarre is rich, and Master Bosha very loyal to her," said Nikys. "So not the first two. And I have trouble imagining any compulsion that would force him to write such a thing against her will."

Penric shrugged. "If he's a scribe, an offer to break his fingers might suffice. Or to blind him." While this was delivered in Penric's voice, the casual bloody-mindedness hinted it might be Desdemona talking.

It wasn't as if Nikys had spoken that much with Surakos Bosha, despite him being an ironic, watchful presence wherever Tanar went.

So she couldn't *support* the conviction with which she said, "No." She added after a reluctant moment, "Although if someone threatened to break Tanar's fingers, it's hard to tell what might happen." Since *someone wouldn't live long* wasn't a thing she could say out loud. "But I can't picture how such an event might come about. Tanar is well-protected in her lady mother's household." Largely by Bosha himself, Nikys gathered.

"Even metaphorically?" asked Penric. "Pressure put on this Lady Tanar, her secretary writing to her dictation?"

Unhappily, Nikys turned out her hands. "To what end?" And hoped everyone else wasn't thinking the obvious, *Entrapment.*

The duke's canny eyes studied Nikys. "If General Arisaydia received this, as he apparently was intended to, what do you think he would do?"

Nikys hesitated.

Jurgo prodded, "Desert his post and attempt a rescue?"

"No."

"Lead his troops in some illicit sortie?"

"Never."

"How much would this impede his duties?"

"Not at all," said Nikys, both in simple honesty, and in aid of the duke's trust in his new general, "because he is Adelis. But he would be distracted and disturbed, as any man would."

"So no good could come from forwarding this to him."

"Except that he may find out from some less friendly source, at a worse time. Must, or what's the point of taking a hostage?"

"Hm."

"Unless," Nikys drew breath, "our mother was rescued already, and the report of that could come with it."

"I cannot lend troops for such a move, not against Cedonia."

"I know. I have a less costly and risky plan." At least, less costly or risky to Jurgo. "Allow me and Learned Penric to cross the border in secret and bring her out."

The duke glanced aside at Penric, whose mouth was set in a grim line, and did not scoff. "Wouldn't that just risk giving Adelis's enemies two hostages instead of one?"

Nikys demurred, "Given the weight of the first to him—to us—adding a second scarcely tilts the scale more."

"That risk could be averted," Penric said in a neutral tone, "by just sending me."

Nikys shook her head. "You don't know the country or the people, but I do. More to the point, they do not know you. This is too dangerous a business to expect them to trust some complete stranger." Of which Penric was one of the strangest. Although he could be convincing at need—she remembered that from Patos.

To Nikys's intense relief, neither man tried to gainsay this.

"So what is your scheme?" asked Jurgo, glancing between them.

"As far as I've come in an hour's thought," said Nikys, "Learned Penric and I could make our way much as we did before, passing ourselves off in whatever way seems best, to Lady Tanar's estate outside Thasalon. Take shelter and guidance there for the next step, that of getting on and then off the island with my mother. Repeat the stages in the opposite direction."

"Preferably better-funded this time," Penric put in. "Including a purse adequate for bribes. Still much cheaper than sending troops."

"Troops," Jurgo depressed this ploy, "were never an option. But the risk you'd bring to your proposed hosts seems beyond that invited by a mere friendly warning." He rattled the letter by way of emphasis.

"Yes," said Nikys, "and no. If Tanar is still considering my mother as her prospective mother-in-law."

"Was your brother's courtship prospering so much?"

"We'd hoped so. Before it was so brutally cut short."

"Mm, yes, that. The barriers between the general and the lady would seem insurmountable now." He touched his temple, and Nikys wondered if he was thinking of Adelis's disfigurement from the burn-scarring, as well as the new political divide.

"Now, certainly. But who knows what the future may bring?"

Jurgo didn't answer, and considering all the awful possibilities that might be a poor direction to bend his thoughts. He twisted in his seat to stare at Penric. "So are you volunteering, sorcerer? I thought you meant to go back to Adria."

"I must certainly report my actions to my Temple superiors," said Penric, glancing skyward as if to find those worthies there, "upon my return from Thasalon."

Jurgo smirked. "I see." He looked down at his sandals, looked up. "And here I thought you might have sought me out to report some happy news. That you had found reason to petition the Temple to allow you to stay in Orbas, for example." It was no secret that Jurgo had been wooing Learned Penric to join his ducal menagerie of scholars, writers, and artists, famous living ornaments to his court.

"That gift is not in my hands," said Penric, with a grave glance at Nikys. Implying that it was in hers?

Jurgo drummed his thick fingers upon his knee. "How soon would you imagine departing?"

"As soon as sensible preparation allows," said Nikys. "If there's one thing I've learned from my brother's military trade, it's that swift is better than slow." At once true, and another reminder of how valuable Adelis was to Jurgo.

Jurgo rubbed his lips, and Nikys hung suspended in the hot sunlight, watching his decision forming but unable to predict its direction. "Very well," said Jurgo at last. "Find my secretary Stobrek and work out the purse needed for the undertaking."

"*Thank you,* my lord," gasped Nikys, and would have fallen to her knees to kiss his ducal ring in wild relief, except he was already grunting to his feet, looking abstracted.

His look refocused on Penric. "Do you really think this can be done?"

"I . . . " Penric's teeth closed, fencing his reply.

"Let me rephrase that," said the duke. "Does Desdemona think it can be done?"

Penric's expression flickered from dismay to tranquility. "Yes, my lord. Or Ruchia does."

" . . . Ruchia? And which one was she, again?"

"The Temple divine who held Desdemona just before me. She was a scholar in her own right. And, er, an agent of my Order who completed many varied tasks, in the forty years of her career as a sorceress." Pen grimaced, and added, "Oh, just spit it out, Pen. She was a spy, and a good one, too."

*That* was Desdemona, without question.

Even Jurgo caught it, by the wry smile that turned his mouth. "Let us all hope so."

# III

IT WAS NOON the following day when Penric and Nikys boarded a small private coach in Vilnoc to make their way west. In this region it was less than three hundred miles in a straight line from one coast of the peninsula to the other, but even the Old Cedonian military roads up through its former province of Orbas were neither straight nor level. The team was reduced from a smart trot to a laboring pull on the upward slopes, and an even more careful descent, wooden brakes screeching and smoking. It was still vastly faster than walking, and more comfortable than mule-back. Much as tertiary fever was better than plague, Pen reflected as the coach bumped and rocked.

Pen shoved with his foot at his restocked medical case that had slid across the floor. Bringing it along had seemed prudent, even if the last thing he wished to do was practice medicine again.

*Oh, you're beyond the need for practice by now, lad,* murmured Des, in her acerb version of encouragement, and Pen let his tired lips twitch in thanks.

Nikys fussed with the few belongings they'd thought they could carry over the more rugged mountains when they made the turn north to slip over the border. Their boots and riding clothes for that part of the trek were packed away. For the coach, Nikys wore a belted dress, with a sort of loose surcoat flung over it for protection from the road dirt, which would have made a more convincing apron without its fine court embroidery. Pen had obtained a man's tunic and loose trousers of this country, the latter cuffed and buttoned at the ankle to hastily alter for his height. The simple cut left his status ambiguous, and told nothing of his calling.

Nikys was still strained in his presence, a tension seemingly made worse, not better, by her sudden need for him. He'd not seen her look so fraught since his first sight of her in the villa garden in Patos, despairing over her unjustly blinded brother. She let the noise of the coach be an excuse for not attempting to talk, and Pen allowed it. He didn't think she'd slept at all last night, for after the first change of horses she leaned over in her seat and dozed despite the rattling.

Pen studied the horribly awkward angle of her neck, and slipped across to supply himself as a human pillow. She turned over and curled up with her head on his thigh, with a wheeze that he was pleased to take as gratitude. He let his hand slide over her torso to hold her secure, rewarded when she slipped into a deeper sleep. He alternated between staring out the window at the bony countryside, and regarding the unbony woman in his lap. Profoundly loyal she was, to those few she took as her own; her brother, her mother. Pen had no idea how he was ever to get himself on that short roster. By an effort doomed to be unappreciated, he kept his free hand from playing with her tumbled hair, black and shining as the best fresh ink.

When the coach halted at the next change and the sharp voices of the ostlers echoed outside, she stirred at last, with a sinuous stretch and an enchanting purring noise. She lay a moment in muddled relaxation, fingers clutching him like a real pillow; then, alas, her disordered world crashed back in upon her. She jerked upright with a yelp, clipping Pen's chin with her head in passing, and flinched to the other side of the seat.

"Ow," Pen complained mildly, rubbing his jaw. She stared at him a little wildly for a moment, and he added, "You fell asleep. Looked like you needed it."

"Oh," she said, partly regaining her composure. She rubbed her head in turn and managed an "Oh, sorry. Strange dream."

"No matter."

They both descended for the usual visit to the coaching inn's privy, a turn about the yard, and hastily quaffed purchased drinks, in this place beakers of over-watered wine. By the time they reboarded the vehicle, she'd put herself to rights again, seeming better for her nap.

"We've hardly had time to talk about how we are to explain ourselves to people," she said as they settled to endure the next stage. "I don't think we can pass as brother and sister." She glanced doubtfully across at his pale cool blondness, back to her own terracotta Cedonian warmth, and pulled straight a stray black lock, glancing up at it before letting it curl back. "Not even half-siblings. And I'd rather we weren't husband and wife."

"Yes," said Pen wryly, "you told me that once before."

She bit her lip, flushing. "You know what I mean."

"I do," he sighed. Teasing Nikys had its charms, but now was so clearly not the time. "Keep it simple, I expect. Don't say anything. People will make up their own explanations."

"So I fear," she murmured ruefully.

"You don't have to care, and they don't either. We're just passing through. While being your husband would give me an unassailable right to protect you, being your courier will serve in most cases." He hesitated. "As always, it's best not to mention my calling. To anyone. Not even to your friends, unless some urgent need arises." His sorcerer's Temple braids were hidden in the very bottom of his medical case, though he had brought no white robes. If it ever came to the valise being violently turned out, it was likely the assailant would be discovering Pen's abilities in more direct ways.

Penric contemplated the unknowns ahead of them. He'd studied the duke's maps last night, planning their route much more logically than their prior lurching flight, but what of all the human hazards?

"This Master Bosha you keep mentioning," he said slowly. "The castrate secretary. Is he a slave, then?" Both those Cedonian customs were alien to Pen's mountainous home country, a land of obstreperous small freeholders scraping out their livings from soil almost as rocky, though damper and colder, than Cedonia's.

"Very much not!" said Nikys, sounding surprised by the question. "Although he has been a servant of the Xarre family for a long time. Since Tanar was six, she once told me, and she's now twenty, so over fourteen years."

Pen did a little historical arithmetic. "That would have been about the year the present emperor took power." Bloodily, although that was the way in Thasalon as often as not. "Any connection?"

"I know nothing about Surakos Bosha's family background. It was a very disrupted year in the capital." Nikys frowned in thought. "I don't think he's low-born. He had a good education somewhere. There are hints he was once one of those men of good family who are cut by choice, to improve their chances of rising very high in the imperial bureaucracy."

Pen made an effort not to cross his legs. "That's more dedication to a career than I would have. Although there is a group of Temple singers in Lodi who have also freely chosen to be made castrates, consecrated to their craft and their god. Male sopranos. I've heard them sing twice, at festivals there. Hauntingly beautiful. I admit, I would not argue their calling with them." Because song, being a gift of the spirit, was considered a most acceptable offering to the gods.

Nikys nodded. "Some do that in Thasalon as well. I don't think that's what he came from, though. He's no soprano." She stared across at Pen in an unsettling manner. "I thought he was the strangest man I ever met, until I met you."

Pen cleared his throat, restraining himself from pursuing that comparison.

But Nikys went on unprompted. "He's still the palest, not even excepting you. He's a true albino. Like a white rabbit, or white horse."

*A gelding, perhaps*, murmured Des, all fake innocence. *I wonder who rides him?*

*Tasteless, Des.* Or had that been Mira? *Hush, I need to hear this.*

"His hair is pure white. At night his skin seems bleached like the moon, although it's rather pink in bright light. Which he avoids—he burns in the sun worse than you do." She frowned in speculation at Pen. "Do you suppose the people in your home country could be part albino?"

"Not as far as I know," said Pen. "Because real albinos do turn up, as rarities, I have heard, and they are considered just as odd there. If not as sunburned."

Pen tried to picture a man who would take up a tender trade as a wealthy young lady's private secretary. Plump, probably—he'd heard cut men were prone to run to fat as they aged—rabbity, maybe timid and twitchy. Odd. Well, he'd deal with the fellow when he came to him.

"What more can you tell me of Lady Tanar?" he went on. Because they would be wagering their lives, as well as their cause, upon her goodwill and power to aid them. "Should we be looking to her mother for command of resources? Did Lady Xarre favor Adelis's suit? Or would she thwart her daughter's dangerous charity, if she finds out?" This was no girls' prank they were engaged in, but something perilously close to treason. With all the gruesome Cedonian penalties that applied, if discovered.

Nikys pressed her lips together in disturbing doubt. "That's a decision I'd leave to Tanar. I've only met Lady Xarre the once. She's long widowed, and lives retired now, seldom leaving her estate. Doesn't dabble in the Thasalon court, even though she has the rank for it. I understand she's very active in ordering her financial affairs, through a troop of trusted retainers. She makes Tanar her apprentice in all her doings, since Tanar is her only heir, which seems to me very much more to the point than making her learn embroidery." Nikys paused as if to consider this. "Tanar thinks so, too."

"And did Adelis?"

"I don't think Adelis was quite aware of it, never having been a soldier's wife." As widowed Nikys once had been, aye? "But she would have been very well fitted for managing all the tasks of his own wide holdings." She scowled. "Before he was stripped of them." And then, "Our other mother—Adelis's lady mother—did such for our father."

Since all of Penric's worldly goods could fit on six mules, and had, this was not work he knew. He supposed it was much like his older brother Rolsch's duties back at Jurald Court, multiplied by several. Or several dozen, it sounded like.

Pen wondered if it would be better to route around these untrusted allies and proceed directly to the island. Somehow.

*Local knowledge is never to be scorned,* murmured Des, or with luck Ruchia. *If not to be relied upon blindly, either.*

That was assuming Nikys's mother was actually on Limnos, and the whole thing not a trap from the beginning.

*If it is a trap,* said Des serenely, *it was made to fit Adelis. Not us.*

Des, it seemed, was much less terrified by this return to Cedonia than he was. Of course, a demon could not be killed, exactly. *Are you saying I would be a surprise?*

*Oh, Pen. You have been a surprise from the beginning.*

# IV

THE DWINDLING late-summer light ended their first day of travel much too soon, Nikys thought. Pushing through the darkness on Orbas's difficult hill roads would be so slow as to not be worth it, Penric persuaded her, and they should not arrive at their hardest stretch over the border mountains already exhausted. What passed for coaching inns in Orbas were more primitive than those they'd encountered in Cedonia, and Penric in his role of her courier was hard-pressed to get her a private chamber, but Nikys scarcely cared. She'd have slept in the stable if she'd had to. They took the road again in the damp gray of dawn.

Even Penric was slow to come awake in the initial hour, but he soon glued himself to the window like the foreign sightseer he wasn't, asking questions about the passing countryside Nikys mostly couldn't answer. But when they'd resettled themselves in the coach after the first change, his boundless curiosity took another turn.

"Were both your mothers called Madame Arisaydia? Because I'd think that would be confusing." At her stare, he added, "In my country men only have one wife at a time. Officially, anyway. Although I suppose my mother and my sister-in-law shared out their name for some while before my mother died, and you were always having to clarify which one you meant."

"No," said Nikys. "Adelis's mother was Lady Arisaydia, or Lady Florina. Or Florie, to my father. Concubines keep their patronymics. So my mother was always Idrene Gardiki." *Is*, Nikys fiercely vowed. "Though my surname was Arisaydia, of course, before I was married." She frowned out the other window at the vexingly endless rocky hillsides. "My other brother was Gardiki for just a brief time before he was adopted by his grandmother's family, and after that he was Rodoa. Ikos Rodoa." She prayed he was well out of this. With luck, he'd be working somewhere on the far northern peninsula, and would not even have heard of their mother's arrest. This dangerous mess was much too far over his head for him to mix into.

A startled silence, then Pen said, "Who? What? I thought you and Adelis were the old general's only children."

"That's right." She glanced across at him, trying to decide if his expression was dismay or just surprise. "To be fair, I didn't know he existed either, till he came to my father's funeral. My mother never spoke of him because the separation had made her sad, she said, but when he reached his majority he could come on his own, and did. He visited us a few times after that, when his travels took him nearby. He's a master bridgebuilder, now, and goes to work all over Cedonia. For various towns, usually."

"Uh ... older brother? Surely not younger. Was your mother a young widow, too?"

Nikys smiled. "Not exactly. Although only by ill-chance. She was actually the daughter of one of my father's senior officers. She fell in love with a junior officer. The way one does, I suppose." Nikys tried to remember if she'd ever been so smitten by the army lads at that age. She'd never been that carried away, to be sure. Firmly, she kept herself from glancing at Penric's long, blond, and entirely unmilitary elegance. "They meant to marry, or so she said. It likely would not have been opposed even though her family thought her too young, but he was ordered out suddenly to, gods, I don't even remember which clash she told me, and killed in the battle. He was the Rodoa family's only son—only surviving child, I believe—so when my mother turned out to be pregnant, they took her in. Except, although the grandmother desperately wanted the boy, she didn't really want my mother—they didn't even offer to make her a ghost bride."

"I don't know what that is." A short hesitation. "Oh, thank you Des. They really do that?" He turned to Nikys. "Marry people to dead people?"

"Not often. It's a sort of adoption, as much as anything. If they'd had the ceremony—it's sometimes held at the graveside, but more often with a memori tablet—my mother would have become a daughter-in-law of the house. With certain rights of support and inheritance, among other things. Without that, she was used more as an unpaid servant. It was a very uncomfortable time for her, I gather. So after Ikos was weaned, and my father sent Lady Florina to convey his offer—really, their offer—my mother let herself be persuaded, even though it meant giving up her firstborn. Grandmother Rodoa was all for it, naturally."

Penric's face scrunched up as he wrapped his mind around this bit of family history. "It sounds complicated."

Nikys shrugged. "I suppose. But Ikos was why my father and Lady Florina became so interested in my mother—proof that she could bear children, which was what they both wanted. It all seemed to work out for everyone in the end, somehow. Certainly for me."

He smiled crookedly, giving a conceding nod. "An excellent result."

She tried not to be warmed by the compliment. She was *using* this man, this sorcerer, she reminded herself. She couldn't remember, in the chaos of the past two days, if she'd ever offered him any payment or reward for risking his life in this frightening venture. Even soldiers were paid, after all—quite insistent upon it if the army payroll was in arrears, as it so often was.

She dismissed her conscience, ruthlessly. She was ready to use anything and anyone to hand, if it would help her to carry out this rescue.

And thus what, exactly, was her ground for scorning his lewd use of Mira, or Mira's lewd use of him, to get them all past the border before?

The courtesan hadn't just been a costume, or a ploy. She was in some strange sense still alive, inside his crowded head. And always would be, along with the rest of her barely understood sisterhood. To convert Nikys's *I fear they know too much* to *I hope they know enough* had only taken one cryptic note.

She settled back with a sigh, willing the team to trot faster.

At the western end of the main road from Vilnoc, service for coaches terminated at the grubby garrison town that guarded the three-way border between Orbas, Cedonia, and Grabyat to the southwest. Adelis had passed through here just a few weeks ago with Jurgo's troop, in aid of the ally in that next realm. Nikys did not dare ask after him. Finding the army post and its commander, Nikys and Penric presented the sealed letter from the duke commanding all aid be given to them, which proved to be a sergeant, a muleteer, and four sturdy animals.

Another dawn start brought them, by dusk, to the broken spine of the last ridge between Orbas and Cedonia, where they camped for the night. Neither the sergeant nor his assistant asked any questions; Nikys gathered they were used often as guides to slip spies over the border.

"It's likely a regular business," murmured Penric. "You wonder if the empire uses the same route, or if they have their own favorite backdoor for their agents."

Adelis might have known.

Nikys could see why they'd waited for daylight for the next leg, emphasis on the leg as they were forced to dismount and lead the mules over the worst ledges. There was no breath left for conversation. They really couldn't have taken this route the other way three months ago, when Penric was still recovering from the injury to his heart; another point, Nikys grudgingly conceded, to Mira.

In the late afternoon, they paused in their equally rugged descent for the sergeant and the muleteer to scout ahead and be sure the military road, along which Imperial soldiers ran regular patrols, was temporarily unpeopled. It proved a bare cart-track. They skittered across, the muleteer coming behind to blot out their prints, and worked their way as quickly as possible down out of sight.

Nightfall brought them to a village where they could hire horses from an incurious farmer, whom Nikys thought likely a retired soldier, anyone's guess from which army. After the briefest introduction, with names notably absent, and the purchase of some grain, the sergeant, the muleteer, and their animals faded away into the darkness, not lingering to be seen and reported by less indifferent eyes. This time Nikys and Penric really slept the night in the stable, and were grateful for it.

Another long day's ride downhill brought them to the first good coach road north of the border, which ran on west to Thasalon. They dismissed their guide and his horses with a double fee, half for the mounts and half for the silence. A larger town and a busier inn allowed them to take two adjoining rooms, wash, and change into their next set of clothes and new personas.

After their late supper, Penric bade Nikys a polite goodnight and left her to lock the connecting door behind him. She sat staring numbly at it for a while, too exhausted to stand up after three solid days of grueling riding. This was, she realized, the first and possibly last time she would be alone with the sorcerer. With the man. The most wasted opportunity ever . . .

The coach-hire the next morning seemed to care only that their coin was good, which thanks to Jurgo's generous purse it was, and to get them on their way as efficiently and lucratively as possible. They would reach the hinterlands of Thasalon by sundown. Still unremarked.

While not having to stop and let Penric steal them funds from local temples was certainly a boon, this round, Nikys suspected the return journey might not run so smoothly.

# V

IN THE MOONLESS SHADOWS, Penric looked up and down the long wall that surrounded what Nikys claimed was the Xarre estate a few miles east of Thasalon. He hoped she was right in her identification; all the walls in this suburban area had looked alike to him. They'd dismissed their coach half a mile back, to conceal their destination from the curious postilion, and it had made a long, nervous trudge in the gloom.

He extended his hand to the lock on the postern gate, and thought, *Des.*

The heavy iron mechanism fell open to this well-practiced magic. Pen held the thick plank door ajar for Nikys, and she hoisted their luggage and slipped inside. Pen closed it as silently as possible after them.

Pen concealed their cases behind a healthy flowering bush, outlier of the extensive garden. "Can you see well enough not to trip?" he whispered.

"Not really," Nikys murmured back. He reached for her hand and led her off down the winding paths that were not dark to him.

There were supposed to be guards, she'd told him, if more like caretakers than soldiers, and dogs let loose at night. No sign of the first, but within minutes a pair of the second came bounding up, snarling. A quick tap of nerve-tweak stopped their alarm-barks, followed up barely soon enough by a brief shamanic geas to persuade them that these intruders were not enemies, but the best of friends. So they were slammed into not by an attack, but by an attack of sociability. Tails wagged like cudgels, thumping into Pen's thighs as the beasts swirled around them. A couple of haunches of beef might have worked as well as pacifiers, Pen thought, had he possessed them.

"These aren't dogs, they're *ponies*," gasped Pen, fighting for his balance.

"Mastiffs," nodded Nikys. "Ew, stop licking me, you huge thing!"

Pen fended off tongues the size of washing cloths, and a miasma of slime and dog-breath. With this unwanted, but at least silent, honor guard panting around them, they made their way to another long, blank wall, the exterior of the residence proper. In the usual Cedonian style, the manse was built around an inner court, giving a cold stone shoulder to the outside. But it was three floors high, and a lot larger than Pen was used to seeing. There were neither windows nor entries on this side of the ground floor, locked or no, but the stories above were pierced with a number of long doors opening onto wooden balconies. Golden candlelight filtered through a few of the delicate carved lattices.

Nikys squinted into the shadows and counted down the doors. "That one," she whispered, pointing up to one of the glowing screens. "Second floor."

The wall was entirely without handy ladders or climbing vines. "You do know my powers don't extend to flying, right?"

"You were a mountaineer. You said?" Her look up at him was far too expectant.

"I was younger. And lighter. And stupider." Nonetheless, he approached and studied the problem, mapping out the slight cracks and irregularities in the stuccoed surface. *Maybe.* Although a stone tossed up against the shutters might do to draw attention, he'd be happier to assure himself first it was the right attention.

"Could you stand on my shoulders to get a start up? You're not that heavy a man . . . "

Pen disliked this picture, but there seemed no other way. He had her brace against the wall, planning his leap to linger on this prop as briefly as possible. He took a deep breath and bounded, one, two— he could feel her straining body dip beneath his feet—and just caught one hand-grip on the balcony's edge. Then another. A foot-shove against the wall, alarming when a bit of old stucco gave way. Then heave *up* and over the balustrade.

He landed crouching as quietly as he could, then unfolded to tiptoe over and try to peek through the lattice. A well-appointed sitting room, it looked like, the scent of expensive beeswax candles, but he saw no identifiable figures.

He tapped cautiously on the carving. "Hello?"

Only Des allowed him to evade, narrowly, the silent thrust of a thin knife blade through the lattice.

He yelped, and yelped again as the door slammed open, bashing him hard in the nose. A swift figure, a swirl of fabrics, and he was spun about. A wiry arm snaked up through one of his own, yanking back and immobilizing it, and the blade snapped to his neck.

And stopped, although pressing alarmingly into his skin. A hot huff of breath puffed against his ear.

*Don't move!* said Des, redundantly. *That blade is poisoned!*

All of Penric's carefully rehearsed introductions flew wide into the night, and he gasped out only, "I'm with Nikys!"

A hesitation, thank the Bastard, though the grip didn't slacken. "On your knees," came an edgy tenor voice, sounding as sharp and dangerous as the blade. "Face the light."

Pen descended at once, free hand going up palm-out in surrender. Or prayer, either one just now. The steel grasp released him. Quick steps circled him, and Pen looked up past fine linen trousers and a fall of an embroidered silk outer robe to a beardless, scowling face as pale as the absent moon. Thick white hair was drawn back from the brow in some queue or braid.

A female voice sounded from within the chamber: "Sura, what is it?"

"An intruder. It seems."

"Visitors, I assure you!" protested Pen.

"You pick an odd way of presenting yourself."

"We are on an odd errand."

The other leaf of the lattice swung open. "Stay inside, Lady Tanar!" the man commanded.

*Ah*, said Des. *At least we seem to be in the right place. Good.*

Disregarding this, the woman emerged. Slender, a little shorter than Nikys, also hung about with rich fabrics, loosed in the cooling late-summer night. She evaded the man's half-hearted attempt to strongarm her back within, instead tripping to the balcony rail and peering over into the shadows. "Nikys?"

"Tanar?"

"I thought you were in Orbas!"

"We were. We got your note to Adelis. And traveled as quickly as we could. Can you come and let me in before your dogs drown me in drool? We probably should not be seen before we can talk."

"Oh, dear. Stay there, I'll be right down."

Lady Tanar darted back inside. The white-haired man made a futile noise of protest, half jerking in her wake, but then turned back to guard his prisoner, the unknown threat. He'd recognized Nikys's voice, apparently. Pen tried to feel reassured by that.

"Can I get up now?" he asked humbly.

The man thought about this for a moment. "Slowly."

Pen complied, entering the sitting chamber at his gesture. One pale hand made the knife disappear inside his robe, and the man rolled his shoulders, allowing his murderous air to dissipate.

*He's carrying four blades concealed*, Des reported. *And every one is poisoned.* She considered. *Drugged, anyway. They are not all the same.*

In the better light from the mirrored wall sconces, Pen could see the man's irises were a thin carmine; likely they showed pink when the pupil contracted in daylight. His pinched eyebrows, too, were white. His face was fine-boned and regular, if tense. An old scar puckered the left side of his mouth, giving an impression of a permanent smirk, belied just now by the downturned right. His snowy braided queue, tied off with colored silk, reached halfway to his waist.

*My word*, said Des. *That one's almost as pretty as you, Pen.*

Pen ignored this. But he bid a glum goodbye to his prior mental image of the pudgy, timid eunuch secretary, swapping it out for this overdressed white snake of an assassin standing taut before him. "Master Bosha, I presume?"

A short nod. "And who are you?"

"My name is Penric. I've taken the duties of Madame Khatai's courier for this journey."

"Do you know what this journey is in aid of?"

"Yes."

The carmine eyes narrowed. "I see." He reached into his robe—Pen tensed—but the manicured hand emerged holding only a fine cotton handkerchief. Ironed and scented. He handed it blandly across to Pen. "Don't drip on the carpet."

"Ah. Thank you." Pen mopped at his upper lip, wet with blood. His price for the shamanic compulsion on the dogs, but let Bosha assume it was from the violent encounter with the door; maybe he'd feel guilty. Likely it was the result of both. The cloth grew saturated before the trickle stopped, at about the same time the door onto the courtyard gallery opened and Lady Tanar slid through, followed by Nikys.

Nikys pressed her hand to her breast and sighed out relief as Tanar closed the door and locked it, as though they had reached a safe refuge after their arduous journey. Pen was not so confident.

Urgently, Tanar turned to Nikys. "How is Adelis? Where is Adelis? We heard he was blinded in Patos, and then we heard he'd turned up somehow in Orbas, and none of it made *sense*."

Nikys took a breath as if to answer this, but then looked imploringly at Penric.

He managed, "The seething vinegar was inadequately applied, and thanks to his sister's good nursing, he recovered his sight. As soon as that was apparent, he fled to Orbas to save the emperor's agents from coming back and trying again." The official story. That Penric had rebuilt the young general's half-boiled eyes with the most delicate and difficult week of uphill medical magics he had ever brought off was not something he wished to confide. Here or anywhere.

Nikys's mouth compressed in silent disagreement with this reticence, but she yielded to his tacit wishes. "Duke Jurgo employed Adelis at once, and has sent him off to command his expedition against the Rusylli incursion in Grabyat. Adelis having defeated the Rusylli once before, to no imperial thanks. I can only hope Jurgo will do him better. He could hardly do him worse."

Bosha's lopsided lip seemed to twist in a real smirk, contemplating the gratitude of princes. He stood back with his arms folded, his attention never straying far from Penric.

"Adelis was weeks gone by the time your note came to my hand," Nikys went on. "In exchange for not distracting him with the news, the duke supported Penric's and my journey to try to get our mother out of Cedonia, and then to Orbas with me. Somehow." She looked back and forth between Tanar and Bosha. "I don't know how much aid you can give without danger to yourselves, but whatever help you can spare, I beg it of you now."

"Of course!" cried Tanar, notably not seconded by Bosha. "You poor dear. All the way from Orbas, so swiftly? Here, you must be exhausted, come, sit. You should drink something." She looked more doubtfully at Penric. "You too, ah, Master Penric." A vague courtesy title, flattering if he were a mere servant. Pen didn't think she took him for a mere servant. But he followed Nikys to the small round table with chairs placed to the side of the room, suitable for two people to take a light repast. Bosha, without comment, set two more chairs around it, brought a carafe of sweet red wine and a pitcher of drinking water from a sideboard, and served out glass goblets of the mixture all around.

*That's not poisoned, is it, Des?* Pen asked in worry.

*Not so far,* she returned darkly. *I'll stand sentinel.*

Tanar touched her lips, and asked in a lower tone, "Was he terribly burned?"

Pen watched Nikys struggle not to answer with the truth, *Hideously.* "It was not good. He was in dreadful pain for a while. But the scars are healing mostly flat, and confined to the upper half of his face, and the redness is supposed to fade in time. Except for his eyes; they didn't come back brown. They are a kind of garnet color now. It unnerves people, but he says that's fine, given his profession."

Tanar's own gaze flicked to Bosha and away. "That's all right. I've always thought red was a lovely color for eyes."

Bosha spread his hand on his heart and offered her an ironic seated bow, which she dismissed with an amused quirk of her lips.

"And if he has already taken up a new command, he must have made an excellent recovery." She smiled in relief, sitting more upright.

"I thought it miraculous, myself," said Nikys, steadfastly.

*No remark, Pen?* murmured Des, preening a trifle.

*Hush.*

Nikys turned more intently to Tanar. "What more have you found out about my mother? Does she know what happened to Adelis and me? Is she still on Limnos? Has anything worse chanced?"

"And how did you find out about her?" Pen put in.

Tanar glanced at Bosha much the way Nikys had lately glanced at Pen, seeking some permission. So, the two shared their secrets?

Bosha, after a contemplative sip of watered wine, chose to answer Pen: "My elder sister is an acolyte of the Daughter's Order on Limnos. I visit her now and then. She was thus aware of Lady Tanar's interest in General Arisaydia, so when Madame Gardiki was brought in, she sent me a private note."

"I didn't think men were allowed to enter the Order's precincts," said Pen, confused.

Bosha cast him a head-tilt, and said dryly, "That is correct."

Pen gulped back an apology, in a dim notion that it would just make things worse. *Likely so,* murmured Des. He flushed slightly. Bosha seemed more grimly amused than offended at his discomfiture.

Bosha added to Nikys, "Your mother is still at the Order. Unharmed as far as we know. We haven't followed up with further inquiries, because such are dangerous should they fall into the wrong hands."

Penric wondered just whose hands those were, and what weapons they held. He supposed he'd find out in due course. Preferably not the hard way.

Bosha addressed the air between Nikys and Penric: "So what is your plan for freeing her?"

Nikys scrubbed her fingers through her curls, in disarray after the day's travel. "All my mind has been fixed on just getting here. We get out to the island somehow, get her out somehow. Penric thinks we should make the return journey by sea, being already there."

"By choice not on a Cedonian ship," Pen put in. "Adriac, with luck"—Nikys shot him a sharp look—"but it will depend on what we can find most swiftly to hand."

"Will that be the safest course?" said Tanar doubtfully. "I mean... storms. Pirates."

"Storms I can do nothing about," Penric granted. "Pirates are no problem." Once they drew close enough, anyway. Letting a chaos demon loose to do her worst in some other ship's rigging than the one they were on ought to have remarkable results.

*Oh, yes,* murmured Des, in gleeful anticipation; Pen gathered she'd be disappointed if pirates *didn't* show up.

Nikys nodded untroubled understanding at this last. Tanar and Bosha stared, startled.

After a moment, Bosha went on, "So, you arrive, you leave, and in between, what? A miracle occurs? Your plan seems to be missing its middle."

"I have never been to Thasalon before," said Pen, carefully not saying, *You are its middle.* He suspected Bosha suspected this. "I must rely on Nikys and local knowledge for this part, but I'll do all I can in support of her."

"Penric smuggled Adelis and me out of Cedonia to Orbas the first time," Nikys put in, "and he'd never been there before either. He is not without skills." Of course, not saying what kind rather left this assertion dangling in air.

Tanar nodded, accepting this without question. Bosha as plainly did not.

Tanar rubbed her delicate neck. Her girlish figure could not compete with Nikys's lush build, but her shining hair, braided up on her head in a complex weave with a glimmer of pearls, had reddish highlights in the candle-glow that Pen thought might show auburn in daylight, and her eyes were a clear hazel tending to the gold side. Fine skin, good teeth. It seemed it was not just her fortune that had attracted Adelis to her, and besides, at the time of his late courtship, his wealth had matched hers. Penric had more trouble imagining what had attracted Tanar to Adelis.

*Oh, come, Pen,* Des scoffed. *Adelis is a very compelling man. Profoundly irritating at moments, I'll give you that, but when not being an ass, and you must allow he's had a great deal to throw him off-balance of late, ladies might find him quite magnetic.*

*Even disfigured as he is now? Stripped of his Cedonian properties?*

*Of course. Really, after eleven years with us, I should think you would understand women better.*

Lady Tanar still seemed to care about him, anyway, which was entirely to their benefit.

*More interestingly, in two years no other suitor has nipped in and carried her off,* Des pointed out. *I can't imagine it's for lack of trying, not with her purse.*

Tanar placed a small, decisive fist upon the table. "It's plain we can do nothing more tonight. I think it's best if you stay right in here with us, Nikys, concealed. You can sleep with me. Sura can find a place for your, um, traveling companion." She eyed Pen more doubtfully, but gestured at them both. "Is this all you came with?"

Pen thought of the duke's coins, sewn in hems or otherwise concealed about both their persons, but said only, "We left our luggage in the outer garden."

"Won't there be servants about?" asked Nikys. "Can they be trusted?"

"Sura will keep them out from underfoot," said Tanar, with an assured nod. "He generally does anyway." She rose, and the rest of them perforce followed.

"Best not to involve them yet," said Bosha. "That being the case, do show me to your belongings, Master Penric."

"Certainly, Master Bosha."

Bosha lit and took up a small glass candle lantern to guide Pen out into the darkened gallery. His footfalls moved soft across the boards, and Pen tried to match the quiet as he followed the eunuch down the end stairs, through a crooked passage, and to a door in the outer end wall, locked and barred for the night. Pen wondered if Nikys had brought them in this way, might he not have come so close to being knifed? He studied Bosha's pale braid, swinging down his back as they followed through what was no dark to Des, and gave it no better than even odds.

They wound through the garden to the concealing bush. Pen collected his medical case himself, and his other satchel, leaving Bosha to take up Nikys's valise. Bosha lifted it and gazed thoughtfully around.

"How did you gain entry through the outer wall?"

"Nikys knew of the postern door."

"It should have been locked."

"I'm good with locks."

"Is that so."

They'd just started back when the dogs came rushing up again. Still barkless, fortunately, although they managed a growl at Bosha, returned in kind. Enough of the geas lingered that they still fawned around Pen.

"Our dogs are not normally so useless, either," said Bosha, wading through them after his uninvited guest.

"Animals like me. And I think they recognized Nikys," Pen offered.

As the main house loomed before them, Bosha added in a cool tone, "You should not have been able to defeat that lock. Past the lock, you should not have slipped by the dogs. Past the dogs"—he turned his head—"you should not have been able to mount the balcony. On the balcony, you should not have been able to evade my knife. Yet you somehow did all of these things, Master Penric."

" . . . Madame Khatai did not choose me for her courier for no reason, sir."

"Hnh." Bosha added after a moment, "I quite dislike being troubled to be the last man between the hazards of the world and Lady Tanar. It takes the maids so much effort to scrub the blood out of the floorboards."

Was that a jest? Pen cleared his throat. "It's a rich estate. Are thieves a common problem for you here?"

Bosha shrugged. "Ordinary thieves are a task for the other retainers. Lady Xarre's mandate to me is more exclusive."

"Is her daughter Tanar under some special threat?"

"Say constant, rather. One too-persistent rejected suitor, last year, actually tried a more direct abduction. Why he thought he would gain forgiveness, after, I cannot imagine. Or that his hirelings would keep his secrets. We left the bodies at his front gate to be found in the morning. I believe he took the hint."

*Not a jest, then,* murmured Des. Pen would rather she didn't sound so pleased.

"I see," said Pen, wondering what hint he was supposed to be taking.

*Oh, I think it's quite clear,* said Des. . . . *You know, I'm beginning to like this fellow. If there are any markers for a child of the Bastard he has missed, I can't picture them. Now I am curious about his birth.*

*We're not asking, Des.*

Back in the sitting chamber, Bosha knocked on an adjoining door, evidently to the lady's bedchamber. Tanar opened it brightly, received Nikys's case, and bade them both a cheery goodnight. Pen could hear her and Nikys's voices, quietly speaking, as the door swung shut again. Bosha led to a matching door on the opposite inner wall, opening it to another bedchamber.

He lit a brace of candles, and Penric took in a carved writing table, shelves crammed with books and papers, chests and a wardrobe along the walls, a washstand, and a narrow bed piled with folded clothing. Bosha removed the garments perfunctorily to the tops of a couple of the chests, and gestured. "You can have my bed."

"Where will you sleep?"

"Where I usually do." He plucked nightclothes from a hook on the inside of the wardrobe and vanished back to the sitting room, shutting the door behind him.

Nonplussed, but mortally tired, Pen took advantage of the washstand, then changed into his own nightshirt. He poked briefly around the room. Bosha seemed to own a great deal more clothing than an average servant, much more finely made. The books and papers were too many to take in, but seemed mostly of a utilitarian nature—apparently, he really was Tanar's secretary. Among his other more disturbing duties. A number of drawers and chests were locked, which wouldn't have slowed Pen down had he further reason to pry.

Curious, and concerned because while the eunuch had put himself between Pen and Tanar, fair enough, he had also put himself between Pen and *Nikys*, Pen cracked the door to the sitting room and checked. Bosha, wearing a nightshirt of fine lawn, was just unrolling a wool-stuffed linen mattress down before Lady Tanar's door. An unsheathed short sword with a chased blade sat propped by the doorjamb.

*Is that one tainted too, Des?*

*Seems to be. I long to ask him what he is using, and how he compounds it. You ought to find that professionally interesting as well.*

*Do you think he brews up his own drugs?* Those locked chests were suddenly more interesting.

*Do you imagine he doesn't?*

A faint sound of feminine voices penetrated from the closed door beyond. Pen bet Bosha wasn't above putting his ear to it.

*Nor are you, Pen dear, but it seems the position is taken.*

Pen was too exhausted to fret further tonight. Judging that they were both about as sincere as two strange cats, he exchanged polite nods with Bosha and withdrew.

# VI

WHILE WAITING for the men to return with their baggage, Tanar drew Nikys into her bedchamber. She sat before her dressing table and began, a bit awkwardly, to take down her braids for the night.

"Shall I help you?" asked Nikys, moving behind her.

"Oh, would you please? Sura usually does it, but with you here he won't intrude."

"My pleasure." Nikys began to withdraw the pearl pins and drop them into the enameled bowl that Tanar shifted closer.

To watch Nikys, Tanar angled the glass mirror in its wooden arms and sat straight. "It's so good to see you well, though I'm sorry it took such a terrifying errand to bring you to me again. Adelis was the only one of my suitors with the wit to offer me a *sister*."

Nikys smiled, flattered. In their early acquaintance Tanar had looked up to her—ten years older and once married—as a fount of female wisdom on how men and women dealt with each other in the bedchamber. Nikys had eventually determined that this was not because Tanar had been left untutored, but rather that she was collecting intelligence from as many sources as possible. Preparing for her life's journey, like Penric studying Duke Jurgo's maps before they'd left Vilnoc. That Nikys had elected to be frank and clear, just as she would have wished for herself, had been much valued.

"Adelis..." Tanar began again more tentatively. "Do you know how he still feels about me? I wrote him a few times while he was on campaign, but received no reply."

"That's just Adelis," Nikys reassured her, beginning to unwind auburn braids. "He doesn't reply to me either when he's in the field, but I know he saves my letters." Now lost with the rest of their possessions. "He was hurried off to Patos so swiftly after the Rusylli campaign, with no triumphal celebration even offered in the capital. And then he had to master his new command. I think he was already starting to be wary. If he suspected trouble was coming down on him, he wouldn't have wanted to involve you."

Tanar's face set in a grave grimace. "I'm very afraid I might have been involved despite myself. Did you know Minister Methani's nephew, Lord Bordane, has been one of my more persistent suitors?"

Adelis had suspected that Methani's cabal, close around the emperor at court, had engineered his downfall by the subtle half-forged correspondence with the Duke of Adria. That was to say, Adelis's letter to Adria had been forged; the return reply had been condemningly real, and guided forthwith into his enemies' outstretched hands.

"It's a hideous thought," continued Tanar, "but as soon as I had heard what had happened to Adelis in Patos, I wondered how much might have been a ploy to get him permanently out of Lord Bordane's way." She raised quietly stricken eyes to Nikys's, in the mirror.

Nikys considered this, watching the guilty fear fleeting in Tanar's face. "That might have been a factor," she said hesitantly, "but it certainly wasn't that alone. Adelis and Methani had been clashing at court for years before this. Adelis's recent success against the Rusylli, and so his rising popularity with his troops, are far more likely to have set this off. I can't speak for Lord Bordane, but I guarantee Methani's more worried about threats to the emperor from a potential usurper than about his nephew's love-life." Imagined threats, curse him—all of this horror done for fears made of vapor and slander. "The latter might simply have been a bonus, from their point of view." Granted Methani would not be immune to the appeal of bringing Tanar's wealth into his clan.

Tanar took this in, and slowly nodded. More relieved by this honesty than by some airy denial, and no wonder Nikys liked her. Had Adelis appreciated her character, as well as her lively beauty?

"Is Lord Bordane still persistent?" Nikys took up the hairbrush from the table and began untangling Tanar's tresses.

Tanar made a moue. "Among others. Up until my last birthday Mother held them all off for me, playing the rigid guardian, but now I'm at my legal majority, they know I could consent on my own. They try all kinds of tricks to get me alone to hear their pleas. Sura is most annoyed." Her puff of disdain transmuted to a purr of pleasure as Nikys changed to longer, more soothing strokes. "Oh, that's almost as good as Sura."

That a eunuch servant acted sometimes as a lady's maid was no very unusual thing. Tanar's morning habit of brushing and braiding Bosha's white hair in turn had been more startling, when Nikys had glimpsed it on her last overnight visit. It was evidently a custom lingering from when Tanar had been a tyrannical six-year-old princess of the house, treating her new guardian, to his bemusement, as something between a playmate, a large doll, and a compliant slave. Most other innocent intimacies from that era had fallen away with Tanar's more conscious maturity, to Bosha's silent regret, Nikys gathered.

"Do none of your other suitors tempt you?"

Tanar shrugged. "I confess, your brother was the first man to really do so."

"It's become rather hopeless," Nikys observed, reluctantly conscientious. "It will be long before he can rebuild his fortune, if ever. You are anchored to Cedonia by your own possessions, and he cannot cross the border."

"Politics change." Her soft mouth set mulishly. "I can afford to wait."

"Do you want him to wait? Should I tell him so?" Nikys hesitated, though her hands kept moving. "Do you love him that much?"

Tanar, after a moment, returned candor for candor. "I'm not sure. Setting all the pretty poetry aside as beguiling blither, because I've never met anyone who seems to actually think like that, I don't know what love is supposed to be. I care that he should be well. The thought of him being injured or killed distresses me. When we had the news of his blinding"—a shudder passed through her—"I cried and carried on till poor Sura was quite alarmed. Of *course* I knew enough to compose myself before I left our chambers." She tossed her head in some remembered irritation.

After a few more strokes, she added in a lower voice, "I thought for a while, before Patos, that I might use *waiting for Adelis* as a stick to fend off the others, but not if it could call down more danger on his head. Because assassins can cross borders where armies cannot."

Nikys sighed, unable to gainsay this, but pointed out, "Given the hazards of his profession, I think that should be one of your lesser worries." And, more thoughtfully: "It might be better for a soldier's wife not to love too much."

Tanar's gaze sought hers in the mirror, just obliquely enough to ask: "Do you still miss your husband Kymis?"

Nikys drew a cool breath through her nostrils. So many memories, and the good ones, in a strange way, almost more painful than the bad, so that she preferred to put them all away in the same locked box. "Not so much now. The present drives out the past, a little more each day."

A knock sounded at the chamber door, and Tanar went to receive Nikys's valise from the hands of her servant, whom she bade a fond goodnight. Both women broke off to share out the washstand and don nightgowns. Tanar's spacious bed seemed the most inviting road-weary Nikys had ever seen, and she fell into it gratefully as Tanar blew out the candles.

In the darkness, Tanar remarked, "Your courier fellow, Penric—Daughter's blessings, what a fetching young man. I've not seen that color of hair or eyes except among the emperor's southern-island guard, and nothing like so bright."

"Not so young," said Nikys. "He's thirty." *And it's the Bastard's blessings. Theologically speaking. Maybe that explains it all...*

"Really? The same age as you?" Tanar seemed to mull this. In a tone of sly humor, she murmured, "Do you fancy him?"

Nikys made a neutral noise.

"Because you're a widow, as free as a woman can be. I don't suppose there's any insurmountable barrier of rank between you." An envious sigh. "And he looked as if he liked you. I quite think you could have him, if you wanted him," she rippled on in cheerful, grating speculation. "Do you know very much about his background?"

"I'm beginning to."

Tanar nudged her with her elbow. "Do tell?"

"Not my tale." Starting with, *He's the agent who carried the fatal letter from the duke of Adria*, descending through *He's a Temple sorcerer with ten other women's ghosts living inside his head*, and going on to *He could knock a dozen soldiers to the ground with a twitch of his eyebrow*, and Master Bosha *really* wouldn't like that news. Not to mention being a physician of near-miraculous powers too broken to practice his craft, a scholar in half-a-dozen languages with enough reputation to be coveted by the duke of Orbas, and a man so very, very far away from home. "It's complicated."

Tanar made a noise of disappointment, but pressed no further.

After a little, Tanar added, "I was so sorry I hadn't had a chance to meet Madame Gardiki. Adelis spoke of inviting your mother to Thasalon for the purpose, but then the Rusylli interrupted. And all the rest followed."

"Well. I can't say he's ever mentioned wanting to do so for any other woman. I think she would like you."

A hopeful sort of "Mm?"

"Do you really think we will be able to get her out?" All the worrisome unknowns still ahead of them made Nikys's head throb to contemplate. Bosha had placed his elegant thumb square upon the problem. *And then a miracle occurs.*

*No.* As they gained more information, they would find a route through. Somehow. Step by step. She couldn't work miracles, but she knew she could work *work*.

Tanar, Nikys thought, also hesitated between kindness and candor. Nikys could not tell which side Tanar imagined she was coming down on when she at last stated confidently, "Sura will know how."

Nikys let that sit unchallenged. She had put hope before prudence, or why else had she come this far? A few more breaths, in the dark. Hope or prayer, she offered up: "I always wanted to have a sister, too."

"Let us try to make that happen, then," said Tanar softly.

# VII

PEN WOKE to early morning light filtering through the shutters, and low voices from the sitting room. He snapped awake and went to check through the adjoining door, to see Bosha, barefoot and wearing his trousers but no shirt, turning away from the gallery door having received a large tray from some servant, which he set on the round table.

Bosha also sported a long, old scar running diagonally across his back, crooked from some crude sewing-up. Like the one on his lip? Pen didn't even need to say *Sight, Des,* to be given a deeper view. Sword cut, surely. As Bosha turned, raising his face sharply to Pen, Pen also marked a set of scars of the same age on his arms. *Defensive wounds, would you say, Des?*

*Oh, aye.*

Even inured by his anatomical training, it seemed rude to Pen to glance below the man's waistband, but Des had no such inhibitions. The significant scar there seemed older, surgical and clean. No signs, as Pen had for an instant feared, of being relic of some brutal battlefield mutilation, as sometimes happened. Bosha was otherwise intact, not always the case either, the more ruthless and complete cuttings leading to incontinence and those ugly jokes about stinking court eunuchs. Of which Des, partly through Mira but largely through Vasia, one of Des's old Cedonian riders, knew many, and *I don't want to hear them, Des.*

*Suit yourself,* Des sniffed. *But all that we know, you'll know in the end.*

*Not while I have to look the man in the face.* He added no softening courtesies to that one, and trusted Des took the hint.

Bosha, unaware of this uncanny inspection, gave Pen a nod by way of greeting, which Pen returned. He pulled on a long-sleeved linen shirt, gathered at the wrists into ruffles, and added as his somewhat bed-rumpled head emerged, "Let the ladies know the tea is here. I'll be back shortly. Don't answer the door." He padded out barefoot, face tight with thought.

Pen went back to Bosha's bedchamber-that-wasn't and quickly dressed himself, before going to tap on the sitting room's opposite door. Tanar poked her head out, received the news about the tea with sunny pleasure, and went back in. Light feminine voices and mysterious rattling-about preceded, eventually, the emergence of the women. Nikys, Pen noted, looked very fine first thing in the morning. And less tense and tired today than on most of the other mornings of their journey, good.

Nikys wore her day garb, Tanar a pink concoction that Pen, or rather, Des, decoded as a dressing-gown, not some fanciful court wear. Only two teacups had arrived with the pot and covered plates and basket, so Pen adroitly evaded sitting lest Lady Tanar feel compelled to try to give up her cup to her other guest.

The social dilemma was solved in a few minutes when Bosha returned with spare cups hooked on the fingers of one hand and a larger pot in the other. Three cups, not two, Pen noted as they were dealt out. The plates and basket proved to contain new-baked rolls, slices of soft white cheese, boiled eggs, olives, and fresh grapes, in sufficient abundance to share around without constraint. Also some of those ghastly dried fish blocks, which Pen avoided and everyone else seemed to think were food. Practical munching replaced conversation for a little.

Bosha rose immediately at a firm rap on the chamber door, seeming unsurprised, though Tanar jerked around in alarm. He opened the door only wide enough to admit the visitor, favoring her with that hand-over-the-heart bow—Pen could not decide if the gesture was ironic or sincere—and closed it with a click in her wake. Nikys and Tanar stood up respectfully, and Pen copied them.

Lady Xarre, without doubt. Tanar, Nikys had told Pen, was the child of the lady's later age much as Adelis had been for Lady Florina. It had been a second marriage for both her and Lord Xarre, who had died when Tanar was four or five. Something of a love match, Nikys had implied. No mention of non-surviving older siblings.

Pen's first impression of *elderly* was not quite correct, he judged. Lady Xarre was a finely dressed, slightly built older woman, to be sure, her graying hair wound up in jewel-pinned braids. The carved wooden cane upon which she leaned was not an affectation, but a needed prop, for Bosha took her other arm and supported her to his chair with no demur on her part.

Des's quick glance by Sight reported, *Very bad hip joints.* Back when he was training and practicing in Martensbridge, Pen had enjoyed some luck persuading such deteriorations to rebuild themselves from within by repeated small applications of uphill magic over weeks or months. Which wasn't time he was going to have, here, so there was no point thinking about it, right? He arranged his lips into a wary smile as she settled herself and looked up at him, and across at Nikys who, following Tanar, had sat again.

"My lady," murmured Bosha. "Madame Khatai you know; may I present to you Master Penric, her courier."

"Lady Xarre," Pen managed.

"Master Penric." At Lady Xarre's wave Pen, too, ducked a bow and reseated himself.

Bosha poured tea for his senior mistress and took a pose leaning against the wall with his arms folded. Pen had seen servants who could fade into the furniture doing that; Bosha really wasn't one of them.

"Surakos told me we had unexpected visitors," Lady Xarre began mildly.

Nikys lifted her chin. "Uninvited, I am afraid. You have my apologies, but under the circumstances I cannot offer regrets."

"Not entirely uninvited. It appears." She cast a pointed glance at Tanar, who squirmed, thus answering the question of whether that note to Nikys had been authorized by Lady Xarre or not. "But not unwelcome, I promise you." Hard to tell how sincere that was. "Given the circumstances. But we are truly in want of first-hand news of the events in Patos, and after." No mistaking the sincerity of that. "You know court rumors. What are not lies outright are invariably so muddled as to be almost worse."

Nikys nodded. She took a deep breath, and launched into a clipped description of the disaster in Patos starting from Adelis's arrest through to his return to Nikys's house, blinded and scalded. She left out the screaming and begging-for-death parts. Pen thought Lady Xarre and Bosha could fill in the lacunae.

"And where do you come into this tale, Master Penric?" Lady Xarre inquired of him.

Nikys bit her lip, caught between her promises to Pen and her unwillingness to lie to her hostess. Pen took up the banner: "Madame Khatai hired me on as a sort of male attendant to her injured brother. I was able to assist her in the sickroom, and later, when General Arisaydia's sight came back, on their flight to Orbas." Which wasn't even untrue.

"That must have been a difficult journey," said Lady Xarre.

"Yes," said Nikys. Pen was a little disappointed that she did not add, *We wouldn't have made it without Penric*, but he had after all asked her not to draw undue attention to him. No one to blame but himself.

Lady Xarre accepted this uninviting monosyllable with a purse of her lips, and did not press for details. She turned to Pen instead. "So much for Orbas. But why were you willing to come here to Thasalon, Master Penric?"

Pen thought over the impossible chaos his life had become ever since he'd first set foot in Cedonia, and decided to try a shorter truth. "I'm courting Madame Khatai."

Pen wished Nikys looked half so delighted with this statement as Tanar did. Lady Xarre smiled dryly. Pen couldn't tell if Bosha's expression was a smirk or just his lip scar.

"Have you known each other long, then?" asked Lady Xarre.

Nikys answered, "No. We just met in Patos."

Her voice still as pleasantly level, Lady Xarre said, "Do you trust him?"

Nikys's eyes squeezed closed, opened. "With my life, yes," she said, with gratifying firmness. "With my future... I'm still thinking."

Lady Xarre chuckled. "Wise girl." She drained her cup—Bosha bent to refill it—and leaned back in her chair. "I confess," she said, "I, too, would be happy to see Madame Gardiki safe with her son and daughter in Orbas. Could she somehow be magically transported there."

Pen flinched. Nikys coughed, and drank tea.

"Surakos reports you seemed a trifle unclear about the intervening steps."

Pen suspected Surakos had been a lot more blunt than that. "We actually hope to borrow his knowledge, as neither Madame Khatai nor I have even been to Limnos, and he has. Everything has to start with understanding both the physical layout and the human defenses. The Order's house cannot be as impenetrable as a prison or a fortress, if it hosts visitors and pilgrims. Not to mention the need for transporting food and supplies in and out for its inhabitants— how many?"

Lady Xarre waved at Bosha, who dutifully replied, "About three hundred Temple-sworn divines, acolytes, and dedicats, and perhaps an equal number of lay dedicats in service to them. All women, within the precincts. The complex of buildings sits on a notable promontory. Beyond the single drawbridge there is a rambling villa for male dedicats of the goddess, and guards. No men ever set foot past the bridge."

That was more populated than Pen had been picturing. "Do men ever try? People being what they are. In disguise, perhaps."

Bosha really smirked, this time. "People being what they are, the Order has a cadre of sacred dogs that roam the entry courtyard, trained to sniff out males. All bitches."

In both senses, Pen gathered. "That actually works?"

"Extremely well, I'm told."

Tanar looked up. "Do you confuse them, Sura dear?"

"I admit, I once made some amusing experiments borrowing your perfume, but in any case I am known, there."

"Did the perfume work?" Pen asked, intent.

"I couldn't really tell." Rose-colored eyes glanced from under lowered lids. "I suspect it would not work for you."

*But I have other ways of controlling dogs.* "Do you know, or have you a guess, where and how Madame Gardiki may be kept within the walls?"

Bosha shrugged. "She may have the freedom of the precincts, and mix with the residents. Some long-term lady prisoners have in the past, if they were judged docile enough. More likely, being new and untried, she would be kept in a locked chamber. Possibly on the side overlooking the sea. The Order is mainly guarded by its, ah, geology. And the water, wind, and currents. The island is only five miles long."

At Pen's prodding, Bosha went on to describe more details of the architecture and the residents' daily rounds of work and prayer. He seemed a remarkably observant man. Pen was getting less and less surprised at this.

"And how do the prelates of the Daughter's Order feel about their goddess's house being used as an imperial prison?"

Bosha cocked his head. "Interesting question. But since the imperial court is one of the main financial supports of the retreat, I don't suppose they can refuse the duty."

"The visitors who go in and out—are they counted?"

"Yes. There is a visitor's book, which gets marked off. And rechecked at sunset, when the drawbridge is raised for the night. The ladies do value their privacy."

Pen sat back and rubbed his knuckles across his lips. *Des, do you see any possibilities?*

*Do you even remember who you are talking to, lad?* and that was, without question, Learned Ruchia's voice that scoffed at him. *I can see six offhand, but let's start with the quietest. The one that involves setting the place afire being the very last resort.*

*I should think so!* Pen shuddered at this hypothetical offense to the Lady of Spring.

*Let me ask Nikys a few questions.*

Pen yielded control of his mouth to his demon, and turned. "Nikys, what does your mother look like? Is she tall, short, fat, thin? Skin color, eyes and hair?"

"She's a little taller than I am, and, um, not so round. Her coloring is much like mine."

"Is she very level-headed in emergencies?"

"Well, she raised Adelis and me." Nikys's enchanting grin, too seldom seen of late, flickered. "Following my father around to various army camps, to boot. I'm too young to remember the one time we were all in the baggage train when it was attacked, though I've heard the stories. Drema was always the practical one, of our two mothers. Florma was the nervous one." Their children's old nicknames for Idrene and Lady Florina. "I think my mother would have liked to be more nervous, at times, but the role was taken. So she mostly ended up reassuring us and Florma all together."

"I see." He glanced at Lady Xarre's cane, propped against her chair. "How fit is she, physically? Can she walk, run, climb, ride?"

"Fit enough. She's only just fifty now. She can do all those things, though not like a young man, of course." She mulled. "Maybe not what you mean by climb. Not even when she was young. Me either. Stairs we can manage."

Des hummed aloud. "I think a substitution removal might just work, here."

"Beg pardon?" said Nikys.

"Two pilgrims enter the precincts to make prayer. A woman and her niece. Mm, cousin. Friend, anyway. We find Madame Gardiki and exchange clothes, and other things as needed. Later, two women sign out again, and make their way to their boat. Except the woman left in the cell is not Madame Gardiki. I escape at my leisure, and rejoin you." Pen wasn't sure whose voice was speaking, now.

"What?" said Nikys. "You don't look anything like my mother!"

"It's not as if we could leave you. That would be like trading a gold coin for a gold coin."

Tanar said tentatively, "Might I do?"

Lady Xarre and Bosha both replied, instantly and in unison, "No!"

Tanar ducked her chin, peeved. "I would like to do something. I could be the only person here with the right to drink from the goddess's well, after all."

"No," Bosha repeated. "There must be nothing whatsoever to connect this escapade with the Xarre household. Or with my sister Hekat at the Order, for that matter. She's the only member of my family I could ever stand, and vice versa. I am wholly loth to risk her." He frowned back at Tanar, and at Pen. "And if you are imagining involving me any further in this, may I point out that I am a line leading straight back to both."

"Yes, you are much too physically memorable," agreed Pen. Although evidently an adept and ruthless bodyguard, which was an undoubted value.

"So are you," Nikys pointed out.

"Appearances can be changed. In both directions. Sometimes by quite simple means. My hair and skin could be colored, or we might obtain a blond wig. I have Mira's clogs in my luggage, which could boost your mother's height to mimic mine. Eyes, well, who notices eyes?"

"Yours?" said Nikys. "Everybody."

Pen was a little miffed when all in the room nodded solemn agreement.

But Bosha pushed off from his wall. "I might have a solution for that." He trod off to his bedchamber, returning with a small case in his hand. He opened it to display a pair of spectacles in fine brass frames, but the lenses were dark green glass.

"Oh!" said Pen, bending to peer closely. "That's very clever! I know a lens-grinder in Martensbridge who would like to know about that. Not that the sun is a great hazard in the cantons, although sometimes the sun on the snow is blinding."

"You have sun and snow at the same time?" said Nikys in some wonder. "What a strange country you come from, Pen."

Pen noted that slip of the tongue, *Pen*, and cut off a smile.

"They were a gift from Lady Xarre," said Bosha. "When I first became a retainer of the household. Because my eyes watered and hurt in the noonday light. In twenty-six years before that, no one had ever thought of offering me such an aid. I've no desire to give them to you, but if it will get you out of here faster, I will."

"They can be replaced, Surakos dear," murmured Lady Xarre.

A hand-on-heart silent nod of thanks. Ah, no, that wasn't irony, was it.

Pen picked them up with care and tried them on. The lenses were flat, thankfully, without any headache-inducing distortions. He blinked around at his viridescent audience.

"If you want unmemorable," said Nikys, "that's not it either."

"So much the better. People will remember the spectacles but not the face behind them."

"Maybe... So would you be Mira again?"

The other three people in the room stared at him curiously, and Bastard's tears—or belly-laugh, whichever—that wasn't a story he wanted told here. Or anywhere. "Not Mira, gods forfend, not at the Daughter's Order. Learned Ruchia. She'll know what to do, for one thing."

Nikys nodded, satisfied. Everyone else kept staring.

"Dyes," said Tanar after a moment. "Now that *is* something I might help with!"

# VIII

NIKYS had been in Tanar's stillroom before. Penric had not, and looked surprised when he was shown past Bosha's bedchamber through the next door down to find the workbench, the shelves crammed with neatly labeled jars and notebooks, the chests with dozens of tiny drawers, and the neat array of tools. The room even featured a little stove with a vent to the outside. Tanar opened the shutters to let in the light; only a window, here, no balcony.

"This is as well-stocked as any apothecary shop," said Penric, gazing around. Nikys expected he was qualified to judge.

"Yes," said Tanar cheerfully. "I first became interested in the art when I made Sura teach me how he concocted his, hm, medicines. Then I followed Karaji around and had her show me how she made all the dyes for the household's spinning and weaving. Then Mama permitted me a real apothecary as a tutor—she came out once a week for, oh, almost three years. So I can make all the household's remedies. I'm better at it than Sura, now."

The retainer gifted her with a conceding eyebrow-lift—proud teacher?—and she tossed her head in pleased reply.

Penric's smile had grown oddly fixed. "Can you cook, too?"

"Oh, yes. Mother agrees I should learn every skill I can. Because even when supervising servants, one needs to understand their tasks. And who knows what all an officer's wife might be called upon to do?"

"A general's wife," stated Bosha, as if repeating himself from some prior and fruitless protest, "would surely have proper help."

Nikys laughed. "So people imagine. I think Tanar has a better grip on the possibilities."

"Mother made it a bargain," explained Tanar. "She would trade me a tutor in whatever I fancied in exchange for me studying her bookkeeping, which I do not love. It all worked out. Except for the horseshoeing, that time."

"Horseshoeing?" said Nikys. Even she hadn't heard this tale. Bosha, who evidently had, hid his mouth behind his hand.

"We had a very patient old pony, and a very patient old farrier. Who both grew much less patient as the day wore on. I still don't think I could shoe a horse, but if ever my horse threw a shoe, I wager I could nail it back on without laming the poor beast, so there's that much." She looked around. "But I like the stillroom best."

Nikys directed Pen to light the stove. The two women donned aprons and set about mixing up an array of samples. They then made him sit on a stool and remove his shirt, testing the colors on his skin until they achieved a tolerable match for Nikys. While Tanar expanded the recipe, Nikys, who had done the task before, combed an inky black dye through Penric's unbound hair.

"Such a shame," Tanar murmured over her shoulder, watching this eclipse.

"My hair has been recolored so many times since I came to Cedonia I'm surprised it hasn't all fallen out," sighed Penric. "I'm tempted to shave my head to defend myself."

"Don't you dare," said Nikys, giving a lock a sharp tug, forgetting that she wasn't supposed to care. Pen, the rat, noticed, because he pressed down a smile.

"With the fixative I'm using these dyes should stand up to water and washing for a few days," said Tanar. "Be careful not to let them rub off on anything where someone might notice."

Once the skin treatment was satisfactorily started, Tanar and Bosha vanished out the gallery door together. Nikys, trying not to think too much about this excuse for so pleasurably touching him, ended up coloring Pen's face, neck, hands, arms and shoulders, then started at his feet, working up his long legs to his knees.

Pen swallowed. She braced herself for who-knew-what—

whatever had possessed him to tell the world he was courting her?—but he said, unexpectedly, "Did you know Bosha carries poisoned blades?"

"I knew he went armed. I mean, he needs to. I didn't know about the other." Although it made sense to Nikys. The eunuch was not a man who could expect mercy if he lost a fight, and Tanar was not a charge he dared fail.

"Do you think Tanar brews his poisons?"

Nikys tilted her head, considering this. "Very possibly. She'd love to think she was doing something for him, in exchange for all he does for her."

"That doesn't bother you?"

"It seems a very good skill for a woman who, by marriage or some other ill-chance, could well be tossed into the imperial court at Thasalon. Which is the most poisonous place I've ever been, even without the aid of apothecaries."

"Could be hard on an unsatisfactory husband. Doesn't it make you worry for Adelis?"

Nikys's lips twitched. "Not really. Adelis is not the sort of man who inspires poisoning. He's the sort of man who inspires hitting on the head with a skillet."

Penric muffled a too-agreeing snort. "So speaks his loving sister. Have you ever done so?"

"Not since we were twelve, I admit." She added after a moment, "Then he grew too tall to reach. Bad angle for the swing."

"I'll keep that in mind."

"You're safe. You're even taller."

A snicker. But then, annoyingly, he rose, leaving her with dye dripping through her fingers, and began tapping his way around the cabinets. A pause, a familiar click, and he drew one door wide and stuck his head in.

"Hey! I imagine that was locked for a reason!"

"Oh," he breathed, "indeed it was." He sounded a little too delighted. "What do you make of it all, Des? . . . Really? . . . Huh."

"Stop snooping," she said, undercutting her indignation by adding, "Someone might come back."

After a long look he closed it up again, to her relief, and troubled to relock it, too.

"You can't go about piebald. Come back here."

Dutifully, he returned, sat, and gave her back his leg. "Interesting."

And left it at that, till she gave in and growled, "All right, what? You're obviously itching to tell."

"Fast-acting paralytics, mostly, according to Des. The death is in the dose, as they say. Even packed in a grooved blade, I don't think such low amounts would kill. *Clever* bastard."

Nikys reflected. "Right. All Bosha'd have to do is land one nick to slow his opponent down. Then kill him with his steel, if he had to. No question of poisoning would ever arise, after. And if someone got his blade away from him, they couldn't kill him with it. Not with the venom, at least."

Penric, who had opened his mouth, said plaintively, "I was going to explain that."

"No need. Have you ever listened to a crowd of drunken army louts bragging about their exploits to each other? One learns a lot." Not that the men noticed.

"Since escaping my brother Drovo-the-aspiring-mercenary at a fairly early age, I've mostly managed to avoid such experiences."

"Lucky you."

Pen was sitting drying, and Nikys was fanning him to speed the process, when Tanar and Bosha came back with piles of clothing in their arms. They proved to be borrowings from some senior female servants, sober and sedate. The key factor in selection, once Nikys and Tanar bound Pen's dye-damp hair in a cloth and marshaled him through a try-on, turned out to be length, but he only needed the one change. Pen seemed much more adept outfitting the persona he'd dubbed *Learned Ruchia* than the first time, when trying to dress, and perhaps evoke, the courtesan Mira. Was he a fast learner—well, Nikys knew he was—or was Ruchia simply closer to himself? Or were all his internal ladies equally present to him?

Partway into this process, Bosha, who had kept his amusement almost under control, though Pen had certainly noticed the voiceless sniggers, inclined his head in a shadow-bow and withdrew through the gallery door. After some fussing about and much debate, they finished the transformation. Pen took a turn around the small stillroom practicing the management of his draperies and a very convincing feminine walk.

"I really do believe you will be able to slip into the Order's precincts," said Tanar, admiring her handiwork. "But will you be able to get out again safely? By yourself?"

Bosha reentered through his own chamber door in time to hear this, and leaned against the jamb. "I expect so. As Madame Khatai says, he has skills." Nikys looked up to see him twirling Pen's Temple braids around one long index finger. "And now we know what kind."

Pen went rigid, and so, for a moment, did Nikys, chilled with a sudden realization of how very, very *dangerous* an act it might be to bait Pen. But Pen only licked his lips and said, flatly, "Give those back."

"Certainly." Bosha handed them across at arm's length. Two arms' lengths, counting Pen's side.

Tanar, goggling, said, "Are those sorcerer's braids?"

"Yes," said Pen shortly.

"Are they real?" A reasonable question, given all the exercises in disguise.

"Yes."

"That explains a lot," murmured Bosha, folding his arms, and himself back to the doorjamb.

"Oh my goodness!" said Tanar. "I've never met a sorcerer to talk to. Nikys, did you know? Yes, of course you do." Tanar looked thrilled. Bosha did not.

"Do you normally rifle through your guests' luggage?" said Pen testily.

"Do you normally light a fire without using a taper or spill?" Bosha inquired in turn.

" . . . Oh."

"Yes, he does," said Nikys. And when had she, and Pen, become so used to this simple domestic convenience that she asked, and he complied, routinely? "Oh, Pen, I'm sorry. I didn't think."

"It's all right," he said, though his voice was still a little choked. "Neither did I. Though I didn't realize he was watching."

"It answers so many questions," said Bosha, "and yet raises so many more. Given where I found them in your case. Temple physician, as well?"

"Not . . . exactly."

"In all but final oath," Nikys put in on Pen's behalf.

"Because the cadre of physicians, I am given to understand, are the very most adept of Temple sorcerers."

"You understand correctly," said Pen. His mouth reset in a thin line, and only Nikys knew how deep a scar that was for him. Bosha would blunder around and never know why the conversation had turned so sour. That wasn't even touching on the disaster that could ensue should Bosha learn Pen had come to Patos as an agent of the duke of Adria. And still might be one.

She cut in ruthlessly. "Your many questions may be answered in full—should we meet again for Tanar and Adelis's wedding. Here, now, it's better not to know."

Nikys wondered what it said for Bosha's mind that, with a slow nod, he accepted this.


Nikys said farewell to Tanar in her bedchamber. They exchanged fierce hugs.

"Take care," said Tanar, releasing her. "I'm happier now I know more about your courier. A Temple sorcerer, really? *And* a physician?"

"He healed Adelis's eyes," Nikys confirmed. "It wasn't a matter of the executioner doing a poor job. I swear they were half boiled-away."

Tanar gasped.

"It was awful beyond belief. I saw. Pen practically rebuilt them, with his sorcery." She felt strangely glad she was able to finally tell someone. Justice? Bragging? She hardly knew.

"But Adelis's eyes are all right now?"

"He sees perfectly. He just looks different."

Tanar nodded, accepting this with a practical air. "And your fetching physician—has he asked you to marry him yet?"

Nikys thought back to that exhausted, difficult conversation she and Pen had scraped through upon arriving safely in Orbas. "I suppose so."

"You *suppose*? How can you not know?"

"Well, I do know. Yes."

"What, and you didn't seize him with both hands? Sorcerer, physician, that astonishing sunburst of hair? So tall. And those *eyes*. Is it true sorcerers can do amazing things in bed?"

"I . . . don't know. Probably." And did *not* say, *General Chadro certainly seemed to think so.*

"I'd think you'd at least be more curious." Tanar huffed a disappointed sigh.

"As you are?" Nikys muffled a laugh, and Tanar smiled sheepishly. Nikys went on, "But it's never just Penric. He comes as a set. His chaos demon isn't only a power, she's a person. He's even named her. Desdemona."

Tanar pressed her fingers to her lips, stifling a giggle. "Clever!"

"But there are two people living in his head, not just one. All the time." Well, twelve... thirteen, but there was no way now to go into the full roster. "She's been riding along with him in secret all this visit, your third guest."

Tanar's head tilted. "But not secret to you."

"...No."

"And, clearly, not dangerous enough to warn us." Tanar raised her face, and her eyebrows, in something not quite a question.

"That's a point," Nikys conceded, in not quite an answer. "But I wouldn't just be marrying him. I'd be marrying *her*. The chaos demon. Do you see?"

"I... oh." If this did not take Tanar aback, it at least slowed her down. "Well, you are a careful woman, and the gods attest you have suffered much. I suppose you know your own mind." Her tone hooked a lingering doubt onto the end of this statement.

Nikys shrugged rueful agreement with the unspoken codicil. Who could foresee regrets? Her marriage to Kymis had seemed fine, had *been* fine, until its ghastly truncation. To give one's heart to any living being, even a simple cat, was to risk such loss. Which brought her around once again: "So what would you have me tell Adelis?"

Tanar bit her lip and looked down. "Tell him..." She looked up to meet Nikys's eyes. "Tell him I will wait."

"Are you so sure? It could be a long time. Or never. I've seldom met a young woman who wasn't wild to escape her mother's household and become mistress of her own."

"No matter what she had to marry to do so?" Tanar inquired, amused. "That road is not for me. Daughter and Mother be thanked. My mother and I don't exactly have to live atop each other, here. And she indulges all my interests. Or at least, she praises my successes, and says nothing of all my false starts. Which have been many and sometimes embarrassing, but she claims it's all learning."

Nikys captured and gripped her waving hands. "I'll pass your message along, then, when I get the chance."

Nikys picked up her repacked valise and followed Tanar out to the sitting room, where Penric, all fitted out as Ruchia, and Bosha awaited. To curtail the number of Xarre servants to see them, it had been decided that Bosha himself would drive them to the village on the coast where they could take ship to Limnos, and play male escort to the two lady pilgrims. Nikys trusted that Penric's god—and hers, and possibly Bosha's as well, she'd never asked—appreciated the ironies in that, and would protect them along their way in exchange for, if nothing else, the amusement. When they took the channel boat in the morning, Bosha would travel not with their party, but merely at the same time, as discreetly as he'd ever guarded Tanar.

Bosha had traded his more flamboyant robes for a trim sleeveless tunic and matching trousers in dark dyes, with a long-sleeved linen shirt despite the heat. The somber servant's garb somehow managed to make him an even more striking figure. Tanar evidently thought so, too, for she picked an imaginary speck of lint off his tunic and said, "You look very fine."

He placed his hands on her shoulders in turn. "Take care while I'm gone. Sleep in Lady Xarre's chambers. Obey her."

"I always do."

"No, you don't."

"I will this time. Just for you, Mother Hen." She tapped his nose. "You take care of yourself as well. Don't drag back all bloody again. And I absolutely forbid you to get yourself killed. That's an order!"

That hand-to-heart bow was all the answer he gave. As Tanar turned away, his habitual smirk slipped into a smile of such surpassing tenderness that Nikys's breath caught.

It was gone in a moment, the sardonic mask back in place. She might have thought she'd imagined it, except that she doubted she could ever forget it.

*Oh.*

*I think I need to think about this.*

It was then time to be smuggled back through the garden to the postern gate, and on out to the side street.

"Wait here," Bosha instructed them. "I'll bring the cart around." He locked the gate after them with a firm clack.

Penric set down his case and satchel, passed the fold of his dress's draperies over his coiled black hair, and leaned against the garden wall. Nikys did the same. At length, she rested her head back upon the day-warmed stone and sighed, "That may be the most forlorn hope I have ever witnessed."

"Hm?" said Pen.

"Bosha and Tanar. He is in love with her, I believe. And he knows it."

Pen's grunt was neither surprised nor disagreeing. "A highborn heiress and a cut servant twice her age? Forlorn indeed. Surely he knows that, too."

"Oh, yes." Nikys went on thoughtfully, "I'm not so sure she knows she's in love with him."

In a distant tone, Pen remarked, "A person might observe that every other name out of her mouth was not 'Adelis'. Is this a cause for concern?"

"Mm, of a sort. I'll have to think of some non-misleading way of letting my brother know they come as a pair or not at all." She added after a moment, "Rather like you and Des."

A convulsive snort. "Bosha and Tanar are nothing at all like me and Des!"

She cocked an eyebrow up at his indignation. "And what does Des have to say to that?"

A little silence. "Des says you're a very shrewd girl and she likes you." A short pause. "And if I would just get my eyes off your, Des, that's rude! I am not that shallow. Yes, he is." Pen clamped his teeth.

Nikys let that one go by, though the corners of her mouth inched up.

He cleared his throat, and resumed, "I think it would be unwise to make assumptions. Bosha seemed very loyal to Lady Xarre, as well. You might note he went to her without telling Tanar, this morning."

"As was his clear duty and, as it turned out, astute. Good for all of us. Was that a point?"

"More of a line. But it's best not to meddle with things half understood," said Pen. Nikys wasn't sure whether it was Pen or Des who then added, "Or else I would recommend they run off somewhere far away and set up an apothecary shop. They could just live over it, together."

"In a set of rooms?"

"Mm. Tanar could spend the day brewing medicines, and Bosha could, I don't know, assassinate the customers. They'd be happy."

Nikys caught a black laugh in her hand too late to stuff it back into her mouth.

And then the cart was turning onto the street, and other peoples' troubles had to make way for her own. The last leg of this mortal relay.

Maybe.

# IX

PEN CRANED HIS NECK as they rattled into the small port village of Guza, on the Cedonian shore opposite Limnos. Dusk muffled its streets in shadows. The sea remained luminous; four miles out, the island bulked as a mysterious silhouette against the horizon. Guza earned much of its living serving Limnos, its Order, and the steady stream of pilgrims making their way to its sacred well. Spring was the busy season for such travelers, but the clear skies and calm waters of summer drew a second wave. In the grimmer winds of winter, Bosha had told them, such traffic shut down.

A hospice of the Daughter's Order in Guza was devoted to housing pilgrims, with a reputation for being the cleanest, cheapest, and safest place to stay overnight. Pen was not willing to test his disguise in the close confines of a women's dormitory, however, where the goddess might not be the sole one to take vigorous offense if he slipped up. Bosha dropped them instead at the inn that was not the mainstay of the sailors, and went off to find secure stabling for Lady Xarre's horse and cart.

Pen had hoped to find separate rooms for all three of them, but was lucky to get even one. The chamber in the eaves held a bed and a straw-stuffed pallet brought-in which, between them, filled the floor. Ruchia advised him to take the offer of plain cold food and drink carried up by a maid in place of a trip to the taproom, and Nikys seemed relieved to go along with this. When Bosha arrived, they made a picnic of it. Pen suspected the retainer dined at home as finely as his mistresses and often with them, but he made no comment on the simplicity of this meal.

Then came the problem of apportioning beds, which brought back memories of the flight to Orbas with Adelis. Nikys, both practiced at the arguments and plainly very, very tired of them, took over, bluntly assigning herself to the pallet and the two men to the bed.

"And don't stare at me like a pair of five-year-olds told to eat their vegetables," she added tartly, blocking protest. Fortunately, Bosha seemed used to following the orders of irate women. It would have made for the most awkward night's sleep imaginable, if Pen hadn't been so fatigued he dropped like a log within moments of hitting the sheets.

He'd no idea of how Bosha had fared, come dawn. The man's eyes were always red.

The small boats that ferried travelers out to the island left Guza as early as they could make up a passenger list. Several of the captains and crews were themselves women, much favored by some of the pilgrims. Bosha directed them aboard one of these not because he knew it, he said, but because he didn't, and vice versa. As soon as the craft cast off, he clambered over the barrels and crates to crouch in the shadow of the sail, augmented by a wide-brimmed hat that he pulled down over his flushed face.

The little fleet sailed out in the morning and back at dusk, giving their supercargo as long a day as possible to visit ashore. Some pilgrims stayed over, either at the fishing village that served the Order, or at the upper hamlet that lay outside its precincts, and a very few, by arrangement, within the walls, most of the latter being themselves Temple functionaries. Pen kept peeking over the green spectacles to take in as much of the glorious sea light as he could, until Nikys appeared with a straw hat she'd found somewhere, jammed it over his head declaring he was going to fry like an egg, and made him join Bosha in the shade.

They had each supplied themselves with a thin blue scarf, conveniently for sale at a booth on the Guza wharf, marking them as supplicants. Bosha had draped his over his head, secured by his hat and pulled down over his face. He raised this curtain to frown briefly at Pen, then let it drop back. With every inch of skin covered with, mostly, dark cloth, including gloves, he looked hot and very uncomfortable.

"Would you like your spectacles for a while?" murmured Pen.

"No," he muttered back. "If you're going to carry out this play, stay in your character."

*He's right about that*, said Des.

"I didn't realize this would be such an ordeal for you." The brilliant morning sun reflecting off the sea would have bathed the man in burns, uncovered. Pen wasn't sure how well Tanar's dye would protect him, either.

"My sister's birthday is in late fall. It's not usually this bad, then."

Nikys sat down on Pen's other side. She seemed to be growing tenser the closer they drew to their goal. Pen nudged her in an attempt at silent reassurance, barely acknowledged by a lip-twitch that did not linger.

With a few barked orders, the boat came about. The sail slid aside like a screen, giving their first view of the Daughter's retreat on Limnos.

Pen looked up. And up. And up. His jaw unhinged. "Five gods preserve me," he breathed.

From the sea, a nearly sheer rock face soared so high into the air that the gray stone buildings atop, roofed with faded blue tile, looked like architect's models. The precipice stood out from the island like the column of a giant's temple.

"That has to be a thousand feet up," Pen marveled.

"Just about that," said Bosha, raising his scarf again to follow Pen's gaze.

"How do people get *up* there?"

"There is a stairway cut into the cliff that winds up it in switchbacks. You'll be able to make it out when we get closer. Over two thousand steps, and every step a prayer."

"A curse, surely, by the end!" said Pen, appalled.

Bosha let him dwell in his horror for a long moment, then added airily, "Or you could pay a coin to the donkey drivers to take you up the road from the village."

Pen, well taken-in, shot him a glare.

The smirk curled back on teeth. "Some rare persons on a pilgrimage of atonement do climb the stairs, I'm told. On their hands and knees. This is less an act of humility than terror, as there are no railings. There are places so narrow that people coming up and people coming down have to crawl over each other."

"I believe we will take the donkeys," said Nikys primly.

"Good decision."

"I'm not sure how such wild feats are supposed to impress the gods," mused Pen, squinting upward, "who are present everywhere the same. Though my subtler seminary teachers advised me that any useful effect is upon the supplicant, not some holy audience. It's all in whether the given action fills a person or empties them, leaving room for a god to enter. You could sit by yourself in a quiet room and have as good a chance at it. A man could walk up those two thousand steps on his hands singing hymns the whole way and have none."

Bosha eyed him curiously. "Could you have such a chance? Learned divine as you apparently are."

"No. Sorcerers are always too full." Pen sighed. "It's all indirection, for my god and me. Maddeningly so, sometimes."

So far up, trees looked like bits of parsley set around a roast. It took study, counting the rows of windows and filigree of wooden balconies, to realize how large the buildings actually were, rising six or eight floors high above the rock base on this side.

"I'm surprised it hasn't been seized for an imperial fortress," said Pen.

"It was, once," said Bosha. "Although not by Cedonia. By one of its enemies. Two hundred years ago. A long tapestry tells the story, up in the halls, that all the pilgrims to Limnos go view."

"So what is the tale?" asked Pen.

"Ah. The ravine was bridged by ladders, and the Daughter's women suffered the usual rapine, slaughter, and carrying-off into slavery. About a week after, the entire garrison was felled by plague. Of a thousand men, there were only thirteen survivors. It was considered a miracle of the Daughter, in vengeance for the affront. The Order has never been attacked since."

Nikys hummed. "Or a very, very angry woman poisoning the sacred well."

The lip-scar stretched. "So I would make it."

"No reason it can't be both," said Pen, judiciously. "And every reason it could. The gods have no hands but ours, they say." He held up his fingers and wiggled them.

"Not mine," growled Bosha, and retreated back under his blue curtain.

# X

AS THEIR BOAT took its turn at the Limnos dock and the passengers wobbled their way to shore, Nikys wasn't sure if she was heartsick, homesick, or seasick. Or all of them. The tension in her shoulders made her feel like a plaster statue whose head could crack away at a careless knock. As her feet found the grainy cobblestones, she took a deep breath.

Penric-as-Ruchia captured her hand and gripped it. "Hey," he murmured. "It will be very well."

There was no rational reason at all to believe that. Sorcerers, as far as she knew, didn't possess the powers of seers. But she stretched her neck a little without her head coming off.

Bosha took care to exit the boat apart from them, but it was easy enough to follow the handful of other pilgrims straggling up through the village to the donkey livery. They ducked around the side of the last whitewashed house and handed off their luggage to him, barring one sack containing Mira's clogs, Pen's tunic and trousers, and a packed lunch atop not just for concealment.

"Where will you wait for us?" asked Nikys. "I only saw the one tavern."

"Not there," said Bosha. "Too many people would notice me. A little way up there's a path, and some crevices in the rocks. I'll just evict the adders, and I'll have a dark, cool place to wait out the sun. I should be able to mark you coming back down."

"This island has adders?" said Nikys nervously. She might have taken this for more of Bosha's sly humor, but he was the only one among them wearing boots.

"Not on the road." He smirked, probably. It was hard to be sure.

"Your sorcerer will doubtless protect you. ... Animals like him, he tells me."

Ignoring this edged dig, Pen drew her off.

"But who will protect him?" Nikys worried, glancing back over her shoulder. The man had already disappeared.

"From the adders? They'll probably welcome him as a cousin. Given the inventory of tainted blades he's carrying."

"He drugs his belt-knife?"

"Oh, that one's clean. But there's one around his neck, one at his back, one in his boot, and that pouch at his belt is full of nasty little larding-needles."

Nikys considered this. "Good."

'Livery' was perhaps too grand a name for what proved to be a collection of animals tethered in the shade of some olive trees, together with a few rowdy boys for groom-guides, and an adult couple who collected the coins from the pilgrims and portioned out the mounts. The poorer or more fit travelers simply walked up the winding road, although there was also a cart for the aged or infirm. They endured a short delay while a longer-legged donkey was found for the very tall woman with the weak eyes, but soon both Pen and Nikys clambered aboard sidewise saddles like little wooden seats, arranged their skirts, and lurched off towed by a lad.

The road bent back and forth across the sparse hillside like a shuttle on a loom, covering what might have been two miles in a straight line, and a thousand vertical feet. The view across the strait to the mainland of Cedonia was superb, sky and sea a vibrant clear blue that reminded Nikys of Pen's eyes, the land aglow with white light. It only seemed forever before they rounded the last turn and approached the hamlet outside the walls of the Daughter's Order.

She searched for any signs of guards they would somehow have to circumvent, later. A few men in blue tunics of the Order were about, bearing weapons, and under a plane tree four bored soldiers in imperial uniforms played at dice. They paused to look over the latest arrivals to be unloaded, but, after the first flicker of attention, their interest seemed more lewd than suspicious.

Truly, even were he mad enough to do so, it was far too early for Adelis to be arriving with any sort of attack force. Which the sentinels could watch coming up the road long before it arrived.

*Except Adelis wouldn't march up the hill in broad daylight. He'd land his troop on the far side of the island in the dark and infiltrate by surprise.* So perhaps the soldiers' present relaxation was justified.

The long drawbridge lay down across a plunging cleft, cool and green in its shadowy depths. Nikys gripped Pen's elbow as if assisting her friend while they waited for a blue-clad man to push a cart holding a barrel across, handing it off at the stone archway to a waiting woman. They exchanged brief Daughter's salutes, a tap to the forehead, as well as the load. Nikys and Pen followed it inside.

The forecourt was sunny, paved with interlaced tiles in blue, white, and yellow. On the other side stood a podium womaned by an acolyte wearing a blue scarf, smiling welcome at the visitors and waiting to assist them in signing the guest book, a large ledger. The only hazard was the startling pack of perhaps a dozen guard dogs.

Nikys had vaguely expected something like the Xarre mastiffs, huge and threatening. Instead, these were small beasts, their long coats beautifully brushed, with bright black eyes and pink tongues. It was like being swarmed by a throng of white silk floor mops.

Pen made a faint *urk* sound, and acquired a look of concentration. The dogs' suspicion turned to joy as they rioted around him, snuffling and panting. A couple of them darted in to lick his ankles. Producing a credible feminine *eep*, not wholly feigned, Pen shook his skirts and attempted to gently shove them away with a long sandaled foot. Which would have been all right had their pink tongues not come away with a distinct brown tint. Nikys swallowed horror and bent to them, waving her arms and hissing, "Shoo. Shoo!" They tried to lick her fingers.

To Nikys's intense relief, a woman came in behind them shepherding four young girls, who squealed at their canine reception. Girls and dogs fell upon each other with equal delight, exchanging petting and cooing for licks and wriggles, and Pen escaped.

As planned, Nikys signed in for the both of them, her false name and his, so that there would be no discrepancy in handwriting when it came time to sign out. Assuming anyone actually compared such things. *They will later on, when they discover Mother missing.*

"And what do you pray to our Lady for today?" the acolyte asked cheerfully.

"Oh, nothing for myself. My friend Ruchia is praying for aid for her weak eyes. I'm just here to help her."

Pen nodded amiably, and, by whatever restraint—maybe Des— managed not to add any rambling comments. He pulled a handkerchief from his sleeve and pressed it to his nose just in time to dam the beginning trickle of blood.

"Oh dear, are you all right?" said the acolyte. "Do you need to go sit down?"

Pen shook his head, emitting a muffled negative noise. "S'tops in a mom'nt."

Reluctantly, the acolyte released them to the first stage of the pilgrims' tour, pointing out the entry to the tapestry gallery. Nikys fished out her coin purse and withdrew an offering for the box set up next to the podium, turning her hand to make sure the acolyte caught the heavy gold glint. The acolyte was all smiles as she sent them on their way, though she added a recommendation to the tall girl to return if she felt unwell and someone would guide her to the infirmary.

The famous tapestry was arranged on a long wall, with a series of arched windows opposite that illuminated without allowing direct sunlight to fade it. Penric actually took the time to look at it all, strolling slowly through thirty feet of closely embroidered narrative, murmuring interpretations under his breath. Nikys wasn't sure if he was just doing an excellent job of playing a pilgrim, or if he was overcome with scholarly distraction, again.

One could make out views of the soldiers landing in the fishing cove below, ravaging through something very like the present village. Scaling ladders and smoke. Women screaming, captured by the hair by what appeared to be brutal ogres. A picture of the sacred well, with the goddess looming over it crying in dismay. Her face was portrayed so vaguely as to be a near-blank, because the Nominalist Controversy had taken some vicious turns in Cedonia, but what could be seen of Her posture somehow conveyed profound emotion. Toward the end, many detailed little ogre figures writhed in visible agony and vomited red threads. Lots of red threads.

"I didn't know needlework could be so hostile," murmured Pen, bending to examine these. "Definitely a sermon, there." He licked his lips a touch nervously.

The last image was of the goddess smiling benignly, presiding over billowing smoke from pyres and the restoration of Her refuge. Pen contemplated this and signed himself, hand passing over his forehead for the Daughter, lips for the Bastard, navel for the Mother, groin for the Father, and heart for the Son, bowing slightly and giving his forehead an extra tap.

Then twice with the back of his thumb on his lips for the luck of his own god, however ambiguous. Because Penric never seemed to forget, though others did, that his powers were lent ultimately by the white god, to Whom he must someday render up an account.

It was an unexpected insight, and Nikys eyed him sideways. She had met him first as physician, then as sorcerer, but he was equally, it seemed, a learned divine. Maybe she hadn't given enough credence to this third pillar of his character.

The gallery let them out down some bluish granite steps into the court of the sacred well, recognizable from the tapestry. But so much more stunning in reality. She and Pen both stopped short and gawped.

From the middle of a white marble circle some eight feet in diameter bubbled up clear, bright waters. *Welling* indeed. Through five ports, it spilled over into an encircling basin. From there, channels led away variously into the surrounding precincts, doubtless including baths and laundries. One spout emptied into a sink with silver ladles hung around it. From there it trickled into something resembling a marble laundry trough, beautifully carved with emblems of the goddess, in which a pilgrim seeking more complete consolation could immerse her whole body.

The music of the waters was the only sound in the hushed court, apart from distant bird-calls. It seemed strange that so glaringly bright a place could feel holy, but it did.

"How," muttered Pen through his teeth, "does the water get *up* here?"

Another acolyte, attendant and guardian-on-duty of the waters, rose from a porphyry bench under a portico and cordially came forward. "We consider it a miracle of the Lady. Four hundred years ago, this place was nothing but a dry and desolate crag. The spring appeared following an earthquake. The inhabitants of Limnos noticed a new waterfall appearing over the side of the pinnacle, and came to investigate. We have celebrated the blessings of the Daughter of Spring here ever since." The wave of an inviting hand. "Drink, then, if you come in good faith, and pray with Her cleansing waters on your lips." Her gesture went on to encompass an array of intricately woven prayer rugs set beyond the well. An older woman, the blue scarf about her neck, was just lumbering up from one, a thoughtful expression on her face.

Nikys took the ladle that was extended and hesitated. The attendant, eyes twinkling, murmured behind her hand, "After the boats and that climb up the hill, most visitors are very thirsty. It's permitted to drink your fill."

Smiling thanks, she did so. Penric watched her cautiously. Moved by impulse, she dipped her ladle and handed it to him. He received it with a grateful nod, and again when she refilled it.

They both wiped their mouths, then proceeded to the prayer rugs, because the attendant was watching them in expectation. Penric, after a contemplative moment, went down not just on his knees but prone, arms wide in the attitude of utmost supplication. Nikys went down on her knees facing the bright fountain and held up her hands palm-out, five fingers spread wide.

For all her anxieties, she had not thought of what to pray. She had nothing.

With the Daughter's water still on her lips, it seemed wrong to perform some dissembling dumb-show. One didn't need to be a virgin to pray here, after all, merely to have once been one. *Because the gods are parsimonious.*

*And, sometimes, merciful.*

She considered offering the goddess an apology for this sacrilegious invasion. Could they buy dispensation by coming to remove what was certainly a greater insult, using Her shrine for a prison?

... *No.* This was the goddess, not Duke Jurgo. Nikys wasn't here to bargain for something to which she had no native right, trading favors. The court of the sacred well wasn't a marketplace. There was no way to put a value on what she sought.

*And no need, child.*

Nikys trembled, not sure whose thought that was.

*Lady. I do not sin against You, and no forgiveness is required. I am here to do today exactly what a daughter ought. I lay my actions as an offering at Your feet, because we should give to the gods the very best of what is in us.*

*There is no offense to You in me.*

And she knew it to be true.

Penric sighed, rolled over, and sat up, then looked alarmed. "Why are you crying?" he whispered.

"Am I?" said Nikys. She wiped at her cheeks to find them wet. *Daughter's waters, given back.* Her head, and heart, felt overfull in a very different way than before. "It's all right."

"I can take—"

She reached out and caught his hand, laid a finger to stop his anxious lips. "No. It's really all right. We can go, now." She echoed his own words back to him. "It will be very well." This time, she stood first, and pulled him up after her.

# XI

DES WAS CRYING, too. Pen was surrounded, inside and out, by crying women. It was appalling.

His demon's response at least was familiar from their previous sidewise encounters with something like this. *Or Someone like this.* Demons were terrified of gods, the one power that could destroy them. Des's shaking was simple fear. Or maybe not-so-simple fear. Interestingly, she wasn't curled in as tight a ball within him as usual. If she'd had a body other than his own, he'd have imagined her prone, arms out hugging the floor tiles, face turned away, all abject surrender.

Nikys . . . was something else altogether. Whatever it was, it didn't include a speck of fear. Which was unnerving in its own right.

She wasn't gulping or sobbing or shaking, but water still trickled in fine silver rivulets from the corners of her dark eyes. Anxiously, he drew her away to a bench in the shade of a colonnade, as far as they could get from the well and its attendant. The acolyte was watching them with a curious frown, but then her attention was drawn away by the entry of the woman with the four daughters, still overexcited from their happy encounter with the dogs.

He extended his arm around Nikys's shoulders, hovering tentatively, offering consolation if she wished it. She must have wished something, because she dove into his embrace, her hands going out to grip his draperies. It was not so much a gesture of affection as of drowning. "Whatever did you pray to the goddess to grant?" Pen whispered.

"Nothing." She shook her head. "I made an offering. I suppose."

The five functions of prayer, Pen had been taught, were service, supplication, gratitude, divination, and atonement, of which supplication and divination were the most begged and the least answered. Atonement grew in importance as one moved through life. So what song of service or gratitude was this?

"What did you feel?"

"I can't say."

"Too difficult? Or too private?"

"Both." She looked away. "I can't make claims. Putting myself forward. It might have just been heatstroke."

Pen felt her forehead, then his own. Each were equally warm in this bright day, and he spared a hope that Bosha had found a nice deep crevice. "As I once said to a man who'd had a similar experience: Do not deny the gods. And they will not deny you."

She raised her face, lips parting in surprise. "You believe me?"

"I don't have to believe. I know. Or rather, Des saw. She's almost spasming inside me right now. She'll recover in a while. She does that."

Gazing at him in consternation, she said, "You've encountered something like this before?"

"Three times. One does not forget."

She mumbled into his bodice, "It was surely no more than the brush of the hem of Her cloak."

"Mm, but it's a very great cloak. It covers the width of the world." He sighed. "Or so I imagine. The most I will ever get is a waft from the flutter of the hem in passing." As now?

Her look grew a trifle wild-eyed. "You understand this?"

"Understand?" He snorted. "As much as I might drink the sea." Envy? . . . maybe.

She swallowed, and got out, "What did you pray for?"

"It was groveling. Mostly. Lots and lots of groveling. That tapestry is downright menacing."

She tried to choke down her laugh and ended up snorting it through her nose. "You shouldn't... I shouldn't..."

"Yes, you should. Joy is a mark of Them, you see. It will likely keep leaking out of you for some while."

"Oh..." She took a breath, sat up, reordered herself. "And you deal with this sort of thing all the time?"

"Not all the time, white god forfend. Very rarely. I would not survive the overload."

"Why are you still sane?" Her lips pursed, then sneaked up. "Oh. Maybe I answered my own question."

"Now, now. Be nice." He couldn't help it; her grin was infectious. He reached out and lightly brushed the last of the silver from her soft cheeks with the backs of his knuckles. He did not blot the cool away. He tried not to feel like a greedy child snitching a treat from his sister's plate.

*Maybe not greedy. Maybe just hungry.*

The both gazed out at the court. The four girls had been dissuaded from trying to swim around the annular basin like the line of dolphins that decorated it, but were being permitted to wade and splash in the trough, skirts hiked up, shrieking. There wouldn't be a dry stitch on them, presently. Sandals were strewn everywhere. The acolyte and their mother looked on laughing.

"You know," said Nikys, "I had worked out an elaborate ruse about asking the way to the garderobe, but I don't think it will be needed. Let's just go."

"Aye."

She seemed to find it very natural to twine her arm through that of her tall friend as they quietly moved into the shadowy interior of the next building.

"Where should we look first?" said Pen.

"You're asking me? The goddess didn't exactly give me a map."

"Ah, They never do," sighed Pen. "It's practically another mark."

She finally dared to say it out loud, if very quietly: "...I think She gave me a blessing."

His lips curved up. "Even better."

She seemed to take this in, all the way, for after a breath she nodded. Then said, "So did you have a plan?"

He wrinkled his nose in doubt as they stopped and looked around the next small courtyard. "Bosha thought they'd keep your mother on the side toward the sea, where the drop is most difficult. The top four or five floors have balconies, giving potential access. Or egress. So less likely those. I'd say start on the bottom floor on the east side. Poke around, see what we find."

"What if we're stopped?"

The place was far from unpeopled, although the women they glimpsed all seemed to be hurrying about their business, with scant attention given to the pair of pilgrims not yet too far out of place. "Keep that garderobe story in reserve. It may not be a waste of invention after all."

When they came to the dimmer interior corridors, Pen shoved the green spectacles up on his head under the fold of his drapery. "I shall be glad to be rid of these. Give them back to Bosha if you can. Though not before you reach the boat."

"Of course. I hope he's all right."

After two false casts, they came to a promising stairway. Pen knew they were going the right way when the descent through fine masonry changed to one carved through solid rock. At the very bottom, the stairs turned out onto a long corridor.

On its right side, a few niches reflected an aqueous blue daylight into the corridor. A gallery of near-identical doors lay along it. The left was lined with windowless cells, some with doors across, some open, all apparently used for storage. A scattering of wall sconces were frugally unlit.

"How do we find the right door?" whispered Nikys.

"Hers will be locked, with one person behind it, most likely. If it's unlocked or no one is home, then not." Or so he hoped. *Des, I need you. Rise and shine, love.*

Reluctantly, his demon unfolded within him, still surly from her fright. *Cajoler,* she muttered, but lent him her powers. The first door on their right was both locked and unpeopled, so he opened it to scout the terrain.

As he'd guessed, it was a dormitory cell for lay dedicats. Two narrow beds, simple furnishings, an upright loom against one wall with a colorful prayer rug in progress. A small window through two feet of solid rock gave a fine sea view, and a draught of pure air. Cool, serene. Less delightful in the winter, no doubt. Significantly, no area for the preparation of food.

"The dedicats must take their meals in a common refectory somewhere," he whispered to Nikys. "Suggests your mother's may be brought to her."

He locked up after them, then ran a survey of the rest of the doors, which numbered fifteen.

"There are three doors both locked and with someone inside," he muttered to Nikys. He pointed them out. "Could be dedicats ill, or resting up for night duties. You pick."

"Me!"

"Yes."

She huffed in doubt, walked up to one, hesitated, then moved to the next. "Try here."

He didn't insult her by asking *Are you sure?* She had as good a chance at guessing as he did, and maybe better. But as he unlocked the door, swung it open, and shepherded her in ahead of him, he braced for a cry of *Oh, dear, this isn't the garderobe, sorry!* and a quick retreat.

It only got as far as "Oh—!" before she broke from him and sprinted forward.

Pen came after and eased the door closed. "Keep your voices down," he warned.

A woman lying on a cot turned toward them. Her face was first weary, then wild, as she rolled to her feet and held out her arms in time to receive the pelting Nikys.

"Oh, gods, Nikys! Did they take you, too? I thought you were safely in Orbas! Oh, gods, no . . . " The mutual embraces held power beyond the mere grip of them, and Pen stood witness in shy silence. No such reunion would ever be his again, his own mother being three years in the cold ground of a country that scarcely still seemed home. Tears started in Nikys's eyes, if not the same as before. Or maybe more closely related than Pen thought.

"No, no, I'm not a prisoner," Nikys gasped into her mother's ear, both women's sets of hands frantically feeling up and down as if to assure their owners of the other's life, health, hope. "We've come to get you out of here."

"What?" Idrene stood back, though not letting go of her daughter's shoulders.

Penric smiled and advanced, feeling dimly that the first thing a man said to his intended's respected mother probably shouldn't be *Quick, take your clothes off!* "I am so pleased to meet you, Madame Gardiki. I'm"—he hastily dumped every confusing and irrelevant honorific—"Nikys's friend Penric."

Nikys looked at him. "Yes," she said. "You are."

Madame Gardiki gave him an utterly baffled smile, reminding him of the false cordiality they'd offered to the Xarre mastiffs, as he laid the spectacles on the washstand, tossed his sack on the bed, shrugged down his draperies, and undid the blue scarf around his neck.

"Plan is you are to exchange clothes with me. You go with Nikys. Two pilgrims enter, two pilgrims leave. I stay in your cell and pretend to be you for as long as I can."

"But how do you get out?"

"I have a scheme."

*No, you don't*, scoffed Des. *It's all improvisation from here.*

"He'll manage, Mother," said Nikys. He hoped that heartening confidence wasn't feigned.

"He? . . . Oh." She stepped back a pace as he continued to disrobe, pulling off his belt and shucking the dress up over his head. With Ruchia's loose, demure clothing, they hadn't bothered with stuffing a breast-band. He was down to his trews when he realized what a bizarre figure he must present. Sky-blue eyes glittering out of a ruddy face, black bun on his nape, chest hair a smattering of gold, piebald with richly colored arms and shins but thighs and torso milk white.

Nikys, thankfully, took over the task of coaxing Idrene out of her own clothes. "It's all right, Mother, Pen's a physician."

"Yes, and I'm an army wife, but I've never seen anything like *that*." She seemed to have grasped the escape scheme at once; her distraction was all for Pen. "A physician, really? He seems too young."

"I'm almost thirty-one," Pen told her, waiting to pass along his garments. His torso was narrower than hers, but longer, but Cedonian styles were forgiving. Nikys excavated down to her mother's shift and tossed her dress his way, taking Ruchia's in trade.

Given Idrene Gardiki's still-handsome appearance at fifty, she must have been stunning at twenty. No wonder the old general had been beguiled. Not to mention young officer Rodoa before him. Her loose black hair had a mere smattering of gray in it, and Pen had kept his draperies over his head throughout, so that substitution shouldn't be a problem. It would only take a moment to wind a similar bun. At least they'd matched her skin. Her features were sharper than Nikys's, if not much like Pen's, but the green spectacles would hide a lot. The bodice of Ruchia's dress would be better-filled, but not unduly so. The clogs would still leave her wanting an inch or two of height, but if they avoided the two welcoming acolytes on the way out, and chanced a different donkey-lad for the trip down, she should pass. Pen had made sure to speak as little as possible. *Check, check, check...*

"Tell me what your daily routine has been in here, Madame Gardiki. I must know what to expect."

"Fear and boredom, mostly. I've been here three weeks—I've been scratching the days on the wall down out of sight behind the bed. Five gods, dear Nikys, how did you get here so fast?"

"We had help. You'll meet some of it in a bit. I'll tell you all the rest later."

"Do they carry in your meals on a tray?" asked Pen. "Who brings it?"

Idrene nodded. "Yes, three times a day. They haven't been starving me, except of news. I'd only just heard, at home, that Adelis had been arrested in Patos, and—dear Mother's mercy, was he really blinded? Because the men who came to arrest me said he'd fled to Orbas, and there was no word of you at all, and *nothing* made sense." Nikys guided Ruchia's dress over her head. "Darling, I'm going to trip on this hem."

"No, we brought shoes. Keep going."

She shoved her arms through the wide sleeves, and went on, "A dedicat brings the tray, but there are always these two large women with her who aren't of the Order. None of them talk to me, though I think the dedicat is curious."

"Always the same women?" said Pen.

"Usually."

"So they'd recognize I wasn't you if they saw me closely?"

"Yes, probably..." She eyed him as he adjusted her belt around his waist. "Yes. Although you make a convincing woman in general."

"I've had practice." Pen grimaced. "How soon are they due back?"

"Sunset."

"You two should be almost back to Guza by then. I might be able to fake my way through one meal. Maybe more."

"How will you catch up with us? Where will you catch up with us?" said Nikys, a distraught edge leaking into her voice.

"Akylaxio, I hope." A larger seaport up the Cedonian coast from Guza. "But if Bosha can find you what seems a good safe ship there heading north, don't wait for me. Keep going. It might be as late as Orbas."

"We're going to Orbas?" said Idrene faintly.

"Yes, Adelis has taken service with Duke Jurgo," said Nikys.

"He's better? But what—" She broke off as Nikys started yanking her hair into a bun.

"His eyesight is restored, though his face is scarred."

"That hardly seems possible."

"It was magical."

"Yes, but—"

"I mean actually magical. Pen is a sorcerer as well as a physician." She added as he opened his mouth to object, "In all but final oath."

Idrene rolled her eyes toward Pen. "Wherever did you find him?"

"He found us. Long story, which I will tell you *later*." She made her mother sit on the cot, and knelt to fit the raised clogs.

"Oh, mustn't forget this," said Pen, drawing the thong of his coin purse over his head. He advanced to fit it over Madame Gardiki's, and she cast him up a look of surprise, fingering the leather bag and testing its heavy weight in her palm. "If you should get separated from Nikys, gods forbid, you shouldn't be without resources."

"But what will you have?"

"I've a coin belt around my waist." The narrow cloth band held the rest of Duke Jurgo's largess. "Nikys has another. We did come prepared." And what a huge difference that had made, although it helped that they had not been sucked dry by need for bribes. Yet. "Might be wise to hide the thong under your scarf. I did." He handed her the blue cloth, which she draped around her neck, tucking the purse in her bodice.

At last the dual transformation was completed. Nikys walked around her mother. "That's not bad, really." She frowned at Pen. "She can pass as you, at a distance. I'm not so sure you can pass as her."

"That is not your problem. You have enough on your plate. Get yourselves to Orbas before Methani even knows you're gone."

"Oh, you think it was old Methani behind all this?" said Idrene, eyes narrowing behind the green spectacles. "Plausible."

Pen herded them both toward the door. "Madame Gardiki, so good to have met you. I trust I will see you again soon."

She made a vague protesting noise, then threw up her hands, muttering, " 'Over the wall, boys, follow me.' *Yet again*." Plainly a quote of some personal significance. He hoped he'd get its story later.

Nikys stopped in front of Pen, glowering up at him. She bit her lip. Drew breath. "I absolutely forbid you to get yourself killed, either, you know."

Was that how a woman said *I love you* without saying *I love you*? Pen thought it must be so.

He grinned and touched his hand to his heart, echoing her echo. Then tapped her lips twice with his thumb, for whatever blessing he could muster. "Our god guard you on your way. And the rest of His kin."

When he closed and locked the door behind them, the cell felt very silent and empty.

# XII

AS SHE GUIDED her mother into the dim blue corridor, the goddess's blessing still seemed to bubble in Nikys's veins like some fizzy wine. The elated confidence in which it cloaked her should not become overconfidence, she reminded herself sternly, because that would be to take more than was offered. She still had to control an irrational urge to smile.

Idrene pulled the green spectacles down her nose and peered over them. "How does he see in these things?"

"They will be better outside, which is where they are intended to be used," Nikys whispered back. "Although Pen can also see in the dark. One of his handier skills."

Idrene glanced back to her door at click of its lock latching, apparently by itself. "I must hear more about that strange young man."

"You shall," Nikys promised with certainty, "when we get to a place we can talk. For now, don't speak to anyone if you can avoid it. Don't rush and don't linger. Pen said—or maybe it was Ruchia—we should move as though we had bespoken dinner in the village tavern, and didn't want to be late."

Idrene nodded. "Who's Ruch—never mind. Later."

Nikys led back the way they had come in, minus the wrong turns. In the court of the sacred well, a last few pilgrims had arrived and were occupying the attendant's attention. The only signs of the woman with the four daughters were the puddles left around the trough, drying more slowly as the afternoon shadows moved across the tiles. They sped past the tapestry in reverse order. Idrene eyed it sideways, reaching out for a bare touch. "Hm. Maybe it's as well it wasn't Adelis to come to my rescue."

In the forecourt, while Nikys signed them out in the ledger, the silky dogs sniffed Idrene indifferently. Nikys received many tickling licks on her sandaled feet. She wasn't sure if it was for Pen's lingering geas or some scent of the goddess, but the dogs whined in disappointment as she left.

Then across the drawbridge, under the benign eyes of the armed male dedicats guarding it. This wasn't the end of their escape, Nikys reminded herself, just the first stage, though Idrene vented a long exhalation as they stepped onto the gravel.

Nikys made straight for the top depot of the donkey livery. As they were led down the winding road once more, Idrene adjusted her spectacles and stared around, concealing tension. The time it took to descend the hill seemed unnaturally longer than it had taken to ascend. Doubtless an illusion. The whole east side of the island lay in its own shadow by the time they found Bosha, sitting with their luggage in the lee of the same house as before.

He rose as they approached and gave them a polite bow, though his hand did not touch his heart. Apparently that enigmatic gesture was reserved for Tanar and Lady Xarre.

As Idrene stopped warily, blinking, as one tended to do at first sight of the albino's singular features, Nikys hurried to introduce them. "Mother, this is Master Surakos Bosha, Lady Tanar's secretary. He's been helping us, by the kind courtesy of Lady Xarre."

"Madame Gardiki. A pleasure." The light voice was smoothly cultured, and Nikys wondered again at his origins.

"Oh." Her mother relaxed, returning a nod. "Yes, I see! A few of Adelis's letters from Thasalon mentioned you, Master Bosha." She added aside to Nikys, "Not that he wrote that often. I'm sure his fingers weren't broken, though in that case he could still have dictated something to a scribe."

"I know he wrote you from Patos. I made him."

"Ah, that accounts for it. Thank you, dear."

Bosha glanced up the hill toward the just-visible blue roofs of the Order, reflecting the last gleams of sun. How soon would the gaolers be bringing the prisoner's supper? "I suggest we get off Limnos first. All else can follow."

"Yes," agreed Idrene, fervently.

Bosha took charge of their luggage servant-fashion, and they followed him to the dock.

As the boat heeled in the soft evening breeze, they were again surrounded by strangers within earshot. Still no chance to talk. The late afternoon light was warmer in color, but not much of an improvement for Bosha, who pulled down his hat and sought what shade the deck provided. While the crew moved about them, exchanging cheerful calls, and the rigging creaked and the waves slapped, Nikys and Idrene held hands in silence.

Nikys wondered how far the blessing of the goddess extended. Her Order? The island? Or, as Penric had claimed, the width of the world?

With the sea light in her eyes that he so plainly loved, Nikys meditated on Penric. After that overwhelming moment of prayer in the well court, the validation and valediction he had so casually bestowed on her had stunned her almost as much. It was the most outrageous claim she had ever made in her life: to be, however briefly, god-touched.

*He believed me.*

If he had not . . . she still would have known. *But he believed me.* It seemed an intimacy strangely deeper than a kiss.

No, better . . . he *knew*, as she had. She thought she'd plumbed his depths—she could, after all, list every one of his demon's former sorcerous riders by name, in order, and was slowly gathering their biographies, but . . . What other mysteries did that packed blond head hold? *If you let him sail back to Adria, you'll never find out, now will you?* She sighed.

Aside from one slightly seasick passenger who almost tottered over the gangplank, saved by the conducting sailor-girl, they landed without incident. Nikys looked back at the distant hump of Limnos, dark against the glowing sunset. Had Pen brought off his plan of passing for her mother at dinner, or were the Order's residents just now starting to search for their missing prisoner? And if so, had Pen escaped arrest or not? Firmly, she reminded herself of his victory over the bottle dungeon. The memory didn't help that much.

"Should we take some of that?" asked Idrene, as Bosha hoisted their belongings once more.

"No, Madame. I'm going to fetch the cart. You'll best serve by picking up some food and drink we can eat on the road. Meet me where the south shore road leaves the village." He glanced west. "I'm loth to lose any light we have left." Though full dark would still overtake them long before they reached Akylaxio, and the new moon would be no help. That town was walled, thus the gates would be shut at dark and require some negotiation for admittance, or else a wait till dawn.

The Guza street markets were deserted at this hour, so Nikys returned to the same inn where they'd stayed before. She was made to pay a gallingly stiff price for the basket that she would not be returning. Idrene stayed outside on the bench. But the two women wearing the blue scarves and weary demeanors of pilgrims returning after their long day's outing drew few glances.

Bosha arrived at almost the same time as they did where the houses straggled off along the south road. He jumped down and handed them up into the cart. It was a small, light, open vehicle, with an oiled sailcloth hood that might be raised to protect passengers from the elements, and well-sprung. Bosha, hat now not shielding him from the sun so much as concealing his memorable white hair, played driver with bland assurance, clicking Lady Xarre's well-bred horse into a trot. Nikys and Idrene settled back into the padded rear seat with near-matching huffs of relief.

"I can't believe we're really doing this," said Idrene.

"I've done it before, with Adelis and Penric. I can't say I've become used to it."

Idrene turned to her, the public mask dropping from her urgent face. "Tell me everything that befell you!"

"You first."

"Hah. I imagine that will take less time." Her hand clenched on her knee. "I had no warning, just a troop of imperial soldiers pounding on our door, shouting for admittance. They told me they had an order for my arrest, but didn't even say where I was going. They may not have known. I'd barely time to pack a few necessities and tell off the servants. The boys were reasonably restrained—perhaps your father's shadow daunted them—but they ransacked the house for papers and correspondence. Thank goodness there are copies of my most important documents at the notary's."

"It was the same when the governor's men came to our villa in Patos, after Adelis was arrested at the barracks," said Nikys. "They seized every paper they could find, including all my old letters from Kymis. I was so furious about that. But they didn't steal much, and no one was raped, not even the maidservants. Although most of them quit right after. I couldn't blame them."

Idrene nodded. "I have no idea what's left at home by now. It's been three weeks." She blew out her breath. "Such a bother. I believe if they'd burned the place to the ground, it would be less a burden on my mind."

Nikys, who'd thought her mother would be as hard to extract from the house she'd shared with Florina as a whelk from its shell, was startled at this assertion.

"I wonder if I'll ever get anything back," Idrene went on. "If we're in Orbas for long, the house will surely be stripped, confiscated, and sold." She scowled. "After that, they hauled me out to that island, and then it was three weeks of pacing the cell staring at that sea-moat, and to think I used to like sea views, and no one telling me *anything*. Mend that, I beg you."

Bosha's back was very straight, but Nikys fancied that if he could swivel his ears like the horse, they'd be pointed their way. He had a very good memory, she recalled Tanar bragging.

Nikys began to recount the tale from Adelis's arrest to their arrival in Orbas, in much greater detail than she'd confided to Tanar. It ended up more scrambled than she'd hoped, as her mother kept interrupting with muddling questions that made her lose the thread. She began to have more sympathy for Tanar when she realized that every other name out of her own mouth wasn't *Adelis* either. She glided very lightly over their interlude in Sosie, which had revealed some truly unexpected skills on Penric's part. She dwelt more on the frightening injury he had taken in the uncanny fight with that other sorcerer. Less on how frightening it had been when his magics had brought down *half a hillside*.

"The poor fellow, what a welcome to Cedonia!" Idrene commented. "First he gets his skull cracked, then tossed into a bottle dungeon, then this!"

"He can turn his healing on himself," said Nikys. "Fortunately. Or his demon does. She seems to favor him greatly." Her frequent backtrackings trying to explain Desdemona to her mother were responsible for much of the muddle. Appropriate for a chaos demon, Nikys supposed.

Gleaming reflections from the sea, glimpsed to their right, were keeping the road visible well into the long twilight. Bosha pulled the cart off at a sheltered spot, tended to the horse, then climbed in to sit backward on his seat as Nikys shared out the food and drink from the basket. Idrene made polite inquiries into the healths of Lady Tanar and Lady Xarre, about which Bosha as politely assured her, as though they were sitting down in some gracious dining room.

"I hope I may yet get a chance to meet them, someday," Idrene sighed.

"You would quite like Lady Tanar," said Nikys. "And she, you. I should write when we reach Orbas, to tell her of our safe arrival."

Bosha sat bolt-up. "I would beseech you not to, Madame Khatai! This has all been dangerous enough. Vile suitors I can fend off. I did as much for Lady Xarre, when she first employed me in her early widowhood. The imperial government outmatches me."

Nikys took in the well-hidden implications of that, and slowly swallowed her mouthful of dried apricot. "Surely Lady Xarre's wealth buys some protection?" Or was Bosha the protection that it bought? *No . . .* She didn't imagine he was underpaid, yet that sort of loyalty wasn't bought with coin, but rather, kind.

Bosha, a trifle self-consciously, eased back. "But it draws down greater dangers. Men may strive to marry a fortune if they can, but are willing to try less pleasing methods to secure it if they can't. A charge of treason, no matter how contrived, makes a fine shield for stripping the accused of his property. Or hers."

"As even my son lately found," Idrene agreed grimly. "And him a general."

"I once thought his rank might be enough to make him safe," said Bosha, "and safe for Lady Tanar, but the events in Patos proved otherwise, if they blinded the man on the basis of one forged letter."

"Learned Penric says he's very sorry about that," Nikys put in. She had been forced to reveal Penric's Adriac origins to her mother, and therefore to the listening Bosha, or there would have been no explaining him at all. "The reply he carried from Adria was in good faith, he claims, but Adelis's enemies had it off him within half an hour of his setting foot in the country. He thinks their agent was watching him the whole time."

"No doubt," said Bosha. "Events have overturned nearly everything, but with the amount of paper they seized from both your houses, they could have manufactured something just as lethal. When I worked in the Thasalon chancellery, we could have done it with six lines." He chased a bite of cheese with a bite of bread.

Nikys's eyebrows rose. "I didn't know you had served in the imperial bureaucracy."

He shrugged. "Almost eight years. It's not a secret. Although my career was under the reign of the prior emperor, and was truncated when he was."

"And as violently?" inquired Idrene, much interested.

"Only because my father chose to throw in our family's lot with one of the losing pretenders. I might have been able to weather the storm otherwise." He grimaced. "Or had I not let him draw me home when the wrong soldiers arrived. Bad day. I barely escaped with my life." He took a swallow of barley-water. "Cured me of ambition."

Idrene looked as though she had no trouble filling in the horrors he'd left out. Nikys did some mental calculations.

"Was that when you went into Lady Xarre's service?"

"Indirectly. I'd fled the debacle—"

Nikys translated that as *slaughter*.

"—at my family's estate, and ended up taking shelter that night in the Xarre garden. In what turned out to be Lady Tanar's tree house, which was not at all what a boy would have imagined as a tree house. I thought the reason all the furnishings seemed so small was because I was delirious. Which I did become, later on."

He eyed his appreciative female audience hanging on his tale, and unfolded a trifle more. "When Lady Tanar found me there the next day, I begged her to hide me. I'd some dim notion of making it seem like a game to her. She entered into it with more enthusiasm than I quite... quite knew what to do with. Smuggled me food and drink and bandages." He touched the left side of his mouth, which quirked up. "My physician was six, and had never sewn anything but a hem before, but she did her best. I can still picture the charmingly intense look of concentration on her face as she bent over me. Stabbing me repeatedly." His amusement slipped to a grimace. "And my blood up to her wrists. That was disturbing. In retrospect. At the time I had other things on my mind.

"Really, it was the first thing I ever taught her. How to sew up skin. She was a shockingly quick study. It set the tone for our future dealings in a way, hm, that I've never been able to get back under my control since." He looked up, producing an awkward smile. "And that's my one and only war story, in full."

Nikys wagered not. Neither sole nor complete, though evidently pivotal.

"And here I am telling it to the general's widow. You lived through those times. I'm sure you've seen worse."

"No," said Idrene, with a thoughtful look at him. "Merely more."

He hesitated, then inclined his head in delicate appreciation.

"How did you get out of the tree house?" Nikys couldn't help asking.

"Ah. The game couldn't last, of course. After about two weeks I grew so feverish Lady Tanar became frightened enough to ask for help. Of her mother, fortunately for me. I think the servants would have turned me over to the soldiers, or just tossed me into the street. Lady Xarre chose otherwise. I was kept discreetly in her household until I recovered. I found ways to make myself useful, and stayed."

So much so that he was still there fourteen years later?

"Lady Xarre took a risk," Idrene observed. Her tone made it an observation of fact, not a judgment.

Bosha opened his hands. "Time went on, the capital settled back down. I was forgotten soon enough. My family were not great lords. None of my older brothers survived to renew the threat. Nor was I going to start the clan over."

Which was one reason the court bureaucracy favored eunuchs for high posts; they could not put the aggrandizement of their nonexistent children over the needs of the empire. Despite all, the clan game was still played, with families cutting and placing a spare son in such service to later boost brothers or nephews. Nikys wondered if the Boshas had once had some such plan for their odd fifth son. It seemed to have gone profoundly awry, if so.

"My father lived for a while, after. I was glad of that." His crooked lips drew back in a smile that was all sharp edges, like a poisoned blade. "Long enough to know I was his sole remaining son."

He turned about and climbed down from the cart to ready the horse for the next stage.

Which raised another question, which Nikys absolutely could not ask: had Bosha been a *volunteer*, exactly, for his bureaucratic career? Or had he been pressured or forced into it by a family overburdened with sons competing for their inheritances? That, too, happened sometimes.

*No*, she thought, contemplating his story. *I've no need to ask.*

The starlight scintillated overhead as they took the road again, but the deep shadows on the ground slowed them to a walking pace. At times even the earnest carthorse balked, and Bosha would go to its head to lead it, murmuring reassurances in the fuzzy flicking ears. Nikys hoped the pale man's misery in bright light was repaid by better vision at night.

At least they were making steady progress away from Limnos. She hesitated to call it the right direction, as they would have to double back north by ship to circumnavigate the Cedonian peninsula and reach Orbas again. If they had to sail without Penric would there be some safe way to leave him word which ship they'd taken?

Would he be safe at all, or was he being as overconfident as whatever error had led him to that first ugly sojourn in the bottle dungeon? His powers were astonishing, but subtle, and she knew he could be taken by surprise, or overwhelmed by numbers. Her mind's eye went on to produce an unwanted string of vivid playlets of how this might happen, growing more and more horrific and bizarre. And unlikely, she told herself sternly. He would not end up smashed on the rocks, or drowned in the sea, or beaten by brutal soldiers till the blood ran down to flood those blue eyes with opaque red. He had skills. He had tricks. He had Desdemona.

So few people knew how *valuable* that bright blond head was, that was the trouble. How irreplaceable. The notion of him being killed by ruffians wholly ignorant of what they destroyed was the most sickening of all.

She wished her imagination came with a lever to shut it off, like an irrigation gate. This nightmare garden needed no watering.

The darkness was cooling rapidly. Nikys leaned against her mother, who leaned equally exhausted against her, and not just to share heat. As the horse plodded on, Nikys wondered if she had just traded a gold coin for a gold coin.

# XIII

DES FELT THE PRESENCE of the women in the corridor before Pen heard the key in the lock. Swiftly, he huddled himself up on the cot facing the wall, drapery drawn over his head, simulating a prisoner in deep depression at her fate. Rather as Idrene had looked when they'd first come in, come to think.

He trusted he wouldn't have to attempt a geas. Apart from the challenge of trying to cast it on three subjects at once, the trouble with using a geas on a person—as contrasted with an animal—was that when it wore off, the person *remembered*.

"Madame Gardiki?" The dedicat's voice was not unkind. The other two presences seemed bored but watchful. "Your dinner is here."

Idrene's voice had been a warm alto. Pen lightened his baritone and shoved his face into his pillow. "Just leave it on the table. I'll get to it." And, after a calculatedly reluctant moment, "Thank you."

Rattling and bustle, as they took the old meal tray and left the new one, refilled the pitcher of drinking water, refreshed the ewer on the washstand, swapped out the chamber pot in the discreet commode chair in the corner. Herded back to the doorway. The dedicat's voice, tentatively: "Is there anything else you need tonight, Madame?"

Pen shook his head into his pillow.

"Goddess bless," said the dedicat, and withdrew with her silent outriders.

*Oh, She does!* thought Pen as the lock clicked over once more. It was the one thing he'd wanted most from this dangerous masquerade: a clear half-day's start for Idrene and Nikys. The attendants would not return till dawn, barring some random bed-check. Should that occur, Des could rust the lock to slow their entry, and he could . . . well, no. That would trap him on the wrong side of the door. Hiding under the bed was bound to fail, being the first place to search. Cabinets and chests would be as bad, had they existed.

Pen went to the deep window and looked out. In the last level light, a few golden sails hurried toward the harbor of Guza. He wondered if Nikys was aboard one, or if they'd already landed. The specks were much too far away to make out figures aboard.

The window had wooden shutters on this side to close against the drafts. Would parchment or glass be substituted in winter? If not, it would make for a gloomy chamber. The opening was taller than wide. He could not fit in his shoulders square-on, but turning sideways he might slip through easily. Lying along the grainy sill, he put his head out for a survey.

He looked into a wide gulf of air, across the darkening blue strait, and down a dizzying slide of stone to a distant necklace of rocks with the white lace of surf foaming over them. Mountaineer or no, the drop was as appalling as it was awe-inspiring. A thin crinkle might be the lower reaches of the penitential steps. An upper course, hacked into bare rock, still lay sixty feet below his window. He shuddered, and determinedly found another direction to study.

Left and right, he could just make out the apertures of the fourteen other windows cut on this level. No ledges, no handholds to even begin to entice him out. He was secretly relieved. Twisting his neck, he studied the jutting joists and braces of the balconies twenty feet up. A man with a grappling hook and a death wish might make something of that, but he had brought neither.

His escape, when it came, would have to be through the corridor. Somewhere to his left, the precipitous stairway must rise to the level of the buildings and climax at a gate other than the closely guarded, and presently raised, drawbridge. Such a postern was doubtless locked and barred for the night, which was fine from this side even without magic.

That exit would leave him to make his way down all two thousand steps in the moonless night. Never had he been more grateful for Des's dark vision. At least it seemed unlikely he'd have to crawl over any other climbers on the curves.

Feeling heartened to have a clear plan, he washed his hands, sat, and consumed Madame Gardiki's dinner. It was a cut above the seminary food in his old student refectory; probably the same as the ladies of the Order were sitting down to eat together somewhere. The portions could have stood to be a little more generous. A search of the room after he'd cleaned his plate turned up only a small bag of almonds, which he methodically cracked and ate by way of dessert.

There would still be too many women abroad in the precincts to venture out yet. He emptied his own clothes out of his sack and gratefully put them on, then used Madame Gardiki's hairbrush to tidy his still-black hair and tie it into a proper queue. Gathering up her few belongings, he put them in the sack by way of trade. He might have a chance to give them back to her. Her dress he would put back on over his tunic and trousers, to give the proper silhouette to any watchers he might encounter in the darkened halls, later.

That left her shawl. He eyed the window, and thought he might put the wrap to best use by pitching it out to be found on the rocks below. Leaving her gaolers to wonder if they were searching for an escapee, or the body of a suicide carried off by the tide, a theory supported by her still-locked door. That should be good for some splendid misdirection.

Satisfied, Pen drank a couple of glasses of water to assure he wouldn't oversleep past dawn, then lay down on the cot for a restoring nap.

❖ ❖ ❖

Someone was calling him. *Ake...p...ake...up...wake...up! Des...?*

A heavy hand gripped his shoulder, and Pen froze, mentally scrambling to prepare some burst of action. Or magic. Or both.

*About time!* cried Des.

And then an anxious male voice murmured, "Mother...?"

*...Oh*, said Des. *Dear.*

It was not a voice Pen recognized. Certainly not Adelis's. Pen let his snatched-up chaos carefully leak away. Sighed. And said to the wall, "By which I'd guess you must be Ikos Rodoa."

The figure, a black hulk in the darkness, gasped and recoiled. The faint starlight and sea-light glimmering in from the window barely allowed eyes to distinguish shadow from substance, though Pen thought he might have sensed him by the smell, a long workday's worth of dried sweat. *Des, light.*

The colorless clarity of Pen's night-sight sprang forth, revealing a sturdy man with broad shoulders, Cedonian-dark hair, and rounded features that might be pleasant were they not clenched in dismay. The man whipped a blade from his belt, but did not at once attack, possibly because he could not tell Pen's head from his tail in the gloom.

Not quite sure what was going to happen when he remedied that, Pen said, "I'm a friend. Don't cry out," and allowed the pair of candles on the washstand to flare to life. The sudden yellow glare seemed searing to dark-adapted eyes, and they both blinked and scrunched their lids against it. The wavering knife blade winked flame.

Why did every Cedonian he met start by trying to stab him? Slowly, Pen rolled over and sat up on the edge of the bed, holding his hands open and still.

"You're not my mother!"

Pen suppressed an acerb reply in favor of efficiency. "Madame Gardiki escaped earlier. Your effort is admirable but a bit late." Wait. The door... the door was still locked. The rush of shock at last cleared the sleep fog from his brain, and he added sharply, "How in five gods' names did you get in here?"

The man pointed mutely at the window.

Pen jerked up and strode to stare out, to be confronted with a confusing mess of cables, pulleys, and a couple of dangling loops that resembled, and may have been, canvas saddle girths. He followed four long ropes upward to where they were apparently hooked to some balcony joists. He didn't look down again, because that would be too unsettling. "Ah," he said, a little thickly. "That's right. You're the bridgebuilder." He drew back inside.

"Who in the Bastard's hell are you?" Ikos demanded.

*Or out of it*, murmured Des, as intent and perplexed as Pen.

"My name is Penric. I'm . . . helping Nikys rescue her mother."

The dark eyes flickered at his half-sister's familiar name, if Pen was guessing this right. "Why?"

The simple answer had worked before, and had the advantage of being true. "I'm courting Nikys."

"Oh." Ikos sheathed his knife and raised a large hand to scratch through his mop of short-cut hair. "Time someone did that." His eyes narrowed. "D'you know what's going on? I'd stopped in at Mother's house a few weeks ago. Neighbor said she was arrested, and General Arisaydia blinded in Patos. Why they'd take her if he'd already been blinded made no sense to me, but I followed on and tracked her here. Took me another week to figure how to get her out."

At his expectant look, Pen said, "Adelis's sight recovered, and he and Nikys escaped to Orbas."

"Huh! *That's* a miracle. But that explains. Those idiots at Thasalon court have sure made themselves an enemy now." He nodded shortly.

Pen was rather fascinated by just how fast Ikos connected the political gaps in this complicated tale. But then, he was a Cedonian born and bred.

Ikos frowned around. "Is that water?" He strode to the washstand and drank directly from the pitcher, long gulps, then paused to stare, puzzled, at the candles.

Pen quickly redirected his attention. "When you got Madame Gardiki out"—had he planned to transport her on that terrible contraption, like a timber being raised into place?—"what were you going to do with her?"

"Couldn't take her home, they'd look there. Eventually. Same problem hiding her in my work crew. I figured to send her to some friends in Trigonie. I built a bridge there two years ago."

All right, that was reasonable, although there was a bit of a gap between dangling from a balcony on Limnos to surprising some host in the duchy of Trigonie. It didn't sound much more tenuous than any of Pen's plans. Each of their schemes, it seemed, were sound in their ways. Until they'd run headlong into each other . . .

And now there was a problem. Two problems.

Ikos evidently felt it, too. Propping his fists on his hips, he looked Pen up and down. "Brother-in-law, eh?"

Pen mentally fitted the term on Ikos in turn, and felt disoriented. "If she'll have me."

"Then I suppose she'd be upset with me if I left you here. Mother'd likely have words, too." He sighed in a very traditional male-put-upon-by-women manner. Possibly not completely sincere. Given the amount of trouble he'd put himself to, unasked, to arrive in this spot.

Pen had one dress between them, and he didn't think it would fit Ikos, shorter and squarer than Penric anyway. Pen would have to use his dark-sight to guide the two of them through the precincts as quickly and quietly as possible, and take a chance on encounters with the residents. Maybe Ikos would have a clue where the stair-postern lay.

"We had better go out together," said Pen.

"Aye," Ikos reluctantly agreed.

Pen started for the door. Ikos started for the window.

They both stopped. "Where're you going?" asked Ikos. He pointed seaward. "Way out's that way."

"You . . . propose to take us both in your, uh, device?" Des actually screeched: *He's not getting me up in that thing!* Pen winced.

"Why not? I was going to take my mother. It's perfectly safe to twice her weight and mine. I tested it." He rubbed his stubbled jaw. "What's the matter? Got no head for heights?"

"I do reasonably well at them," said Pen, while Des gibbered, *No, no, no!* "But that's a lot of height out there." If it was true a dying man saw his life flash before his eyes, Pen thought that fall might give enough time for all thirteen of his and Des's.

Ikos shrugged. "Way I figure, once a drop is enough to kill you, any more you add makes no difference."

"A reasonable argument."

*No it's not, it's insane!*

Pen went to take another look at the contraption, and check the clock of the stars. The two girths, he judged, must be intended as seats like bosun's chairs. The succession of pulleys was more complex, the logic of their sequencing not immediately obvious to his untrained eyes. It was certainly an ingenious device.

Des radiated something like murderousness at his open intrigue.

Pen raised his glance to the horizon to check for any recognizable constellations, and drew a harsh breath. The stars to the east were melting away into the steel gray of dawn. He turned back to the room. "It's much later than I'd thought."

Ikos tilted one hand back and forth. "The stairs were about what I'd calculated, but walking my way across under the balconies took longer than I'd planned. May be faster going back for the practice." He hesitated. "Slower for the added weight."

"I think we'd better try my way."

"Which is what?"

"Sneaking."

Ikos's mouth screwed up in misgiving. "How're you getting out the door?" He paused. "How'd you get in here, for that matter?"

"I'm good with locks."

"Well, so would I be, if I had my tool belt with me. Left it behind for the weight, though." His eyes narrowed at Penric. "How do I know there aren't half-a-dozen guardsmen the other side of that door, waiting for me?"

"There aren't. Yet. Besides, if this were that sort of trap, better to have them on this side of the door. You'd be trussed like a chicken already."

A long, thoughtful silence. "I like my way better."

How was he to persuade Ikos to trust him in three minutes, when three months had not sufficed for his sister Nikys? Pen sucked breath through his teeth. Threw up his hands. "Fine. Your way. So long as it's *now*."

*No!* cried Des as he crossed the room, wadded up the shawl, and pitched it out, to Ikos's evident bafflement. He reconsidered his sack. If he was staging a convincing suicide, the personal effects would need to be left in place, right. He grabbed it up and circled the room again, putting things back. Shoved the sack and dress under the mattress. "Right, ready—"

The lock rattled. Pen whipped his head around and rusted it stuck before Des could even voice an objection. "We just ran out of time," he whispered. "Go." He held a finger to his lips as thumps sounded on the door.

Ikos oozed sideways through the window. Penric glanced back. On the other side of the door, the sturdier attendant was trying her hand turning the big iron key. Pen ran a hair-thin line of rust through its barrel and grinned as it snapped off in the lock. He was fairly sure the sharp words that resulted, muffled by the door, weren't ones a lady was supposed to say in the Daughter's Order. Or anywhere else.

He added an extra burst of corrosion to guarantee the half-key would stay jammed in the face of anything short of a hammer and chisel, drill, and crowbar. Or an ax.

Ikos's feet kicked and disappeared. Pen eased his torso through, watching the man, one arm wrapped around a rope or vice versa, bend up and thread his legs through the loop of a girth. He wriggled it under his hips, straightened his spine and shoulders, and braced the other arm over the suspending eye and swivel and across his chest. He rotated dizzyingly, snaked his hand around the second suspension rope, and swung the girth toward Pen. "Just like that," he whispered. "Then hold still and leave the rest to me. You can't help, and I don't need interference."

Des wailed as Pen copied the procedure. The girth closed up tight around his narrow hips as it took his weight. He clamped both arms around the suspending lines, gripping each other.

It wasn't often that he spoke sharply to his demon, but he did now. *Des, we're committed. Settle down and keep your chaos strictly to yourself until I say otherwise!*

A sense of a whimper, and a tight, unhappy ball within him. She would be surly for days, unless he made it up to her somehow. A process she would probably seek to stretch out to the maximum benefit to herself, once she regained her tone of mind. Minds. Apology-gifts to a nonmaterial person took some ingenuity.

Assuming they survived. Well . . . assuming he survived.

*I do not wish to end up in an ugly engineer*, she whined. *Or a dolphin.*

*I don't think he's ugly. Sawed-off and tough-looking, sure.* Pen chose not to look down to try to spot dolphins frolicking in the distant waters.

Ikos set about hauling on one pulley-rope after another, in some balanced pattern known only to himself. The swaying jerks of the girth at each yank did unpleasant things to Pen's stomach. But, slowly and methodically, they began inching upward.

As they passed the window above Madame Gardiki's room, Pen held his breath, but no awakening dedicats or acolytes tripped over to look through and take in the sunrise. And the man-rise. He could do things to disable their alarm cries like the Xarre mastiffs, but if it seemed an offense to him, it was possible the goddess would think so as well.

At least, Pen consoled himself, he had spared Madame Gardiki this ordeal. Unless she would have enjoyed it. From their few minutes of acquaintance, it was hard to know. She might have liked the part about seeing her elder son hard at work, and cleverly. Pen was pretty sure she wouldn't have liked his risks.

Pen rotated toward the sea view, watching the thin red line of light start to glow behind the Cedonian mainland, eating up the steel gray. On any other occasion, the return of the sun would be a delight. Pen longed for an eclipse. The new moon was in the wrong place for it, alas.

The vertical progression lurched to a halt just under the balconies, and Ikos commenced a complicated dance with his pulleys of tightening three lines so as to loosen and ease the one in the rear from its joist, unhook and extend it forward, rehook it, and repeat. They moved north in the thinning shadows at an excruciating pace. Ikos, above him, was breathing heavily and sweating. Pen tried to estimate the distance and time left to make the end of the row, racing the advent of the sun like very anxious, very careful slugs.

The gaolers with breakfast would be a good long stretch getting through the door. First would come time wasted trying to extract the broken key, initially seeming an annoyance rather than an emergency, then more in futile attempts to unstick the lock. Some running back and forth to find the tools for the job, and wake the women in charge of them. The hinges had been on the inside, inaccessible, or he'd have rusted them as well. The planks were thick oak, which were going to need that ax. Or a battering ram. Only once they'd broken through could they know their prisoner was missing— or suicided—and set up a cry. The echoes of woodchopping would be Pen's sign that he and Ikos had very little time left.

A red-gold sliver crested the distant hills, then became a crescent, a ball, and then too bright to look upon. The boundary of blue shadow on the slope below dropped like night's floodwaters receding. From behind the thick walls of the Order, occasional light voices echoed, too muted to make out words. In some courtyard beyond the blue roofs, a choir of several voices began a hymn, echoing and eerie with the distance. No ax-blows yet.

Ikos, just above Pen, kept grimly working. Penric, reminded of his duties as a divine and otherwise feeling to be inert cargo, began praying. There was nothing in the least rote about his morning's tally of the gods here, no.

Within Penric, Desdemona moaned. He could feel the chaos roiling within her, a growing pressure like a bad stomach about to heave up. *My demon is seasick.* The last thing in the world he needed was for her to begin vomiting unshaped disorder into the rigging that suspended them above a plummeting death. Or anywhere else nearby. He stared around like a frantic nurse looking for a bucket.

The most likely thing in sight was a trio of seagulls, rising with the morning breeze and cruising the balconies for scraps. He wondered if the ladies of the Order ever amused themselves throwing tidbits to them to be caught in midair. The pale scavenger birds were shore pests, considered sacred to the Bastard as the only god who would have them. Bastard's vermin were always allowable sacrifices.

*All right, Des,* Pen thought in some exasperation. *You may have one seagull. Just one.*

A burst of gratitude and chaos caught a bird on the wing as it swooped above the balcony under which they were making their transit. With a loud pop, it exploded in a shower of feathers, blood and bones turning to dust as they fell in the white flutter. Pen winced.

That was a lot of chaos. Des must have really been in distress. *Feel better now?*

The response, had it been aloud, would have approximated the hostile noise one would expect from a friend bent over a ship's rail who'd just delivered an offering to the sea.

Ikos stared up through the gaps in the boards with a disconcerted expression, but any exclamation was caught by strong teeth biting his lip.

From inside the open door to the balcony, a startled female voice said, "What?"

Another more distant voice called, "Hekat, are you coming?"

"I'll catch up in a moment. You go on ahead."

The sound of a door closing. Pen and Ikos both froze as footsteps rapped out onto the balcony boards.

Pen caught sight of the blue tunic and skirt of an acolyte as the woman bent over to pick up a few blown feathers and roll them in her fingers. She looked up. She looked down.

Both men peered back through the board-gaps. Ikos tried a friendly smile. It just made him look like a bandit delighted with the prospect of cutting a throat.

Middle-aged acolyte. How many women named Hekat could there be in this order? Dozens, for all Pen know. She wasn't an albino. But there might, unless he was fooling himself, be a faint echo of her brother in the fine frame of her face, much the way Ikos's more robust bones echoed Nikys's. Pen feared to attempt the delicate seizure of her vocal cords with Des in such disarray. As she opened her mouth to cry out, he was driven to take a different chance.

He tapped his lips twice, looked up into the brown eye he could see, and said clearly, "Surakos."

Slowly, the mouth closed, though the stare intensified.

Ikos swiveled his head and glared at Pen in complete mystification. Pen held up a hand begging silence.

"*What*," she breathed, "has Sura to do with *this*?" A wave of her hand encompassed the lunatic configuration of tackle and men hanging from her balcony joists.

"It would take about an hour to explain in full." Which they surely did not have. "But I promise you, when he comes out for your birthday in the autumn, he'll tell you everything. It should be safe for him to speak by then."

There. The birthday visit was personal information that no one who did not know Bosha could be privy to. Would it be coin enough to buy her trust?

"Why is it unsafe now?"

At least he had her attention focused on her brother, and not on the intruders' blasphemy. "Thasalon court politics."

That eye-scrunch might be a wince. "Oh, gods," she said, in a voice of loathing. "Not again."

"He'll be all right if you say nothing of what you've just seen. Except to the Lady of Spring. You can pray to your goddess. She might even speak for us."

Now the eye grew indignant. "Do you expect me to believe you have some sort of, of holy dispensation for this?"

Pen knew they did, or at least Nikys had, but it seemed unwise to test the gods. Or the acolyte. "I make no claims. Sura can tell all."

She sat with a thump, fingering her handful of feathers. "He'd better," she muttered, and Pen knew they were safe. He motioned for Ikos to continue.

Ikos shot him a hot look that suggested Surakos wasn't the only one who would be interrogated later. But he started working his pulleys and hooks again, and they recommenced their onward lurch.

Acolyte Hekat went to the gap between her balcony and the next—and last, thankfully—and hung her head over to watch their progress. "That's the most bizarre thing I've ever seen. What in the world is it in aid of?"

"Right now, removing two men from a place they should not be as expeditiously as possible. With our heartfelt apologies, I assure you."

"Were you looking at that seagull?"

"What seagull?" Pen produced an innocent blink.

She sucked breath through her teeth and gave him a gimlet glower reminding him of how the Jurald Court cook used to successfully squeeze confessions out of him about the missing pastries. Followed by a cuff to his ear and, usually, another pastry to eat on his exit. "Is Sura going to explain that, too?"

"If I get another opportunity to see him, I'll make sure he can," Pen promised.

When they swayed out of her view, she was still sitting cross-legged rolling the feathers in her hand.

Pen discovered Ikos's plan for descending from the balcony end to the stairs when they arrived, and it was even more horrifying than he would have guessed. It consisted of Ikos lengthening Pen's suspension rope and setting him in motion like a pendulum, *swinging* some twenty or more feet over to where the rising steps curved out of sight to their pilgrim-gate. "It's perfectly safe," the bridgebuilder asserted in a whisper. "Just don't get out of your girth till you've found your feet. If you slip before then, we just try again."

Pen managed his landing on the third attempt. Desdemona, crying, insisted she wanted another seagull, but he held her off.

There followed a heart-stopping interlude watching Ikos twist himself around under the balcony, fiddle with ropes, and loosen all four hooks of his evil contraption. Pen had to detach his girth and clip its doubled line to a mysterious eye-bolt in the rock face, which held it taut for Ikos as he slid down with his machine in tow. An unclipping and undoing, a rapid winding-up of rope around the engineer's arm, and the loosed end cleared its joist and fell, leaving nothing at all in its wake. Ikos somehow drew the eyebolt anchor out of its socket in three pieces, leaving only an anonymous square hole. Pen couldn't quite see if there were any other such holes pocking the rockface.

Then another maddening delay while Ikos sat down and carefully wound and folded it all into a tight, heavy bundle, no trailing ends. Pen supposed it was how he'd packed the thing up here. In the dark, all last night. Pen really wanted to take it away from him and just heave it into the sea, but Ruchia, managing to get her one-twelfth voice heard through the general cacophony that was the upset Des, agreed it would be better to leave no evidences at all. As Ikos had already concluded, apparently.

Ikos made a final survey of the balconies, then frowned aside at Penric. "Wordy bastard, aren't you?"

*In so many ways.* "It's my stock-in-trade."

"I'll be wanting to hear more about that, later."

"I hope you'll get a chance."

Pen reflected on all that the weary Ikos had done, starting last night at dusk. And for weeks beforehand, it seemed. All that patient labor, and no pleased mother to show for it at the end after all. He regarded the start of the two thousand steps, and murmured, "Would you like me to carry that pack?"

Ikos huffed, thick eyebrows rising in surprise at him. "Aye."

Two pilgrims on the steps. It would be no unusual thing to see (and mock, probably) and their details would be indistinguishable from a distance. Pen felt very penitential indeed as he hoisted the contraption, which turned out to weigh about thirty pounds mostly in coiled rope, on his back. As he started down in front of Ikos, he could finally hear the faint crunch of ax-blows leaking from one far window.

A last look up before the rising stone eclipsed her found Acolyte Hekat still leaning on her railing, looking down studying them. He made the tally of the gods broadly over his chest at her, tapping his lips twice by way of farewell.

She touched her fingers to her forehead in return salute, and Pen thought her brother might not be the only member of her family with a strong ironic streak.

# XIV

CLOSE TO AKYLAXIO, Master Bosha found another sheltered spot to conceal the cart, where they lay up to wait out the dawn. The stop afforded more an uncomfortable doze than a sleep; still, better than nothing. His timing was good, Nikys thought, for they entered the city gates at the dewy hour when the guards were busy overseeing the influx of country folk bringing food and goods to the day-markets. Their tense wait to pass within was recompensed by being cloaked in the crowd.

The guards did not yet seem to be scrutinizing middle-aged women. If things had gone as Penric had planned, Idrene might only just now have been discovered missing on Limnos.

It didn't seem wise to assume all had gone as planned.

Still, there had to be a minimum and a maximum. If the escape was discovered at breakfast, a certain amount of time would first be spent searching the Order's precincts, and then the island. Any alarm would have the same watery barrier to pass that they had. Minister Methani's women gaolers might have to send to their master in Thasalon for instructions, though Nikys expected they'd delay that in the hopes that their report could include the prisoner being found. The period for any pursuit reaching Akylaxio could stretch out for days.

The minimum was all Nikys must worry about. If Pen had been

seized last night, a military courier could have docked at Guza bare hours behind them. Although such a message couldn't have overtaken them yet, or their reception at the city gates would have been very different. If Pen had been captured... she really wasn't sure if she should be worrying for Pen, or for Limnos. But even sorcerers couldn't fly out a window, or across a strait.

The cries of gulls and the smell of the shore announced the harbor, and Nikys stretched her neck to take it in. Bigger and busier than little Guza, smaller than Patos, much less than the maze of docks and warehouses and forests of masts that crowded great Thasalon's entrepôt. Two piers in deep-enough water allowed direct loading and unloading of vessels, and men and cranes were already noisily doing so for the handful of ships tied up. The port was active enough to rate full-time bureaucratic customs officers, although they inspected mainly for contraband and tax evaders. But they would also keep both provincial and imperial lists of wanted fugitives and criminals.

Bosha, Nikys gathered, was only slightly more familiar with Akylaxio than she was, but he found a clean-looking inn close to the harbor, and, playing servant, escorted both women inside to secure a room in which to rest and hide. He carried up their luggage, not speaking until the door closed behind them.

"I'll find a place to put up the horse and cart," he said, "then reconnoiter the harbor. I brought papers that we can finish filling out when I've found a ship." He took a sheaf from his tunic and laid it on the washstand. "Think of what names and personas you want to travel under. Don't leave the room till I get back. I'll send up a maid to see about food and drink."

"Thank you, Master Bosha," said Idrene formally, by way of accepting this program, and he nodded and departed.

Nikys went over and peeked out the window, which gave onto the other roofs of the town, mostly flat and filled with drying laundry, pots of herbs, and other useful implements. She picked up and examined the papers, which already bore seals and signatures... some of Lady Xarre's wealth was in shipping, yes, so these probably weren't even forged, wholly. Although she didn't doubt such skills were also in Bosha's repertoire, at need.

Nikys and Idrene took the chance to wash, eat, and, both familiar with the challenges of the army baggage train, reorganize their meager belongings for a quick removal when the order came. A cat-nap would be due after, to make up for the prior night.

Idrene examined Pen's medical case with interest. "This seems well thought-out. I can believe he really is a physician."

"In all but final oath. And you're snooping, Mother."

"Of course." She held up Pen's braids, which she'd unearthed in the depths, contemplating them with less irony than Bosha had. "And really a Temple sorcerer. Not hedge. Hedge would be too risky. Temple is probably all right. So, you say you're courting?"

"He says he's courting me. I didn't say I was courting him." She removed the braids from her mother's grip and restored them to their place.

"I thought you wanted to remarry. That was why Adelis invited you to Patos, wasn't it? To meet eligible men? Or at least that's the tale you both told me."

"Yes, but all the men he introduced to me were army officers. I wasn't going to travel down that road again."

"Did you tell Adelis that?"

"Not . . . exactly. I didn't want to dishearten him. He *was* trying to help."

"And also, you won a trip to Patos," said Idrene, amused. She plunked down on the edge of the bed, patting the place beside her by way of invitation.

Ruefully, Nikys shrugged and sat. "I wasn't going to say that."

"True, though?"

"Yes," Nikys admitted. "Although after Adelis was blinded, I had quite different reasons to be grateful I was there."

"Yes . . ." said Idrene, her humor melting into pensiveness. "Hideous as it all was, I'm glad you were at his side. I think things would have gone much worse for him without you. Well, your Penric certainly has nothing of the camp about him. So has he actually asked you to wed him?"

"Yes."

"And you didn't agree to it? Why? Has he some hidden defect of character?"

"Not . . . not hidden. Just complicated. He's only loaned to the duke of Adria, but he is truly subordinate to the archdivine. He either has to go to a great deal of trouble to renegotiate his Temple oaths, or I would have to follow him to Adria. I don't want to go to Adria, for all he claims he'd teach me their tongue."

"Oh. Yes. Of course he'd have to speak Adriac. But it's not his native place, you say?"

"No, he's from the cantons, some obscure mountain town. But he trained in the Weald. He speaks Wealdean, Adriac, Cedonian, Darthacan, Ibran, Roknari, and I'm not sure what all else by now. He's a notable scholar."

Idrene took this in, thoughtfully. "It's true I had my fill of being dragged from pillar to post after my father, and later yours. As a home, the army has its drawbacks. And I should not like to shift myself to Orbas only for you to run off to live in Adria."

"Penric wants me to live in the air, like a bird, for all I can tell from what he's offered."

"Bachelor habits of mind, I daresay. Well, then, your solution is easy. Insist he stay in Orbas for you, and give you a house as a bride-gift. If he won't or can't, then bid him a fond goodbye."

"Mother! I'm not selling myself to the man!"

Her mother's voice went a touch drier. "But you shouldn't be selling yourself short, either. And if you don't like that bargain, perhaps it's not such a sticking-point after all, hm?"

"Mm." This was already shaping up to be one of *those* conversations with Idrene. Nikys was almost sorry she'd started it. *Or not.* Considering how close they'd come to never having such a chance again.

Idrene lowered her voice. "But you should know, Florina's jewelry is in a box walled under the plaster on the west side of her old writing cabinet. Because everyone knows to dig up the root cellar for such things. We'd always meant for you to have it for a second dowry, when you remarried. If ever you can return there before I do, find it and take it. Married or not!"

"Yes, Mother," said Nikys, thrown aback. Florma had owned some extraordinary pieces, she recalled, some of it preserved from her own noble dowry, some gifts from her husband as he rose in rank and wealth. At the least reckoning, there might be the value of a modest house out of them, with something left over.

"So there's another resource for you. Not any more chancy than marrying some chancy man. If I were you, I'd send your sorcerer to fetch it for you. Like a hero in a tale given a task to win his princess."

"He's not *my*—and I wouldn't want him to risk his life on a *third* trip to Cedonia!" She glared indignantly, which only made her mother smile.

"So, no Adria, but we have established Learned Penric is more valuable to you than jewels. Or a house. That's a start. What else?"

Nikys sighed, unwillingly driven to recite her next verse. "I wouldn't just be marrying him. I'd be marrying Desdemona. She's going to be inside his head always. Closer than a wife, more intimate than anything I can imagine."

Idrene shrugged. "Any number of women have to learn how to share their husbands with another. I grant most of them are not chaos demons. Sometimes it works very well, sometimes it works very badly, mostly it falls somewhere between. My experience, happily, was on the better end."

"How did you decide, when you went with Father?"

"Several long, frank talks, to start."

"And he persuaded you?"

"Oh, five gods forfend, I didn't talk with the general! What a pointless waste of breath that would have been. I talked with *Florina*." Idrene waved a hand. "It helped that Florina was the shrewd and experienced woman she was." She eyed Nikys. "So . . . you seem to think this demon is a person, or persons. A woman. Can she talk, then?"

"Yes, we've talked before this. But she has to use Penric's mouth to do so. With his permission. So it's not as if I could speak with her privately. He's always with her, and she's always with him. She'd be there with us in bed, too, I might point out."

"Oh, hm, yes. That does become very personal, doesn't it?" Idrene did not expand on this, to Nikys's relief. Though she added cheerily, "On the positive side, she could never give birth to heirs rival to your own children."

Nikys set her teeth.

Yet the notion did plant itself in Nikys's mind. If her dilemma was with the demon, perhaps it was with the demon she should be talking? It would, necessarily, be a council of three. Or fourteen.

*But not impossible.* And she'd seen Penric demolish impossibilities before.

*I've spoken with a goddess. A demon cannot be more daunting.*

It was the strangest thought she'd had in a week of strangeness. Like a seed putting out slow shoots, down into the earth and up to the sky. She left it in the tender darkness for now.

"So, no Adria, better than jewels, you'd have to sleep with a chaos demon. Although I must say, it sounds as if you've rubbed along with her fairly well so far. And she did heal Adelis." This news, apparently, had gone a long way toward reconciling Idrene to Penric's uncanny aspects.

"She and Pen together. They seem to work as a yoked pair on that sort of thing."

"An astonishing one, if so. Anything else?"

Nikys looked away. This far into her heart's fears, she might as well unburden herself of the whole basket. "You know Kymis and I were never able to get a child. I keep wondering if that was my fault. . . . I could be condemning Pen to childlessness."

The puff through Idrene's nose held a sad familiarity. "I imagine Florma could have given you the best counsel on that. It's no small worry, I know. But it seems to me you have its solution already. As a physician, couldn't your Penric determine the true cause? The Temple rations out its mage-physicians like water in the desert, but you hold this one in your hand."

"Mother!" Nikys flushed. "I can't ask the man to, to look up my private parts!"

"Why not? I don't imagine he'd object. As either physician or man. What, you mean you haven't tried him out in bed yet? I would have, in your place."

"Yes, Drema, we know," sighed Nikys. "And I'm sure Ikos thanks you for it." She nudged her mother in fond exasperation. "I'm not sure I'd have your courage. Or whatever it was that carried you through. Bloody-minded determination."

Idrene chuckled. "Ikos has grown into such a dear man. So that worked out well in the end. It was rough along the way in parts, but of all my many regrets, Ikos was never one. Look at it this way. Either your fears are justified, in which case you run no risk, or they are not, and so they are settled in your favor. Or do you judge Learned Penric would run away at the news he was to be a father?"

". . . No. Absolutely not. He may even have it in his mind."

"Another thing you haven't talked about with him? This list is getting long, dear Nikys."

She hunched. "I'd be betting my whole life on the man. I did that once with Kymis. And then he went and *died* on me." The furious helplessness of that loss still reverberated, when she made the mistake of remembering.

"Oh." Idrene's smile grew crooked. "I know the answer for that one. It worked quite well for Florina. And your father. And Ikos's father, too."

Nikys raised her face. "You do? What?"

She tapped Nikys's forehead in a gesture not quite a blessing. And said, in a voice as arid as Nikys had ever heard from her, "Die first."

# XV

AS THE SUN CLIMBED, Penric and Ikos descended, negotiating the narrowest passages of the pilgrim stairs, scarcely wider than Pen's aching shoulders, to where they widened out. The elevation was much reduced by this point. Desdemona had calmed somewhat. So Pen finally asked her, *Grant you the machine was strange, and I know you've never liked heights, but why the extreme fear, Des?*

*It was an extreme drop.*

*You couldn't have died no matter what went wrong.*

A reluctant hesitation. *Sugane died from a fall.*

Des's very first human rider had been a Cedonian mountain woman of the northern peninsula. Pen still had to work to keep her broad country accent from leaking into his Cedonian, although he'd smoothed it out quite a bit through listening to Nikys's and Adelis's Thasalon-trained voices.

*A day or so after*, Des went on. *She was brought to Litikone's house, which was how I came to jump to her. It's not a memory I've shared with you. It wouldn't help you.*

Des tended to keep that final part of all her riders' histories not secret, Pen thought, so much as private. *Do you think your chaos might have contributed to the accident? You wouldn't have had it under such good control back then.*

A shifty pause. *Might have. It was almost two centuries ago. Even demons forget.*

Not much, in Pen's observation. But even demons mourned, and had a long time to do so. Grief, guilt, regret... not everything they learned how to do from their human riders was a boon. He did not press.

Ikos called a halt where the stairs twisted back to become more of a trail through scree, zig-zagging down leftward toward what Pen thought might be a boat landing. He could glimpse a timber dock, but no boats, set in a ragged bite of shoreline that could barely be called a cove.

"I'll have my pack, now," said Ikos, holding out a hand.

Pen's legs were quivering custard and his mouth was dry, but he offered gamely, "I could haul it a bit farther. Where are we going?"

"I'm going to my boat." Ikos gestured right to where a faint path led away to some hidden track above the water.

Yes, of course Ikos, with his meticulous planning, would have a boat waiting to take his mother off the island. Unlike Pen, whose plans had been more nebulous at this point, involving blending with departing pilgrims.

"You can go anywhere else you please." Standing a couple of steps above Pen, Ikos could frown down at him. "Sorcerer."

"Ah, hm. When did you figure that out?"

"Candles don't light themselves. Seagulls don't burst in midair, no matter what crap they've been eating. And I still don't know what kind of spell you cast on that poor acolyte, but I want no parts of it. I know sorcerers leak bad luck, and I don't want yours anywhere near a boat I'm on."

"I didn't put any kind of a geas on Acolyte Hekat!" Pen protested. Not that he had a way of proving it to Ikos. There were good reasons sorcerers learned to be discreet. "And I'm not a hedge sorcerer. I'm Temple-trained. Learned Penric kin Jurald, formerly of Martensbridge, sworn divine of the Bastard's Order." And of the white god in Person, but that was another story. He left off his younger-brother courtesy title of *Lord*, as he usually did, since Ikos seemed a man who would not be impressed by such empty baubles.

Pen had come far from Jurald Court, tucked in its valley in the distant cantons.

*In so many ways,* murmured Des.

"Formerly of Martensbridge? Wherever that is," said Ikos skeptically. "Where're you from now?"

"That's unsettled at present. I'm waiting for Nikys to decide. If she says yes, probably Orbas, for the time being. If no... I don't know."

Ikos's face screwed up. "Why hasn't she said yes? Widow 'n all."

"I wish I knew," Pen sighed, ignoring Des's *Do you want a list?* "I'm working on her. And not with magic, I might point out. Self-evidently."

"Hm..."

"The point is, I promise I can keep my demon's chaos off your boat. It might be hard on a passing seagull. Or a shark, or whatever. But I'm certainly not going to befoul or sink a ship I'm sailing in!" He added, prudentially, "Though neither sorcerers nor gods have any control over the weather."

Ikos folded his arms. "I've got no reason to trust anything you've said is true."

"I trust you." *More or less.* "I rode in your evil device. Isn't that proof enough?"

"It was perfectly safe!" snapped Ikos. "You're here, aren't you?"

"So is my magic. You're here, aren't you?"

Ikos's head went back and his lips tightened, but he did not at once reply.

"Look." Pen scratched his hot and sticky scalp. His fingers came away darkened. "How do you decide anything is sound? You test it, don't you?"

"If I'm trying out new gear," said Ikos, "I usually test it to destruction. To be sure."

"Ah. If you had two sorcerers, you could try that, I suppose. You see the problem."

Ikos snorted.

"I was thinking more along the lines of a question." *Ask me anything* seemed a dangerously open-ended invitation, so Pen left it at that.

"Doesn't work too well if I'm trying to decide whether you're telling the truth in the first place," Ikos pointed out. "But, I don't know... What's Nikys's objection to you? You being a learned divine and all. Seems to me the sort of thing women ought to like." His lips tweaked up. "No complaining you come home from work all smelly, eh?"

Pen suspected that had not been a compliment. "I can't say," he replied, if not with truth then with precision. "But when Nikys received the letter reporting her mother had been arrested and taken to Limnos, I was the first person she came to for help. If you don't trust me, could you trust her?"

Ikos considered. Or wavered. Or at any rate, thought about it. "I like the girl," he said at last. "Pretty solid."

"I know."

"Huh."

"You have a boat, and I urgently need to get to Akylaxio. I could pay for your time and trouble." Pen did not suggest a price; no need for anyone to know how much of Duke Jurgo's purse he was still carrying.

"Not my boat. It belongs to some friends."

"All right, I could pay them."

Ikos pursed his lips. "Doubt they'll like to have a sorcerer aboard, either."

"You don't have to mention my calling. Or anything else about me, really."

"You want me to lie to my friends?"

"You want to listen to this same argument all over again, at length? If you think you're tired of it, imagine how I feel. You don't have to lie. Just... leave it out."

"Which tells me something about you, I suppose." Nothing that Ikos approved of, by the sardonic expression on his sweaty copper face.

Pen waved his hands in frustration. "I'm supposed to meet your mother and Nikys in Akylaxio, to escort them on to Orbas. It could be a chance for you to see them. Your last for a while."

"Oh." A pause. "Why didn't you say so first?"

While Pen was still mentally flailing for a reply, Ikos led off down the side path. "Come on, then," he said over his shoulder. A tight smile. "You can carry the machine."

❖ ❖ ❖

Pen scrambled after his guide for about two miles on the scrubby trail following the shoreline. In a tiny cove, they found the boat attended by three men as sunbaked and tough-looking as Ikos. The crew waved and exchanged laconic greetings with him, but stared at Pen.

"That your mother, is it?" said one. "There's things you haven't told us about your family, Ikos, my lad."

Ikos shrugged. "Change of plans. It seems my mother's gone to Akylaxio. We need to get there."

"What, after all your trouble?"

"Aye. I'm not best pleased about it either." He jerked a thumb over his shoulder. "This one says he'll pay for the ride."

The dickering was short, since Pen, wildly anxious to be gone, closed the deal at the first suggested price. The fellows, who could have been brothers to the hardy fishermen Pen had observed putting out from Guza, presumably had been told by Ikos what risks they ran, or if not, it wasn't for Pen to apprise them.

Riding in the clear water as if floating on air, the boat might well be just such a day-fishing vessel, smelling of sun-warmed tar and timber, salt and fish-scales. It would have been substantial for the cold lakes of the cantons, but seemed disturbingly undersized for this vast blue sea. When they cast off and raised its one sail, Pen hunkered up in the shifting shade and left its management to the men who, he hoped, knew what they were doing. Ikos doubtless thought it was perfectly safe, because he curled up on a folded sack and fell into a doze. Either that or he was just too exhausted to care.

Had Nikys and Idrene reached Akylaxio unharmed? Or had they run afoul of some trouble or delay in that long night-ride they'd planned up the coast road? Lamed horse, cart-wheel come off, a tumble into a ditch? Or bandits? Pen expected Bosha could speedily dispose of one bandit, or two, but what if there'd been, say, six, or a dozen?

*Two ex-army widows are not going to make for easy victims*, Des pointed out. *I doubt Bosha would end up doing all the work himself.*

That was not quite reassuring. Although Pen was subtly impressed with what little he'd seen of Idrene's cool head so far. And Ikos, who knew her better, had plainly believed she'd handle his vile machine without panicking. Or puking. (Des growled.) If it was true that women turned into their mothers as they aged, Pen's future with Nikys might prove even better than he'd hoped.

If they both lived to see it. Or even start it.

The women couldn't yet have been overtaken by official pursuit, more dangerous than bandits, he persuaded himself. At this hour, Idrene's gaolers should still be searching Limnos. As the boat tacked southward to parallel the coast, he leaned up to watch as the island fell behind them.

And so he was the first to spot the slim, speedy patrol galley, ten oars on a side and sail set as well, as it rounded Limnos's rocky, surf-splashed curve. No fishing or cargo vessel, that. It reeked of military purpose. A distant figure in its prow pointed an arm at them and shouted something, and the galley began to angle in their direction.

Pen crept over and shook Ikos by the shoulder. "We seem to have company. Might be trouble."

Ikos stood up on his knees by the thwart, scowled, and swore.

*I could take care of them if you wanted*, Des suggested. *Just like pirates.* An unsettling sense of the chaos demon licking her nonexistent lips. *Ripped sails. Snapped stays. Fouled oars. Popped pegs. Opened seams in the hull. Fires in the galley. So many amusing things to be done . . .*

No wonder captains didn't want sorcerers aboard.

Ruchia was the only part of Des to protest. *Stay calm. If they've anything to do with us, they are looking for an escaped woman. No women on this boat. Let them search, and then go away.*

*Yes*, Pen agreed with Ruchia. He offered a sop. *And should things go badly, there might be an opportunity later for even* more *chaos.*

Not at all fooled, Des gave way, grumbling.

Ikos's crewmates didn't look any happier than he did at this visitor. Pen had heard that Cedonian islanders sometimes supplemented fishing with less benign sources of income. Smuggling. Or even piracy. But—he glanced around their lightly laden vessel—they didn't seem to be carrying any obvious contraband today.

And no escaped prisoners, either.

"Where did that thing come from?" Pen asked Ikos. The galley looked all-business, and they clearly stood no chance of outrunning it in this mild weather.

"Imperial navy keeps a station around the other side of the island," Ikos replied. "Not a full garrison. Couriers, mainly, and vessels to carry the alarm to the mainland if a threat should heave over the horizon." He added after a moment, "I checked. Didn't you?"

Pen let that poke pass.

When the galley drew close enough for shouts of *Heave-to!* to carry across the water, Ikos's crew reluctantly did so. Oars were raised, and some officers clustered at the rail, looking down into their open boat. A young sailor in an imperial uniform climbed along a rope net and made a daring leap aboard.

"We're searching for a woman." He gave a brief, tolerably accurate description of Idrene. His first close look around verified there was no one of that sex aboard, although he stared hard at Pen, distracted for a moment by his foreign eyes. Which were not the brown of his quarry, so he went on, "She might be drowned by this time. If you find her body, bring it to the officers at the Limnos cove. There's a reward. Pass the word."

Ikos's crew mumbled some interest in that last, and the sailor caught the rope tossed from his galley and managed the harder trick of returning upward, without even dipping himself in the waves. Ikos pushed off with one of their own oars, and, as soon as they were clear, the galley's oar bank came down and bit the water once more. Going who-knew-where, but, as Ruchia had predicted, *away*.

And not ahead of them toward Akylaxio, or at least, not yet.

Penric exhaled and sat, bonelessly.

Ikos sank down beside him. Judging by his wheezing, Pen was not the only one with his heart thumping in his ears.

"Word will reach the mainland by nightfall, then," said Ikos.

"Yes. Although word of what is an open question. It looks as though they bit on my suicide lure, at least in part." But not conclusively. Still, the pursuers would have to search everywhere, and Idrene and Nikys were in just one place. Would they imagine Idrene had fled inland, or realize that she sought a ship?

"If m'mother had been aboard with me just now," Ikos observed after a distant minute, "that would not have gone well."

"Quite," agreed Pen. "I plan to dedicate a hymn to the white god, when I get a chance to breathe."

Ikos cocked his head. "The Bastard your god, too?" And answered his own question, "Yes, of course, must be. If you're His divine. So, having His ear, so to speak, can you ask Him to bless this voyage?"

Pen gestured the tally of the gods, and tapped his lips twice with this thumb. "By every sign," he said, "He already has."

" . . . Aye."

They sat together in reflective silence as the boat tacked south.

# XVI

NIKYS SNAPPED AWAKE at a rap on the chamber door, her sleep-slurry washed away by alarm. Thankfully, it was Bosha. She snared a quick look out the window to check the time as Idrene sat up on the edge of the bed, yawning, and Bosha took off his hat and settled on a stool. Late afternoon; they'd slept a good stretch. Perhaps two more hours till sunset?

"What did you find?" asked Idrene.

Bosha grimaced. "Nothing good yet. Of the ships now at dock, three are headed the wrong way, one is not suitable for unescorted women, and the last is a Xarre-owned vessel. You will understand if I'd prefer not to place you there, but in any case, its next port of call is Thasalon, which you'd best avoid."

Idrene nodded. Nikys couldn't decide whether to be worried or relieved. Sooner away was better, but a delay might allow Penric to catch up with them. . . . If nothing awful had befallen him.

"How long, do you think," said Idrene, "should we wait for a better chance before giving up and heading east overland? Could you drive us to a coach road?"

"Maybe," said Bosha, obviously not liking this much better than putting them on a Xarre ship. "But your description will certainly reach any border before you. This whole scheme depends on speed."

Indeed, outrunning pursuit was all their hope. Resisting it, should it catch them, was out of the question without Penric, and even more terrifying to contemplate with him.

"Three ships are putting out on this tide," said Bosha. "I'm told Akylaxio gets half-a-dozen seagoing merchanters a day docking to load or offload. A couple of day-coasters call regularly"—local ships that passed to and from the smaller towns and islands—"but that's not a first choice."

Not a good choice at all. They would repeat the same risks at every port, and accumulate delays.

Idrene rubbed her sleep-creased cheeks. "Let's give it till tomorrow morning to see what else arrives. Then take counsel and decide." She rose to splash her face at the basin, then went to peer out the window. "I confess, I'm growing mortally tired of being trapped in small rooms."

Bosha gave her a sympathetic nod, and with the women's collaboration turned to filling out as much of their documents as he could. It seemed he could alter his handwriting at will, Nikys noticed. He put down his quill and looked up at a fresh tap on the chamber door. "That may be dinner." He rose to open it, though his other hand hovered on the hilt at his belt.

But it wasn't the maidservant who stumbled through. It was Penric. And...

"Ikos!" Idrene shrieked, dashing across the room and falling upon him.

He seized her in return, huffing relief. "So it was all true...!"

"Keep your voices down," Penric and Bosha chorused.

Bosha glanced at this new man and opened his hand in pressing query to Penric, who shrugged and closed the door firmly behind them. "Brother," he muttered. "The other brother."

"Oh. The bridgebuilder? But what...?"

"He was a surprise to me, too."

Penric was altered in coloration yet again, his hair now a sandy brown, sticky with salt, and his head and arms and feet paler, but mottled, like a peculiar tan or a mild skin disorder. He was back in his tunic and trousers, noticeably grubbier.

Ikos looked, and smelled, as if he were home from a very bad, very long day at work, stubbled and sunburned, clothes crusty with dried sweat. Nikys hugged him anyway. Pen looked on as if... envious? Breaking away from Ikos because Idrene was elbowing in again, Nikys's fingers stretched and closed. She didn't need her hands to assure herself of Pen's reality; her eyes were enough, in this company. For a moment she wished her company anywhere but here.

Idrene's anxious questions tumbled over one another. "What are you doing here, you shouldn't be within a hundred miles of me, whatever are you two doing together, how did you *get* here?"

"Fishing boat," said Ikos, choosing the simplest from this spate. "From Limnos."

"I was worried how we'd get into Akylaxio discreetly," Penric put in, "but it turns out that a brace of those big tuna fish make an excuse to dock at any harbor, no questions asked. We picked them up along the way. Ye *gods*, they're huge in a small boat. For a moment I thought they'd sink us. I'd only seen them laid out flat in the markets at Lodi, before."

"You stopped to go fishing?" said Idrene, sounding bewildered.

"No," said Ikos distantly, "we didn't stop. They leaped into the boat all on their own, and died at our feet. Smiling. Apparently."

That... ah, that wasn't a joke. Or sarcasm. Nikys had seen that round-eyed look on people before, and what did it say that she recognized it? He wasn't poleaxed, just Penric'd. Her lips stretched up unwilled.

"We left the lads to sell the fish," Ikos went on, "and strolled around at random till he found you."

"It wasn't random," Pen protested, "it was logic. Mostly. But tell me everything that's happened to you!"

They ended up with Idrene and Nikys seated on the edge of the bed, Penric on the stool, and Ikos at Idrene's feet, her hand fondling his hair, urgently swapping tales. Bosha leaned silently against the wall with his arms folded, taking in, Nikys thought, everything, although even his set face screwed up with consternation at parts. He did not look best pleased when he learned about the encounter with his sister Hekat, nor Pen's promise that her brother would tell her all about it on his next visit. "All that seems safe," Pen temporized, which did not improve matters.

Bosha broke off to answer the door and receive the dinner tray from the maid, and order more food, very necessary as the two men fell upon the offering like starved wolves.

The second round of dinner was delivered and consumed before they came to the end of Penric's and Ikos's intertwined and often clashing explanations, frequently dislocated by Idrene's many questions. "You do make me wish I'd been able to ride in your machine," Idrene told Ikos. "It sounds splendid. Perhaps, at some happier time, you might get a chance to demonstrate it for me." Ikos smiled. Penric rubbed his jaw, squeezing some remark to unintelligibility.

Nikys left out from her account only her strange experience in the court of the sacred well, and Pen did not press her on it, to her silent gratitude. She turned at last to Ikos.

"But you say you have a boat?"

He shook his head. "Not my boat, and nothing that could take you to Orbas."

Pen scratched his scalp and grimaced. "I'm thinking I want to find a bathhouse before I board anything. I'll circle back through the harbor and see what's come in since the last check, after."

Idrene was clearly torn between sending Ikos with him, or keeping her son at her side for every possible moment before they had to part. But Ikos stretched, his joints making disturbing muffled crunching noises, sniffed his armpit without prompting, and chose to depart with Penric.

Nikys fell backward on the bed, floating between elation and new terror. The latter hardly seemed fair. Given how she'd fretted at Penric's absence, surely his presence should be the cure? Perhaps this was what a gambler felt when he laid his whole stake on one last throw of the dice. Not a thrill she relished, it seemed.

It was nearly dark, Nikys was anxious, Idrene was pacing from wall to wall, and Bosha was staying out of her way, when the two men returned, much cleaner.

And triumphant. Penric barely closed the door behind him before he blurted, "Two more ships have docked. One is Roknari—"

A general flinch.

"—but the other is Saonese. Heading homeward, near full-laden. It's not going to Orbas, but it is planning a stop at the Carpagamon islands, and from there it should be no challenge to double back to the duchy."

"Do you speak Saonese?" asked Nikys. A difficult dialect of Darthacan; she had a working command of the latter.

"Oh, yes, it's practically my father-tongue. Jurald is a Saonese name, you know. And there was Learned Amberein, one of Des's riders before me. The purser thought I was an expatriate fellow-countryman. I didn't correct him. Time for that later. Anyway, they keep a few cabins aboard for independent merchants transshipping cargo. Only one free, but I booked it. More space than a coach, at least. Another may open up later in the voyage. They sail on the morning tide."

"Should we go there now?" asked Idrene, looking ready to dive for their baggage.

Pen shook his head. "The Customs shed closes at dark. We're supposed to board in the morning."

Bosha drummed his pale fingers on his thigh. "That could be cutting things fine."

"Yes." Pen bit his lip. "Though it would be the usual course for passengers."

"Mm," said Bosha. There seemed no choice but to accept this delay. Nikys wondered if she'd sleep at all tonight.

Pen had secured a chamber across the hall for the two men and Bosha, though Ikos lingered with Idrene and Nikys. He'd been supposed to be at his next worksite two weeks ago, although he claimed his crew could begin surveying without him. They would say their goodbyes indoors in private tomorrow; he planned to watch over their departure from a distance with Bosha till they were safely away.

They talked in low tones until his head was nodding, and his mother sent him to bed with a kiss the like of which he'd probably not had from her since he was four. It seemed to please them both. It often felt to Nikys that her elder brother's relationship with their mother was less, not more, complicated than her own for its long gap, but she could not begrudge it.

# XVII

PEN FOLLOWED HIS FELLOWS into the women's chamber at dawn, for breakfast and for Bosha to put the finishing touches on their papers. There was nothing more to pack, but Nikys pulled Pen's Temple braids from his medical case and held them up in doubt.

"The customs officers may search our baggage. Is there some better way to hide these, Pen?"

Pen sighed and took them from her. "I suppose I'd better abandon them. They can be replaced when we get home." And when had he started thinking of Orbas, of all places, as home? "It's more imperative just now to conceal that I'm a Temple sorcerer than to prove I am."

The other side of Bosha's lip curled. "Give them to me for a moment." A bit reluctantly, Pen handed them over, and Bosha examined the knot holding the loops. A few moves of those deft, pale fingers, and the cord fell into one long length. "Madame Khatai, might you sit here?" He gestured to the stool.

Her eyes rolling in curiosity, Nikys sat as instructed. Bosha plucked her hairbrush from her valise and busied himself about her head. Idrene drifted over to watch. Within a few minutes, he had somehow turned her hair into a raised confection with the braids visible as no more than a few fashionable glints holding the black curls.

"Oh, that's charming!" exclaimed Idrene. Pen had to agree.

Nikys smiled, reaching up for an uncertain prod. The arrangement held firm. "Very clever, Master Bosha. Thank you!"

"Do encourage General Arisaydia in his quest for Lady Tanar's hand, Madame Khatai."

"Do you favor him for her, then?" Nikys's smile didn't alter, but Pen thought she was listening for every nuance in the answer. Because Bosha would have them. And Bosha's opinion in this affair mattered far more than was obvious.

"She's had much worse, sniffing about her." He rubbed his neck beneath his white braid. "You know, her latest interest is in going up onto the roof to learn celestial navigation. She conscripts one of Lady Xarre's captains for her lessons, when he stops in to give his reports. If she's not married to your brother, or some man of like merit, with her vast vitality diverted to children, I'm afraid she will insist on apprenticing as an officer on one of Lady Xarre's ships. And if denied, would run off to become a pirate queen."

This was *probably* a joke, Pen thought. Probably. Hard to tell with Bosha. Or with Tanar, for that matter.

Nikys dimpled. "Do pirate queens keep secretaries?"

"I dread finding out." His smile faded altogether. "Although childbed is the one place even I cannot go to defend her. Perhaps the high seas would be better after all."

Idrene said gently, "We cannot protect anyone from being alive, Master Bosha. No matter how much we might wish to." Her eyes fell on her own children.

His lips stretched in an expression Pen would hesitate to call amused. "I can try."

And then it was time for final farewells, teary when Idrene and Nikys embraced the sheepish, but gratified, Ikos. Pen stifled his jealousy. He, after all, would be the one getting to keep the women.

*If I can.* He hoisted the baggage and shuffled after them to the stairs.

The blue Cedonian sky was hazier this morning as they walked down to the harbor. If this heralded some change in the fine weather, Pen thought, eyeing it, it wasn't going to be soon enough to impede their departure.

The squawks of white gulls played over the clatter of men and equipment on the two piers readying ships for sea. Crates of goods from last night's unlading were piled up ashore, waiting for their carriers to come take them to their inland destinations. A crew of men unpacked an arriving wagon, lifting long ceramic flasks of wine from their straw bed and carting them off to a dock. Another crew wrestled with ingots of copper, distinctive with their green patina and red scratches, stacking them on a handcart. Ikos watched it all with great professional interest, as he and the behatted Bosha, mismatched sightseers, veered off to loiter on a low wall as if enjoying the maritime spectacle.

"All this way," mourned Pen, "and I never saw great Thasalon."

"Since any view we're like to get would be from inside an imperial prison," said Idrene, "best not to make that wish."

"Aye," Pen sighed.

Idrene clutched the packet with their papers as they approached the Customs shed. Nikys raised her chin and inhaled.

At a clatter of hooves on the cobblestones behind them, Penric wheeled around. And froze.

A man in the uniform of an imperial courier dismounted from his sweating horse and tied its reins to a bollard, looking over the docks and ships with sharp, flashing eyes. Turning to his saddlebags, he withdrew a leather dispatch case. He began to walk purposefully toward the Customs shed.

"Keep smiling, don't panic, and play along," Pen muttered through his teeth to Nikys and Idrene as they paused to see what had distracted him, and stiffened in turn. "I can take care of this."

Nikys gripped Idrene's hand. In caution? In reassurance?

*This one is going to be costly*, warned Des, fully alert. It wasn't an attempt to dissuade him.

*Not nearly as costly as failing*, Pen thought grimly back.

*Aye.*

*Sight, Des.*

Pen set down their baggage and moved to intercept the courier, plastering a smile on his features. That strange, compelling, colorful interior view of a soul's essence, hidden within the outer material form, flickered into focus in Pen's mind's eye. "Oh, **officer!**" he called, the reverberations of the shamanic weirding voice entering his tones even as he pushed the words out. They touched the man like tendrils, barely catching on that firm sense of duty. His head jerked toward Pen, and he frowned, but stopped.

"Good morning," Pen continued. "Have you ridden from Guza?"

Pen felt the assent swirling within the man even as he returned in a quelling growl, "What is it to you?"

"I think **you want to let me see that paper**," Pen purred, holding out his hand as though such an exchange were the most natural thing in the world. The fellow shook his head as if throwing off an insect, but, slowly, opened his case. "**You need to deliver that paper to me.**"

The courier extracted a document, stood at some echo of attention, and held it out. Pen took it and ran his eyes hastily through what he guessed was some standard Cedonian bureaucratic preamble—Bosha would know—to the critical paragraph, a description of Idrene in much the same terms as the sailor had given them yesterday afternoon. The official detainment order for the customs inspectors, clearly.

Pen twitched it behind him and set it alight. It was a puff of ash before it reached the cobbles.

"**You have delivered your urgent message to the Customs-shed officer**," Pen continued, driving the words, and the geas of persuasion, as deep into his target as possible. The tendrils set like hooks, like sucking mouths, into the officer's spirit, and Pen winced. Geases could be nasty almost-organisms, at times, parasitizing the life of their victim for their own prolongation. A true shaman could create one that would last for weeks. Pen hoped for a day. "**You have done your duty. Now you need to take care of your loyal horse.**" A geas worked best when laid in alignment with the subject's natural inclinations. "**And then go drink a flagon of wine. You've earned it. You delivered your message in Akylaxio just as ordered.**" Pen simulated a Cedonian military salute, which the man, his eyes slightly dazed, returned.

Blinking, the man returned to his horse, untied it, and led it off. By the time he reached the street, his steps were a firm stride again. He didn't look back. He might bear other copies of the circular to deliver further along the coast, but their existence did not concern Pen.

Still sitting on the wall overlooking it all, both Bosha and Ikos swiveled their heads in worry to watch the officer. Not looking back at them, Pen managed an *it's all right, stand down* wave, which he hoped they interpreted correctly.

It wasn't entirely all right. Memory alteration fiddled not only with free will but with the very essence of a soul, and thus bordered on sacrilege. *Good intentions* and even *good results* were valid theological defenses only up to a point. Pen could hope he'd not transgressed beyond it. He wouldn't say *pray*, as he'd decided long ago not to bother the gods with questions when he didn't really want to hear the answers.

The blood was already starting to trickle. Pen snorted and sucked it back to send down his throat. "Now I need to get out of sight for a few minutes," he told the women. "Quickly."

Nikys, who had watched him with the sacred dogs, understood at once. She dropped Idrene's hand and grabbed Pen's, towing him back toward the stacks of crates as the trickle turned into a flood and Pen choked, gasped, and choked again. His eyes watered wildly. He clapped his other hand to his mouth as he coughed out blood. It stained his palm in quick stripes as he reached the shelter and dropped to his knees, then his hands and knees, coughing wetly. The scarlet splattered onto the stones, spreading.

And kept coming. Struggling for breath between spasms, Pen

wondered if he could actually drown himself. There was a new hazard for the list . . .

"Mother's tears, Pen!" gasped Nikys, holding his quaking shoulders. "This is much worse than before."

And Idrene's startled voice, "Is he *dying*?"

It must look as if he were hacking out his lungs in gobbets. Which, admittedly, sounded much more dramatic than *It's a nosebleed.* Pen wheezed and shook his head. "Ugly magic," he got out between coughs. "High cost. Des hates it." Shamanic magics did not come naturally to a chaos demon, and Pen suspected his body paid a premium price for his use of them at all. It was as if chaos and blood were coins of two different realms, and the moneylender charged an extortionate fee for their exchange.

*Should I do something?* Des asked, anxious. *There are harbor rats lurking about . . .*

*Don't.* Trying to divert or delay his somatic payment for this magic with some uphill healing had unpleasant side-effects, afterward. Better than dying, to be sure, but still better was to pay off the debt at once. It just looked alarming.

He studied the cup or so of blood splashed on the ground under his face. All right, *was* alarming. But his desperate coughing ceased, his lungs stopped pulsing, and the blood issuing from his stinging nose dwindled to mere drips, then tailed off altogether. He let Nikys roll him into her arms, smiling weakly up at her distraught face.

He should explain about the nosebleed, but her lap was such a lovely soft cushion . . .

*Malingerer,* scoffed Des.

*Are you going to tell on me?*

*Never.* He knew he was going to be all right when his demon's temporary fright faded back into amusement. *Enjoy your treat. After all, so do I.*

*Not thinking about that, Des. It throws me off my stride.*

*As you wish.*

"Bastard's teeth, is all that red gush his?" asked Ikos's voice, much too close to Pen's ear.

"You were supposed to steer clear of us." Pen cracked open his eyes. "You two." Bosha had taken up a guard stance at the entry of the space between the crate stacks. Pen added to Ikos, "This, by the way, is what happens to me when I force a geas on an unwilling person. So you see I didn't cast one on Acolyte Hekat yesterday."

"Huh." His face retreated out of Pen's sight.

"Should I follow that courier and do anything about him?" Bosha asked over his shoulder in a neutral tone.

Was he offering to assassinate the man? *Dear me, he is!* crowed Des. *What a handy fellow to have around.* Pen hastened to explain that his geas made further intervention unnecessary, which Bosha, after a considering moment, accepted.

Ikos returned with what proved to be his shirt, wetted with seawater, and handed it to Pen without comment.

"Do I look a fright?"

Nikys nodded, her clutch not slackening.

"I'd best tidy up. I don't want to be kept from boarding because they fear I have some sort of plague. Aside from being a sorcerer." Deciding, since it was Ikos's shirt, that he couldn't make it much worse, Pen wiped the gore from his face and hands—he'd managed to keep most of the splash off his tunic—then let Nikys have it to finish the job to her satisfaction.

*One gives you the shirt off his back*, mused Des, *and the other offers to help you bury bodies. I do believe you have made some new friends, Pen!*

*Hush*, Pen thought back. But he believed so, too. Or a brother-in-law and a... did Idrene realize they were going to acquire a eunuch-in-law?

*I imagine she will*, said Des. *She seems quite as shrewd as Nikys.*

He grinned and let Ikos and Nikys pull him to his feet. The gray dizziness passed off as he caught his breath.

When he had composed himself, the three taking ship continued the interrupted trek for the Customs shed, leaving Ikos and Bosha to lurk warily among the crates. Pen let Idrene, all assured-army-widow this morning, although of a different and fictional officer, present their papers to the clerk. They all watched in feigned indifference as their baggage was turned out onto the table, but it was soon clear this modest party bore no contraband. The clerk grew interested in Pen's medical case, though not for any official reason, and seemed content with Pen's explanation that he was an aspiring student of the healing arts.

Then it was time to traverse the dock to the gangplank of the Saonese ship, and be herded up it by sailors ready to get underway. Three sturdy masts, Pen observed with approval, and even larger than the cargo vessel on which he'd traveled from Lodi to Patos not four months past, which now seemed a century ago. Making this Pen's second sea voyage ever. Would it be as life-altering as the first?

# XVIII

A BENCH ran along the taffrail at the stern of the big merchanter. After stowing their scant baggage in their cabin, they all went out and sat upon it to watch the sailors work the ship out of the harbor. Nikys contemplated the receding shore, as did Idrene. Their hands found each other, as if to assure that this one part of their lives, at least, was not lost to them. Pen leaned his head back under the wide sky and gazed up. Distant figures, no matter how carefully watched-for, grew indistinguishable, then the town became a blur on the sun-hazed coast, and then the coast, too, dropped below the horizon. They were away.

It felt to Nikys as though her body had been bound strangling-tight by wires, and one by one, each wire was being clipped off till none were left. She breathed, shook out her arms, sensed her blood move freely. Stretched her neck. Exhaled.

"Penric . . ." No, that wasn't right. "Desdemona. Can I talk with you?"

"Mm?" Pen turned his head. "Of course. Any time."

She stood. "Let's go to the cabin."

Pen followed her up at once, amiable if baffled.

Idrene smiled behind her hand. "Take all the time you like. I've had my fill of tiny rooms. I plan to sit right out here as much as possible, this voyage."

Nikys rolled her eyes, but said, "Thank you, Mother." And meant it.

The cabin was tiny indeed, two pairs of bunks built into the bulkheads facing each other across a narrow aisle. It did have a small, square window on the end, presently hooked open on the sight of the sea falling behind them, stirred by the ship's passage. The air was fresh and fine.

Nikys gestured Pen to one bunk, and sat on the other facing him. With his long legs, they were nearly knee to knee.

Nikys hardly knew where to begin, only that she had to begin. With a feeling of jumping into murky but deep water, she said, "Desdemona, have you ever been married before?"

She wasn't sure if it was Pen or Des responsible for his head going back and his eyebrows up, but she could mark the little changes in the tension of his face as the demon came to the fore. "By which I suppose you are asking if any of my sorceresses were married before?"

"Yes, that. During the time you were with them. I know some were widowed . . . "

Pen held up his fingers to keep count. Or Des held up Pen's fingers. "Of the ten, five were never married. Sugane, Rogaska, of course Mira, Umelan, and Ruchia. Vasia and Aulia were both widowed before they acquired me, and did not remarry after. Litikone, well, I was a very young demon then. With no Temple guidance, I suppose it seemed more like contracting a madness than a power. Her husband became frightened and moved out, which was why she went to Patos to end her days as a servant to Vasia. Who was the first to acquire me purposely, if still untutored.

"Aulia of Brajar was my first trained Temple divine, and what a huge difference that made, but she was already older, and widowed, and very firm of will. Which was how I came to be handed off at her death to the great physician Amberein of Saone. She was still married, with her childbearing behind her of course, but her husband, dear fellow, was already used to dealing with a strong-minded woman. I had not guessed a sorcerer could live in intimacy so well, before. Helvia was another of the same stamp.

"Ruchia . . . was Ruchia, my dearest rider until Pen. The first to really treat me as a partner and a person, if still unnamed. Forty years with her quite spoiled me for anything less."

Pen's hands had lowered to clasp between his knees; he looked up from them. "Six of the ten had borne children, before me. None after, of course."

"Why of course? Is it something to do with the chaos?"

Pen, yes, it was Pen now, cleared his throat. "Yes. Sorceresses who conceive suffer early miscarriages. Unless they are very knowledgeable and adept. Amberein or Helvia could certainly have brought a child to term, but they had already finished their families. Or Ruchia, but she did not choose it. Something emotionally complicated to do with herself being a foundling of the Bastard's orphanage, I gather."

Nikys pursed her lips. "What of sorcerers?"

"Um . . . I'm less sure. Well, no. I've heard of sorcerers who managed to get married, and have families." He added reluctantly, "Though they are more often bachelors or widowers. Or their wives leave them, because it's too much like living with a crazy man." He smiled ruefully as if inviting her to argue with this, and looked more rueful when she only nodded. "*I've* never been married," he pointed out. "Although I am trying to rectify that."

His lips twitched back, as Des said, "Feeling left out, lad?"

"Who wouldn't? Looking at . . ." A feeling gesture at Nikys, and a melting smile.

Nikys resisted melting. Barely. She tried to remember everything on her list. "I don't want to move to Adria."

Pen sat up. "I could transfer to Orbas, with some help from the duke. The duke pressuring his archdivine, rather. Even the Temple hierarchy must give way in the face of the sacrament of marriage. . . . Usually." He added after a moment, "And if not, well, I'm in Orbas, they're in Adria, what are they going to do about it? Although I would like to be able to travel back there someday, at need." He nodded, as though the point were disposed of. Perhaps it was. Though, being Pen, he added after another moment, "I might still like to take you to visit Adria sometime. When it's not having a clash with Cedonia, but then, you're not going to be a Cedonian anymore, are you? It's really a very interesting realm."

Nikys grimaced. "I'd never have left Cedonia, if Cedonia had not betrayed Adelis. No going back now."

"Sometimes," sighed Pen, "that happens. Even without betrayal." Missing the white peaks of his distant cantons? Though Nikys was of the strong opinion that the Mother's Order in Martensbridge had betrayed him too, and first, through their nearly lethal mishandling of his healing skills. And he knew it, or he would not have near-fled that beloved home, either.

Nikys fought her way back to her points. "I want a house." Though she temporized, "Someday, at least. I realize it might not be possible right away."

"Well, so do I."

"Oh. . . . Huh."

"I haven't spent the past decade perching in other people's palaces by choice, exactly. It was just easiest. Convenient to my work."

She supposed that was so. "I think you live mostly inside your own head. It hardly matters where you've put your body."

"So a house will do just fine, then." Another maddening smile.

She swallowed. "Children . . . "

"Those, too." He nodded. "They will go with the house. Like a cat."

"What?"

"That was Pen, not me," Des put in. "I don't know what he's thinking, either. Yes, you do."

Nikys drew breath and faced her darkest fear. Head-on, because it was time. "I may be barren. Kymis and I were never able to get a child." She didn't want to add, *And we tried*, though she supposed it was implied. She had never met a man before Pen so able to toss her like a coin between shyness and exasperation.

"Could be many different reasons for that." He glanced her up and down. Wait, why did it feel as though those blue eyes had just knifed through her? *Sorcerers, agh.* "There's nothing obviously amiss on your side, at least." *Was that all it took?* The eyes crinkled. "It might require some experimenting to be sure. I could help you with that."

Why did he sound just like Drema? If she'd been sitting next to him, she would have hit him. Perhaps she should shift across there, so she could.

She rubbed her forehead. "If I married Penric, he would be my husband. But what would you be, Desdemona? Now you are a person. Not my husband. Not my wife, either. My . . . my big sister?" There was a new thought, oddly warming.

"For you, sweetling," said the demon, with impressive confidence, "I can be anything you like."

She couldn't help what popped out. "Even silent in bed?"

"Yes, please," Pen interjected fervently.

Des grinned. "Yes. Although I predict you'll get over even that need in due course."

"I daresay," sighed Nikys. Considering all she'd become accustomed to so far. Ultimately, he would just become Pen. Or, *Pen!* (Or, maybe sometimes, *Des!*) He was nearly so already. "Spouses do rub each other smooth at the joints, given enough time."

Time. It did not wait for any human want, or grief, or plan. Or careful list. Nearly half her life might be behind her already. It was time to get started on the next half.

"Marry the sorcerer, dear," Des urged, "and put me out of his misery. He'll be glad you did. If he is happy, I can be happy. And so can you."

And that was just how it worked, wasn't it? Happiness handed around and around, never stopping. It wasn't something one could hoard tight like a miser. That would be like trying to hold one's breath for later.

Nikys looked up, and said firmly, "You can't shave your head."

"Wouldn't dream of it," Pen returned instantly. "Although . . . I can't promise I won't go bald, when I get old. Des, could you do something about that?"

"I've never tried. Not an issue that ever came up with my prior riders."

"By the time you grow bald," said Nikys, "I shall doubtless be fat and wrinkled."

"And sweet. Like a winter apple."

"More likely cranky."

"Sweetly cranky."

"Optimist."

"I think people must be, to do this." He'd slid across beside her. Just the sort of thing he would do, if she didn't keep her eye on him.

Not that keeping an eye on all that male elegance was a burden. What had been her first impression of him, back in the garden in Patos? *Ethereal*, that was it. He seemed very human to her now, flesh and blood and long, long bones. Mistakes and miracles, awkwardness and profound grace, sorrow and joy. Beautiful hands, slim-fingered and sensitive and so very skilled at so many things. A woman would have to be a witless fool to let those hands get away.

"It's still a long way home," she pointed out. By this time, her faintly breathed objections must be pure habit, because she was falling toward him all in air.

"Or maybe home is right here in arm's reach," he said. The arm in question curled around her, hugged tight. Like drawing a woman to shore.

She reached back.

# AUTHOR'S NOTE:
## A BUJOLD READING-ORDER GUIDE

### THE FANTASY NOVELS

My fantasy novels are not hard to order. Easiest of all is *The Spirit Ring*, which is a stand-alone, or aquel, as some wag once dubbed books that for some obscure reason failed to spawn a subsequent series. Next easiest are the four volumes of *The Sharing Knife*—in order, *Beguilement*, *Legacy*, *Passage*, and *Horizon*—which I broke down and actually numbered, as this was one continuous tale divided into non-wrist-breaking chunks. The novella "Knife Children" is something of a codicil-tale to the tetralogy.

What were called the Chalion books after the setting of its first two volumes, but which now that the geographic scope has widened I'm dubbing the World of the Five Gods, were written to be stand-alones as part of a larger whole, and can in theory be read in any order. Some readers think the world-building is easier to assimilate when the books are read in publication order, and the second volume certainly contains spoilers for the first (but not the third). In any case, the publication order is:

*The Curse of Chalion*
*Paladin of Souls*
*The Hallowed Hunt*

In terms of internal world chronology, *The Hallowed Hunt* would fall first, the Penric novellas perhaps a hundred and fifty years later, and *The Curse of Chalion* and *Paladin of Souls* would follow a century or so after that.

The internal chronology of the Penric novellas is presently

"Penric's Demon"
"Penric and the Shaman"
"Penric's Fox"
"Penric's Mission"
"Mira's Last Dance"
"The Prisoner of Limnos"
"The Orphans of Raspay"

The first three are collected in the Baen compilation *Penric's Progress*; the second three in *Penric's Travels*.

## OTHER ORIGINAL E-BOOKS

The short story collection *Proto Zoa* contains five very early tales—three (1980s) contemporary fantasy, two science fiction—all previously published but not in this handy format. The novelette "Dreamweaver's Dilemma" may be of interest to Vorkosigan completists, as it is the first story in which that proto-universe began, mentioning Beta Colony but before Barrayar was even thought of.

*Sidelines: Talks and Essays* is just what it says on the tin—a collection of three decades of my nonfiction writings, including convention speeches, essays, travelogues, introductions, and some less formal pieces. I hope it will prove an interesting companion piece to my fiction.

## THE VORKOSIGAN STORIES

Many pixels have been expended debating the 'best' order in which to read what have come to be known as the Vorkosigan Books (or Saga), the Vorkosiverse, the Miles books, and other names. The debate mainly revolves around publication order versus internal-chronological order. I favor internal chronological, with a few adjustments.

It was always my intention to write each book as a stand-alone, so that the reader could theoretically jump in anywhere. While still somewhat true, as the series developed it acquired a number of sub-arcs, closely related tales that were richer for each other. I will list the sub-arcs, and then the books, and then the duplication warnings. (My publishing history has been complex.) And then the publication order, for those who want it.

*Shards of Honor* and *Barrayar*. The first two books in the series proper, they detail the adventures of Cordelia Naismith of Beta Colony and Aral Vorkosigan of Barrayar. *Shards* was my very first novel ever; *Barrayar* was actually my eighth, but continues the tale the next day after the end of *Shards*. For readers who want to be sure of beginning at the beginning, or who are very spoiler-sensitive, start with these two.

*The Warrior's Apprentice* and *The Vor Game* (with, perhaps, the novella "The Mountains of Mourning" tucked in between.) *The Warrior's Apprentice* introduces the character who became the series' linchpin, Miles Vorkosigan; the first book tells how he created a space mercenary fleet by accident; the second how he fixed his mistakes from the first round. Space opera and military-esque adventure (and a number of other things one can best discover for oneself), *The Warrior's Apprentice* makes another good place to jump into the series for readers who prefer a young male protagonist.

After that: *Brothers in Arms* should be read before *Mirror Dance*, and both, ideally, before *Memory*.

*Komarr* makes another alternate entry point for the series, picking up Miles's second career at its start. It should be read before *A Civil Campaign*.

*Borders of Infinity*, a collection of three of the five currently extant novellas, makes a good Miles Vorkosigan early-adventure sampler platter, I always thought, for readers who don't want to commit themselves to length. (But it may make more sense if read after *The Warrior's Apprentice*.) Take care not to confuse the collection-as-a-whole with its title story, "The Borders of Infinity".

*Falling Free* takes place 200 years earlier in the timeline and does not share settings or characters with the main body of the series. Most readers recommend picking up this story later. It should likely be read before *Diplomatic Immunity*, however, which revisits the "quaddies", a bioengineered race of free-fall dwellers, in Miles's time.

The novels in the internal-chronological list below appear in italics; the novellas (officially defined as a story between 17,500 words and 45,000 words) in quote marks.

*Falling Free*
*Shards of Honor*
*Barrayar*
*The Warrior's Apprentice*
"The Mountains of Mourning"
"Weatherman"
*The Vor Game*
*Cetaganda*
*Ethan of Athos*
*Borders of Infinity*
"Labyrinth"
"The Borders of Infinity"
*Brothers in Arms*
*Mirror Dance*
*Memory*
*Komarr*
*A Civil Campaign*
"Winterfair Gifts"
*Diplomatic Immunity*
*Captain Vorpatril's Alliance*

"The Flowers of Vashnoi"
*CryoBurn*
*Gentleman Jole and the Red Queen*

Caveats:

The novella "Weatherman" is an out-take from the beginning of the novel *The Vor Game*. If you already have *The Vor Game*, you likely don't need this.

The original "novel" *Borders of Infinity* was a fix-up collection containing the three novellas "The Mountains of Mourning", "Labyrinth", and "The Borders of Infinity", together with a frame to tie the pieces together. Again, beware duplication. The frame story does not stand alone.

Publication order:

This is also the order in which the works were written, apart from a couple of the novellas, but is not identical to the internal-chronological. It goes:

*Shards of Honor* (June 1986)
*The Warrior's Apprentice* (August 1986)
*Ethan of Athos* (December 1986)
*Falling Free* (April 1988)
*Brothers in Arms* (January 1989)
*Borders of Infinity* (October 1989)
*The Vor Game* (September 1990)
*Barrayar* (October 1991)
*Mirror Dance* (March 1994)
*Cetaganda* (January 1996)
*Memory* (October 1996)
*Komarr* (June 1998)

*A Civil Campaign* (September 1999)
*Diplomatic Immunity* (May 2002)
"Winterfair Gifts" (February 2004)
*CryoBurn* (November 2010)
*Captain Vorpatril's Alliance* (November 2012)
*Gentleman Jole and the Red Queen* (February 2016)
"The Flowers of Vashnoi" (May 2018)

... Thirty-plus years fitted on a page. Huh.

Happy reading!

—Lois McMaster Bujold